REMINISCENCES

OF THE HON.

GALAHAD THREEPWOOD

edited by

N.T.P. MURPHY

PORPOISE BOOKS

© N. T. P. Murphy 1993 & 1995
who asserts his rights as author and editor of this book

Heavy Weather: A Cinema Verity /Juniper Production for BBC Television
Produced by Verity Lambert   Directed by Jack Gold
Screenplay by Douglas Livingstone
Executive Producers: Michael Wearing (BBC)
Michael Wills (Juniper)

Front cover photograph by John Rogers
of Richard Briers as the Hon. Galahad Threepwood
Copyright © BBC Worldwide 1995

Cover design and layout by Brian Sanderson
Typesetting by Elizabeth Wilsey, Wargrave
Linotronic reproduction by LetterWorks, Reading

Printed by Antony Rowe Limited, Chippenham

A CIP catalogue record for this book
is available from the British Library

Porpoise Books
68 Altwood Road
Maidenhead SL6 4PZ
ISBN 1 870304 23 3

The Reminiscences

of the Hon.

Galahad Threepwood

To C.

and

the memory of D.H.

Contents

Illustrations

Introduction

ALTHOUGH the Threepwoods of Blandings Castle in Shropshire have long played an honourable part in their country's affairs, it is only in this century that the family history has been fully documented. From the pen of the pre-eminent social chronicler of our times, Sir Pelham Wodehouse, the world learned of the crises that have from time to time shaken this stately home of England to its foundations.

In immortal prose, Sir Pelham has related stirring accounts of theft, blackmail, imposture and feuds, both porcine and internecine, that purged the emotions of the reader with pity and terror.

The dramatic events that culminated in the marriage of Mr Ronald Fish, Lord Emsworth's nephew, to Miss Susan Cotterleigh (better known under her stage name of Sue Brown) were recounted in *Summer Lightning* and *Heavy Weather*.

In those volumes we read of Mr Galahad Threepwood's Reminiscences, whose publication would have brought scandal and embarrassment on respectable pillars of Society from Cumberland to Kent. After being stolen, mislaid, retrieved, re-stolen, sold and resold, the Reminiscences were eventually consumed by the Empress of Blandings, Lord Emsworth's prize pig – a loss to the literary world on a par with the destruction of the library at Alexandria or the burning of Carlyle's *French Revolution*.

It has been my good fortune to enjoy the friendship of Mrs Ronald Fish for a number of years, and I count it a great honour that it was to me she first made the astounding disclosure that a copy of the legendary Reminiscences was still in existence.

She was kind enough to seek my advice on whether she should now allow them to be published. While this had certainly been the intention of her old friend, she was concerned that, even after all this time, the repercussions on Society might be considerable.

After perusal of the manuscript, I had no hesitation in urging her to put the Reminiscences into the public domain. While publication in the 1930s might not have rocked the chancelleries of Europe, it would certainly have caused a furore amongst the highest in the land. However,

I was convinced that the passage of years and the social revolution since 1945 have now made the Reminiscences a document of historical significance.

I also felt that the noble families of England, far from being ashamed of their grandfathers' excesses in and around the West End of London, would now regard them with amusement and, probably, considerable admiration and envy. Mrs Fish was eventually persuaded to publish, firstly, as a memorial to her old friend and, secondly, to record for posterity a way of life and behaviour that has vanished for ever.

She has also agreed the publication of two letters enclosed with the manuscript. The first, set out in the Prologue, answers the question why Mr Threepwood, despite his publicly-stated intention of never putting pen to paper again, decided to produce another copy of the great work.

The second letter, printed as the Epilogue, recounts two remarkable and hitherto unknown incidents in the life of Lord Emsworth when, as Mr Threepwood so graphically puts it, his brother 'brushed with History'.

Because of the bizarre nature of some of Mr Threepwood's anecdotes and the possibility that this might cast doubt on their veracity, it has been thought prudent to consult other volumes of memoirs and contemporary accounts of the events he describes.

While it has not been possible to verify every incident in Mr Threepwood's narrative (I was refused access to the Dunstable and Parsloe family archives), the documents that were available to me establish conclusively the authenticity of Mr Threepwood's account. A list of the references consulted is set out in the Appendix.

Apart from occasional footnotes to confirm Mr Threepwood's narrative, no alterations or amendments have been made to the text. It is Mrs Fish's hope – and the editor's firm belief – that the Reminiscences will rank with those of Pepys, Aubrey and Evelyn as an imperishable record of an era the like of which we shall never see again.

N.T.P. Murphy
Savage Club
London

Prologue

The letter below is undated but Mrs Fish remembers receiving it some weeks after her marriage in 1929.

King Street,
St James's.

My dear Sue,

By the time you receive this letter, you will have been Mrs Ronnie Fish for a month or so; one of the best things that has happened to the Threepwood family for a long time. I was delighted that young Ronnie had the intelligence to see what had to be done, viz. holding the Empress to ransom till Clarence came up with the money. The boy has more to him than I thought. I just wish I'd showed the sense Ronnie has and run off with your mother as Ronnie ran off with you.

All the goings-on at Blandings this summer must sometimes seem to you like a bad dream; the pest Pilbeam, old Stinker Pyke or Tilbury as he calls himself nowadays, the Empress whizzing about the place as though on wheels, my reminiscences, not to mention Hugo Carmody and Monty Bodkin sticking their well-meaning but ineffectual oars in. I must admit that even I sometimes feared that we were not going to see the happy ending.

Now that all the fuss has died down, you may wonder why you haven't received a wedding present from your old pal. I am giving you one, but it is not the usual toast rack or coffee service because it occurred to me that I could give you something nobody else could – an insurance policy. You see, my dear, although you have your Ronnie with whom I hope you'll be very happy, you have also acquired my sister Julia for a mother-in-law.

You will have realised by now that Julia is a tough nut. Constance, Hermione and the rest of my sisters could step into the part of the Valkyries without rehearsal but, although they are full of rage and fury, it signifies nothing. Julia is different.

You may have become used to her air of patronising good humour, the great lady amusedly trying to make friends with the backward child of one of her tenants. But beneath that smiling exterior is a woman of steel. I was once dragged along to a Shakespeare play where a character said 'Why, I can smile and murder whiles I smile', and thought to myself the expression fitted Julia like a glove.

I saw her as a child bite her governess not once, but twice, with the same serene, angelic look on her face as she wore when she welcomed you back to Blandings after your honeymoon. As someone said, she's vengeance proud and loves not the common people, and I think it will be a long time before she loves you.

I don't say she would actually try and engineer a divorce between you and Ronnie, but I respect her powers and fear them. So I have bent my mind to the problem and I think my counter-measures should prove sufficient to ensure your happiness and her frustration.

After you and Ronnie whizzed off to get married, I returned to King Street and sat down to write another version of my reminiscences. It was a terrible sweat, and they aren't a patch on the manuscript that finished up inside the Empress, but I think they'll do the trick.

Although Julia doesn't care what effect my stories of the old days have on people like Tubby Parsloe or Stinker Pyke, the one thing she can't stand is to have people laughing at her. That is why I took particular care to include one or two incidents about Ronnie's father in Chapter 29.

I am not sending you the manuscript because we both saw how my sisters were quite happy to employ creatures like the unspeakable Pilbeam to steal it. Locked drawers are as nothing to them when they consider the family pride to be at stake.

So, my dear Sue, I have taken the revised, and I'm afraid shorter, manuscript along to Messrs Watson, Watson, Watson, Watson and Watson of Lincoln's Inn. They have been instructed that you and I are the only people allowed to see it. I have apprised them of the situation and Messrs Watson and Watson (there are only two of them left now) have assured me that inquiries made by Lady Julia Fish or anybody else will be given short shrift.

Once the manuscript was safely locked away in the darkest vault, I told Julia what I had done. I think this will be sufficient to ensure your long, happy and untroubled marriage.

If you ever do decide to have a look at the reminiscences, I hope they will provide you with some innocent enjoyment and make you think kindly of one who loved your mother dearly. It is to her that I would have dedicated the book if it had ever been published.

Remember me to Ronnie, my best wishes to you both,

Gally

Chapter 1

Early Days

My first bet and its happy outcome. My brother
Clarence's eviction from the Empire Music Hall.

ONE OF the annoying things about other people's memoirs is the amount of time they devote to their childhood. If they are artistic, they dish out page after page on their early appreciation of the beauties of Nature and the part it played in their sensitive lives. If politicians, they ramble on about the Duke of Wellington, young Mr Gladstone, Garibaldi and the like queuing up to kiss them in their cradle.

I shall not mention the fascinating and influential people I met in my childhood, because I don't remember them. In any event, it is people's adult lives that are of interest, when they do the things that make them worth reading about.

Passing quickly over my early years, I shall merely state that I was born the second son of the 8th Earl of Emsworth at the family home, Blandings Castle in Shropshire. Because my mother, like so many Victorian ladies, was a devotee of the works of the late Lord Tennyson, I was saddled with the names Galahad Montmorency Peveril. My father died in a hunting accident at the age of seventy-seven and the title is now held by my brother Clarence. I am the reluctant possessor of no fewer than ten sisters, most of whom have inherited the forcefulness of character and shortness of temper that made my father such a prominent figure in the county.

A perfectly normal childhood was broken only by such accidents as happen in the best-regulated families. These included nearly drowning in the pond in the kitchen garden and, at the tender age of six or so, being knocked out cold by my sister Hermione using her favourite doll Belinda for the purpose, rather in the manner of a warrior-queen wielding a battle-axe or mace.

On the credit side of the ledger is the time my sister Constance shot her governess, Miss Mapleton, in the bustle with an air-rifle. There was an equally exciting occasion when Uncle Harold, never quite himself after that touch of sunstroke out East, wrecked the Blandings drawing-room while trying to kill a wasp with a meat axe.

It wasn't till my tenth birthday that I came into contact with the things that really matter. We were at Norfolk Street at the time and Clarence had been told off to take me to Truefitt's to get my hair cut. When my turn came, I couldn't help overhearing the conversation the barber was having with the man in the next chair.

I'd noticed him when I came in. A big chap with the largest gold watch I'd ever seen, he was wearing extraordinary clothes. I'd seen some loud tweeds in Shropshire but never any like his. It was a blue herringbone with big orange and red checks, and I thought he must be someone from a circus or a music-hall in his working clothes.

I knew they were talking about racing because I'd heard Jackson, our coachman, grumbling about the horses he backed that never came in. The barber went on for a long time about what he called the 'good 'uns' for the Grand National until the big man lowered his voice and whispered something. The barber was so surprised he repeated the name out loud – 'Billy Buttons'. They didn't say much after that, but I noticed that instead of the man paying the barber, the barber paid him! He said: "All of it – on the nose," and the big man left. It wasn't till years later that I met him again and found it was Dickie Dunn whose path was often to cross mine in the future.

Uncle Robert came to lunch that day and tipped me ten bob. Luckily my parents didn't see him do it, so I went round to the mews and asked Jackson to put it on Billy Buttons. He didn't want to because Father would be furious if he found out, but eventually agreed. The price was 20-1 which meant I'd scoop in a tenner if it came up.

Billy Buttons fell at the last fence and Father discovered all! My sister Constance had been hanging around, heard me talking to Jackson and sneaked. There was a tremendous row; I had to stay in my room for two days and wasn't allowed to go to the Magic Show at the Egyptian Hall.

Jackson was all right. He told Father he was teaching me how easy it was to lose money, and if he hadn't taken the ten bob, one of the other servants would have. Jackson told me afterwards that there was always a way of getting out of trouble, so long as you worked out a good story beforehand. It was a lesson his father had taught him and Jackson said it was more valuable than any I'd learn at school. He told me never to forget it and I never did; I didn't do so badly out of Billy Buttons either.

Years later, when Pitcher Binstead introduced me to Dickie Dunn in Romano's, I told him what happened; how I'd lost my ten bob and missed Maskelyne & Devant at the Egyptian Hall. He smiled reminiscently:

"Yes, it never stood a chance but, if you're a bookie, every time you go for a haircut, the barber keeps you in the chair for hours trying to get a tip out of you. Give them a rank outsider and they're so surprised, they shut up. Besides, it means you get your hair cut for free and most of the time they slip you a quid to put on it."

The Pitcher was grinning at this.

"Quite right, Dickie. I haven't paid for a haircut in years. The only trouble is that occasionally the beggar wins and I have to pay up. Anyway, I taught you that trick and you never even bought me a drink on it. So what are you going to do about this young fellow you diddled out of his last ten bob?"

Dickie Dunn looked around the bar.

"Well, I've had a good day at Sandown, thanks to the mugs in here tonight who couldn't tell a horse from a donkey. I'll tell you what I'll do. You're a young man with a lot of racing ahead of you and I'll give you a choice. I'll give you your tenner now and we'll call it quits, or I'll let you have permanent credit for ten quid on my book. But Lord help you if you ever try and stick me for more!"

It took me only a second to make up my mind.

"Mr Dunn, that's a very fair offer. I'll take the ten pounds credit and I'd like to put it on La Flèche for the Dee Stakes at Chester. Any to come, I'll back it again for the Ascot Gold Cup."

I've never forgotten the way his face changed. He looked round the bar again, but nobody was listening and Pitcher was talking to someone else. Then he leaned over and said quietly:

"That's a very good bet. What have you heard?"

Realising I was going to make London's biggest bookmaker look foolish, I gulped and said:

"Mr Dunn, it's not for me to give you advice. But if you will sit with your back to the bar, you must expect people to look over your shoulder at your betting book. If you sat with your back to the wall, I think you'd find it more profitable."

He roared with laughter, ordered a bottle of champagne and called Pitcher over.

" Pitch," he said, "where did you get this one from? Teaching me my business at his age! Who is he?"

So Pitcher introduced us properly and Dickie Dunn said:

"Well, Gally, you're no knight in shining armour but you've got your wits about you. I'll take your bet and I'll take your advice. And there's a couple of seats at the Alhambra in my name if you want to use them."

And off he went. Pitcher was dying to know what it was all about but I had enough sense to keep my mouth shut.

Good old Dickie! He was the last of the ready-money bookies, an honest man who never welshed or turned down a bet in his life.

Even my brother Clarence sometimes got into trouble in the old days, although you'd never think it to look at him now. Of course he never meant to, but he simply didn't learn and because he didn't gamble, he always had more money than the rest of us. That made him popular with the fast set who could stick him with the bill.

It must have been about '87, when I was in my last half at Eton, that he nearly came unstuck. We were in town for the Harrow match and Clarence had gone out for the evening. I'd been at Lords and came home wondering how to tell Father I needed a new topper. I'd smashed at least three Harrovian hats in the scramble after the match, but a big chap had scragged me properly. Mrs Perkins downstairs said she could sew up most of the rips in my coat, but I was definitely going to need a new hat.

I was lying in bed wondering what Father would say when a growler pulled up outside, followed by a frantic banging on the front door. Wilson opened it and I heard Clarence shouting at him to pay the growler. I looked out to see him rushing upstairs dressed in nothing but his evening shirt, socks, shoes and what looked like a crumpled newspaper!

I followed him to his room to find him sitting on the bed, swathed in a dressing-gown and shuddering violently. He was in a terrible state and I thought he must be tight. But, although he might have been spifflicated earlier on, he was sober enough now. Shock, I suppose. When I heard what had happened, I wasn't at all surprised.

He'd gone to the Gaiety, 'Fun On The Bristol' I think it was, where he'd met Wild Willy. The world knows him now as a pillar of Shropshire society, Sir Willoughby Travers of Easeby Hall, but Wild Willy was what everybody called him then, not to be confused with Willie Wilde of whom, as they say, more anon. Wild Willy was at Oxford with Clarence and they hadn't much in common, but Willy always overspent his allowance by the third of the month and I suppose he wanted Clarence to pay for his supper.

I don't know how much persuasion Clarence needed, but Willy took him to the Coal Hole, still there in the Strand I'm glad to say, and introduced him to sherry cobblers. Even I knew sherry cobblers aren't strong, but Willy insisted on adding a nip of rum to improve the flavour.

Eventually Willy decided they needed a change, so they went on to the Empire. They'd been in the Promenade only ten minutes when Willy called two girls over to join them and ordered champagne to celebrate the occasion.

When I asked Clarence who the girls were, he said he only knew their first names – Bessie and Daisy. They were friendly and obviously very popular because most of the men in the Empire Promenade seemed to know them. Good old Clarence – he was twenty then, but still a child at heart!

After half an hour or so, Wild Willy said he was going and touched Clarence for a sovereign for the cab. Clarence was a bit puzzled because Bessie or Daisy, he couldn't remember which, heard Willy asking for it and got very annoyed. She slapped Willy's face and said it would be two quid at least. Anybody else would have seen what was going on, but Clarence simply gave Willy the two sovs and they left.

Clarence said things got a bit dull after that. He didn't know what to say to Daisy (or Bessie) and after he'd asked if she'd visited the Academy and what dances she had been to that Season, there didn't seem anything else to do so he called for the bill.

The trouble with Clarence is he's too innocent. Anybody else would have kept his wallet out of sight or found an excuse to change a note at the bar where the girl couldn't see it, but not Clarence. She must have seen how much money he had because she suddenly became very friendly.

"The next thing I knew," he said, "she was sitting on my knee, telling me I had nice eyes and I could take her to the Academy whenever I liked. I was never so embarrassed in my life."

After a couple more drinks, she said it was time for her to go home. So Clarence called a waiter, put his hand in his pocket for his wallet again and found it wasn't there. And then he couldn't find his sovereign case either.

He started babbling about where could they be and were they under the table, but the girl took no notice and started putting her cloak on. It was then Clarence made his big mistake. He got down on his hands and knees to look for his wallet, pulling up the tablecloth to look underneath. Unfortunately, it wasn't the tablecloth, it was the girl's skirts! Naturally she drew away, Clarence hung on and the next thing he knew she was standing there in her drawers and stockings, screaming her head off while Clarence was plunging about in a pile of petticoats and skirts.

He couldn't remember much of what happened after that. He found himself struggling with three or four men who picked him up, tore off his coat and trousers and threw him out. So there he was in Leicester Square in nothing but his shirt, socks and shoes, the rain pouring down and the two Empire bouncers telling him he was a dirty beast!

Lord knows what would have happened if Ned de Clifford hadn't been there. He came out with a copy of *The Times,* wrapped it round Clarence and whistled up a growler to bring him home.

Poor Clarence! He gave the Empire a miss from then on, which was a pity because I'd been hoping he'd take me there. Still, I did manage to convince him the Hippodrome was worth a visit. They had a girl juggler there with the finest figure in London and most of it on display. I told Clarence it was a Classical reconstruction and she was meant to be a Roman slave.

Having heard some of the things Wild Willy got up to, I reckon Clarence got off lightly. My old friend Gee-Gee (Sir Stanley Gervase-Gervase) still pales at the recollection of what happened to him in Willy's company at Rosherville Gardens. Unfortunately it is too scurrilous to recount even in these enlightened days.

The experience put Clarence off London for life, whereas I couldn't wait to leave the peace and quiet of Blandings and succumb to the temptations of the big city. However, it was not until a couple of years later that I was able to join that company of free spirits whose activities revolved around the three institutions which were to become such major influences in my life – Romano's Restaurant, the Pelican Club and the *Pink 'Un* newspaper.

Chapter 2

Romano's Restaurant

Paradise in the Strand

I'M NOT sure when I first entered the hallowed portals I came to know so well at 399 Strand, but I remember vividly a large fat man just inside the door having a furious argument with a small, perky-looking chap. It was my first sight of Fatty Coleman and Shifter Goldberg, though of course I didn't know who they were till later.

There was a large goldfish tank just behind the fat man. As I stood there, waiting for Ned de Clifford to pay the cab, the small chap suddenly reached up and pushed the fat man's topper off the back of his head into the tank. The fat man straightened up, unable to believe what had happened and the small man shouted at him:

"Me! Trying to touch me, Fatty! Trying to touch old Shifter for a dollar when there's a dozen mugs in here you haven't even sniffed at yet! Start swimming for your hat and I hope you've been mug enough to pay for it!"

And, with immense dignity, the small chap marched down the corridor to the restaurant. The fat man looked after him helplessly for a moment and cried:

"Go easy, Shifter. I was only trying to save time – and everybody knows you came up on a winner today."

For some reason, this infuriated the little man even more; he stopped in his tracks and shouted back: "It was only twenty-five quid and it's for the wife and kids, not you, Fatty."

This seemed to flabbergast the fat man and also, I noticed, the dozen or so men and girls who were in the bar. One of the girls called out: "I didn't know you were married, Shifter."

I have never seen such scorn on a man's face.

" Of course I'm not married! But my girl-friend is and it's costing me more and more to persuade her little Tommy that he doesn't see me coming out of her room at four o'clock in the morning!" And he resumed his indignant march down to the restaurant.

It was a typical introduction to the home of what Dwarf called 'London's white-shirt-fronted Bohemia'. We all patronised the Empire, the Criterion, the Alhambra and went on to the Pelican or the Gardenia but, from about 1885 till 1905, Romano's was THE place to go. The food wasn't particularly good but the company was superb. It was where we met our friends and a very unusual bunch they were too. You wouldn't take them home to meet your mother, but they had a zest for life that made them well worth knowing.

The Roman, Alfonso Nicolino Romano, was a waiter at the Café Royal who decided to set up on his own. His capital was only four pounds but he took a small scruffy fish-and-chip shop in the Strand and asked his bookmaker George Piesse to lend him the outstanding amount.

To make sure his money was safe, as well as helping the Roman, Piesse started taking his racing pals there. They brought in the racehorse owners who in turn brought in the sporting journalists, who were being crowded out of the Café Royal by the artistic set.

When the *Pink 'Un* crowd came in, its fortune was made. They wrote about it and the Gaiety Girls started lunching there (the Roman knew how much business they brought with them and only charged them half-price). But Romano kept on with his betting and, although he was an excellent judge of wine, he was a rotten judge of horses. So, no matter how successful his restaurant was, he was never able to expand the premises. I was glad he didn't; it would have spoilt the atmosphere of the place.

In the early days there was one central window, flanked by two doors. One door led to the bar, the other to the rooms above.

In the window was a large aquarium into which customers would try and duck each other late in the evening. The unfortunate fish lived on a diet of cigar ash, burnt almonds, lemon rind and other oddments, not to mention Hughie Drummond occasionally trying to join them for a bath. One of my acquaintances once tried to use it for another practical, if disgusting, purpose but Steggles (the Vine Street Inspector) happened to be passing and the chap got himself a hefty fine for indecent behaviour.

On a table in the centre of the room was a silver-plated galleon containing three large bottles of red, amber and green liquid. These went the way of all flesh the night Alfred Cellier came back from Australia to find that his show 'Dorothy' had become a tremendous success. He was, if only fleetingly, a wealthy man and threw a party to celebrate the fact. At some time in the proceedings – my memory is a little blurred – Tubby Parsloe, Hughie Drummond and a few others became convinced the mysterious liquids in the centre-piece were rare liqueurs and decided to sample them.

The stuff turned out to be poisonous and their lives were only saved by the fact that a group of doctors from the Charing Cross Hospital were present, of whom a couple were still sober. The bodies were hauled off and desperate work with emetics and stomach-pumps saved the day. The ravished galleon itself featured in an informal game of football and the Roman had to sell it for scrap.

Somebody was sober enough to collect up the broken glass which you can still see today at the Gaiety Theatre. If they're doing a scene where someone is meant to be drinking champagne, the ice in the ice-bucket is the glass from the bottles destroyed in Romano's all those years ago.

Behind the bar was the restaurant, a long thin room with tables down either side. These were occupied by journalists from the *Pink 'Un* like Shirley Brooks, Shifter, Jimmy Davis and Pot Stephens or men of the theatre like Charlie Harris (The Stage Damager). Charlie always made sure his food was given special attention by waiting till the waiter had finished calling his order down the speaking tube, then grabbing it and shouting *"Pour le patron"* down the line.

There were Guardees like Billy Fitzditto (The Hon. William Fitzwilliam), The Windsor Warrior, Haddocks and The Bonetwister. There were racing men and actors and, at a table reserved for them, were the girls from the Gaiety, Nellie Farren, Jack St John, Bessie Bellwood and the Leamar Sisters.

The higher echelons of the aristocracy were represented by the Dukes of Manchester, Hamilton and Dunstable while the lower ranks included chaps like The Mate (Sir John Astley), Sir Jarge (Sir George Wombwell) and myself. I recall it was Kim Mandeville (Duke of Manchester) who made *homard à l'Americaine* the restaurant's most popular fish dish, while Barney Barnato, the richest but meanest man in London, was happy to pay the Roman half a guinea each for fresh strawberries in December. Sultry Sambo (Sam Lewis), the money-lender of Cork Street, always occupied a corner table where, as he put it, he could keep an eye on his investments.

As was only to be expected, it was in Romano's that the Jubilee Plunger announced his inevitable and often forecast bankruptcy. The Jubilee Plunger (Henry Ernest Benzon, not to be confused with Walton, the Jubilee Juggins) inherited a quarter of a million quid and got through it in two years. He just couldn't walk away from a bet whether it was cards, pigeon-shooting, horses or cock-fighting. We all knew it would happen; we were just surprised he lasted two years.

And it was also in Romano's that old Sir George Chetwynd organised the fund that provided the Plunger with £7 a week for the rest of his life. I am glad to report that Dickie Dunn and several other bookies were among the largest contributors, as was Sam Lewis.

It was there that I first came across that man of wrath, Tubby Parsloe, who I understand is now the Unionist candidate for our local Parliamentary Division. When I first met him, he was walking up and down the restaurant in Romano's with a whisky and soda he certainly hadn't paid for in one hand, a soup tureen on his head, a French loaf over his shoulder, informing the world in a raucous voice that he was an officer of the Blues on Royal Guard.

We all considered it a great honour to be invited to join the Gaiety Girls' table and I was having a drink there with Bessie Bellwood when half a dozen of the other girls joined us, all laughing their heads off. They were followed by George Edwardes who was trying to console a pretty little brunette, clearly the butt of the joke. She was downcast but defiant. How was she to know that silver sables were supposed to be that colour? She had felt it would be rude to express her doubts to the admirer who had given her the cape. So she said nothing and just spent two days picking out all the 'grey hairs' that spoilt it in her eyes.

Later the same day, I was lucky enough to be present at the famous 'Second Civil War', a pitched battle between four peers of the realm and three Members of the Lower House, aided and abetted by an archdeacon with republican sympathies to whom the Roman's champagne had recalled his lost youth a trifle too vividly. The enthusiastic audience included bookmakers' touts, remittance men and journalists from a dozen London papers. It says a good deal for Romano's that, when the combatants were eventually scooped in by the gendarmerie for continuing the battle in the Strand, nobody thought of revealing their real names in the Press or anywhere else.

As a tribute to their loyalty that night, neither shall I, even though the archdeacon under advisement went on to become a bishop, renowned for his fulminations against the evils of drink and disorderly living.

There was always somebody worth meeting or something happening at Romano's. For instance, there was the time that Valerie Rhys, the boisterous bohemian actress of the Alhambra whom I mention elsewhere, celebrated her engagement to Henry Meux, heir to both a baronetcy and the enormous brewing business.

He stood on a table and proudly read out the lines with which *Fun* had commemorated the occasion:

> 'I offer my congratulations, not my stern rebukes
> To one who was once Miss Val Rhys, but is now Madame Meux;
> But on the solemn word of one who says 'I slightly knew her';
> 'Tis not the first or only time that Val has copped the brewer.'

The roars of applause at this re-doubled when the blushing bride-to-be joined him on the table and announced that her future husband was just as good a poet as the anonymous writer of *Fun*. To prove the point, she took off her glittering engagement ring and asked the audience if they had any idea of the beautiful sentiments inscribed therein by the man she loved.

Respecting her emotions – or so they thought – a decorous hush fell over the audience.

"Very well, then," announced the future Lady Meux. "I'll tell you. It's better than Shakespeare and truer to Life.

"The inscription of eternal devotion on this ring is expressed in words so beautiful, so touching, so tender I can hardly bring myself to utter them. But, if only to show the exquisite delicacy of phrasing and poetic touch possessed by my future husband, I shall do so now. It says," and, in the awed silence, she declaimed in ringing tones:

> " 'To bloody old Val,
> From drunken old Hal' !!"

She got the biggest round of applause in her career.

People sometimes ask me what made Romano's different from other restaurants. Apart from the mixed company, very mixed sometimes, it was undoubtedly the Roman himself. He was the most likeable of men and his *bons mots* in strangled Italo-English were famous all over London. People used to think it was all a fake, but I got to know him pretty well and I am convinced that the English we heard was all the Roman knew.

He knew his English was execrable but I think he was clever enough to realise that people liked it. In any event, his normal enthusiasm led him to believe people understood what he was saying, even though the bar would often divide into two camps, arguing fiercely as to the meaning of his latest attack on the language of Shakespeare and Milton.

I remember once he wanted to place a bet on a horse and a bemused silence fell on the bar as he called to a bookie across the room:

"Ere! Missa Bookworm, 'ow much you lay me Sausages?"

It took a good five minutes of puzzled questions, answers and reference to a racing paper before the bookmaker realised the Roman wanted to bet on a horse called 'Isosceles'. He had always called it 'Icicles' himself.

After the galleon with its bottles of mixed liquids had gone the way of all things, the Roman replaced it with what he fondly believed was the latest in interior fashion – a fernery. This consisted of a small pile of bricks, barely covered with earth, with some very tired greenery that struggled for survival. On top reposed a small china alligator which soon disappeared. The Roman mourned its loss and got it into his head that Shifter Goldberg was the culprit. For weeks afterwards the entrance of the little man into Romano's was signalled by an indignant outburst from the proprietor :

"Hi! You! Missa Shif! You gimme back my elevator, or Romano, 'e take out a snubbons."

On one occasion he took a holiday to his native Italy. When he returned, we all gathered round him to hear his experiences.

"What did you see in Venice, Roman?"

"What I see in Venuses? I see 'ouse of him you write plays of, the merchants of Venuses, what you call Shamrocks by Henry Irving Esquire."

The Roman was a kind-hearted chap; with the amount of dud cheques he was given, he had to be. I believe only two or three fellows were ever actually banned from Romano's. One I remember is still with us, John Runciman, the music critic who was barred because he made the mistake of drinking too much before he entered Romano's, instead of getting drunk there as most of us did. This was too much for the Roman who evicted him with the unforgettable words:

"Missa Runtz Esquire, I do not mind a chentleman getting drunk in 'ere. But, whenna you go somewhere else to drink and come to Romano's only to *vommit* – I say 'Outside, Missa Runtz Esquire, if you please!'"

It was the only time I saw him expel someone into the outer darkness. I had feared it was going to be Stiffy Halliday who had, moments before, laid out Dunstable with a cold turkey (Stiffy was never more to be feared than when he had a cold turkey in his hand). But Romano didn't mind the odd fight so long as we kept on buying drinks, and occasionally paid for them.

I won't go into the various manoeuvres we adopted to pay or avoid paying our bills there. Old Otto, the headwaiter, could be persuaded to cash a cheque for a fiver most of the time and we missed him sadly when he died in '93 or '94. Luigi took his place and although Luigi was even then undoubtedly the best headwaiter in London, he wasn't as soft-hearted as Otto had been.

The Roman died in 1901 and was given one of the biggest funerals London had ever seen. Unlucky to the last, poor chap, he was buried on the day Little Eva won the Lincolnshire. The Roman had two thousand to come on it, but his death cancelled the debt.

A new company was formed to take over the restaurant with Teddy Bayly as manager and Luigi as his lieutenant. But Luigi's gifts soon made him manager and he held that position until he moved on to Ciro's. After making that famous, he went on to build up the Criterion for Solly Joel before he bought the Embassy from Albert de Courville. At the Embassy he has achieved the recognition he has deserved for so long as London's leading restaurateur.

They closed the old bar in 1910 and the Romano's we knew and loved ceased to exist. Old Bendi the cellarman hung on as did Villa the sommelier, but the spirit has gone as have many of the clientèle. With a few exceptions such as myself, the survivors of those hectic evenings have joined the ranks of those poor wretches who have been told by their doctors that alcohol is a luxury their bodies can no longer afford.

The restaurant is still there and I pop in occasionally for old times' sake, but there are too many ghosts.

When I leave the old place, I always glance down the Strand to the Law Courts. It is a habit some of us got into after the Roman lost the famous bet about his clock.

We were having a drink one evening when Shifter came in from the *Pink 'Un* office, ordered a whisky, looked up at the clock over the bar, then at his watch and told the Roman his clock was wrong. Romano denied it hotly and Shifter, with a wink at us to keep quiet, told him the Law Courts clock told a very different time. If the Roman didn't believe him, all he had to do was to step outside his own front door and look. Romano dismissed the suggestion out of hand. The Law Courts clock was at the other end of the Strand; there were two churches blocking the way; it was impossible to see the clock from the restaurant.

Shifter was adamant; he would bet Romano a fiver on it. The Roman considered it, thought about the two churches and took the bet. So we all trooped outside and saw, as Shifter had known all along, that the illuminated Law Courts clock was perfectly visible in the darkness.

A month or so later, Pitcher Binstead came in and brought the conversation around to clocks in general and Romano's clock in particular. The Roman listened warily but then leaped into action as Pitcher said it was a pity one couldn't see the Law Courts clock from the restaurant. 'Missa Pitch Esquire' was wrong; it was possible to see the Law Courts clock from his front door, everybody knew that.

Pitcher drew him on like a fisherman playing a trout until the Roman lost his sense of caution. He would bet twenty-five pounds that, if they went out there and then, the illuminated Law Courts clock would be in clear view. And Pitcher took the bet.

We all trooped outside and looked down the Strand. Nothing! The Roman blinked, looked harder, then persuaded Pitcher to walk down the road to Southampton Street. Pitcher good-naturedly agreed but the clock was still invisible. A downcast Romano led the way to the restaurant where he paid Pitcher his pony which, I am glad to say, Pitcher promptly spent on champagne for all those present.

When the restaurant closed that night, the Roman put his coat on and walked down the Strand. He reached the Law Courts and looked up flabbergasted at the darkened clock.

"Whatta has 'appened to the damm light insida it?" he asked the duty policeman nearby.

"Ain't been no light in it for a couple of days now," replied the copper. "A friend of yours, Mr Binstead, asked the same question early on tonight. I thought he would've told you!"

From then on, the Roman refused to listen to any comments on his clock or indeed comments on time-keeping of any sort.

Alfonso Nicolino Romano ('The Roman')

Note. The famous restaurant was demolished in 1956 and a new office block built on the site. Because of the public outcry, it was named Romano House, but even this name has now gone.

On the day the roof came off, the final mark of every building's death, I went down to the cellars and found a single jar of Crosse & Blackwell's pickle standing in the corner of the kitchens. Like the mummified sentry at Pompeii, it was faithful unto death.

For pilgrims who wish to see what it looked like, its neighbours are still there, ornate Victorian buildings in a splendid mixture of Flemish, Venetian, Gothic and Turkish building styles. From the pavement outside 399 Strand, it is still possible to see the Law Courts clock, despite the two churches in the way. *Ed.*

Chapter 3

The Pelican Club

*'They are no members of the common throng
They are all noblemen who have gone wrong!'*
'Pirates of Penzance', W.S. Gilbert

I REMEMBER Sullivan quoting Gilbert's lines to describe the membership of the Pelican Club and I thought then how apposite they were.

However, I should make it clear that we prided ourselves on being the most democratic of clubs. It didn't matter who or what you were, our conditions for membership were based entirely on a certain standard of behaviour. Drinking, gambling and a keen interest in racing were a prerequisite; the ability to pay for your drinks was desirable, but telling a good story was acceptable in lieu.

The Pelican Club, to whose training I owe any success I may have had in coping with those little problems that have confronted me and those I hold dear, was founded on 19 January 1887, a date memorable in the social history of London. The first clubhouse, at 21 Denman Street just off Piccadilly Circus, was a peculiar old building, a cross between a disused Turkish Bath and a Baptist meeting-house. [1]

Shifter Goldberg, with that touch of genius that characterised many of his actions, had realised that the Adelphi Club in Maiden Lane, 'The Spooferies' as everybody called it, was nearing the end of its time. The waiters were starting to demur when called upon to produce tripe-and-onion suppers at seven in the morning; the cleaners were beginning to complain about the number of members they found asleep under the billiard table in the grey light of dawn, and the secretary was even said to be taking steps to enforce the payment of subscriptions!

---

[1] I can confirm Mr Threepwood's description is an accurate one. The building in Denman Street survived till 1977 when I sadly watched its demolition. A tile from the old bar has pride of place on my desk. It is the last relic of the institution which Mr Threepwood and his fellows made famous around the world. *Ed.*

So everyone was anxious for a new club and Shifter opened 21 Denman Street as The Star Club. For the first few weeks it did very well. It must be the only club in London whose inaugural party exhausted not only the stocks of champagne in the bar, but in all the neighbouring taverns and the wine merchant's warehouse as well! Unfortunately Shifter, who believed in wetting his good luck, overdid it and Swears Wells, club manager extraordinary, arrived just in time to become joint proprietor of the newly-named Pelican Club.

Swears Wells had a persuasive manner and, in no time at all, he had a committee any club would be proud of. There was the Marquess of Queensberry (Q); Viscount Mandeville, later Duke of Manchester (Kim); Lord de Clifford (Ned); Lord Churston (Johnny); the Hon. Daniel Finch (Dan); the Hon. Clement Finch (Clem); Sir John Astley (The Mate) and Captain Archibald Drummond (Archie).

They were names that looked wonderful on a prospectus and some of them even had a bank account in credit.

In its early days the club did well. The bills were paid, sometimes, and the staff were willing; indeed some would say almost too willing. I remember, soon after I joined, hearing the members grumbling about the recent grievous loss of a prized Club amenity.

One hot day in July, a new member, elected for the depth of his pocket rather than his charm of manner, wandered into the dining-room with a supercilious air and ordered:

"A really decent lunch, if you can provide such a thing in this place."

The head waiter concealed his emotion, as good head waiters should, and took the order. Our young spark continued in the lordly manner of one who didn't care to be bothered with trifles:

" Whatever soup you've got – and I'll try the fish. And I may as well try the entree – oh, yes," he added in the bored tone of an epicure who wants his palate tempted, "and a bird of course!"

A bird! In July! The head waiter choked back his laughter, fulfilled the order, but charged him three guineas for 'the bird' since, as he pointed out in a grave undertone, it was the close season.

When the news got out, the members were highly indignant. Three guineas was ludicrous. They were unanimous that the unfortunate club parrot which had been pressed into service was worth five guineas at least.

In a moment of weakness (his daughter's a delightful girl) I have agreed not to reveal the name of the wretch concerned. To keep faith with my conscience, I shall merely say that the pompous young man in question has now become a pompous older man; but perhaps some of my readers will remember the incident a few years ago at the installation of a certain Lord Chancellor.

As he mounted the steps to his seat in the House of Lords, the respectful silence was broken by a sotto voce remark from somewhere amongst the peers of the realm assembled below him. The newly-appointed Great Officer of State was seen to stumble slightly and take his seat with a red face and an indignant expression. This did not worry my old friend Barmy Twistleton one little bit. Believing, like the ancient Romans, that it was important for the highest legal luminary in the land to be reminded of human frailty, Barmy felt he was only carrying out his public duty when he murmured the words:

"Who was it ate the Pelican Club parrot?"

Only one candidate for membership of the Pelican was ever blackballed and he was a millionaire. For a club as desperate for wealthy members as we were, this was unprecedented and the incident was widely reported at the time. Swears Wells and Costs Booth both refer to it in their reminiscences, but the name of the unfortunate has never been disclosed. I see no reason for such mealy-mouthed reticence. I am happy to reveal to the world that the man who achieved this unusual distinction is none other than Alaric, Duke of Dunstable and I have no hesitation in saying the members were absolutely right.

Indeed, I will go further and say that a primary qualification of any decent club is to ensure the Duke is not one of its members. Starting off as a young Guardee with an allowance big enough to choke a horse, his reluctance to buy a round of drinks was legendary in the Brigade. He married the only daughter of a wealthy pottery manufacturer; she died and left it all to Dunstable who then came into the title and estates as well.

But, wealthy as he was, the Pelican Club would have none of him. I recall Stiffy Halliday stood on the bar and made such a rousing speech against his candidature that the committee were reaching for the black balls in handfuls and vying with each other to stuff them into the old top hat we used for the purpose.

What with the famous boxing-matches on Sunday nights, the concerts Swears used to organise and one thing and another, the Pelican was the liveliest club in London. And there was always Hughie Drummond to keep members on their toes.

For sheer high spirits, it is difficult to choose between Hughie and Barmy Twistleton. Gross irresponsibility, people like my sisters Hermione and Constance call it but, if adding to the gaiety of London is the measure adopted, then Hughie and Barmy must rank high in the hierarchy of whatever it is. I mention some of Barmy's exploits elsewhere, so this seems an appropriate place to recount some of Hughie's activities in and around 'the village'.

In passing, 'the village' is another common expression of my youth that seems to have vanished with Nineveh and Tyre. I used the phrase 'one of the lads' to a young chap the other day and he looked at me blankly. So I explained that it meant one of the lads of the village. Another blank look made me realise that today's generation doesn't even know what 'the village' is!

I should therefore make it clear that, from about 1870 till 1914, 'the village' was the term used for that area of London stretching from St Paul's in the east to Hyde Park Corner in the west. 'The lads of the village' was the name given to fellows like myself who spent our days and nights making use of the facilities for harmless, and not so harmless, entertainment to be found there.

But to return to Hughie Drummond. Hughie and his brother Archie, both leading lights of the Pelican, were related to the Earl of Perth and the banking Drummonds. I remember Hughie used to glower at the Trafalgar Square bank as he walked past it. He didn't object to their having the money, it was their complete lack of family feeling that annoyed him. He read in the papers once how much profit the bank had made and promptly went along to open an account. They were quite happy to do so until Hughie made it clear he expected special overdraft facilities as a member of the family, such facilities to start from the opening of the account. What riled Hughie was that the director who turned him down as flat as a bed-spread was his elder brother Allan!

Although Archie settled down eventually and lives somewhere near Stroud now I believe, Hughie died unmarried in '99. But he certainly made his mark in his time. He had two favourite occupations that I remember. He used to finish his evenings at the Raleigh by getting himself chucked out, then climb the lamp-post outside, from which vantage-point he would read selected passages out of Howard Vincent's Handbook to the policemen gathered below. (I should add that Vincent was the soldier-turned-barrister-turned-war correspondent who became a Member of Parliament and Director of Criminal Investigation at Scotland Yard.)

It was his *Police Code and Manual* that Hughie used to read aloud to the constables waiting below his lamp-post, laying particular emphasis on the paragraphs dealing with the rights of the citizen to go about his lawful occasions without let or hindrance from the forces of the Law!

Hughie's other enthusiasm was for driving four-wheelers. Although he was a keen pupil of Dickie the Driver (Walter Dickson), his coachmanship was notorious. If, when travelling to Epsom or any other race-meeting within reach of London, we came across a four-wheeler in the ditch, we knew it was odds-on Hughie was somewhere around.

There was one famous occasion for which Swears never forgave him. The Pelicans had laid on a lavish evening of boxing-matches at St James's Palace which the officers of the Brigade had thoroughly enjoyed. Swears, always on the lookout for new members, issued an invitation for them to look in at the Pelican and the Guardees had accepted.

Swears deliberately invited them early so they could see the club before the noisier element came in from Romano's and the Empire. Normally I wouldn't have been there at that time either, but I went along because old Colonel Brabazon was a friend of my father's. (Swears had paid Fatty Coleman a fiver not to be there, I recall.)

Swears really pushed the boat out. The place was sparkling, the waiters were on their best behaviour and Swears was in his element, beaming beatifically on thirty prospective members. They were all admiring his quiet, respectable establishment and old Brabazon had just asked if there were any vacancies for new members when Hughie Drummond interrupted the proceedings.

He had come back early with a few other fellows and noticed a four-wheeler standing outside the club. Hughie looked at the four-wheeler, looked at the steps leading up to the large double doors and decided to enter the club in style. The cabman was persuaded (a sovereign) to hand over his responsibilities, the horse was pulled round to face the steps, Hughie took the reins, his pals got inside and Hughie used the whip.

It was quite an entrance. One moment, there we were in the bar chatting quietly of this and that; the next thing was a tremendous crash of glass, a thundering of hooves, then another violent crash as the four-wheeler smashed straight through the door into the bar where we all stood petrified. Hughie was whooping his head off, his pals inside the growler were cheering and shouting and the Guardees looked as if they'd been caught in a rather nasty Afghan ambush.

Swears, for the one and only time in his life, was speechless. It all got sorted out eventually, but by that time the Guardees had melted away, taking Swears' dreams of financial security with them. [2]

Hughie was always an optimist and matched Shifter Goldberg in his powers of repartee. When he had a painful and difficult operation performed by Sir James Paget, Sir James brought him back to consciousness and gave him the reassuring smile surgeons always give their patients on such occasions. Hughie was not impressed:

"You may well smile now, sir, but you won't think it's so damned funny when it comes to the suit of 'Paget versus Drummond' for your fees!"

I remember vividly Hughie's normal method of entering the club. There would be a shout in the corridor, the glass doors would burst open as Hughie strode in with a ringing 'Hark forward! Hark forward!' and walk past the bar, scything off with his cane any glasses that happened to be on it.

While many of us were pretty good with a bread roll, which can be surprisingly painful if it lands on the end of one's nose, Hughie prided himself on his accuracy with any foodstuff that came to hand. On one occasion, a group of members having supper decided that the food provided for them was more suited as ammunition than sustenance and

---

(2) Mr Threepwood has inserted a footnote here.

'I'm glad to see the old traditions still linger. Last month, a young chap I know in the Brigade tried to drive a taxicab into the Savoy dining-room. He made it through the main doors, but stalled on the carpet inside and the doormen were on to him before he could get the engine started. I won't give his name because his colonel, Old Stuffy, has no sense of humour whatsoever. When I tell you he doesn't even know he's called Old Stuffy, you'll appreciate my reticence.'

the comestibles were flying around the room like edible bats.

When the lighter items had been used up, somebody turned to the heavy artillery (I still believe it was Stiffy Halliday, who always got carried away on such occasions) and grabbed a boar's head from the serving table. He picked off Lord Esmé Gordon as clean as a whistle and the next thing we knew, there was the Marquess's pride and joy flat on his back in the fireplace, out like a light.

In the recrimination and reproaches that followed, Hughie was particularly censorious:

"Play fair! Lay off a bit! I've thrown nothing but jelly all evening. Just as much fun and makes far more mess if you get the right chap!" Which gives you some idea of the members Swears had to cope with.

As well as Master, Pitcher Binstead, Shifter Goldberg and the rest of the *Pink 'Un* lot, the membership included musicians like Arthur Sullivan, dear old Alfred Cellier and Teddy Solomon, and theatrical chaps like Augustus Harris (Druriolanus) and his brother Charlie (The Stage Damager). We had dukes, earls, amateur jockeys and playwrights by the dozen, not to mention a few Rothschilds; in fact, all the young and not-so-young men about Town who found the Pelican provided a liveliness to be found nowhere else in London.

By way of contrast, we also had the two Lewises. Sam Lewis was London's biggest money-lender; George Lewis was solicitor and confidential adviser to Royalty and most of the House of Lords whenever any delicate problems occurred – which often did. (There was a certain lady of the theatre who was most reluctant to return a valuable piece of furniture to its rightful place in the State Room of St James's Palace.)

One member of whom we were particularly proud was Legs Ponderby. When the Savage Club chaps boasted of Sir Henry Irving, we used to boast of Legs Ponderby. Sir Lewis Ponderby was universally known as Legs, short for Hollow Legs from his phenomenal consumption of alcohol. He earned his place in legend and song when, by universal acclaim, he won from Shifter Goldberg the title of the Pelican Club's – and therefore, London's – biggest liar.

This, mark you, was in competition with men like Arthur Roberts, Pitcher Binstead and Swears Wells, whose skill in bending the truth had earned the admiration of bookmakers at every race-course in England. Legs won the title in what he always referred to modestly as 'The Case of Quick Thinking in Cecil Street'. (Conan Doyle's Sherlock Holmes was all the rage then.)

It was Billy Wyndham who told us about it as we hung on his words with bated breath. Billy, whose brother Charlie succeeded as Lord Leconfield in 1901, had a room in Cecil Street, one of those small cul-de-sacs that ran down to the river from the Strand. It has gone now and the Cecil Hotel occupies the site, though they tell me it is soon to be replaced by another ruddy office block. [3]

Billy was in his rooms one evening when there was a bang at the door and Charlie Freeson charged in with a girl-friend, both of them in a terrible state. They had been coming out of the Café Royal when Charlie spotted his wife across the road. The pair of them ducked into a cab but, from the shout his wife gave, he knew they'd been seen. She'd called another cab, set off in pursuit and chased them round the West End! They reckoned she'd seen them turn into Cecil Street, but they had managed to get indoors before she saw where they went.

From behind the curtains they could see her mounting guard at the top of the street. Charlie was sure she'd wait there all night if she had to, so it looked as if the pair of them would have to stay at Billy's.

Well, Billy was a good-natured chap so he let the two love-birds have his bedroom and went off to doss down at his club, taking care to avoid the prowling Mrs Charlie Freeson on the way. He went back the next morning to change and Charlie and his girl were very grateful, especially as he was able to tell them that Charlie's wife had given up her vigil. Charlie told him to go and change and they would all go out to breakfast.

So there the three of them were: Billy changing in his bedroom, Charlie and his light-of-love in the sitting-room, when Legs Ponderby, dishevelled and frantic, burst through the door.

Legs took one look at Charlie and his girl and exclaimed:

"If anyone comes through that door, no matter who they are or what they say, tell them you're waiting for the doctor! Where's Billy?"

They pointed at the bedroom door and Legs charged in to find Billy just putting his tie on.

---

(3) Mr Threepwood's forebodings were correct. The Cecil Hotel was demolished two years later in 1931. Shell-Mex House stands on the site now. *Ed.*

"Into bed with you," shouted Legs. "No time for explanations – into bed with you. I didn't go home last night and my wife's after me! You were run down by a hansom last night and both your legs are broken. You're at death's door. Remember that – because if you don't, I shall be!"

Sure enough, another set of footsteps was heard on the stairs and Legs' wife stormed in. She was a woman I wouldn't like to cross; her normal manner made you think of Boadicea in a bad mood. When she was angry, strong men took to their heels.

Charlie said he had never realised before what the Avenging Angel looked like. She came through the door like a troop of cavalry, but stopped dead when she saw Charlie and the girl standing there, both of them in their street clothes and clearly the height of respectability.

"Lewis! Lewis! Come out here and bring that trollop with – oh!"

Then, Charlie said, she realised things were not quite as she expected and her voice faltered.

"I am – er – looking for my husband. Have you seen Sir Lewis? Is he here?"

Luckily for Legs, Charlie and his girl managed to play it through. The girl put her handkerchief to her eye and sniffed a bit and Charlie said mournfully:

"Clearly you have not heard the dreadful news, madam. We are awaiting the doctor, but we fear there is little he can do. Your husband, gallant and kind fellow that he is, is at the bedside now."

And he pointed towards the bedroom door. In went Legs' wife to find Billy in bed with eyes shut, groaning slightly (he knew Legs' wife) and Legs seated at the bedside, radiating sorrow, sympathy and patient exhaustion in equal measure.

As she stood there, speechless for probably the first time in her life, Legs stood up and said gravely:

"It was good of you to come, my dear, but there is little you or anybody else can do. All night I have watched and prayed by the poor fellow's bedside, but I hold out little hope. See how he groans and tosses in his agony …

(At this point, wishing he were a thousand miles away, Billy groaned and tossed to the satisfaction of all parties concerned.)

"But I am only sorry, my dear," Legs went on, sprouting wings as he spoke and looking like Uriah Heep trying to float a large loan, " that I was unable to inform you earlier and save you needless concern over my absence last night. But the shock of finding my old friend so terribly injured ... It drove every other thought from my mind. How can I apologise for the distress my thoughtlessness must have caused you?"

Well, of course there was nothing really she could say.

"No, Lewis," she replied. "It is I who should apologise. I thought ... well, never mind what I thought. Is there anything I can do? Why do you not come home with me now and your friends outside can watch over the poor man? Perhaps you can return later and see what the doctors say."

At first Legs refused to leave his post. His duty was clear. But, slowly, reluctantly and – oh how gracefully, he yielded! A master of dissimulation, he gave way to her entreaties at last as a loving husband should.

"Perhaps you are right, my dear. I do need some rest; it has been a long and dreadful night. The realisation that this is the awful Fate that comes to us all has led me to forget such things as food, drink or sleep. I shall come with you as you ask. But, my dear, I have made a vow to my wretched friend that I shall not let him face the dreadful hours of darkness alone. Tonight I must leave you again to keep my promise and watch by his bedside. We who are lucky enough to see tomorrow's dawn must think of those poor wretches who are not so fortunate!"

And he got away with it. He spent the next three nights on the town, having the time of his life, basking in the admiration of his fellows and revelling in the new nickname of 'Broken Legs', which was instantly bestowed upon him. And that is how Shifter Goldberg lost his title as the Pelican Club's biggest liar.

Chapter 4

The *Pink 'Un*

The paper everybody read,
with some comments on its unusual staff

A LTHOUGH the *Pink 'Un* is still going under its official title of *The Sporting Times*, it has changed so much that people wonder why there was once so much fuss about it. It is difficult for them to realise what an important part the *Pink 'Un* played in the social history of this country and what a formative influence it was on chaps like me.

The *Pink 'Un* was nearly as powerful an organ as the mighty *Times*, and certainly far more popular. Not in the numbers sold maybe, but in its influence on the social habits of London and, indeed, of the British Empire. It might not tell you much about foreign affairs or politics, but it told you all the things about politicians they didn't want you to know. You never saw it in a drawing-room and my father never allowed it in the house, but you never saw a mess, wardroom or club without it.

The paper was started by Dr Shorthouse as a 'Chronicle of Racing, Literature, Art and the Drama' back in 1865. He was a very good doctor; the trouble was he didn't like doctoring. He was much keener on racing and undoubtedly had a good eye for a horse, but his comments about owners did not make him popular.

Shorthouse eventually went to prison for criminal libel and sold the paper to Outram Wallace, late of the Black Watch, who sold it to John Corlett. The price was fifty pounds, half of which John Corlett (soon to become known as Master) had to borrow.

It was first printed on the famous pink paper, not from policy, but simply because Corlett had bought a batch of pink paper cheap. The following week, at a railway station, he heard a fellow ask for *The Times*. The news-seller offered him the august publication from Printing House Square but the chap refused it vehemently:

"No, not that. The pink 'un."

Corlett recognised a snappy title when he heard it, ordered more paper of the same colour and adopted the new title *The Pink 'Un* the following week. People liked the colour and they also liked the new anecdotal page 'Answers to Queries' written by Shirley Brooks, (Peter Blobbs), eldest son of the famous *Punch* editor. The paper began to prosper and the circulation rose to 4000, then later to 20,000 copies.

Pitcher Binstead reckoned Master's success was based on three things. He was an admirable judge of horses and could write about them in a way that both experts and amateurs enjoyed reading. Secondly, he recruited and managed to control the most colourful set of contributors a newspaper ever had. Thirdly, he told each member of staff to cultivate a personality and stick to it.

And personalities is what they were. Their scurrilous adventures and escapades were faithfully recounted in the *Pink 'Un's* pages and made them famous across the country. Nobody who reckoned himself a man of the world was to be seen without the *Pink 'Un*. Its jokes are still repeated today, as are the expressions it introduced into the language.

The most famous is the term 'The Ashes' for the Test matches against Australia. Back in '82 England, set 85 runs to win, were bowled out by Spofforth seven runs short of their target. It was the first time Australia had beaten a full English team on English soil. Peter Blobbs wrote the following 'In Memoriam' notice for the next number of the *Pink 'Un:*

In Affectionate Remembrance

of

ENGLISH CRICKET

Which Died At

The Oval

On 26th August 1882

Deeply lamented by a large circle of sorrowing
friends and acquaintances

RIP

N.B. The body will be cremated and the ASHES taken to Australia

The idea caught the public imagination and the next year Ivo Bligh (later Lord Darnley) took out a team to Australia to recover the mythical Ashes. Australia won the first game, but England won the next two and the series. The real Ashes came into being when some Melbourne ladies, one of whom became Bligh's wife, burnt a bail used in the last game and presented Bligh with the ashes in a small urn. He died last year – 1928 – and left the urn to the MCC.

It was the *Pink 'Un* which taught its readers that 'oof' meant money, that a 'prosser' was a cadger and 'tart' a lady of easy virtue. Not the most elegant of terms perhaps, but the *Pink 'Un* was never one to pull its punches. The Bright Young Things may mock the respectability of the Victorians, but we had a robustness that is lacking today. The *Pink 'Un* reported what actually happened and what people said about it.

I don't suppose there are many so-called 'fearless' or 'daringly-modern' editors today who would print the joke that adorned the front page of the *Pink 'Un* in the mid-Nineties. It ran:

> 'Last week a man was fined thirty shillings in Clerkenwell Court for docking a dog's tail.
> If that's the going rate, what price the Chief Rabbi?'

The old offices at 52 Fleet Street, now long gone, gave a good indication of the tone of the paper. The ground floor was occupied by a small tailor's shop. To one side a steep staircase led up to a minute lobby with a cubby-hole of an outer office. A small glass window allowed the Cerberus on guard to inspect visitors. Once satisfied that the caller was not a bailiff, bookie's minder, creditor or some other unwelcome visitor, the guardian would pull a string which, by some complicated mechanism of his own devising, opened the inner door.

This led on to a narrow corridor running right and left. To the right, towards the Fleet Street front, was the staff room. It was a low, square, wood-panelled room with a series of pictures round the walls. These included such historic items as a copy of Fred Archer's indentures and photographs of such well-known men about Town as Hughie Drummond, Ballyhooly Martin and others who did little of note in their lives, but added considerably to the gaiety of London's nightlife.

Over the fireplace hung the most eye-catching exhibit to the casual visitor, a poem by Doss Chiderdoss (A.R. Marshall) and the indignant response it had brought from a reader. The poem had dealt with the intimate lingerie of the domestic servant and the response was an indignant letter from 'Parlour Maid' enclosing a be-ribboned, frilled example of the garment under discussion. Poem, letter and sample all hung framed over the marble fireplace.

In the centre of the room was a large dining-table around which the staff sat, with Colonel Newnham-Davis as editor-in-chief at the head. Another door led directly on to the staircase, a facility often used by such members as Shifter Goldberg whenever the voice of the tax collector was heard in the outer office.

Friday was the important day of the *Pink 'Un* week. At ten in the morning or so, most of the half-dozen regular staff would arrive, followed by the Dwarf (Newnham-Davis) at eleven. Pitcher Binstead always came in on the dot of noon. Old Energy (Fred Smith) came in at the same time and they sat down to correct the proofs as they emerged from Newnham-Davis's tray.

Noon was also the time for the heavy tread of the proprietor, John Corlett, to be heard coming up the stairs. He would look first into his own small office which just had room for a large roll-top desk and a safe bearing the legend:

'NOTICE TO BURGLARS. THERE IS NOTHING IN THIS SAFE. WE GO RACING.'

The boy took out the proofs as they were corrected, the room started to fill with visitors who knew that Friday was the one day they could catch the staff at home and, promptly at 12.45, in came the cashier with the welcome white envelopes. The staff then dispersed to lunch in Covent Garden, at Romano's or wherever the Dwarf had advised them in the previous week's epicurean column.

Lunch over, it was back to work signing the corrected proofs, after which the majority of the staff left. Master, Gubbins and Rooty Tooty then got down to the really important business, the selection of horses for the following week's racing. This was taken very seriously and mere humorous writers were pointedly excluded from the arcane discussions that took place over the Racing Calendar.

Racing was the theoretical basis of the whole paper. But it has to be said that, though John Corlett knew as much about horses as anyone, he had little success with his own. Indeed, it became an article of faith amongst his staff that the horse NOT to back in any race was one owned by their worthy proprietor. Despite that, Master's opinion was sought by many owners and trainers who respected his undoubted knowledge of the sport; he was certainly the only *Pink 'Un* who made a profit on his racing-bets.

Of course, the *Pink 'Un* staff being the men they were, payday was never as straightforward as I describe it above.

The cashier, a very hard-tried man called Fred Barnard, always referred to in print as The Economist, had a difficult task. With the constant calls from the staff for a couple of quid 'to get them through till Friday', the petty cash box was always plentifully supplied with IOUs. In theory, these were deducted from the cheques signed on Fridays.

Master ran the paper on a loose rein and, most of the time, the IOUs were quietly torn up and the full amount was paid to the anxious staff member. But occasionally there was too much paper in the box, even for the generous Master, and sad faces and loud grumbles from the staff made it clear to the world that John Corlett's patience had been tried too far.

My old friend Costs (J.B. Booth) remembers one occasion when an IOU of Shifter Goldberg's was not torn up and the little man was furious. He protested to Master, tempers were lost and eventually it seemed as though Shifter had resigned or been sacked – no one was quite sure which.

When the time came for Master and the staff to retire to the Cheshire Cheese for the weekly lunch, Shifter stood at the other end of the bar, wrapped in outraged dignity.

"What's yours, Shif?" grunted Master. But Shifter was implacable. Lowering his head, he butted his ex-editor and proprietor violently in the stomach like an angry ram, exclaiming between butts:

"Am I sacked or not?" (butt), "Tell me!" (butt), "Am I sacked or not?" (butt).

"Stop it – ouch! – stop it, Shifter ! Ouch!" exclaimed John. "Don't be – ouch! – a – ouch! – fool!"

"Am I reinstated or not?" (butt).

"Ouch! – Reinstated!"

As well as becoming famous through their columns, Pitcher, Costs, Shifter and the rest made other people famous too. With acute observation and skilful turn of phrase, they introduced the readers of the *Pink 'Un* to cabmen, hairdressers, stage-door men and other important and hitherto unpublicised participants in London's social life.

Pitcher Binstead, for example, always had his hair cut by the barber at the Tavistock Hotel in Covent Garden. While most men found conversation in the barber's chair tedious, Pitcher brought out the best in his acquaintances at every level of society. From his barber, christened Funny Fred in the *Pink 'Un*, he extracted stories for readers to laugh at and showed them that barbers, costermongers and cabmen were personalities in their own right.

Pitcher's favourite cab-driver, Richard Gilbert, carried him to race-meetings around London for twenty years and provided him with some astonishing stories. It is said a man has no secrets from his valet; I think cabmen must know even more secrets than valets or hotel-keepers, but that is another story.

Lord Brampton (Hanging Harry Hawkins), a feared and fearless judge, was an enthusiastic reader of the *Pink 'Un*. He enjoyed racing to such an extent that questions were asked in Parliament on the curious coincidence by which the learned Lord always found himself on Assize in Newmarket during Race Week. By another strange coincidence, there was always some legal complication which forced an adjournment on the afternoons when racing took place!

Hawkins was a brave man. He tried the Fenian bombers himself rather than put any of his fellow judges at risk, and carried a loaded revolver in his pocket for the duration of the trial and for several months afterwards.

It was from the pages of the *Pink 'Un* that the world learned of his one weakness, a little fox-terrier called Jack, from which he was inseparable. John Corlett (Master) wrote an article about Hawkins, laying it on thick about the respect in which he was held, his dignity, knowledge, integrity and all the rest of it. In typical *Pink 'Un* style, he ended the piece with an account of the part Jack played in the Assize Procession at Maidstone.

Hawkins had been met at the station with all the pomp and ceremony due to a Queen's Justice and the procession formed up to proceed to the Court. There were the High Sheriff, Deputy Sheriff, Judge's Marshal, the Mayor and Councillors, the javelin men, an escort from the local yeomanry and all the rest of it. But this time, things were different.

Instead of entering the carriage provided for him, Hawkins decided to walk to the Court, leading Jack on a piece of string.

The procession set off with tremendous dignity, but had to stop every minute or so to enable Jack to satisfy his apparently insatiable curiosity about every lamp-post on the way. As the embarrassed Mayor said later: " I had no idea we had so many blasted lamp-posts in Maidstone."

One of the things I learned from my association with the staff of the *Pink 'Un* was to broaden my social values. At Blandings things were simple. We were the children of the 8th Earl of Emsworth who held dominion, if not over palm and pine, at least over our bit of Shropshire. Apart from childhood friendships with people like the gardener's boy and James the groom, our social life was restricted, to say the least. We weren't allowed to associate with the local farmers or the shopkeepers in Market Blandings. Our visiting list was restricted to people like the Corbets at Acton Reynold, the Corbetts of Stableford – the 'one-tee Corbets' and the 'two-tee Corbetts' we used to call them – the Actons at Morville, the Parsloes of Matchingham and the Bridgemans of Weston Park along the Shrewsbury road.

Things got worse as we grew older. Clarence never bothered, bless his heart, but my multifarious sisters became snobs of the first water.

I recall a cartoon by du Maurier which sums up their attitude perfectly. It showed a woman and her two daughters walking in the Park and one of the daughters says:

"Look, Mama, there are the Wilkinsons. Should we not acknowledge them? I know they are most anxious to know us."

Mama's reply was firm: "Nonsense, my dear. Ignore them! The people we want to know are the people who don't want to know us!"

The Pelican Club and the *Pink 'Un* taught me differently. People say the Victorians lived for their class system but, in my experience, it was the women who bothered about such things, not the men.

Look at the *Pink 'Un* staff. John Corlett (Master) the proprietor was the son of a sergeant-major; William Mackay (Jim) was a barrister; Gubbins and Finch Mason were Etonians; old Colonel Newnham-Davis (The Dwarf of Blood) was a Harrovian; Shifter had been a prizeman at Oxford; Howlett came from a barber's shop and W.W. Wignall (Freelance) was station-master at Didcot railway station till he

John Corlett, 'Master' of the *Pink 'Un*

won thousands on Thormanby and West Australian in the Derby.

There was no snobbery there and there was no snobbery about Phil May, the man who made the whole of England laugh at his drawings, from Queen Victoria to the costermongers in Covent Garden.

Phil May found the *Pink 'Un* staff more to his taste than his colleagues on *Punch* or the *Daily Graphic*. In any event, Master knew how to deal with him. Although he was the finest cartoonist in London, Phil wouldn't work unless he had to. Newspapers' deadlines were their concern, not his, and he saw no reason why a sketch he had promised for Monday should not be equally funny when he eventually provided it a week later.

Master had a simple solution to ensure the *Pink 'Un* got the Phil May sketches he wanted. He would accost Phil, ask him what drawings he had in his pocket and buy them. If this didn't work, Master would simply put a sovereign on the table and make Phil do a cartoon for it there and then.

I recount elsewhere how Phil wheedled money out of the *Punch* cashier. The *Daily Graphic*, for whom he worked as well, were more ingenious. They found a retainer meant nothing to Phil other than eating and drinking, mainly drinking, at their expense. So they stopped it and told him that the commissionaire at the *Graphic* office had a five pound note given to him each day. At any time of the day or night that Phil turned up, and with Phil it might be at any time, he could collect the fiver on delivery of a cartoon that made the commissionaire laugh. It worked very well.

On one occasion the *Graphic* slipped up. Phil had undertaken to do a series of cartoons for the extra-special Christmas number with which the *Graphic* was going to knock all its rivals sideways. Phil insisted on money down and, foolish trusting men that they were, the *Graphic* people agreed.

Time went by and, as so often happened, Phil completely forgot about it. When the *Graphic* started chasing him all over the place with messenger boys and reproachful telegrams, Phil simply vanished into thin air. Eventually they traced him to a hotel in Bournemouth. The next morning Phil came out on to the hotel verandah to find an unusual sight. Across the road were six sandwichmen, each carrying a large board inscribed in letters a foot high:

'PHIL MAY'.

Phil was a bit surprised but assumed it was a spoof by one of us, so he just waved cheerfully at them. All six promptly did a right-about turn and Phil found himself looking at six boards each with the message:

'DON'T FORGET THE *GRAPHIC* XMAS NUMBER!'

Phil laughed, waved again and went in to have his breakfast, but he soon found that wasn't the end of it. He went for his usual walk along the front and to his dismay acquired a retinue which followed him wherever he went at a respectful, but adamant, twenty yards distance. If he entered a shop, they waited outside. If he paused to light his cigar, they paused also. When he had lunch at a local hostelry, they lined the pavement outside. Pleas, threats, offers of a half-crown per man, later raised to a sovereign each, were met with a polite but firm refusal.

Eventually Phil gave in and sent word out that he would catch the 6.35 back to Town. The message was respectfully acknowledged, but they stayed where they were. Defeated at last, Phil packed his bags and caught a cab to the station – and his six faithful followers went along as well to see him safely on to the train.

Chapter 5

Beside the Seaside, Beside the Sea

A Baroness at Brighton and goings-on at Goodwood

IN THE 1890s Brighton was known as 'London by the Sea', described by Labby Labouchere as 'four miles long, one mile in depth, with a Sassoon at each end and another in the middle.' People didn't go abroad for their holidays then, winter sports were yet to come and the Riviera was only just becoming fashionable. Brighton was the place to go and the 'church parade' along the front was as smart as that in Hyde Park.

It was in the summer of '94, in the bow window of the Old Ship, that old Johnnie Toole invited me to join him at dinner with Henry Irving. They were the two best-known actor-managers in London and Toole's Theatre in William IV Street even had its own pub on the corner. The theatre was pulled down years ago but the pub is still there. It's called The Final because they had a special licence by which it stayed open till half an hour after the final curtain across the road. A very sensible idea, I've always thought. [1]

I accepted the invitation gladly, especially when Toole told me two ladies would be joining us. He wouldn't say who they were, merely that I'd enjoy their company. He was right; they turned out to be Florence St John, one of the most beautiful actresses of the day, and Baroness Burdett-Coutts.

I held the Baroness in awe, as any young man would. To dine with the richest woman in England, who was born before Waterloo was fought, had proposed marriage to the Duke of Wellington, had supported just about every charity in the country and was the first woman to be made a baroness in her own right, was an unexpected honour.

---

(1) Toole's Theatre in King William IV Street was demolished in 1896 but The Final, one of the smallest pubs in London, survived till the rebuilding of the Coutts' Bank block in 1973. On its last day I drank a glass of beer to the memory of Toole and the loss of another London landmark. *Ed.*

She must have been in her eighties then, but she had all her wits about her. After introductions in the foyer she said:

"Mr Threepwood, I suggest you take me in to dinner. Then you can sit beside me and listen to the stories of an old woman, while you admire Miss St John across the table. I'm sure you'd prefer that to having to look at me all the time!"

It was a delightful meal. With her reputation for supporting so many worthy causes, I feared we might be on water, but not a bit of it. She didn't join us in the burgundy, asking our forgiveness for sticking to the habits of old age. I only hope I will be able to enjoy the same excellent habits in my later years.

She had Bernkasteler with the fish, vintage champagne with the roast, followed by a small pot of tea at the end of the meal. Apparently it was her invariable diet. We got along famously and I asked her which of the three drinks she preferred.

" It depends who is asking the question, Mr Threepwood. If it is the Queen or the Prince of Wales, I say it is the Bernkasteler I prefer – because each of them thinks they made it popular in this country. And my reply makes them happy.

"If it is a supporter of one of my charitable causes, a bishop say, or a worthy lady who looks upon alcohol as the Devil's drink, I assure them earnestly that I drink wine only because my doctors order me to do so. And I tell them I always finish my dinner with a strong pot of tea because it is what I enjoy most. And then they are happy.

"But, Mr Threepwood, if it is a young man like you who is asking – then I say that every woman knows champagne is the most romantic drink in the world and he is happy. It is what he wants to hear, so he goes off and spends money he hasn't got buying champagne for charming young ladies like Miss St John over there. Of course, as to his motives for doing so, I should not like to venture an opinion. Am I right, Mr Threepwood?"

She looked at me very hard and I have to admit I blushed. I didn't know what to say but she did not hesitate.

"Mr Irving, I'll trouble you for that five pounds for my charities. Mr Threepwood has gone a pretty pink."

Irving and Toole burst into laughter and explained that since I was a newcomer to their group, the Baroness had decided to take advantage of the occasion. She had bet Irving five pounds that, old though she might be, she could still make a man blush when she wanted to.

She rose from the table soon afterwards, asking my assistance to the stairs. I was honoured and bold enough to tell her as much. She smiled and said:

"You have a ready tongue, Mr Threepwood and it is a gift I hope you will not abuse." After a pause she added: "Well, not too much, anyway."

And we both laughed. She bade me good-night with the words:

"I have enjoyed this evening, Mr Threepwood. If Miss St John leaves early, make sure you ask Mr Irving to tell you the story about my Bethnal Green children's home."

I never saw her again, but made a point of attending her funeral in the Abbey in '06. A great lady. She could tell the tale with the best of them!

I went back to the table to find Mons Marius, who was playing at the Royal that week, had arrived to take Florence St John home. I had been looking forward to impressing her with my charm and personality, but I liked Mons and I liked the way he and Florence looked at each other, so I smiled and said good-night with the others.

The evening seemed just about over, but, remembering what the Baroness had told me, I asked Irving about her Bethnal Green children's home. He let out a guffaw that turned every head in our direction.

"She told you to ask me that, did she? Well, you must have made a good impression on her. I don't think you know it either, do you, Johnnie?"

Old Johnnie Toole shook his head so Irving leaned forward and told us the story. As well as endowing bishoprics and churches from South Africa to Australia, the Baroness had always taken a deep interest in the London poor. I'd forgotten till Irving reminded me that it was she who'd stopped the scandal of chimney-sweeps putting their apprentices up chimneys. She'd worked on the cause with Shaftesbury and Dickens and lobbied every Cabinet Minister in turn. Sensible woman that she was, she knew enough not to rely on promises alone so, when the Bill came up, she visited every MP in London, asking each to give it his support. It was probably the only Bill never to be debated and was carried by acclamation without a single dissenting vote.

Anyway, Irving continued, the Baroness had founded a girls' orphanage down in Bethnal Green. With her support it had done fairly well, but one day the matron told her they needed a couple of dozen lengths of blue calico to make drawers for the little girls.

"Now, young Threepwood," Irving said, bending those extraordinary eyebrows on me, " I bet you didn't know that up until the 1850s or so, ladies didn't wear drawers. Not quite sure why not, probably wore so much anyway. Still, there it is. So," he continued, "the Baroness says – 'Drawers? Drawers? Quite unnecessary. I have never worn drawers in my life.'

" 'Maybe so,' says the matron, 'but then it is hardly likely that your ladyship spends much of your time upon the swings in the public parks!' "

Fashions in women's underclothing seem to change constantly although, as I learned on one memorable occasion, they were not always considered important or even necessary in Paris.

It was in the summer of '95 or '96 that I was fortunate enough to attend a special rehearsal at the Duke of York's theatre; it was called the Trafalgar Square then, but the name never caught on. I'd heard about the rehearsal from Fred Storey and cadged an invitation.

Looking for something to follow 'Go Bang!', Herbert Pearson had gone over to Paris to book the famous Moulin Rouge dancers, but La Goulue was having a baby so Pearson booked her rival Nini Patte-en-l'air and her girls instead. Since we all wanted to have a look at them, there was quite a crowd in the stalls including Letty Lind, Jessie Bond and the other girls from 'Go Bang!' who'd come along to see what all the fuss was about.

The troupe had arrived in London only the night before and Nini came on stage to tell us their dancing clothes, skirts and petticoats, etc. hadn't been delivered yet. But because so many of us had turned up to welcome them to London, the girls would go through their routine in their normal clothes to show us what had made the Moulin Rouge dancers so famous. They certainly did.

The music started and they began their routine – but they never finished it. It soon became apparent that we were seeing something never seen before on the London stage. The conductor of the orchestra turned as crimson as a turkey cock in a violent sunset and the orchestra became so intrigued by what was happening above their heads that, one by one, they stopped playing. Only the hero on the triangle in the corner carried on tapping away by himself. Eventually Pearson leapt into the breach. To Madame Nini's great bewilderment and subsequent indignation, he stopped the rehearsal until 'such time as adequate clothing was available'. He was most grateful to the ladies but, as he said in a masterly understatement:

"We have seen all, indeed more than is necessary, thank you."

At Brighton in the old days you were sure to see everybody who mattered, although Le Touquet and Deauville have now replaced it as the smart place to go for a weekend.

I suppose it does make things easier if there is a stretch of water to separate one from those little problems that can make life difficult. That is the view held by a disreputable friend of mine who includes in the phrase 'little problems' his wife, other wives' husbands, his creditors and bookmakers to whom he owes money.

Yet creditors never seemed to be a problem at Brighton. The explanation was given me one night in the Savoy by Dickie Dunn, who stopped at my table where I was dining a delightful little member of the theatrical profession. Dickie, very much a family man, wasn't going to talk about the advantages of Brighton before a young lady, so he waited till she went off to check her back-hair or whatever women do, before giving me the benefit of his experience.

"I've been young myself and it's not for a tired old bookie to tell you how to run your life, but if you take that little stepper down to Brighton, make sure you've got your running shoes on. Her brother's a waiter at the Old Ship, her old man's the head porter at the Albion and he'd make three of you, so take it careful!"

I was grateful for the advice and asked him what made Brighton so special.

"Well," he said, "I suppose it comes down to this. If you get into trouble at Brighton, it's trouble, just like anywhere else. The difference is that you can walk along the front and meet a dozen London tailors, each of them wondering if it's their unpaid-for trousers you're sporting so proudly. But they won't say a thing about it. Why? Because they are down for the same reason you are and they're probably not using their real names either!

"It's a sort of gentlemen's agreement. You meet them in the hotel restaurant, they'll give you a polite good morning and nothing more will be said. But it works both ways.

"One young chap I know thought he had it made when he found himself sitting next to an old fellow whom he happened to owe quite a bit. The old boy was with the prettiest little thing you ever saw and the young chap thought he'd do himself a bit of good. So, when they met in the bar later, he hinted gently that keeping the information from the old boy's wife and business partners ought to be worth a little something off the account.

"The old boy was livid. It turned out the girl really was his wife and they were on their honeymoon. He was so furious that he went back to London, bought in all the young chap's debts from his other creditors and saw him into the Bankruptcy Court. So don't be too clever.

"Of course," Dickie went on, " there are times when it would be stupid not to take advantage of things. Young Lord Thingummy was telling me about one time he was down at Brighton, looking forward to admiring the sunrise from the same window as a little blonde friend of his. As he put out his boots in the hotel that night, the bedroom door opposite opened and there was his father, the giddy dook himself, doing the same thing.

"Young Thingummy's a quick thinker and recovered first. Looking hard at the very high-heeled shoes in his father's other hand, he said:

'Ah, good evening, father. I see you have brought mother down with you. I hope she is in good health?'

The duke looked at him blankly, then spotted the pair of equally high heels beside his son's boots.

'Nicely, thank you my boy, nicely. I, er, I see you have got married without telling us and here you are on your honeymoon. Let's talk it over tomorrow morning when I look forward to giving you a cheque to mark the happy occasion.'"

I laughed and asked Dickie who they were, but he refused to tell me. All he would say was that since he had paid out most of the money the son had got, he felt he had an interest.

"A double interest really, I suppose," he added. "It was Goodwood Week and I paid out a thousand to the duke on a ten to one shot on

Tuesday. But I got most of my notes back from the young fellow by the last race on Friday. I like to keep things in the family when I can!

"What really made me laugh," Dickie concluded, "was something I knew and young-fellow-me-lad Thingummy didn't. He and his old man were keeping it in the family all right – the two girls were sisters and I happen to know they'd tossed to see which one would get His Grace. If someone isn't careful, the House of Lords is going to have a nice time sorting that lot out. It'll make Roger Tichborne's case look easy."

It was at Brighton that I first saw Fred Archer, who I still believe was the best jockey the Turf has seen, though Donoghue is becoming nearly as popular today. John Corlett always held that it was the excessive dieting to keep his weight down that led Archer to take his own life; he also reckoned Archer should have accepted the offers made to him by the Duchess of Montrose. It was well known that she was fond of Archer and anxious to look after him, make him a trainer or something, anything to stop him starving himself to death.

I didn't move in the top circles then any more than I do now, but I used to be roped in to do the rounds of the London Season. I remember once in Londonderry House watching six duchesses come up the staircase to be presented to the Prince. All of them were in full fig, which really was full fig in those days, and Hughie Drummond murmured in my ear:

"Look at those tiaras, Gally. Any one of them would buy a Derby winner and keep you and me in good champagne for the rest of our lives. There's no justice."

I don't know if the Duchess of Montrose had a tiara. I suppose she must have done, although by the time I met her, the odds are she'd have cheerfully put it on a horse if Archer was riding. It was on the Hill at Goodwood that Pitcher Binstead introduced me to her. She certainly didn't look like a member of N.P. Willis's Upper Ten; more like one of Sally Army Booth's Submerged Tenth.

Pitcher and I had walked up there because, as he said, not only could you see the entire course, you could also see which way the bookies sneaked off if they decided to welsh on your little transaction.

As we reached the crest, Pitcher stopped and raised his topper respectfully to a little brown-faced woman dressed in what looked like a charwoman's cast-offs. This was in the days before sunbathing when every lady wanted to look as pale as possible. The Duchess didn't bother with that sort of thing. She looked as though she'd just finished cleaning out a stable and perhaps she had, but she certainly knew her racing, and she and Pitcher fell into an animated discussion on the prospects for the next race.

Just below us was a group of toughs, clearly of the Submerged Tenth, and I would have given them a wide berth, but Pitcher was a big burly chap and nobody was going to mix it with him easily. As Pitcher and the Duchess paused in their conversation, we heard one of the toughs say in the most indignant tones:

"Well, I asks yer! When yer've paid tuppence for a bed for the night, yer'd think at least yer ruddy trousers would be safe, wouldn't yer?"

All three of us burst into laughter. When the Duchess had recovered, she turned to Pitcher:

"Now, Mr Binstead, you see why I prefer the Hill to the Enclosure. The dresses may not be so elegant but the conversation is far more interesting. The tips are often better as well. I don't know about you gentlemen but I think I'll put something on Two Coppers in the race after next!"

She was certainly an unusual duchess. Perhaps she would have looked after Fred Archer properly; we shall never know. Although he knew racing inside out, Archer was very naive in some ways. Pitcher always insisted that the Duchess had offered to marry Archer and that he was very taken with the idea, until he discovered he wouldn't become a duke. He'd probably have been as good as some of the ones I know.

Goodwood Week always seems to produce a crop of engagements; one I particularly remember was young Southborne's. I first ran into him in Romano's when he was celebrating his accession to the title with some other young members of the Upper House. They were on their second or third bottle when Fatty Coleman wandered through from the bar to see what all the noise was about.

He was a bit of a philosopher, was old Fatty, and knew them all. He walked over to the table, beamed down on them and said:

"Dear old chaps! Dear old chaps! What a fine sight. Nine hereditary legislators – and not an ounce of brains amongst the lot of you. What a prospect. Thank God for the House of Commons!"

Young Southborne was a nice enough chap, but could never make up his mind about anything. He'd got himself engaged to a splendid girl, but couldn't bring himself to name the day and she'd handed him the mitten. But she still loved him, Lord knows why, and she'd told me one day in a fit of confidence that she was determined to marry him. She knew he wasn't the cleverest man in the world, or the best-looking, and he wasn't all that rich – but he was the one she wanted.

It was all good spirited stuff, especially when you remember this was back in the '90s when girls didn't say that sort of thing. You sat back and waited for the right chap to come along and ask you. If your parents didn't think much of him, then you sighed, wept a silent tear and wrote him a letter saying you'd always look upon him as a dear friend but you were unable to go against the wishes of dear Papa, etc. But this girl had bright red hair and I've found that girls with red hair have a habit of getting their own way.

I was honoured by her confidence (I think it stemmed from too much dance champagne), wished her well and sat back to watch events. She got him all right, just as she said she would. She made sure they were both invited down to Heron's Hill, the Matchelows' place in Sussex, for Goodwood Week. I was staying there as well and one morning after breakfast, up got young Southborne and blushingly announced their forthcoming nuptials. As he stammered away, she looked at him with pride and love in her face. She clearly saw something in him nobody else did. Women are funny creatures.

We all made a fuss of them and said the things one does say on these occasions. It wasn't till later that I had a chance to ask her what had happened.

"Gally Threepwood," she said, "I've never been a Suffragette, but they certainly have the right idea. If a man can persuade a woman into matrimony, why can't a woman persuade a man? I knew he was too shy to ask me, so I decided to ask him and he said yes."

I was naturally staggered by this; all I could say was:

"What! Just like that?"

"No, not just like that," she replied. " I got him into my bedroom last night, locked the door behind me, took the key out and put it to him. If he promised to set a date, all well and good. If he didn't, I'd throw the key out of the window and start screaming. I meant it too, and he saw I did. There's always a way round these things if one looks hard enough!"

She was a relative of Barmy Twistleton, which may explain it, but I still put it down to her red hair. Marriage was the making of Southborne; perhaps it might have been the making of me.

Chapter 6

Brighton Again

Jellied Eels – By Appointment

IT WAS at Brighton that I was introduced to a side of English social life far removed from both the Pelican Club and Blandings Castle.

It happened the day Pitcher introduced me to the Duchess of Montrose. It hadn't been a good afternoon; Two Coppers had trailed in last, as did every other horse I'd backed, and I'd lost every penny. I was just glad I'd had the sense to buy a return ticket and wouldn't have to hoof it for fifty miles.

I was waiting at the station, feeling very hungry and sorry for myself, when a chap selling jellied eels pushed his barrow into the station-yard. There was nobody else around so he latched on to me, parked his barrow and went into his patter. After I'd heard it twice through, I walked over to him:

"You're wasting your time with me – I'm broke. I've got my return ticket and nothing else. I haven't even got the fare for a cab when I get back to Town. If you want to sell your jellied eels, you'd be better off trying the pubs along the front."

He replied with a face as lugubrious as mine:

"Guv, I've been selling jellied eels in Brighton for ten years and tonight's the worst I've ever seen. There's about four and sixpence free money between here and the Metropole, and that's in the hands of the pub-keepers. The bookies skinned us all today and they left sharp on the six thirty-three. Two Coppers! That ruddy horse wasn't worth a penny."

We were clearly fellow sufferers in adversity so I asked how much he'd had on.

" All I had, Guv! All I ruddy well had. A sov and tenpence, the whole of yesterday's takings, and I'm still owing on the eels and barrow!"

It's all comparative, I suppose, and we were both victims of misfortune so I told him of my hard luck. We vented our joint wrath on all racehorses, Two Coppers in particular, exchanged views and generally chummed up.

At last he made the big gesture. Would I like some jellied eels – for free from a brother-sufferer at the hands of Two Coppers? Payment could wait. He had the eels, I was hungry. It was charity at its most practical and I tucked in as though I'd hadn't eaten in weeks. Having satisfied my hunger – with jellied eels, it's the slice of bread you get with them that hits the spot – I thanked him and gave him my card with an IOU on the back.

" When you get back to Town," I said, "that's good for ten bob at Romano's," and I went off to catch my train.

I didn't see him for some time, although Luigi told me he'd been in to redeem the IOU, for which Luigi was grateful for settlement. It must have been a couple of months later that some of us went down to Aldgate to see a young boxing prospect we thought might do well at our Pelican Sunday night matches. The lad certainly showed promise, so Swears went round the back to make arrangements while the rest of us waited in front. And there on the pavement, plying his trade, was my benefactor from Brighton. I went over to say hello and he greeted me warmly.

After thanking me for the ten bob, he offered me his wares. I wasn't as hungry as I had been at Brighton, but it would have been churlish to refuse, so I ordered six penn'orth and called the other fellows over to join us.

It so happened that the Dwarf was with us that night, better known to the world as Lieutenant Colonel Newnham-Davis, whose recommendation could make or break any restaurant in London. It also fell out that the Dwarf hadn't dined and had never tried jellied eels, so he was quite intrigued by the idea and thoroughly enjoyed them. So much so that he graciously told the chap he would be recommending his wares in the next edition of the *Pink 'Un*.

The jellied eel chap wasn't as overcome with gratitude as the Dwarf expected, so I explained that a barrow wasn't quite the same as a restaurant in the West End. It was very kind of Dwarf and so on, but you couldn't really expect the Smart Set and their girls to chase around Aldgate East on the off-chance of finding an itinerant jellied eel barrow.

It was at this point Pitcher suddenly muttered a warning. While listening to this unusual epicurean discussion, he had been keeping his eyes open. It *was* Aldgate, the pubs were emptying and Pitcher had noticed a group of toughs eyeing us from across the road. I suppose in our toppers and cloaks we were a bit conspicuous, and it was clear there was going to be trouble. (This was a few weeks after The Major had been badly beaten up in the Haymarket when a gang went for his watch and the old boy had put up a fight for it.)

Most of us had been around long enough to know what to do, so we formed up, back to back, with our sticks at the ready. Never despise the old-fashioned evening cane by the way; it is a useful weapon if used properly. Don't try to use it as a club. Thrust with it like a sword; it can be very effective. We weren't too bothered since Swears came back just then and he knows a bit about scrapping. In fact, I saw him slip on the famous brass knuckle-duster he maintained was part of his regular dress whenever he came east of St Paul's.

We needn't have worried. The jellied eel chap was clearly sent by Heaven to act as the Threepwood guardian angel, because he shouted across the road:

"Get out of here, Joey, and take that lot with you. These ain't ordinary customers – they're friends o' mine! Any more of your goings-on and I'll have a word with Uncle Jack. You want to steal somebody's watch, push off and hit some harmless old fellow over the head. That's more your style."

And off they went without another word.

We all expressed our gratitude and the Dwarf said he didn't care whether the chap had a barrow or a café, he'd write up his jellied eels anyway. Pitcher put his hand in his pocket as we all did, but the chap would have none of it. He beckoned me aside and asked if I would do him a favour. I said I would certainly try and asked what it was.

To cut a long story short, while he would be glad of any financial contribution we cared to make, there was something else he would far rather have. All his life, he said, he had envied those shops up West that had the Royal Coat of Arms, which he had been told meant they sold to the Queen herself. He knew he had a long way to go, but he had to start somewhere – and he had noticed from my card that I was an Honourable. What would I feel about him putting a notice on his barrow, saying he was jellied eel seller 'By Appointment' to me?

I didn't know what to say. He wasn't pulling my leg and he had twice helped me out of a jam. But the proud name of Threepwood on a jellied eel barrow! I was never much of a chap for family pride and tradition and that sort of thing, but this was a bit too much.

Then something else struck me. He was doing something I'd never managed to do, he was earning an honest living and who knew where he might not end up. Billy Harris, the sausage manufacturer, started with a barrow to become one of the wealthiest men in London and an acquaintance of the Prince of Wales, even though Billy did attend race-meetings in a fur coat over full evening dress. This chap was paying me a compliment I couldn't refuse. He couldn't get the Queen's name so he had asked for mine instead! So I said of course he could use my name if he thought it would be any good to him, we all shook his hand, Pitcher slipped him something as well and we got a growler back to the Strand.

I didn't see him for a bit after that, though some other fellows did and pulled my leg about the barrow with my name on it. I just grinned, made up some story and let it go. It wasn't till Ladies Day at Ascot that we met again and it could have been a more comfortable encounter.

We were strolling across to the Paddock, Clarence, my sisters Connie, Julia, Hermione and myself, when Connie suddenly stopped, looked hard at something in the crowd and turned on me in a fury:

"I know you're a disgrace to the family, Galahad, but I never thought you'd sink to such depths! How dare you drag our name through the mud like this?"

And there was my chum with his barrow painted as large as life:

'Jellied Eels.
The best in London.
By Appointment to
The HON. GALAHAD THREEPWOOD.'

To make matters worse, he greeted me like a long-lost brother, shook me warmly by the hand and told me he was doing a roaring trade, especially among the nobs, as he called them. One or two had queried his right to put my name up but he had reassured them. I would be glad to hear that everybody was buying his jellied eels and would the lady like some with his compliments?

Connie was nearly purple with rage so I declined his offer, told him I'd see him later and pulled Connie and the rest of them away. As you can imagine, I had a bad afternoon. Clarence just thought the whole thing was a joke and saw no harm in it, but my sisters didn't see it that way at all.

It was when the Prince walked past that Connie went through the roof. She was certain she saw him look at us, say something to Mrs Keppel and then they'd both laughed.

Connie exploded. She was going to have my poor chum arrested, she was going to sue him for libel, she would make sure he never dared use the family name again. She only regretted she couldn't stop me using it as well, since I was clearly determined to do all I could to drag it down.

With my sister Constance one has to fight fire with fire. I wasn't too pleased about the poor chap either, but I'd given my word and I wasn't going to let Connie bully him.

"Connie," I said. "You've made up my mind for me. If you had been reasonable about it and just asked me nicely, I'd have gone along and asked him to stop. And I'm sure he would have done. But you've gone too far. I'd never realised what a rotten snob you've become. You need a sharp lesson and you're going to get one.

"I'm going down to the Silver Ring," I said, "and I'm going to offer my name and patronage to any bookie who feels it worth his while. I should clear about a tenner from each of them and if Dickie Dunn's there, he'll make it twenty at least. And then, Connie, I shall go round every three-card trick man, barrel organ and sideshow I can find on the course. And I'll see what terms they'll give me to let them put up a notice with my name on it.

"I should clear quite a bit, one way or another. Of course, it means you'll never be able to attend Ascot or any other race-meeting ever again, but that's your hard luck."

I was so angry that I would have done it too. I let it sink in for a bit, then I offered her the alternative. If she, Hermione and Julia were so upset about it, they could jolly well stump up to buy the chap off. And that's what we did, once I'd persuaded her that fifty quid was the least the chap would take.

He was very understanding about it and accepted my apologies readily. It all worked out nicely because the fifty quid was enough to buy a shop, which is what he'd always wanted.

He did very well with it too; in fact he's got a couple of others now, although he has a long way to go before he catches up with Billy Harris. I went down for the grand opening and he treated me royally. Best stout and oysters I'd had in years, I recall.

We got our own back on Connie as well, because it was only *my* name the chap promised not to use. Halfway along Aldgate High Street, you will find a fish restaurant proudly displaying the Threepwood coat of arms. Below it is a plaque with the words:

'This establishment was founded through the good offices of
Lady Constance Threepwood
Lady Julia Threepwood
Lady Hermione Threepwood
of Blandings Castle.'

It's a pity none of them is ever likely to see it, especially as the jellied eels are the best in London.

Chapter 7

South Africa

Barnatos, Boers and bubonic plague

IN 1900 I met the only girl I ever wanted to marry, but my family disapproved and shipped me out to South Africa where I spent the first few months in an alcoholic haze. I went unwillingly, unlike thousands of my compatriots who wanted to fight the Boers or find diamonds.

I met quite a few members of the Pelican Club out there, some of them in the Army, others having a look at the place like me. I had a job as ADC to a general for a bit, but things were dull in Cape Town and I packed it in and went up-country on the famous two-day train journey to Johannesburg.

Jo'burg was a rough place – I picked up more fleas than a terrier at the Gold Fields Hotel – but I ran into a fellow called Cohen whom I'd met occasionally in Romano's and he showed me the ropes. He was an odd chap who'd been in at the start of the diamond boom, but never managed to do much good out of it. He knew all the diamond millionaires, but they'd hung on to their money while he had lost his. Just unlucky, I suppose. He returned to London eventually and went to prison, I recall, for criminal libel.

From about 1890 onwards, London saw plenty of South African diamond millionaires and a pretty rough lot they were. They were the 'new money' of the time, replacing the old 'from millhand to millionaire' lot whom my father used to snub so unmercifully. Tommy Blunt (he's Sir Thomas now), who married Julia Coombe-Crombie from Dreever Castle, is the sort of chap I mean. Made piles of money and reckons he knows everything.

I suppose the Barnatos (their name was Isaacs originally) made the biggest splash. They left Whitechapel for South Africa and came back fifteen years later to live in Park Lane.

I remember Cohen telling me how he and one of the Barnatos, both of them fresh out from London, had found themselves the proud possessors of a half-mile or so of South African desert. They had been told it was an endless source of diamonds but all they could find were a few unpleasant insects and the odd snake.

They dug a few holes here and there, but found nothing and were beginning to work out how they could palm the swindle off on to somebody else. But they were clever chaps and they noticed a local Boer farmer riding by every week to various native encampments. It was clear that whatever he was doing, he was doing very well out of it, so the pair of them pooled what was left of their cash and bought the farmer's pony.

The next day they took the pony along the track the farmer used and let it pick its own way. It took them to half a dozen kraals, in each of which were natives with diamonds to sell to the first-comer. They finished the day as rich men.

Barney Barnato, who came back as chairman of De Beers and one of the wealthiest men in the world, was an odd chap. No matter how much he made, and he made plenty, he hated sharing it, refusing to discuss anything to do with money – horses, business, musical comedies, anything. I once visited Paris with Swears Wells, who knew Barney well, and we went out to Longchamps for the racing. When Swears saw Barney had a horse running, he became very excited:

"Barney doesn't enter a horse in a race unless he thinks he's going to get his money back – and it's a good long price too!"

We couldn't find Barney anywhere but we did run into Woolf Joel, Barney's nephew, who wasn't very helpful – or so he thought:

"Oh, Barney says it's utterly useless; it doesn't have a dog's chance. Save your money. Don't touch it."

And he wandered off. I was going to take his advice but Swears knew better.

"Gally, my boy, whatever you've got on you, slap it all on that horse! Barney's a fine fellow, but he's the meanest man in the world. He believes that telling people he's got a good 'un in a race is giving them money out of his own pocket. If he says the horse is rubbish, that's the one to back."

We did and it came in at a nice 11-1.

The rest of the family are different from old Barney, I'm glad to say. Jack, Solly and Woolf Joel are pleasant enough fellows and young Babe Barnato, the racing driver, cuts quite a dash nowadays. He raced the

Blue Train from Calais to the Mediterranean and my nephew Ronald tells me that he set another record the other day, managing to reach a hundred miles an hour along Park Lane.

The Boer War had been going some time when I arrived and there were a lot of other chaps out there, either Regular Army fellows with their regiments or people like young Herbert Buckmaster who wanted to see a bit of action. Many of them joined what were accurately called units of Irregular Cavalry. The most popular of these was the ILH, the Imperial Light Horse, a very tough lot whom I got to know when they were at Maitland Camp near Cape Town.

They included fellows like Bill Seeton, the Irishman who went through three fortunes before he was thirty and Fred Adams, a mining engineer, who originally intended to join the Boers till a friend tossed him for it and won him over. There were ex-troopers of the British South African Police, chaps from the Klondyke gold rush, American cowboys who wanted to see what all the fuss was about, some of Teddy Roosevelt's Rough Riders and quite a few who'd been in the Jameson Raid.

And of course there was Tommy Crean. He was the pride of the Irish Rugby team, led them in their famous win at Blackheath in 1894 and dropped the goal that gave Ireland victory. He joined the ILH as a trooper but soon became its Medical Officer and won a well-deserved Victoria Cross at Tygerskloof.

Cape Town was a dull place. There was only one gaming-house called Hildebrand's, which ran a pretty rough game of Faro, and a couple of so-called theatres. One of them, the Alhambra, was a favourite with the New Zealand troops, who exercised an effective form of theatrical criticism by jumping on the stage and throwing into the orchestra pit any acts they didn't approve of. It's a pity the habit never caught on in London.

I did a bit of big-game shooting and even got involved in the odd Boer skirmish, but eventually they had to invalid me out along with many others. It was a pretty depressing time. Just about everybody I knew was suffering from malaria, jaundice or dysentery, which killed off far more fellows than the Boers ever did.

I had just decided to move on when Cape Town was hit by bubonic plague. I didn't get it, but the cook in my hotel did, and that was enough to get everybody staying in the place taken off in carts to the Contact Camp in the Karoo. It was a bit like the Great Plague in London. Every house or hotel where the plague was found had a big yellow cross painted on it, the 'plague carts' we travelled in were given a wide berth and the streets were empty.

We were given some tents, food, cooking equipment and left to our own devices for a fortnight to see whether we were infectious or not. It was tedious for a few days, but things improved enormously when another camp appeared, full of British girls, nurses from Cape Town whose cook had caught it like ours. It was astonishing how morale rose and how keen chaps became to show off their camping skills.

Young Buckmaster was in the same camp and I am glad to say came out of it as I did. He attributed his immunity to alternate doses of whisky and quinine taken every hour. A useful preventative, but I query the need for the quinine; whisky on its own will defeat most germs.

Look at Freddie Potts who went to stay with his brother Eustace at a villa near Grasse in '98. One day Eustace, who was a rabid teetotaller, gave his cook twenty francs to get something good for dinner. The chap went off, spotted a dead hedgehog by the roadside and decided the twenty francs were better off in his pocket. That night he served up hedgehog *à la maison,* pretending it was chicken or something. Eustace, whose teetotalism had rendered him susceptible to every ill the flesh is heir to, nearly died. Freddie, on the other hand, had drunk nothing but whisky for years and positively thrived on the hedgehog, finishing it cold the following day.

Buck and I were glad to leave South Africa. It was all very well everybody at home singing 'Goodbye, Dolly Gray' (originally written to encourage American troops in the Spanish-American War incidentally), but it was a very different matter when you were lying in hospital with dysentery. Things weren't improved by the positive invasion of South Africa by smart and utterly useless Society ladies who came out 'to help'. It got so bad that Milner and Lord Roberts had to take steps to get rid of them.

The women made themselves unpopular by insisting that Church parades should be compulsory and alcohol banned in Army canteens. They used to visit hospitals, dressed in pink silk tea-gowns and their London jewellery and sit on the wounded officers' beds playing Bridge with them. If they felt particularly charitable, they'd even venture into the soldiers' wards and dab a few faces with sponges under the impression they were Florence Nightingale reducing some poor hero's fever.

One chap I used to keep supplied with tobacco (his father was a tenant farmer of ours), got his own back one day on a particularly tiresome Angel of Mercy:

" Yes, mum, you can wash my face if you want to, but it's been done eleven times already this afternoon. Now, what I really want is someone to wash my feet. They haven't been done for three weeks and I think I've got ringworm!"

Chapter 8

My First Trip to America – 1

San Francisco, The Wild West and some old pals

BUCK Buckmaster went back to England, but I had nothing to go
home for – a certain girl had married someone else – so I decided
to have a look at America, arriving in San Francisco just in time to see
James J. Jeffries beat Gus Ruhlin in five rounds.

Like everywhere else San Francisco has a smart side, Nob Hill
overlooking the bay, and a rough side, the section below Market 'south
of the slot'. (The 'slot' is the cable-slot that pulls the famous cable-cars
up and down the incredibly steep hills.) In those days the Athletic Club
'south of the slot' was where the fighters trained and it was there that I
met an old friend, William Brady, who got me a card for the Bohemian
Club, a splendid body of men who based their activities on the old
Pelican, and introduced me to everybody who was anybody.

William Brady, not to be confused with Diamond Jim Brady the
railroad chap, is the nearest equivalent of our C.B. Cochran, though
some would say that Florenz Ziegfeld also deserves the title. Like Cocky
Cochran, he seems to have one ambition – to produce shows of any
sort. From the experience of my Pelican chums, I would have thought
the theatre was even riskier than staging boxing matches, but Brady
disagreed and managed to do both. [1]

He started his theatrical career by talking his way into a part in 'The
White Slave' back in '82, telling them he'd been on the stage since
childhood. Absolute lie of course but, as he said, persuading people into
believing what you want them to believe is what acting is all about.

I asked him if he managed it with bookmakers, but he said they were
different. We swapped experiences of telling the tale and he demonstrated
what a wonderful country America is. If we get into bother in London,
we have to leave the country and go across to Boulogne. In America all
they have to do is to cross the State line, though Brady did add that you

---

(1) William Brady (1863-1950) was still producing plays in 1939. *Ed.*

had to remember that bookies' minders could cross the State line too.

After 'The White Slave' he'd played a few more bit parts, then decided to go into management. 'The White Slave' was a pirated version of Dion Bouccicault's 'Octaroon', but it did so well on the West Coast that Brady decided to try the same trick again, taking Bouccicault's 'After Dark' out on the road without going through the formality of asking Bouccicault for permission.

He made quite a bit out of it till word got back to New York and lawyers started writing rude letters all over the place and making life difficult. So he decided to make the big, generous gesture and bought out the rights.

He told me it was the wisest thing he ever did. The play was going well and he had Gentleman Jim Corbett under a cast-iron contract. He re-wrote the play, put in a scene for Corbett, sacked the leading man and played the part himself : "It's criminal the way these dummies reckon a good set of teeth and curly hair are worth fifty bucks a week, Gally. There ought to be a law!"

He made a packet out of it and managed to buy the rights to 'Trilby' which made him even more money. After that he moved to New York, took over the Manhattan Theatre and hasn't looked back since. He's got two or three New York theatres now and is still surrounded by pretty girls, all looking for jobs.

What with half a dozen shows on the road and two heavy-weight boxing champions under contract, he reckoned he'd got things sewn up nicely. He maintained the secret of success was to find out what the public wants to see, then buy it. It may be a pretty girl, it may be a boxer or a wrestler; it doesn't matter which. Buy it, then sit back and charge people to come and see it. I'm sure he's right but I don't see my family lending me the money to buy in Carpentier or Jessie Matthews.

I suppose Brady's best remembered for managing Corbett, who took the title from John L. Sullivan in the famous fight in September '92. It was the sensation of the day because Sullivan, the first boxer to be recognised as heavy-weight champion of the world, had held the title for ten years.

Of course he had put on a lot of weight, hadn't done much training and he didn't have Corbett's intelligence. The Boston Strong Boy's usual tactics of rushing at his opponent, flailing his fists and shouting:

"Stand up and fight, you bastard!" were of little avail with someone who could move as quickly as Corbett could. He didn't just stand there and punch; he used the ring and wore Sullivan down in twenty-one rounds.

Everybody wanted to see the man who'd beaten Sullivan and Brady made a packet touring the new champion. Corbett fought exhibition bouts by day, to which the boxing enthusiasts came, and appeared on stage at night and pulled the theatre-goers in.

I first met Brady when he brought Corbett over to Drury Lane in '94. We all went along to see the new champion who was a good-looking chap, and the girls swooned over him. I was the intermediary when old Jem Mace, who'd held the championship in the 1860s, wanted to meet the man who'd beaten Sullivan and I arranged for him to come on the stage at Islington where Corbett was playing.

Old Jem made a splendid speech saying that, as the last English world-champion, he took pleasure in recognising Corbett as a worthy successor and presented him with a gold-headed cane. Corbett and Brady never forgot the status this gave them and Brady reckoned he was in my debt from then on.

The '90s were a busy decade in the boxing world. In '92 Corbett beat Sullivan; in '97 Fitzsimmons beat Corbett and Jeffries beat Fitzsimmons two years later. So you can imagine the excitement over the Jeffries–Ruhlin fight, especially as it was the first time San Francisco had staged a heavy-weight championship. Brady had Jeffries under contract as well and was confident he would win, as indeed he easily did.

People often don't appreciate what a difference a good manager can make to a boxer. It was Jeffries who went in the ring with Fitzsimmons in '99, but it was Brady who won the fight. I believe much of Brady's success was due to his theatrical experience, because he fixed the fight as only a theatre producer could. Cocky Cochran would probably have done just the same.

Brady knew Fitzsimmons was over-confident and out of training, and he knew that Jeffries, though far the better man, was very nervous. So Brady, just as Cochran would have done, decided to adjust the odds. He began by keeping the Press away from Jeffries and letting slip the information that Jeffries wasn't training and was in poor physical shape. In fact he had Jeffries, a big chap, in the peak of condition.

The evening of the fight came and Brady made Jeffries change early and spread his enormous frame over the couch in the dressing-room. Then Brady went off to Fitzsimmons' dressing-room, started an argument over some minor point in the rules and invented some pretext to bring Fitzsimmons back to Jeffries' dressing-room. As they came through the door Jeffries, who had been carefully coached in what he had to do, jumped to his feet so Fitzsimmons could see how fit and how big he was. He came up to his startled opponent till he towered over him, angrily demanded to know the reason for the intrusion, grabbed him by the lapels and shoved him against the wall with a thump that made his jaw sag. Fitzsimmons left the room a worried and anxious man.

Half an hour later, Jeffries went into the ring and took the title from his demoralised opponent in eleven rounds. He kept it for six years, retiring undefeated in 1905.

People have forgotten the way Jeffries changed boxing style. It was Tommy Ryan, a brilliant middle-weight champion, who taught him the 'Jeffries Crouch' that boxers use today. The old-fashioned way was to stand straight up to your opponent, head back and fists in the air in front of you. Ryan taught Jeffries to crouch, one shoulder forward, head tucked well down and both arms guarding the head and body. Although universal now, it was new then.

It was the same when Lord Marcus Beresford brought Tod Sloan over to ride for him. Everybody joked about a monkey on a stick but, my word, Sloan's famous crouch, stirrups right up, riding forward on the horse's shoulders certainly made a difference. The Americans have taught us a lot, including how to mix cocktails, of which more anon.

I thoroughly enjoyed myself in San Francisco, especially as I was there between earthquakes. The really big one that ruined most of the city didn't come along till 1906, long after I'd left, but Brady was in the middle of it and told me about it years later. He had gone out to the West Coast to keep an eye on a young actor of his, Douglas Fairbanks, who they tell me has now become a big name in the film world. I only saw him once, playing the hero in Brady's production of 'A Gentleman of Leisure', set in an English castle remarkably like Blandings.

Brady had come to San Francisco to tell Fairbanks to stop chasing girls and start doing some acting, but had been unable to find him. Knowing Fairbanks liked the high life, Brady was looking round the big hotels and bars when the earthquake struck. As one would, he forgot about Fairbanks but, when it was over, resumed his search, hoping to find Fairbanks still alive.

The whole city was in chaos, but he struck lucky. Outside one hotel was a crowd of people frightened to go back indoors. In the middle of them Brady spotted Enrico Caruso who had electrified the opera house in 'Carmen' the night before. He sat there in his night-gown, dressing-gown and slippers, clutching a photograph of his mother, all he had had time to grab before he escaped. He had come to the conclusion that San Francisco wasn't for him and was asking everybody the time of the first train back to New York.

As Brady commiserated with Caruso, Fairbanks strolled out of the hotel entrance without a care in the world. He was as bright as a button, beautifully dressed in top hat, white tie and tails. It turned out he had been entertaining a young lady. They had been aware of something strange happening, but they'd been too engrossed in what they were doing to take much notice! Since he didn't know the real reason for Fairbanks' dress, Caruso was terribly impressed:

"Meester Fairbanks! What style! What bravado! You must be the only man in the world who puts on evening dress for an earthquake."

I would have liked to stay longer in San Francisco but I had an invitation to stay with Oliver Wallop up in Wyoming.

It was a long but interesting journey. I ran into Barmy Twistleton in Arizona, holding down a job as cowboy or wrangler or something of the sort. It wouldn't have done for me, but Barmy thrived on it. He told me the local whisky was pretty rough but, by adding a judicious amount of bitters to every bottle, he'd convinced the rest of the ranch that he had a private supply of ten-year old best Scotch.

He reckoned that if nobody caught on, he'd soon have enough money to buy his ticket back to New York to see the girl he'd fallen for. It was the usual story. The parents thought he was marvellous till they found out he had an elder brother who would scoop the title. When they discovered that, they went off Barmy considerably.

I gave Barmy a tip I'd found useful in San Francisco. Over in America, people use the word 'Honourable' for Governors of States, ambassadors, senators and the like. In order to help things along, I'd written to Pitcher Binstead to send me out a bit of parchment, telling the world that I was his personal representative and under the special protection of King Edward, etc.

He told me in his letter that it cost him nearly two quid in drinks at Romano's, but there were five noble titles in full at the bottom of it. The fact that they were the signatures of the five poorest peers in England, whose IOUs wouldn't be accepted by a three-card trick man on a hard day, didn't really matter.

Of course I never used it socially but, as I told Barmy, it did come in handy when one found oneself in the hands of the local gendarmerie. Barmy said that everybody in the local bars knew him too well by then to try and pretend that the word 'Honourable' meant anything other than well-born English bum. But he thanked me anyway and said he'd try it out when he moved on.

I'd found it useful when, on Brady's recommendation, I'd visited a bar in San Francisco called Mike's Place, where they served a thing called a Dynamite Dew-Drop. They were also proud of their Dreamland Special and a concoction called Undertaker's Joy. Things had become a little hazy after the first few drinks, though I do recall trying to kill a chap twice my size, dressed in a cap and sweater. I can just remember the pair of us bouncing whisky bottles off each other's heads, but everything after that is a blur.

The judge was very reasonable the following morning, especially when I produced Pitcher's parchment and told him I was merely carrying out an investigation into the abuse of alcohol in the United States. Of course what really helped was tipping him the wink on the odds for the Jeffries fight, but Pitcher's parchment certainly paved the way. It changed what could have been a very sordid affair into a delightful social occasion.

The judge was kind enough to ask my views on the matter and I told him that I felt a local bye-law should be passed immediately, under which the ingredients of Dynamite Dew-Drops, Dreamland Specials and Undertaker's Joys should be clearly set out to give unsuspecting customers half a chance. He agreed with me completely and took a careful note of the three names. And since he felt, with a devotion to duty that did the American judiciary credit, that personal experience was the only way, he joined me in Mike's Bar after the court had gone into recess.

But my advice to readers is – stick to whisky, except when someone else is buying, when it is only good manners to take whatever you're given.

Barmy had seen quite a bit of America. He'd worked in a drug-store as a soda-jerk and then got a job on a local newspaper which had been interesting, especially when the editor pulled out all the stops in his hard-hitting editorials. The results could be quite dramatic.

When Frank Boyd was working on *The Hawk* for Gus Moore, Moore had put in something about Charlie Mitchell that caused the fur to fly and he had to spend the next month out of London. Well, I suppose it was a bit foolish going out of your way to offend a man who'd fought Corbett for the world championship, but at least you knew he'd only kill you with his fists.

Barmy's paper was in one of those small Western cattle towns where things get a bit rough. The editor reckoned that if he didn't get a bullet through the office window at least once a month, his editorials criticising the local vested interests must have fallen off and clearly lacked that extra degree of pith and vigour which makes all the difference.

Barmy would have stayed, but a friendly bar-tender tipped him the wink that a lynching-party had been proposed to muzzle the freedom of the Press once and for all. The suggestion had gained much local support, so Barmy and a chap called Painter decided to move on and go prospecting in the Mojave Desert instead. They hadn't found anything but their only worries were snakes, mosquitoes and the odd Indian, which were annoying, but not half as annoying as waking up with a rope round your neck.

We had a splendid time catching up on mutual acquaintances. I'd met our old school-fellow, Mugsy Bostock, in South Africa where, through some oversight on the part of the Colonial Office, he was exercising dominion over palm and pine and generally making life miserable for those of our coloured brethren unfortunate enough to live in his district or province or whatever it was.

He was still the same beetle-browed bully he'd been at school, which tendency both Barmy and I had tried to correct with a fives bat applied to the right spot. From the look of hatred Mugsy had given me when I saw him in Johannesburg, it seemed that the memory lingered on.

(Mugsy has now become Sir Aylmer Bostock, so they tell me.)

There are few pleasures in life more enjoyable than pulling mutually-disliked acquaintances to pieces and we recollected with glee how Mugsy had got his come-uppance. He was always on the lookout for kids whose lives he could make a misery, and one day a new boy with golden hair and blue eyes arrived, who made Little Lord Fauntleroy look like Attila the Hun. Mugsy was on to him at once, pulling his hair, twisting his arm and generally trying to show him who was boss. Before we knew what was happening, this frail child turned around and gave Mugsy a black eye with the sweetest left hook you saw in all your puff. He turned out to be a junior bantam-weight champion, transferred to us because his father thought the air was better in our part of the world.

Barmy felt it showed there was some justice in the world, and expressed the hope that Mugsy had profited by it and become more spiritual in his dealings with his fellow men. I had to say from what I had seen of Mugsy in South Africa, I doubted it. However, I'd done my best to ensure that there wasn't a bar or club from Cape Town to Jo'burg where the story wasn't known. And I was able to announce that Mugsy, who always hated his nickname, was, through unstinting effort on my part, now known by it throughout the length and breadth of the colony. Barmy agreed one can't take too much trouble in keeping stinkers like Mugsy in their place.

It was sad leaving old Barmy, but he gave me a whale of a send-off. He told his fellow cowboys that I was the British Ambassador who had come to Arizona to buy up every cow in the State for the British Army. So there were thirty cowboys to see me off, all of them firing their revolvers in the air and whooping their heads off. It could have been a pretty dull journey north but, luckily, there were a couple of pretty girls on board going to Seattle to open in a new show. They invited me to share their carriage and proved to be delightful company.

Chapter 9

My First Trip to America – 2

Wyoming, the Wallops and Buffalo Bill

I REACHED Wyoming a couple of days later and parted from the girls with mutual regrets. Of course I had told them that I wasn't the British Ambassador and never would be, but I made up for it by telling them all about the wealthy American wives so many of the aristocracy had brought over to England.

They regretted they'd never have the chance, but I assured them that chorus girls were equally popular as wives for the House of Lords, and Edna May and 'The Belle of New York' had made American shows all the rage.

They had seen Lillie Langtry on her last American tour – they hadn't thought much of her, although they were envious of her having a town in Texas named after her – and I was able to give them the inside story of the famous row she'd had with the Prince of Wales in the Café Royal. I'd only met her a few times but a lot of my pals had known her *very* well before she married Shuggy de Bathe. (She died in the South of France while these memoirs were being written. Another part of my youth gone.)

I gave them both my card with a note to Brady scribbled on the back and told them to look him up if they ever tried for a job in New York. I'm delighted to say one of them did, came to England and married into the aristocracy as well. But that story comes later.

When I eventually got to Sheridan, way up near the Montana border, Oliver Wallop was there to drive me the sixteen miles to his ranch at Big Horn. He was, and still is, an extraordinary chap with colossal energy. He didn't mind living in the back of beyond one little bit; he revelled in it. It wouldn't suit me, but it made me realise what I might have been or might have done.

I hadn't seen Oliver for years. I was still at school when he went out, but I've known the family all my life and even stayed at their country place at Farleigh Wallop, which hasn't been bought or sold since the

Conquest, which is more than you can say about Blandings.

There's a lot of them, nearly as many as there are Threepwoods, but at least the dozen Wallops are split evenly between girls and boys; Clarence and I are outnumbered ten to two by our sisters. I knew the youngest brother Freddie best, since he and I joined the Bachelors' Club together. Oliver is a member of the Bachelors' too, but I doubt if he has got his money's worth out of it.

Oliver, the third son of the Earl of Portsmouth, (against the odds, he's come into the title now), left Oxford in '84, came out to America and decided he liked it. He has always been a superb horseman and in this part of the world, that's the big thing.

I don't know how much money he had when he came over, but it can't have been much because he spent three months simply following the Canadian Pacific Railway line on foot. He got board and lodging at farms and ranches along the way by breaking in horses and got some real rogues, but he said it was astonishing how many so-called wild horses responded well to what he called 'good manners'. He reckoned cowboys bullied their horses, whereas he found quiet words and gentle handling worked just as well. I remembered something I'd heard years ago from one of the Blandings grooms and asked Oliver if he used the 'Horse's Word'. He looked at me very hard and hinted that might have something to do with it.

I've heard rumours of the 'Word' all my life. I believe Rarey, the fellow who ran the livery stables just off Seven Dials, would pass it on for fifty quid, but I've never really had the need for it myself, nor fifty quid to spare if it comes to that.

Oliver borrowed enough to buy a ranch, but nearly went bust in '86 when the snows lasted for months and there was no grass for the animals. The clever ranchers learned to grow hay to get them through the winters, though the old-fashioned lot didn't like it because it meant enclosing land and that was against the 'free range' philosophy they'd been brought up on. By the time I arrived, however, all the big ranchers were growing alfalfa or whatever it's called, for winter feed.

I'd assumed everybody would be wearing guns all the time but Oliver told me he'd never carried a revolver; in his experience it was the people who carried a Colt who got killed. He found a shotgun for game and a rifle for protection were perfectly adequate. He'd seen lots of lynchings in his time and showed me a scalp he'd kept when two Sioux Indians attacked a Crow Indian just a few yards from his ranch-house.

He made a point of keeping on the right side of the Indians because they knew the country and it was safer. There were still many people who remembered the Custer disaster which took place just a few miles from Oliver's place, and the 1890 rising was a recent memory.

He took me over to Cody, a small town founded by Buffalo Bill, stopping at a small railway station on the way to introduce me to the famous (or infamous) Martha Jane Burke, otherwise known as Calamity Jane. She was an astonishingly ugly woman who smoked a corn-cob pipe, but Oliver told me she'd been married ten times or more. Shows what personality can do, I suppose. It must make a difference if the girl who proposes to you has killed half a dozen men with her guns already!

Oliver said we were to meet his wife's newly-married sister at Cody. He refused to tell me who her husband was, so I got the surprise of my life when he turned out to be another old chum of mine from the Bachelors', Malcolm Moncrieffe.

Malcolm was one of the enormous family of Moncrieffes of Moncrieffe who cut quite a swathe in my time. His father, old Sir Thomas, had eight boys and eight girls, the latter being known collectively as 'the beautiful Moncrieffes'. Most of the girls married titles, including Harriet whose famous divorce from Sir Charles Mordaunt led to the Prince of Wales appearing in the witness box for the first time. He wasn't actually named as a co-respondent, but it was all very shocking at the time and I remember how horrified my parents were.

Malcolm went out to America just after Oliver to take a neighbouring ranch. They formed a polo team of cowboys who could beat anyone in America and organised a hunt as well, though it was pretty rough as I recall. Anything from a bulldog to a prairie dog was enlisted and they went after anything that could give them a run, though they found mountain wolves had a bad habit of eating the hounds before the hounds could eat them. Malcolm had just returned from England, so he brought us up to date on all the London gossip. Of course the death of the old Queen was the biggest shock; we knew she was going to die one day but somehow we all thought she would go on for ever.

Charlie Beresford (son of the Marquess of Waterford) who alternated between being an MP and an admiral, was still crowing over the War

Office about the old Queen's funeral. When the coffin was taken down to Windsor, the train was delayed or the horses had been standing too long. The result was that when they put the coffin on the Army gun-carriage, the horses were too cold and wouldn't move. Somebody called over the Naval Guard of Honour who had the horses out, picked up the traces and were off at a funeral march up the hill before you could say 'God help the Army!'

The row was still rumbling on, and the story round the clubs was that the King had let it be known that he wasn't surprised the Army had so much trouble stopping the Boers. Perhaps the Navy should have taken charge in South Africa instead. Tremendous mutterings in Whitehall at this, apparently.

Oliver, Malcolm and myself had a splendid evening, though we all agreed that we preferred Scotch to bourbon. We tried Barmy Twistleton's trick of adding bitters, but it tasted even worse so we just settled for plain bourbon and wished we had some fresh mint so we could make mint juleps, which Oliver and I agreed were one of America's gifts to the world.

Oliver told us about the great Cattle Rush in the early '80s in which Hughie Lonsdale, 'Sporting Joe' (Heneage Finch, 7th Earl of Aylesford) brother of my Pelican chums Dan and Clem Finch, and most of the House of Lords seem to have been involved. *Punch* published a cartoon depicting the Upper House wearing cowboy gear instead of robes and Cheyenne used to be called the Westminster of the West because of the number of younger sons of the nobility who went out there.

It all started back in '77 when Mortal Ruin (Moreton Frewin) and his brother came out to set up as ranchers. It was the first of his many weird ventures; if he made money on one, he lost it in another, yet they tell me he was a brilliant financier when he put his mind to it. He could certainly tell the tale, and I suppose it didn't do any harm to be Lady Randolph Churchill's brother-in-law.

His pals spread the word back in England what a wonderful place Wyoming was, and Hughie Lonsdale came out on his famous hunting trip with Lord Rodney, Charlie Fitzwilliam, Jimmy Burke-Roche and Maurice de Bunsen. (He's Sir Maurice now, a retired Foreign Office bigwig.)

It was a very odd affair, by all accounts. At one end of the scale, de Bunsen distinguished himself by stalking and killing the milk cow they'd taken along with them, an incident about which my spies tell me he is still very sensitive.

Jimmy Roche, on the other hand, took to it like a duck to water and scared everybody to death with his habit of panicking a herd of buffalo, selecting the animal he wanted, then riding into the middle of the stampeding herd to kill it at close range with a single shot from his revolver. Even the Indian guides hadn't seen that before. (He came into the Fermoy title but didn't enjoy it for long. He died in 1920.)

Oliver also confirmed the story about Little Henry that Hughie Lonsdale had told us so often in the Pelican. Hughie and Roche had gone out hunting one afternoon, leaving Grace, Hughie's wife, alone in the camp. On the way back, the guide stopped to examine the tracks of a solitary horseman. He became very excited and said the tracks belonged to Little Henry, a notorious horse-thief and murderer with a price of five thousand dollars on his head – and the tracks were heading towards the camp where Grace was alone with the rest of the horses and guns!

They galloped on, dismounted out of sight of the camp, took their rifles and crept up to see Little Henry taking a cup of tea with Grace Lonsdale as though paying a formal call at Eaton Square. The guide wanted to shoot him there and then to get the reward, but Hughie and Roche weren't having that. They walked in with their rifles at the ready till Hughie shouted, dropped his rifle and ran towards Little Henry, clapped him on the back and shook him warmly by the hand. As Roche and Grace looked on in amazement, Hughie explained that he and Little Henry had been at Eton together!

When Hughie Lonsdale had told us the story we'd all assumed he was just pulling our legs, but Oliver confirmed the Little Henry tale so perhaps it was true after all. As he said, was it any more unlikely than three members of the Bachelors' meeting in a small hotel on the other side of the world? Though he hoped none of us would suffer the same fate as Little Henry, who was eventually shot by Bat Masterson in Dodge City.

The great Western ranching craze went phutt in the blizzards of 1886 that killed nearly all the cattle in the north-west; not even Sporting Joe, Earl of Aylesford, with all his money could weather that one. One of Oliver's cowhands used to work for Sporting Joe and told us stories about 'the Jedge' as they called him. Every time a cowboy called at the ranch a new bottle was opened, and it didn't stop at just one bottle either. Oliver's hand remembers waking up one morning 'to find the bottles lyin' around thick as fleas, the boys two deep on the floor snorin' like mad buffaloes and the Jedge with a bottle in each hand over in the corner'. So no one had been really surprised when Sporting Joe died down in Texas soon afterwards.

We shook our heads mournfully over this but, as we agreed, what else could you expect after such a divorce scandal. Way before my time of course, but anyone who had been involved in a divorce as messy as his, which finished up with the Prince of Wales challenging Randolph Churchill to a duel, had little to look forward to in England.

We stayed at Cody's Irma Hotel, named after Buffalo Bill's favourite daughter, which was quite good as American hotels go and even had a telephone system. It was only for internal use, but it certainly seemed effective, though Malcolm Moncrieffe had to smile when the desk-clerk told him why the machine in his room wasn't working. A cowboy had been in the previous night, found it annoying and emptied his revolver into it. We went along to have a look and, sure enough, there was this battered mechanism on the wall with six bullet holes in it.

We stayed on a couple of days to meet Bill Cody who was passing through. He was beginning to look his age and he'd lost his ringing voice, but it was still a thrill to meet my boyhood hero on his home ground. I'd seen his Wild West Show when it first came to Earl's Court in 1887 and I'd met him in '92 when Ned de Clifford brought him and his troupe along to the Pelican. Bill Cody, or Colonel Cody, as Oliver advised us to address him, remembered the evening well and told me that they'd nearly had to cancel next day's show because of the hangovers everybody had.

I recall he asked after his old showman rival, George Sanger, with whom he'd had the big lawsuit; I suppose it's forgotten now so I'd better say what it was all about. Sanger's circus hadn't been doing too well in London, so he'd decided to run a Wild West Show in imitation of Cody's. When Cody came back to England on his second tour, he reckoned he was losing business, so went to law to stop Sanger calling his show by the same name. At one point in the case, Cody's counsel made much of his position as Deputy Governor of Wyoming or whatever it was, and insisted that Sanger refer to him as the The Honourable Colonel Cody.

Sanger went off the deep end and told the judge that if that ruddy cowboy was going to call himself an Honourable, then he was going to call himself Lord George Sanger. He insisted on the title from that day on and Lord George Sanger's Circus is still going strong. To everyone's surprise, Queen Victoria found it all very funny and let it be known she had no objection to a circus-manager taking the style and address of a duke's younger son.

As well as being a great showman, Cody was also a great whisky man and he matched the three of us drink for drink. At one point he suggested a shooting match but Oliver managed to talk him out of it, much to our surprise and disappointment.

We couldn't see what Oliver was playing at till he pointed out to us the following morning that, while he trusted Cody's shooting, he didn't trust ours. We didn't understand what he meant till he told us the form the shooting match would take. Drunk or sober, he said, Cody was one of the best trick-shots in the world. He would challenge us to hold a playing card in our hand and he would put three bullets through it. Then he'd put a tin can on our heads – and he'd knock that off as well.

We saw what he was getting at when he concluded:

"And, Gally, while I'm perfectly happy to let Bill shoot cans off your head at twenty yards, are you sure you could do the same to him? He built this place and I'd hate to see you strung up for killing Buffalo Bill in his home town!"

How right he was. I didn't know what sort of mark I'd make in the world, if any, but I certainly didn't want to be remembered for that.

Chapter 10

My First Trip to America – 3

*Chicago to New York. New York Society and noble marriages.
A kind deed brings its reward. I play Svengali*

FROM Wyoming I travelled to New York via Chicago, which at that time was reckoned to be the fastest-growing, busiest city in America. Chicago, the hub of the Union, they used to call it. Understandable, I suppose, when you remember it is halfway across America, has the Mississippi river running south to the Gulf and the Great Lakes linking it to Canada and the Atlantic.

Its relationship with New York struck me as much like Manchester's to London. 'What Chicago-Manchester says today, New York-London says tomorrow', that sort of thing. As one chap said, you make your money in Chicago, you spend it in New York.

Everybody had tremendous civic pride which was all very laudable, though it got a bit wearing at times being told how much bigger and better it was than anywhere else. They told me the Chicago fire of 1871 had been the biggest America had seen, for what that's worth, then told me how they had buckled down and re-built the place as the second biggest city in America. They were terribly proud of the 1892 Exposition and their skyscrapers, which were the first I'd seen, were certainly very impressive.

Somebody took me along to admire the new library. I find libraries dull places and this was duller than most, probably because the basis of it was a collection of books sent over by Tom Hughes, the fellow who wrote *Tom Brown's School Days*. He was a very worthy chap, a big pal of Charles Kingsley's and that lot. I suppose the world needs people like that, but I always found them very poor company.

Like Moreton Frewin (it was certainly the only thing they had in common), Hughes came out to America to start a new community in Tennessee. It was going to be a new Utopia based on peace, love, trust, common ownership, the dignity of labour and all the rest of it. He called it Rugby after his old school but it failed, losing him a lot of money as such ventures always do.

America seems to go in for such 'ideal' communities. Emerson and Hawthorne's Brook Farm and Bronson Alcott's Fruitlands were two among dozens, but they never seem to work. I suppose some people want to lead the simple life as Thoreau did at Walden. On one of the many occasions my sisters urged me to get a job, I silenced them by saying I was merely following the dictates of Henry David Thoreau. What they forgot, as so many people do, is that Thoreau believed that the less labour a man did, over and above the absolute necessity, the better for him and the community at large. Now that is something I can agree with.

It was at a party in Chicago that I first met Gordon Selfridge. As a young man he had joined Marshall Field, America's biggest store, and became a partner by the time he was twenty-eight. When I met him, he had just opened his own place, which was doing very well, but he didn't want to enter into rivalry with Marshall Field and was wondering what to do next.

I'm proud to say I played a part in persuading him to open his present gigantic store in London by telling him that Burbidge at Harrod's and the 'Universal Provider' (William Whiteley) could do with some competition. I never liked Whiteley and I went off Harrod's when they treated Fatty Coleman so badly in '98.

That was the year Harrod's installed the first moving staircase in London, escalators they call them now. Harrod's made a tremendous fuss about it, advertisements in all the papers and that sort of thing, which included the statement that a member of staff would be in attendance at each escalator with *sal volatile* and brandy for any customers overcome by the experience. Fatty Coleman, who never missed a chance of a free drink, spent an enjoyable morning swooning up and down the building and being revived by solicitous members of staff. It wasn't till lunch-time that they realised what he was up to and chucked him out on his ear.

As all the world knows, Selfridge took my advice and opened his Oxford Street shop in 1909. He certainly gave Harrod's and Whiteley something to think about; London hadn't seen publicity like it since Barnum's Circus. He opened the store with the biggest fanfare London had ever heard by hiring the trumpeters of every military band within

100 miles. When Blériot flew the Channel, his aeroplane was in Selfridge's window the following day. When Marconi perfected his radio transmissions, Selfridge hired him to give demonstrations and thousands of customers thronged the shop to watch. Nowadays he's probably best known for squiring the Dolly Sisters around, but who can blame him for that?

From Chicago I travelled on to New York, the first of my many visits there, and ran into my old pal Barmy Twistleton again, who had unexpectedly come into the title. He was now officially engaged to his girl in New York, her parents having withdrawn their objections once they found he was a full-scale English earl. After she had broken off their engagement half a dozen times, mainly because he found poker games more attractive than dining with her parents, they got married and are now living down at Bishop's Ickenham in Hampshire.

I was given cards for the Lamb's and Strollers' clubs and everyone made me very welcome, although lots of chaps asked if I had come wife-hunting. I didn't blame them. Everybody remembers how many peers of the realm married Gaiety girls; fewer remember how many married wealthy American women. Even my own nephew Freddie is married to the daughter of an American millionaire manufacturer of dog-biscuits, though I am delighted to say that he makes Freddie work. He sells dog-biscuits and, to the surprise of all who know him, does quite well at it.

The American marriages of so many of my noble contemporaries is an aspect of social history that you won't find in many history books, but it has always struck me as a superb example of poetic justice, or poetic irony, or whatever it is called.

In the 1870s, the Stately Homes of England of which the poetess Mrs Hemans spoke so highly, were in a pretty bad way financially. The agricultural depression had reduced rent-rolls by as much as 80%, a disaster directly attributable to the import of cheap beef and wheat from America. Yet, ironically, many of those same Stately Homes survived through a series of judicious marriages between their noble owners and the daughters of American millionaires.

The first was that of Henry Wodehouse, the Earl of Kimberley's cousin, who married Mary Livingstone of Georgia, but such alliances became the fashion in 1874 when Jennie Jerome married Randolph

Churchill, the Duke of Marlborough's brother. I suppose it can be said to have ended in 1910 when Mildred Carter married young Archie Acheson, the Earl of Gosford's heir which, I'm afraid, didn't work out too well. She sued him for divorce last year on grounds of desertion. Can't really blame her. He told her he was going to China for a holiday and stayed there three years. [1]

In the intervening years, under the approving eye of Edward VII, no fewer than 118 American girls married into the British aristocracy and nine of them became duchesses. The three Paget brothers all married Americans and the Churchills, always a radical lot, married no fewer than four of them.

The newspapers had a field day and somebody in New York even published a guide to the British aristocracy for American mothers, listing the habits, appearance and financial status of every name in Debrett. I was chagrined to find it thought little of my personal habits and less of my financial prospects.

The understanding was that the girl got a title for her trouble and the groom got American money for his. But young Kim Mandeville, the son of my Pelican chum who had also married American money, went too far. He went over and told the New York newspapers that he was looking for an American wife, any wife, so long as she had enough money. This was too blatant, even for them. Everybody knew our dukes and earls wanted to marry money, but none of them had admitted it so openly before.

Kim found a wealthy bride eventually, though like his father before him, he was declared bankrupt on the eve of the wedding. It wasn't a formality, he really was bankrupt. Most of us owed our tailors, but Kim's housekeeper sued him for her wages – that was real shortage of cash! [2]

---

(1) Archibald Acheson, who became Earl of Gosford in 1922, later married another American, Mrs Beatrice Breese of New York. He went to live in America, ran a wine-shop in Manhattan and joined the City Police at the age of 65. *Ed.*

(2) Kim Mandeville was the 9th Duke of Manchester. Both the 8th and 9th Dukes went through the Bankruptcy Court and both found rich American wives. The 9th Duke married Helena Zimmerman of Cincinnati in 1900 with a marriage settlement of £400,000. She divorced him in 1931 after which he married another American, Kathleen Dawes.

All this was in 1900 and very fresh in people's minds when I arrived in New York. It had got to the point that they didn't believe any Englishman with a handle to his name, even a humble Hon. like me, could visit America for any other purpose than to look for a wealthy wife. Yet the irony is that the cause of the whole thing was the snobbery of Mrs Astor of New York!

Many of my American chums still speak with bated breath of the life-and-death struggles to get into 'the Four Hundred', the term coined to describe the four hundred people who supposedly made up New York Society. Mrs Astor, with the biggest fortune in America behind her, decided she would become leader of New York Society, and for forty years that's what she was. Her balls were the biggest event in America's social life, far outweighing anything that the President might do in Washington. It was her social secretary, Ward McAllister, who told the Press that her ballroom held four hundred people and Society consisted of those fortunate enough to be invited. If you weren't on Mrs Astor's visiting list, you were not in Society; it was as simple as that. But some people had other ideas.

The struggle was between Old Money and New Money. Before the American Civil War there were only a dozen or so millionaires in America. By the 1870s there were hundreds of them, and their wives made them move to New York, determined to break into Society. The Knickerbockers, or the 'Nobs', were the conservative old New Yorkers led by Mrs Astor. The newly-moneyed people were called the 'Swells'.

Led by fellows like Leonard Jerome, the Swells started playing polo, racing yachts, building those extraordinary French *châteaux* along Fifth Avenue and generally throwing their money about. They started a club at Tuxedo outside New York rather on the lines of our Queen's Club, making a tremendous fuss about the so-called informality of the place and wearing dinner-jackets instead of white tie, which is why Americans call a dinner-jacket a tuxedo.

In 1935 he was sentenced to nine months in Wormwood Scrubs for pawning jewellery belonging to his trustees. The sentence was overturned in the Court of Appeal and the Duke came out after a month looking far fitter than when he had gone in. He was the original of the caricatures of fortune-hunting Englishmen drawn by Charles Dana Gibson. He died in 1947. *Ed.*

But Mrs Astor refused to recognise the existence of the Swells, no matter how much money they had. The upshot was that three ambitious mothers whom she had snubbed, Mrs Jerome, Mrs Yznaga and Mrs Stevens, brought their girls over to London. The Prince of Wales met their daughters, liked what he saw (especially the Jerome girls) and all doors in London Society were open to them. Two of the Jerome girls married titles, as did both the Yznaga girls, while Minnie Stevens finished up as Lady Paget.

And that's how it all started. The girls whom Mrs Astor refused to recognise came over to England and married titles instead. A sort of divine retribution, I suppose.

Mrs Astor fought back by putting her servants into Windsor livery and having her carriages painted the same colour. (Mrs John Astor and Mrs Clarence McKay followed her example by sporting replicas of the Queen's crown on formal occasions instead of tiaras.) But the Jeromes had broken Mrs Astor's dictatorship, the lure of a title was too strong and one of her own family is now in the House of Lords.

By the time I arrived, old Mrs Astor's reign was over. She was still alive but had become insane. Her madness, appropriately enough, took the form of wandering round the house in full evening dress and jewellery, greeting imaginary guests. Rather sad, really.

The leadership of New York Society had passed to the 'Great Triumvirate' of Mrs Stuyvesant Fish, Mrs Oelrichs and Mrs Oliver Belmont (better known as the mother of Consuelo, Duchess of Marlborough). Mrs Stuyvesant Fish, said to have the sharpest tongue in New York, was held in awe by everybody, but there were strong rumours of a mysterious power behind the throne who stood no nonsense from her, and thus held the *entrée* to New York Society in his hand.

I was fortunate enough to meet this illustrious individual when I called at the Fish place on Fifth Avenue, which was more like Versailles than a town house. When I tell you it was twice the size of the monstrosities the South African diamond millionaires built along Park Lane, you'll understand what I mean.

As I was handing my card to a footman, another figure approached and bowed:

"Good morning, Mr Threepwood. We have not had the pleasure of seeing you here before, sir. May I welcome you to New York."

It was Morton, Mrs Fish's English butler, a man of such immense dignity that he made Gilbert's Pooh-Bah look like a street urchin and the only person in the world of whom La Fish was afraid. His habitual comment on her suggestions for some enormous extravagant party became legendary:

"Just as you wish, madam. But I should inform you it is not done in the best English households."

We may have won the Empire by the Thin Red Line and the playing-fields of Eton, but American social life is ruled by that race of supermen, the English butlers, who bestride the narrow world like Colossi.

Even Chet Tipton, hardly the most reflective of men, recognised their importance. One night, in a mood of philosophic reflection induced by mixing whisky with vintage port to see what it tasted like, he pronounced gravely that, in his opinion, the English butler stood second only to the dry Martini as the greatest civilising force in America.

Morton greeted me like a wealthy uncle of whom he had expectations. He conducted me to the presence, announcing me as though I were Emperor of All the Russias, and informed Mrs Fish that I was free to come to dinner, making it sound as if she was extremely lucky I could fit her in.

On my next visit to the Fish mansion, Morton was there again with lots of sound advice on the people I was going to meet. Although I knew I possessed a personality full of wit and charm and all the rest of it, I was puzzled by his warmth. Could it be that I reminded him of home, the gas-lit streets of Piccadilly, the smell of fish-and-chip shops or the rolling countryside of Shropshire?

So I said how grateful I was for his advice and what a help it was in a strange city. He smiled benignly, like a bishop approving a curate's sound views on a rival bishop:

"It is I who am under an obligation, Mr Threepwood. I look upon you as the founder of my fortunes!"

I asked him what on earth he meant and he smiled again:

"I suppose there is no reason why you should remember me, sir, but you were once glad of my assistance. I was in service with the Earl of Wivenhoe at Hammer's Easton on the occasion that you and Mr Benger put one of his lordship's pigs in Major Basham's bedroom.

Having some difficulty in smuggling the animal into the house without detection, you called upon my services to ensure the coast was clear before you took it up the back staircase.

"You were kind enough to press a note into my hand, with a strong recommendation for a double at Hurst Park the following week. I do not normally bet on horses, but I did as you advised and your optimism was fully justified. I acquired sufficient funds to buy my ticket to America where my services, as you can see, were very soon taken up.

"If you require any introductions or assistance during your stay in New York, you have only to say the word."

Upon which he bowed like a maharajah acknowledging the presence of an inferior, a trick only butlers are able to achieve, and led me through to the drawing-room. He kept his word too. Invitations were showered upon me and even my hotel made a pleasing little ceremony of tearing up the bill. (I discovered later that Morton had told them that I had been sent over by the King to see if the hotel would suit him when, or if, he ever visited New York.)

So there I was in New York Society, hostesses clamouring for my company and all the rest of it – all due to a single kindly act. By kindly act, I do not mean slipping Morton a fiver, but being worried enough about Plug Basham's mood of depression to do something about it, i.e. putting a phosphorescent-painted pig in his bedroom in an effort to jerk him out of his lethargy and take an interest in things.

Some of the formal functions were a bit stolid for my taste, but the Lambs' and Strollers' were full of lively chaps and I met a few of my old Pelican chums, including Chet (Chester) Plimsoll. He missed London sorely, he told me, but wasn't sure if he dared come back.

Like so many of his fellows, he worked too hard and married too often, as wealthy Americans tend to do. When Chet had been over in London for a break between wives, he discovered the joys of *haute cuisine* as practised by Escoffier at the Savoy. Chet dined there every night and invariably had double helpings, because there was nothing like it in New York and it seemed a shame to waste the opportunity.

The result was that Chet, always a fairly well-built chap, started to put on weight. He didn't want to cut himself off from his newly-found delight in food, but he didn't want to end up looking like Tubby Parsloe or Fatty Coleman either, so he went out and bought one of those abdominal belts that you wear under your clothes. You know the sort of thing – 'as recommended by leading doctors and worn by Royalty'. They're supposed to sweat off the fat without discomfort while retaining the figure beautiful.

So there was Chet in the Pelican one night, knocking back his third buttered rum and thinking how much good his abdominal belt was doing him, when Clem Finch came in with the two Horn brothers – Drinking Horn and Hunting Horn, we used to call them. They joined him at the bar and talked of this and that for a while until Hunting Horn drew Chet to one side:

"Chet, old man," he said. "We were talking about you just now and thinking that the way you're going, Fatty Coleman is going to lose his title as our fattest member. Why don't you try one of those abdominal belts you see advertised in the papers? You wear them under your clothes, apparently, and they keep you looking slim while they sweat the fat off. I'd try one if I were you. I'm sure it would make all the difference!"

Old Chet was so depressed by this that he caught the next boat back to America. He reckoned that his New York business kept him so busy that he never had time for a decent meal, and in the evenings he was too tired to enjoy it anyway.

Still, I saw him in Delmonico's occasionally and he coped with most of what the chef served up. He built up a chain of stores right across America before he shuffled off this mortal coil just a few months ago.

I shall finish this chapter with a minor triumph. There aren't too many things in my life I look back on with pride, but I can say I had a hand in a social phenomenon of our times.

I mentioned above that there were two types of aristocratic marriages making the news in those days. One section of the peerage was marrying English chorus girls, while another section was marrying American heiresses. I had a hand in a third variation, the marriage of English peers to American chorus girls. (I don't count Maxine Elliott and her proposals from Rosebery and Curzon. Nobody would ever dream of calling her a chorus girl. Her house parties at Hurstbourne were conducted along *very* strict lines though Winston Churchill, then Home Secretary, used to be allowed to do his favourite party piece – an imitation of an angry bear using one of Maxine Elliott's bear rugs for the purpose. Some of his colleagues reckoned that he was better suited to the stage than he was to Government. I wouldn't like to comment.)

You may remember that I travelled from Arizona to Wyoming in the company of two charming chorus girls. I'd given them my card and told them to go and see William Brady if they ever got to New York. I'd forgotten all about them till I received a message at my hotel to say a young lady had called to see me. It was Camille Clifford, one of the girls in the train, who had seen my name in the social columns and dropped by to say hello. She had come to New York, been to see Brady and had got a walk-on part in his show 'Foxy Grandpa'.

We had lunch at Rector's, and she confided that she still dreamed of going to England and marrying into the aristocracy like the Vanderbilts and the Gaiety girls I had told her about. (I think she had been reading too much Ouida, but who was I to destroy her hopes and dreams?)

She was a nice girl and I promised that, if she could get herself to London, I'd send a letter to Seymour Hicks. The question was – did she have a speciality? Anything that made her different from all the other girls trying to make their name? Could she convince theatrical managers she possessed that certain something the others had not got?

We brooded over this at length and I got the answer halfway through the second bottle. When I'd met her in Arizona, she had reminded me of someone or something and, under the beneficent influence of alcohol, I remembered what it was. She was a perfect double of the Gibson Girl! THAT was the thing to make her name with.

For my younger readers I should explain that in those days, all the older women wanted to look like Queen Alexandra; when she injured her knee, Society ladies started walking with the 'Alexandra limp'. The younger wives dressed like Lillie Langtry and the girls around town tried to look like the Gaiety stars, Connie Gilchrist or Gertie Millar.

But there were no American girls to copy until the artist Charles Dana Gibson came along with his 'Gibson Girl' drawings, which appeared in magazines all over America. Originally modelled on his wife, Nancy Astor's sister, the Gibson Girl was the first in the procession of American styles of beauty led today by Mary Pickford, Clara Bow, Theda Bara and the rest of them. The Gibson Girl of the cartoons was tall, beautiful, elegant. She had a superb figure with a wasp-waist and was depicted wearing a very décolleté long dress. She was aloof, she was enticing, she had what nowadays they call 'It'.

I told Camille to get a dress like those in the drawings, do her hair in the Gibson girl style, and pull her waist in to the eighteen inches or whatever it was that gave the Gibson Girl that unmistakeable figure. The next time she went on stage, she was to delay her entrance until everybody was waiting for her, then she was to walk slowly across the stage as a Gibson Girl would do and see what happened.

She was very nervous but said she'd try it, so long as I promised to go along to give her some moral support. The big night came and there I was in the stalls with most of the Strollers' and Lambs' clubs along for company. The play began, the moment for Camille's entrance arrived – there was a long pause, then she came on and sailed slowly across the stage.

She looked magnificent. I was going to start the applause but there was no need. Before she'd got half-way, every man in the place was on his feet cheering his head off. The Gibson Girl had come to life!

They made her walk to and fro for ten minutes before someone, the leading man I think it was, went up to her, bowed low and led her off the stage. She never said a word, she didn't have to; all she had to do was to be the Gibson Girl. For the rest of the run she was the star of the show. The Press was full of her, Gibson came to see her, approved of what he saw and Seymour Hicks, at my instigation, invited her over to London. [3]

She appeared as the Gibson Girl in his 'The Catch of the Season' at the Vaudeville and then in 'The Belle of Mayfair'. And that was enough. On 11 October 1906, I attended her wedding to Harry Bruce, Lord Aberdare's son. I met her a few months later at Weston Park, the Bradfords' place along the Shrewsbury road from us at Blandings (Harry Bruce was Bradford's brother-in-law). She told me she was the happiest woman in the world. She loved her husband, she had married

---

(3) The following footnote appears in Mr Threepwood's manuscript.

I meet Gibson occasionally when he comes over to stay with the Astors. He tells me that, although his drawings made him famous, he is prouder of the Martini Gibson cocktail named after him. It happened in the Players' Club one night when the bar-tender had run out of olives. He popped in an onion instead and Gibson liked it so much, he insisted on it thereafter and the habit spread. Funny how a name takes on. With the amount and variety I've drunk, you would think there would be a Galahad cocktail somewhere, but no sign of it so far.

into the nobility, life was one grand sweet song and she owed it all to me, or so she said.

She never went back on the stage, although I hear she appeared at the Queen Charlotte Ball the other day as the original Gibson Girl and amazed all the Bright Young Things with her waist which is still only eighteen inches.

It was the first marriage of an American show-girl into the aristocracy and I was proud to play a part in it. But now, as the song says, everybody's doing it. Lord Marshmoreton of Belpher Castle married an American chorus girl called Billie Dore; my old pal Sir Buckstone Abbott married Alice (Toots) Bulpitt who came over in 'The Pink Lady' in 1911, while Northesk made the American dancer Jessica Brown his Countess just a few years ago. And, if I'm any judge, young Charles Cavendish, Devonshire's third boy, is going to break up the Astaires's brother-and-sister dancing act by marrying Adele Astaire.

And it all began at that small railway station in Arizona.

(Photo: Picture Post)

Camille Clifford, 'The Gibson Girl'

Chapter 11

Some Men of My Time – 1
Barmy Twistleton

Frederick Altamont Cornwallis Twistleton, 5th Earl of Ickenham

I AM aware that some people consider my old friend and colleague Barmy Twistleton irresponsible, but he is a man of infinite resource and sagacity. You may finish up feeling as if you've been in an earthquake or swept away by a typhoon, but Barmy will spare no effort to solve those little problems that crop up in Life's long journey. I have no hesitation in stating that Barmy Twistleton is hot stuff.

We were at school together, you will recall, and met again out West. Like me, he was a younger son, but on his brother's death Barmy scooped the pool and returned with an American wife.

He came back to England to sort things out before the wedding, and threw the biggest party Romano's had ever seen. Luigi still shudders at the memory of it. Barmy invited just about everybody, ranging from Natty Rothschild to Dickie Dunn and old Jimmy, the chap who sold the *Pink 'Un* outside Romano's, when he wasn't scraping a living as the worst racing tout in London.

I still think it was all Dickie Dunn's fault. He should have known better than to bet Barmy he couldn't produce some trick that Romano's hadn't seen before. Barmy called for silence, made Dickie repeat the bet so everybody could hear, and took him for fifty quid.

"Right, Dickie!" he said. "Put your money on the counter." Dickie Dunn did so and waited to see what would happen next.

Barmy walked away from the bar and turned round, pulling back his coat to reveal a couple of ruddy great revolvers on his belt.

"Stand away!" he shouted. "From the left! One, two, three, four, five, six!"

He let fly at the row of glass jars that stood along the top of the shelves behind the bar. You never heard such a racket. The shots deafened us, the glass clattered down, the women screamed, Luigi was bellowing at the top of his voice, but Barmy hadn't finished.

"Name your poison, Dickie," he shouted. "Let's try that bottle of absinthe on the next shelf – awful foreign muck!" And a bullet crashed into the absinthe bottle.

"Now for the Calvados!" – and the Calvados vanished with a bang.

It went on for another four bottles until he ran out of bullets. In the stunned silence which followed, Barmy walked up to the counter, picked up Dickie's fifty quid, put it into Luigi's shaking hand and said:

"Mr Dunn is paying for the damage."

In another chapter I mention some stage-effects that went wrong. The most dramatic I ever saw was engineered by Barmy for the best of all motives – to help a pal.

It happened in 1911 when Barmy and I popped over to New York to see the middle-weight championship and ran into old Johnny Schoonmaker, a splendid American whom we had welcomed to our bosom in the old Pelican, where he made his name by showing us how to mix a proper mint julep.

He was keen on racing, and one summer he broke his leg in the middle of the season and had to go into hospital. I went along to visit him with Pitcher Binstead and found he was thoroughly enjoying himself. He'd combined business with pleasure by opening a book for the nurses and the other patients, running it on a barter basis, and taking bets in oranges, cigarettes, chocolates and the like. He was doing very well out of it, although there were complications.

"There's a fellow in the next ward who's had a nice winner in the 2.30," said Johnny. "Only trouble is, he bet a plum-duff on it at odds of 100-8 and I'm dashed if I know what to pay him."

So when Barmy and I met him in Delmonico's, we had a tremendous reunion before going on to the Lambs', the nearest thing in New York to the Savage Club. Johnny liked it because they let him mix his own mint juleps. But behind all the bright chat about old times, it was clear something was worrying him. After the fourth mint julep we discovered it was the old, old problem – his mother-in-law.

I hadn't met Johnny's wife but, like many a wife before and since, she wanted Johnny to work all day long making money, and be on parade every night to help her cut a dash in New York's social whirl.

Her mother encouraged her in this belief, making it clear that she thought Johnny should spend his evenings at the opera or the classical theatre rather than the Lambs' or Delmonico's.

He saw no way out of the difficulty and our hearts bled for him. Barmy seized on the problem at once.

"Johnny, you need help. And," he added modestly, "the last and the best of the Twistletons is at your service. Something must be done. The nub of the matter clearly rests with this mother-in-law of yours. If we can persuade her that the theatre is not as smart as she thinks it is, we shall solve the problem. Tell me, which play are you under starter's orders to attend next?"

"Tomorrow night," muttered Johnny morosely. "First night of a thing called 'The Garden of Allah' at the Century. Lew Waller's in it."

"Ah!" said Barmy, pleased. "Good! You know Waller, don't you, Gally? I think a visit to the theatre is indicated, so you can wish your friend the best of luck on his New York opening."

We asked him what he had in mind, but he refused to be drawn.

"Always remember what 'Bobs' said was the secret of winning battles. 'Time spent in reconnaissance is never wasted', he used to say. I don't know what we will find at the theatre tomorrow, but I am confident we shall find something. Cheer up, Johnny! With Gally Threepwood, the only man who ever got the better of Dickie Dunn, and Frederick Twistleton, Earl of Ickenham, in your corner, you can look forward to a happy, if as yet unknown, outcome."

The next day we went down to the theatre and I sent my card in to Waller. He's dead now, poor chap, but in his day he was London's best heroic actor, played Henry V and D'Artagnan to the manner born and, incidentally, was the first actor to have what they now call a 'fan club'. They were a group of women who went round wearing badges saying 'Keen On Waller'. Waller was highly embarrassed by the whole business because we pulled his leg unmercifully, but then they decided the initials were enough. Londoners laughed their heads off at Society women wearing a badge with 'KOW' on it so the whole thing died, much to Waller's relief.

Anyway, he seemed glad to see someone from London, and we wished him luck and chatted about things for a while. You know what a theatre is like before a first night; people dashing all over the place shouting their heads off and so on. Barmy was amazingly quiet for him and while I was talking to Waller, he wandered around the place looking at what was going on. Eventually he came back to join us in the stalls.

"What," he asked Waller, "is that enormous metal thing on the Prompt side? There's a chap filling it with what looks like sawdust."

Waller explained that the big scene was a desert sand-storm. The heroine would stagger across the stage, dying for lack of water, hear a sand-storm approaching, make sure the audience heard it too – and then this machine would belch out about two tons of sawdust, corn meal and bran all over the stage to show New York what a sand-storm was really like.

Barmy was fascinated. Wasn't it dangerous? What happened if it spewed the wrong way? Waller agreed that it was tricky. It was like a firehose, he said; if the pipe was loose, it would send the stuff all over the place. That's why the stage manager was tightening the fittings to make sure the bran and sawdust went where it should.

I didn't see Barmy for a bit after that, but he came back eventually to wish Waller the best of luck and we left. As we walked out of the theatre, Barmy told me he'd secured a box for that evening so we would have to postpone our visit to a poker game of which we had heard good reports. I didn't see why, but Barmy was adamant.

"Last night we promised good old Johnny we'd do our best. The very least we can do is make sure that we have done it."

And not a word more would he say.

That evening saw us in a box in the Century, looking down at the audience. It was quite a sight. Before the War first-night audiences in New York took a pride in their appearance. Indeed the phrase 'The Diamond Horseshoe' was coined to describe the dress circle of the Metropolitan Opera House. Some journalist worked out that when Caruso or Melba sang there, that horseshoe of seats had enough diamonds on display to pay the National Debt. He also said the amount of bare skin on show would make Casanova blush, but people tended to ignore that bit. The Century audience was equally glittering and we could see Johnny, his wife and a large lady, clearly her mother, in the third row of the stalls.

The play ran its course, the last act came along and the heroine staggered on stage telling us how she had been in the desert for days and was dying of thirst. Then she put one hand to her ear and announced she could hear the sand-storm coming. It was at this point that Barmy grabbed my arm:

"Here we go, Gally!" he whispered. " This is it."

There was a sort of rushing noise and the girl demonstrated how frightened she was by screaming and throwing herself to the ground. The next second the machine started belching out its two tons of bran and sawdust. It was most impressive; the whole stage just vanished in a brown haze. The first instalment went on the stage all right, but then the nozzle swung the wrong way and before you could blink, the machine was blasting out the stuff straight on to the first dozen rows of stalls!

There was nothing anybody could do. The women screamed and the men yelled as they tried to save themselves by getting down behind the seats with their hands over their heads. It seemed like hours, but it was probably only a minute, before someone managed to turn the machine off – and then the row started.

It was like a political meeting I once went to down in Aldgate East. The people in the stalls were bellowing their indignation at the tops of their voices, while those in the circle and balcony were cheering their heads off. I've never heard so many shouts of 'Encore!' in my life. Apart from those in the target area, the audience made it clear this was the best thing they'd ever seen on the New York stage, and they wanted to see it again as often and as soon as possible. It was pandemonium and Barmy sat there with a grin on his face, looking like Napoleon after a good battle.

Eventually things calmed down. The curtain descended, the lights went up, the noise died away and Barmy said:

"I think we'd better be shifting, Gally. I'm not sure someone didn't see me this morning, and I'd hate my pals back home to read that the last of the Twistletons had been lynched by some New York stage-hands."

So we slid out.

Barmy was very modest about the whole thing. Providence had clearly put the sand-storm machine there for a purpose. All he had to do was loosen the bolts on the side nearest the audience so the vibration would swing it that way rather than the other.

"And from now on," he said, "Johnny can tell his mother-in-law he prefers to risk the odd spot of cigar ash in the Lambs' or a waiter in Delmonico's spilling the soup. But at least he won't run the risk of being suffocated by a ton of sawdust in her so-called Temples of Art!"

Which was exactly what Johnny did. He and Barmy became great pals, and Barmy used to go round and help him bath his baby daughter Myra. I haven't seen her for years, but we expect her at Blandings soon.

It was one of Barmy's most spectacular successes and puts him well up my list of England's unsung heroes, though I don't suppose that everybody would take the same view. For example, look at his recent attempt to brighten up the sport of greyhound racing.

A few months ago in Bond Street, I ran into Barmy who celebrated the occasion by inviting me to join him for lunch as the guest of his nephew Pongo. He said Pongo wouldn't object because he, Barmy, controlled Pongo's allowance, so off we went to Buck's Club in Clifford Street.

For those who don't know him, I should mention that Buck, alias Herbert Buckmaster, is the nephew of old Harry Buckmaster who took a pride in being seen with the prettiest blonde of the Gaiety chorus on his arm. I'd got to know young Buck in South Africa, so he insisted we join him for a pre-lunch snifter.

Before the War Buck was probably best known as the lucky chap who married Gladys Cooper, but things went wrong and I'm afraid they were divorced a few years ago. He started Buck's Club in 1919 and it's doing very well, though it will never equal the old Pelican. Still, there are some bright young chaps amongst the members and they do get out and about.

The conversation turned to a mutual acquaintance, Charlie Munn, who had come to Buck a couple of years ago with an interesting proposition. He had seen greyhound racing over in America, wanted to bring it to England and gave Buck the chance to join him.

Buck saw the possibilities, but realised it would ruin the sport of coursing on which he and his pals were very keen. He discussed the matter with some of the coursing set, Osbert and Helena Sefton (she was a Bridgeman and a neighbour of ours in Shropshire), the Duke of Leeds, old General Cator and the like, and they all told him not to touch it. So Charlie Munn went ahead with somebody else and made a packet.

We listened sympathetically and Barmy mentioned that he'd never been to a greyhound track. No reason why he should really; the first track only opened in 1926 and I don't suppose there are more than fifty in the country as I write.

Then young Pongo collected us and we went into lunch, a decent enough meal with the occasional bread roll whistling across the room. An excellent habit in a club, I feel. Nothing makes an unpopular member more conscious of his position than a well-aimed roll when he has just raised his soup spoon to his lips. Barmy and I were brought up on stronger stuff and told young Pongo that a leg of pork or a roast turkey was far more effective, but he just grinned weakly and told us that bread rolls were as far as they went in Buck's.

As we were taking our leave, Barmy raised the matter of greyhounds again. Was I free to accompany him to a track the next day? I couldn't, as it happened; I was bidden to a rather interesting private gambling party where I hoped to improve my financial situation. So Barmy told young Pongo that he was in luck, and could look forward to an instructive and interesting outing under the guidance of a fond uncle. Pongo looked a bit taken aback at this but Barmy was firm.

It was my nephew Ronald who told me the rest of the story. A couple of days later, Pongo had arrived back at Buck's, white and shaken, gasping for strong restoratives, sympathy and plenty of both.

Barmy and young Pongo had travelled out to Shepherd's Bush or wherever the greyhound track was, with Barmy passing the time musing on the merits of scientific experiment *vis-a-vis* greyhounds. Were they, he asked himself, so well trained they would chase only an electric hare, or would their natural instincts predominate? Would they chase anything that ran from them? A deep mystery lay here, Barmy felt, and he knew that Pongo would be as keen as he was on finding the answer.

When they arrived, Pongo said, they had been met by an appalling bounder with two sacks under his coat. Pongo became even more worried when Barmy paid for them, stuck them under his own coat and answered Pongo's questions with the remark that Truth was a jealous mistress to be served at all costs, no matter what temporary inconvenience might ensue.

They watched the first couple of races in silence, then Barmy led

Pongo over to the back straight and took up a position beside the railings. As the dogs were being put into their starting boxes, Barmy pulled out his two sacks and Pongo saw with horror that they were both moving as though something was wriggling inside.

"I think now is the time for our little scientific experiment," said Barmy. "In one bag are a dozen assorted rats; in the other are a couple of good strong hares. The whole menagerie has the personal guarantee of the gentleman we met at the gate who, although his outward appearance may not be all one would wish, is reputed to be the finest rat-catcher in London."

Before young Pongo could say a word, the traps were opened, the dogs raced out, Barmy leaned over the rails and emptied the contents of both sacks on to the track! The results were all that he had hoped for and that Pongo, I must admit with some justification, had feared. I suppose chaos is the only word to describe what ensued, and even that is understating things by a long chalk.

It was difficult to get any sense out of young Pongo, Ronald told me. He just moaned and shut his eyes as though trying to erase some dreadful memory. However, it seemed that an excellent, if somewhat confused, ratting match occupied three of the hounds, who certainly seemed to enjoy killing rats they could catch far more than chasing mechanical hares they couldn't.

The two hares set off up the back straight like good 'uns with a couple of greyhounds in hot pursuit. The hares justified all the claims Barmy's ratcatcher friend had made for them, were ahead at the first bend and kept on down the finishing straight. That was all right until one decided to jump the fence and vanish into the multitude. One hound went after it and they went through the crowd like a dose of salts, culminating, from what I can ascertain, in a spectacular kill somewhere down the High Street a quarter of a mile away.

The second hare, with a spirit of fair play that did it credit, stayed on the track and led its greyhound back to where the scramble for the rats was still in progress. Things wouldn't have been so bad if they'd stayed there, but the rats decided the crowd was a safer bet and made their way under the fence with the hounds in hot pursuit.

Nobody likes rats around their ankles at the best of times, and I suppose the realisation that all bets were off added a sense of grievance to the mass hysteria which gripped the crowd. It was at this point, Pongo said, that shock gave way to fury, and about five thousand enraged enthusiasts decided jointly and severally that their one ambition in life was to string up Barmy and Pongo from the nearest lamp-post.

The details are vague, but Ronald tells me that Pongo lost his hat, collar and coat, and got a superb black eye and half a dozen bruised ribs before the US cavalry arrived in the shape of a certain PC Potter, who hoicked them into protective custody, a most appropriate term in the circumstances.

Pongo said his gratitude to the officer, though fervent, was misplaced. It became clear that the constable, far from regarding Barmy and Pongo as innocent citizens whom it was an honour and a privilege to rescue from the mob, viewed them as villains of the deepest dye. It transpired he had placed a sizeable chunk of his pay on the favourite, and looked forward with the keenest anticipation to seeing Barmy and Pongo sent up the river for twenty years.

Luckily Barmy and even Pongo in his shattered state remembered the cast-iron rules for any imbroglio with the constabulary, viz. stick to firm denial and a false name.

The result was that when they stood in the dock the following morning, listening to Constable Potter accuse them of everything he could think of, starting with a breach of the peace, forming an unlawful assembly and finishing with high treason in that they did put several hundred of His Majesty's lieges in fear of their lives, the old training stood them in good stead. It was as George Robinson of 14 Nasturtium Road, East Dulwich and Edwin Smith of the same address that they bowed their heads and suffered the awful retribution of the law. And since both the said Robinson and Smith appeared to have no previous convictions to their name, they got off with a hefty fine.

Barmy regards it as one of his better days. A scientific truth established, a new experience for Pongo and several hundred others, brightening their drab lives and giving them something to talk about when they went home to their wives and families. And all at the cost of a temporary, if heavy, blow to the exchequer.

Chapter 12

The Pelicans at Henley

Debts, duckings and a young man's fancy

ONE evening, not long after I had joined the Pelican club, I walked in to find Swears Wells and a few others discussing whether they should repeat their trip to Henley. Swears saw me looking curious and explained.

In the summer of '88, the club was just starting to pay its way. (Pitcher and Master snorted a bit at this but Swears ignored them.) But then the bar takings began to drop badly and he and Shifter realised the hot weather had prompted many of the members to leave London. After several whiskies, they saw what had to be done. If the members were going elsewhere to do their drinking, then the club would go there too! Henley was coming up, Swears knew someone who knew someone else who had a houseboat, so a club houseboat at Henley was the answer.

As Swears was the first to admit, the important thing was that the houseboat owner didn't know him, Swears, from Adam. He had never been to Henley so there wouldn't be any of those little misunderstandings that occasionally make life complicated. When I asked what he meant, everyone laughed but Swears just stroked his moustache thoughtfully and said:

"Oh, just little things. Pretty barmaids who might have got the wrong idea from something you said and whose fathers are still trying to find you. Or local tradesmen leaping out at you with accounts for things you only bought so you could pay by cheque and get a bit of change to give the barmaid a good time. Just little things like that, young Gally. You'll find the same problem as you grow older.

"Provincial tradesmen are very narrow-minded," he went on. "The only thing to do is to give a false name, a good London address, and tell them you're thinking of settling in their beastly little town, and they might get your custom if they cash your cheques until such time as your bankers send down your letters of credit."

Shifter agreed: "That's the only thing wrong with this club. If I'm not down in the *Pink 'Un* offices, then every dun in London knows I'll be in Romano's or here. If it wasn't for the fact that I can get out the back doors faster than they can, I don't know how I'd carry on."

This was clearly a sore point with Swears.

"Heaven knows why I let you persuade me to become your partner in this ruddy club, Shifter. We would have been six quid up this evening if it wasn't for you! I checked the till ten minutes ago and they told me you'd borrowed it all. It's bad enough you drinking here as manager for free, without grabbing the only money we've got to spend somewhere else."

Shifter just grinned at this and Swears grew angry:

"I'll tell you one thing that'll take that idiotic grin off your face, Shift. You don't know the name I use when I'm out of town and a bit short of cash or female company. It's your name I always give 'em, Shifter! And there's quite a few hotel-keepers in Brighton waiting for you to settle their bills!"

Shifter waited till we had finished laughing and retorted:

"Sucks to you, Swears! What do you think I've been calling myself down there for the last six months? You use your name anywhere within a mile of the Metropole and there'll be twenty head waiters and a dozen landladies out looking for your blood! And I wouldn't go too near the Metropole either, if I were you. That pretty new barmaid has got three brothers waiting to settle things with Mr E.F. Wells!

"And," he went on, "I only borrowed the six quid from the till after I heard you tell George to hoick it out for you as soon as it reached a tenner. I'm off to Romano's, where I can get a bit of peace and use my own name!"

And he marched out.

Swears grumbled his way upstairs to see if he had any money left, while Pitcher settled down to tell me the rest of the story. Swears had gone ahead and hired the houseboat for forty quid for the week, plus an extra tenner for having it towed up to Henley to a good spot.

"I remember," Pitcher said, "that the chap asked Swears what he meant by a good spot. Did he want it near the finishing-line?

" 'Never mind the finishing-line,' says Swears. 'I want it where it's easy to get to, hard to get away from, and as far as you can get from the pubs where they'll sell drinks cheaper than I will!'

"The chap looked a bit puzzled, but said he'd do his best and would Swears care to pay the fifty quid there and then? Swears jumped to his feet, radiating indignation and hurt pride. Didn't he know who he was dealing with? Didn't he realise that half the House of Lords was coming down – and most of Fleet Street? If this was the way he did business, then no wonder nobody else had hired his rotten houseboat.

"By the time Swears had finished," said Pitcher, "the chap was sure he was going to lose the deal, so he said a tenner on account would be fine. Which was just as well, because that was all we had between us, but Swears handed it over as though it was hardly worth the receipt he was careful to get for it.

"Shift and Swears covered most of their costs from the start, because they charged members a guinea a day to come on board. Some of them reckoned that was a bit steep, but Shifter had invited down the girls from the Alhambra and that soon got the fellows trooping in. Quite a few of them persuaded their lady friends to come along as well, so everything went as merry as a wedding bell.

"Swears even decorated the houseboat with flowers. He said he had found a florist to let him have them on tick, but my own belief is that he sent his man George to steal them from the gardens of the hotel across the river. He got a band from somewhere as well. He told them they could have two guineas a day in cash, but they had to stay teetotal. Or they could take their chance on what they could screw out of the members in tips and free drinks for playing popular tunes.

"They weren't sure which to choose, till Swears told them Alfred Cellier and Jimmy Davis would be coming, plus half the Brigade. All they had to do was play military marches and selections from 'A Gaiety Girl' and 'The Geisha' and they couldn't go wrong.

"We passed the word along to the girls as well. Whenever things got a bit slack, they'd ask for a favourite tune and suggest a sov for the band's trouble. It worked very well till we found out the prettiest girl on board was the cornet player's sister. He was trying to keep an eye on her, to save her – well, her good name, shall we say? And when she took counter-measures by sending him up whisky after whisky to give him something else to think about, that didn't really work either. His playing got so bad, the rest of the band had to duck him in the river to sober him up.

"Still, by and large, it was a splendid week. Swears won a tenner with the fish he caught one morning. He'd laid bets he could land a five-pounder or bigger before breakfast and half a dozen chaps took him on. In passing," said Pitcher, "I'll give you a tip, Gally. Whenever Swears bets he'll do something, bet on him. I wouldn't say it covers horses, but if he's betting on himself, follow him.

"The next morning some of us came down early, and there was Swears with Peter Blobbs and Shifter out in the punt. As we watched, Swears shouted, his rod bent and the next thing you know, there was a fine six-pounder in the net and a dozen witnesses to say Swears had caught it.

"I won't say he cheated, because we could never prove it, but I noticed his man George surreptitiously untying a large fish-cage from the back of the houseboat and I drew my own conclusions. Anyway, I'd backed Swears for a fiver as well, so it wasn't for me to get the judges' decision reversed.

"The other fellows got their own back the next day. They persuaded Swears to try again. Not for a bet, you understand; just to get him out on the water. He and Blobbs and Shifter got into the punt and the next thing you know, a dozen fellows bent down, tipped up the punt and the three of them were in the water.

"A quick dip, inadvertent or otherwise, became quite the fashion before the week was over. Bill Bowman was down, mashing one of the Alhambra girls pretty hard. Halfway through the week his wife suddenly appeared from Town and found them fraternising. She was on the stage as well, Daredevil Esmeralda, who used to dive from the roof at the Hippodrome into a tank of water. She gave the Alhambra girl what for, tore into Billie and generally behaved as an outraged wife should. We didn't think much about it; it happened to most of us at one time or another, though normally it's the husband we have to deal with.

"Billie went off to the bar, Swears got Esmeralda a glass of champagne and Shifter, who always liked big girls, started soothing her and telling her Billie wasn't worth it and she needed somebody like him to appreciate her fine sensitive nature. Billie suddenly reappeared, marched up to her and shouted:

'You've driven me too far and now you can weep over my watery grave', and he jumped into the river!

"You never saw such a commotion. The girls screamed, people started shouting 'Man overboard' and looking for life-belts, while some of us got into the punt to look for him. It was confusion all round, though I did notice that Shifter carried on consoling the widow who had swooned in his arms.

"After about ten minutes of this, we heard a shout from the far bank and there was Billie, thumbing his nose at us and generally enjoying our discomfiture. He'd faked the whole thing just to fool us. Swears broke the news to Esmeralda that she was once again a happily-married woman, adding that her swooning showed her to be a lady of true feeling and delicacy. She was furious! Delicacy be damned! Billie would have been good riddance. She had swooned because she couldn't remember where she had put the receipt for his insurance premium!

"The ducking that could have been serious came the next day. Old Charlie Crocker was acting as treasurer, wearing a good strong leather satchel that Swears had given him. With the barmen we have, Swears thought it better to reduce temptation to a minimum, and it was Charlie's job to collect all the money every half-hour or so and stick it in his satchel.

"Suddenly there was a splash and Charlie was in the water. Before we had time to think, there was another splash and there was Swears's man, George, in the water too, swimming hard towards Charlie. We cheered him on, saw him reach Charlie and they both vanished under water. The next thing we knew, George was swimming back with the satchel firmly in one hand. He'd been with Swears long enough to know what really counted.

"He was quite disconcerted when somebody reminded him about Charlie, but it was all right. Charlie could swim like a fish, it turned out, and was only bothered that Swears wouldn't pay the five per cent of the takings he'd promised him.

"And that," concluded Pitcher, "was why we thought of doing Henley again this year, though it's doubtful if we'd get anybody to hire us a houseboat again. We cut too much of a dash last time, and Swears is still getting writs from the shopkeepers up there."

My first experience of Henley was very different, but just as enjoyable. Tommy Tucker (his real name was William, but we always called him

Tommy) had managed to squeeze me into a house-party that an uncle of his had organised for Regatta Week. It started off quietly, just Tommy and me and a couple of cousins who were rowing in some race or another. The uncle did us proud in the way of catering, and made us honorary members of his club tent at the regatta, so that was all right. We put his name on the bar chits and hoped he wouldn't twig till later.

It was on the second day that an elderly female connection of Tommy's uncle arrived with two of the prettiest daughters you ever saw. I think she had brought them down to meet the two rowing chaps – Tommy's uncle was a rich old bird in the brewing line – but she didn't know about racing-training. Beefy and Bully were interested only in their races and had no time for girls, so Tommy and I had to step into the breach, which was no hardship at all.

I took one look at the younger of the two, Dorothy, and saw something in her eye that made me think a young man's fancy might not be wasted on the desert air. I had a quick word with Tommy; well, to be accurate, we tossed for it and I won. (I used that double-headed penny I got from the cabbie in Covent Garden, but that's another story.) For the next day or so I squired Dorothy around while Tommy looked after Mary; Beefy and Bully kept on winning their races, so everybody was happy.

One evening the racing had gone on a bit late and Tommy's uncle and the girls' mother went home, saying they'd send the carriage back for us. It was a beautiful evening and I suggested to Dorothy she might like a walk along the river-bank to see the last race start. I could see Tommy had had the same idea and he was furious, till I suggested that he and Mary might care to try one of the canoes. Girls have to be held very carefully when they get in and out of canoes, and you have to sit very close when you're in them – so Tommy thought it was a splendid idea.

Dorothy and I started to stroll along the bank, talking of this and that. I gave her my arm as we crossed the rough grass just before the little wood that comes down to the water's edge. We reached the trees and I was screwing up my courage to slip my arm round her waist with the suggestion that we pause to admire the light on the water, when it happened.

She suddenly turned to me with a look of horror:

"Mr Threepwood, I believe a beetle or something has fallen down the back of my dress. What shall I do?"

I didn't know what to say for a moment; then I realised I was in luck.

"Miss Dorothy," I said, "or may I call you Dorothy? Just for the present, you understand. I would not dream of suggesting this under any other circumstances, but if perhaps I were to ..." and my voice faltered.

"What do you mean, Mr Threepwood?" she said.

"Well," I stammered, "if you really want me to get that beetle out for you, I'm afraid it will be necessary to, er, well, er, put my hand down the back of your dress and sort of ..."

She looked at me as if she couldn't believe her ears. "Do you mean, Mr Threepwood, that you propose to put your hand inside my clothing? Is that what you are saying?"

When I said that it was the only option I could see, she lost her patience entirely. She tossed her head and snapped:

"Mr Threepwood, I assume you are drunk or else you would never have suggested such a thing. I shall turn round and I require you to strike me between my shoulder blades. Please do not argue. If you do, I shall scream for help and I'm sure you do not want that!"

She made me hit her with the flat of my hand where she had said. I must have killed the beetle, because she just stood there for a moment and said:

"Thank you. Now I think we should go home. Mother will be waiting."

So we did, without a word passing between us for the rest of the evening. I'm sure there's a moral in the sequel somewhere, but I've never managed to work out what it is.

The next day started off like all the others. We went down to watch the races from the Enclosure; everything seemed just the same, though Dorothy and I didn't have much to say to each other. The last race was late again, so Tommy's uncle and the girls' mother went home early as they had the night before. The four of us sat there in silence for a time till Mary spoke:

"Mr Tucker, I did enjoy our little trip in the canoe yesterday. I know Dorothy would like it too. Why don't you take her?"

Of course Tommy said he'd be delighted, so off they went, leaving

Mary and me sitting there. After a while she said:

"Mr Threepwood, I think I would like to stretch my legs. Shall we go for a little stroll?"

I followed her along the path that Dorothy and I had taken the night before. Crossing the rough grass she took my arm and I asked where we were going. She murmured something I couldn't catch and kept on walking towards the trees. We were well into the wood when she suddenly stopped, gave a little gasp and turned towards me:

"Mr Threepwood, I'm afraid a beetle has fallen down the back of my dress. What shall I do?"

As if in a dream I heard myself saying:

"If you want me to get it out, I'm afraid it will be necessary for me to, er, put my hand, er ... inside your ..."

There was a long silence, then she murmured:

"Oh dear! But maybe you are right. Perhaps we should find somewhere more secluded."

Before I could say another word, she had taken my hand and led me deeper into the wood. She stopped, looked around and said:

"I think we are quite alone here, Mr Threepwood. Perhaps you had better undo the top couple of buttons – so as not to strain the material, you understand."

I did as she asked, but I couldn't see the beetle and told her so.

"Perhaps you had better undo another button, Mr Threepwood, and see what happens."

I never did find that beetle, although I looked for an hour. They left the following morning and I never saw her again. Someone told me that she married Beefy in the end and now she's a grandmother. I wonder if she recalls the incident as fondly as I do.

Chapter 13

Prossing

or
Twenty ways to raise the ready

1. Hurt indignation often pays well.

Master (John Corlett, owner of the *Pink 'Un*) had a hanger-on who cadged a half-crown off him every publishing day, a dole to which he had no claim whatsoever except for Corlett's kind heart. One year Master went off on a long holiday to Morocco. On his reappearance in Fleet Street, his beneficiary was waiting outside the office and received the customary half-crown with some disgust. He looked at it, turned it over, then demanded indignantly:

"What about the arrears, Mr Corlett?"

Master was so flabbergasted, he emptied his loose change into the man's hand before escaping in a hansom.

2. A private carriage inspires confidence.

One day Master and Shirley Brooks were entering Romano's when they were amazed to see Shifter (Willie Goldberg) drive up in a smart private carriage.

"Not a word!" whispered Willie. "It belongs to Bessie Bellwood, and she took me for a drive to her dressmaker's. She's being fitted for a dress, which takes her goodness knows how long, and I'm supposed to be waiting for her. The prestige of the turn-out – liveried coachman and all – has so far raked in on credit two brooms, a pound of lump sugar, a case of whisky, three ready-made greatcoats, a tame monkey, and a four-ounce bottle of camphor liniment – not to mention that the only expense incurred has been beer for the driver!"

3. Keep an eye on racehorse owners.

Brer Rabbit (Captain Fred Russell) was at the Curragh one day when Garry Moore, a well-known amateur, was riding his own horse in the third race. Nobody knew anything about it and betting was slow. Brer

Rabbit followed his usual practice of having a drink in each of the bars around the course to see if he could learn anything, and eventually came to the last one, tucked behind the grandstand. In the corner, away from the crowd, was Garry Moore refreshing himself with a whisky and soda. Russell kept an eye on him and saw him get the soda-water bottle filled with whisky.

Intrigued by this, Russell followed Moore back to his horse-box and saw him empty the bottle down the mare's throat. Russell put every penny he had on Moore's horse, which won easily. As he said:

"I knew Garry wouldn't waste a pint of whisky on a mare that wasn't trying!"

4. Bribery is useful – so long as you don't get found out.
Years ago, John Corlett was approached to stand for Parliament. He wasn't too sure about it, but the proposer said it would be a walkover. There was a certain constituency where corruption was rife. If Master stood, he was to expend nothing other than his proper expenses, even though the other candidates spent thousands. John would come bottom of the poll, but could then appeal and claim the seat, since he would be the only man who hadn't bribed anybody. Master refused the invitation and followed subsequent events with interest.

The election took place, bribery was unblushing, a Royal Committee was appointed, the constituency was disenfranchised and several enthusiasts were sent to gaol.

When the case came to court, one witness told the judge he had received £25 to vote Conservative. He then admitted he had accepted the same amount to vote Liberal.

"And for whom did you vote at the finish?" asked the astonished judge.

The witness drew himself up with tremendous dignity:

"How can you ask such a question, my lord? As any honest man would, I voted according to my conscience."

5. A blank sheet of paper can save the day.
If his money and credit had run out, and he was forced to do some work, Shifter Goldberg would borrow the means for that as well. On one occasion he drove a long-suffering bookmaker too far.

"I don't mind him owing me from last Goodwood, and I don't mind him borrowing a fiver to lay against myself. I don't even mind him borrowing five bob for the train home. But when he borrows the back page of my betting book to write an article on the iniquities of bookmakers – then I do draw the line!"

6. Get yourself libelled.

One of the more disreputable frequenters of Romano's was Captain Flash, an undesirable who had lived on his wits all his life. In return for whisky, he provided Pitcher Binstead with anecdotes of the seamier side of racing, which Pitcher then recounted in the pages of the *Pink 'Un*. In one story, however, he alluded to prison life. When he and I met Captain Flash the next day, the Captain was furious. "Me in prison! Never! It's been my pride that the charges have never stood up in twenty years. There's a nice little libel case here and I'm off to see my shyster about it."

"Come and have a drink," said Pitcher, and led the way into the old Green Dragon. Remembering some of the big libel suits that were receiving publicity at the time, I thought Pitcher was in trouble. I should have known better.

Within ten minutes the 'nice little libel case' had been settled out of court, with damages of two whiskies, a ham sandwich, a public house cigar, a good tip for the 2.30 at Hurst Park the next day and five bob in cash. And the writer of the libel would have kept his five bob if the luck of the toss hadn't gone against him.

7. Keep your pride, even when cadging.

George Robey told me the other day that he was once accosted by a 'resting' brother professional, who announced that he would be working over Easter, if he could only raise the fare to Sheffield.

"Damn it all!" said Robey, "it's not three hours since you cadged a quid off me outside the Cavour – and *then* you were going to Plymouth!"

The brazen one drew himself up to his full height:

"Well, what of it, George? What of it? Even you change your patter sometimes, don't you?"

8. Become a bookmaker.

I have mentioned elsewhere Lord Esmé Gordon, the Marquess of Huntly's son. Esmé was fairly wild, but his brother Granville shocked London even more, by wearing deer-stalking tweeds in Pall Mall and using a bicycle to get round the West End. He lost all his money and sat down to consider his position, coming up with a remedy that could have killed him socially, but which certainly saved him financially. He borrowed £20,000 from Sam Lewis, bought a share in a bookmaking firm and never looked back.

9. Telling the tale.

The brilliant artist, Phil May, was a master at telling the tale, which was just as well because he was always overdrawn on the salaries the newspapers paid him. One hot dry afternoon he decided that things had got so bad that a raid on the *Punch* offices was indicated. I had the story from Pitcher Binstead whom Phil took along to give him moral support in his battle with the *Punch* cashier.

The cashier was the kindest of men, but his nerves were beginning to crack under the strain of coping with Phil May's tangled financial relationship with the magazine.

His attitude to Phil's opening request was sympathetic but firm. He liked Phil, as everybody did, but he genuinely deplored his abysmal ignorance of financial propriety. With sorrow he reminded Phil that only three days before, Phil had drawn thirty pounds on an IOU now on the cashier's desk. Furthermore, he had already drawn seven weeks' salary in advance. In any event, the cashier had closed his books for the day, paid in at the bank and the safe was empty.

Phil took all this in his stride and asked to see the proprietors. Both were away. Where was the editor, Mr Burnand? Gone to the Riviera. So Phil appealed to the finer feelings of the man in front of him. He needed the twenty pounds, Phil began, because there was a bailiff in the kitchen ...

The cashier sighed and reminded Phil that he always had a bailiff in, and had previously made much of the advantages of doing so. The silver was cleaned, the garden was dug and there was someone to wait at table.

Phil was not a whit taken aback:

"Let me finish. There's a bailiff in possession in the back-kitchen with a judgment summons, and he doesn't hit it off with the *other* bailiff in the front-kitchen who's there with a bill-of-sale summons. One pretends to be a teetotaller, the other holds opposing views, and they meet in the hall and argue it out. This very afternoon when I left, they were both drunk and were pulling their coats off to settle things with their fists. How can you expect me to work in an atmosphere like that? And I've left next week's cartoon, one of the best I've ever done, unfinished on my table."

Slowly, reluctantly, the cashier reached into his pocket and produced the four five-pound notes required. Ten minutes later, Phil and Pitcher entered the Café Royal in triumph.

10. Be tactful.
One day Sir Herbert Tree, then at the height of his career, met an old schoolfellow in the Haymarket. The other had become a millionaire but he was all over Tree, told him how famous he was, how well he looked and couldn't have been more effusive if Tree had been a wealthy uncle not long for this world. Tree lapped it up, as anybody would, and invited him to lunch at the Carlton.

As lunch ended and they drew on their cigars, Tree asked:

"There is something I have always wanted to know. How did you become so wealthy? As a boy you were backward, you were dull, you seemed to have nothing. Yet here you are, a millionaire famous across the country. How did you do it?"

The millionaire leaned forward and lowered his voice:

"Herbert," he said, "I will tell you what I have never told anyone before. I owe everything to tact. Look at today. I met you, I told you how well you looked, how famous you were and what a great actor you were – and what did you do? You invited me to a splendid lunch for which you are quite happy to pay. I have a thousand times more money than you have, but my tact made you want to buy me lunch. Tact is the secret."

11. Draw the money, let someone else do the work.
Old Pot (short for Pottinger) Stephens, dramatic critic of the *Pink 'Un* newspaper and a very good one, decided to try his hand as playwright,

as all John Corlett's dramatic critics did. And, somewhat to John's chagrin, many of them were highly successful.

Pot wrote 'Billee Taylor' which, with music by Teddy Solomon, was a big hit. He wrote others equally successful, but since he could never keep hold of the money, he stayed on at the *Pink 'Un* in order to ensure a regular, if small, income. One day he approached John Corlett for the loan of £100 and Master, knowing Pot depended on his job on the paper, let him have it.

When the staff assembled for their next weekly meeting, there was no sign of Pot. In his place sat Jimmy Davis, with a broad smile on his face and a letter from Pot to John Corlett.

It was written from Liverpool, and announced that Pot was catching the boat to America and had arranged for Jimmy Davis to do his work for the next two years. Since he had agreed with Jimmy that he would do the work for a pound a week less than Pot was receiving, the two years' absence would clear the £100 debt nicely!

12. Get hold of a good signature – and hang on to it.
Henry Irving, the kindest of men, hated dismissing anybody, but one chap was so bad in every role that Irving had no choice but to get rid of him. Normally his business manager, Bram Stoker, would have done it, but he was on holiday. (Stoker is famous now as the author of *Dracula*, but was then best known as Irving's assistant.) With considerable reluctance, Irving wrote the letter of dismissal himself.

Although Irving's signature was unmistakeable, his writing was quite illegible and the dismissed actor took full advantage of the fact. For the next three months he managed to convince the Lyceum box-office staff that the letter was a free pass to any part of the house!

The trick was discovered only when Irving noticed him in the best stalls on three successive evenings, accompanied by a charming, if different, companion on each occasion. Even then, the chap might have got away with it if Irving had not mentioned to Stoker his gratification that an actor he had sacked should still feel so kindly towards him.

Stoker made some inquiries and discovered the trick the chap was playing. He was furious, but Irving just laughed.

"Well! Well! Perhaps he is cleverer than I thought. Hmmm! Yes, you must certainly stop him taking our best stalls, but I think such ingenuity deserves some reward. Make sure he only gets the upper balcony in future!"

13. Get a standing order signed.

Sam Lewis, London's biggest money-lender and a member of the Pelican, made his money by playing fair and not being greedy. Indeed he was once publicly congratulated in Court by the Lord Chief Justice on the probity of his business.

After the Pelican closed down, Sam joined Swears's City Athenaeum Club and Swears somehow managed to persuade him to sign a five years banker's order. As Swears said, it was cheaper in the long run and saved all those irritating annual reminders. Although Sam knew better than anybody the chaotic state of Swears's financial arrangements, he good-naturedly agreed.

A couple of years later, just a day or so after the annual payment had been made, Sam died and his solicitor called on Swears to try and get it back again. They exchanged compliments, and Swears told the man of law how popular Sam had been and how he would be missed. But the solicitor, though polite, was adamant.

"It appears his last subscription was only paid two days ago – when in fact, he was already beyond human aid."

"Ah," replied Swears, who saw exactly what the other was getting at. "How true, how true it is we little know what Fate has in store for us. Poor old Sam."

"And I felt I had only to call your attention to the matter for you to instruct your secretary to return the amount."

Swears was firm and completely truthful for a change:

"No," he declaimed. "No, I couldn't do it. It's clear I knew Sam far better than you did. He would turn in his grave if he thought for one moment I would fall for a try-on as weak as that!"

14. Make people feel sorry for you.

Swears Wells, the immortal proprietor of the Pelican Club, usually managed to fend off his debtors with one story or another. On one occasion, however, even his golden tongue proved inadequate and he was hauled off by the bailiff on a debit summons of sixty pounds.

He had enough small change about his person to send messages to six fellows he thought might help. Using official paper with the dread words 'Bankruptcy Court Office' embossed at the head, Swears sent his pleas out across London. Such were the burning words he used to describe his plight, all six messengers returned with sixty pounds each! Swears was deeply gratified by this mark of confidence and decided that an equally gracious gesture was due in return.

He paid the debt of sixty pounds, which staggered the creditor concerned who, knowing Swears, thought he'd be lucky to get twenty, and put sixty in his pocket to console himself for the inconvenience and shock to his nervous system. He then spent another sixty on a splendid dinner for his benefactors, at which he likened them to the gallant Crusading knights who had defended Right against the Infidel. And, in a unique gesture, he gave back thirty pounds to each guest.

Since no one had ever known Swears willingly hand over money to anybody, the incident was around London in a flash. When I expressed amazement, Swears was philosophical:

"Dear boy, one must think of the future. It is just possible, perish the thought, that a similar incident might recur. And now I have six good men and true who vaguely believe they owe *me* thirty quid. It isn't only in Heaven you should lay up treasure for yourself."

15. Making out the cheque to Royalty doesn't work any more.
After an evening of baccarat, a Guardee known to his fellow Pelicans as the Windsor Warrior, found he was down thirty pounds. That was bad enough, but it occurred at Tranby Croft and his creditor was no less than HRH himself. The Guardee's overdraft at Coutts' was as long as your arm, but desperate times require desperate measures. In fear and trembling, he made out the cheque 'Pay His Royal Highness the Prince of Wales the sum of thirty pounds or Order' – and Coutts' paid out.

A week later he once again found himself in dire straits, so he wrote another cheque made out to 'His Royal Highness the Prince of Wales or Bearer'. And it worked again! But then he made the fatal mistake of boasting to his friends how to cash stumers and the bubble burst within a month. Don't try it today.

16. A Royal photograph can be useful.
As is only to be expected, it was Swears Wells who made this discovery.

After the Pelican closed, Swears started another club, the City Athenaeum, commonly and accurately known as 'The Thieves' Kitchen'. He soon found himself heavily in debt to a dozen suppliers with no way of paying them.

One evening a friend dropped in, and left behind a metal photograph frame with a small panel for an inscription. Swears picked it up, looked at it thoughtfully and had a brainwave. He sent George, his man, out to make certain purchases, and invited his biggest creditor to lunch the next day to 'discuss matters'.

As they ate, Swears poured out the story of his sad life and the effect his bankruptcy would have on his poor old mother. He would have to give up his position in Society, he would have to leave London. Why, he would even have to sell his proudest possession, which commemorated an occasion when he was able to be of service to the greatest in the land! But he could give no more details. At least he could keep his self-respect and do his duty as an English gentleman, which precluded him from revealing further information.

At this point Swears paused and let his eyes slide towards the photograph frame in the middle of his mantelpiece. This now contained a signed photograph of the Prince of Wales, while the panel below read:

> 'With gratitude to a trusted and loyal friend.'

Fifteen minutes later, the creditor left with the photograph in its frame, while Swears pocketed a receipt for the total amount owing.

Another trip to purchase frames and photographs, a few minutes forging the Royal signature, the remaining creditors invited to lunch and Swears was back in credit.

17. Sell your moustache.

The Major, old Robert Hope-Johnstone, was a fine figure of a man, a credit to the Army he had served loyally and bravely. But his Army pension was insufficient and he was sorely pressed for cash, even though the Roman, who held him in great respect, used to allow him to slide out without paying his bill. He was once in such dire straits that he sold his famous moustachios and beard to Lord Esmé Gordon, Hughie Lonsdale's brother-in-law, for a fiver. He set one condition – that Esmé perform the dreadful deed himself. Esmé did so, had them mounted by

Rowland Ward, and the trophy decorated the bar of the Pelican thereafter.

18. Make your parents keep their promises.

Bob Bignall made a lot of money from the old Argyll Rooms, until Joe Lyons bought him out and built the Trocadero on the site. Bob sent his son to Cambridge and, in an effort to instil a sense of thrift, said he would double whatever sum his son brought back at the end of the year.

The boy led a riotous life, but turned out to have a genius for backing horses. He came home to little academic acclaim, but with £5000 from a win on the Cambridgeshire, and made poor old Bob pay up.

19. Inherit the stuff.

The present Duke of Portland has been a member of the Bachelors' for many years, and that's where I ran into him first. Of course nowadays he's a terrific nib, with half a dozen country houses, a hundred thousand acres and all the rest of it, but once he too was one of the boys.

I don't suppose many people remember it, but his getting the title was a bit like winning the Irish Sweep. He was the third son of a third son of the third duke, or something like it, and was happily pursuing his career in the Coldstream Guards with little money, lots of debts and nothing on his mind but Gaiety girls and how to raise a bit of extra cash.

One morning his servant came in to wake him with his regular brandy and soda, and greeted him with the astonishing words:

"Good morning, your grace. You are due on parade in an hour and your uniform is laid out."

Of course Bentinck asked what on earth he was talking about, but the chap was adamant. It was in the morning papers. The 5th duke had died and Lieutenant Cavendish-Bentinck of the Coldstream Guards, his second cousin thrice removed, or his third cousin once removed, whatever it was, was now 6th Duke of Portland.

"Right," said the newly ennobled pyjama-clad warrior, "in that case, you drink the brandy and soda and bring me a bottle of Pommery."

20. Never forget an old debt.

A few of us were out on Newmarket Heath one day watching the training gallops. One of our company was Kangaroo Hill, so-called because he had come back from Australia with a stomach like the marsupial's pouch. Some owners rode by, with that stand-offish air that owners have when they are trying to convince everybody their horse is a Derby winner, and Kangaroo looked closely at one chap on a black cob. Then he gave a shout you could hear on the other side of the Heath:

"Hi, you! You there! Pull up, damn you! You, Bentinck, pull up, can't you?"

Well, the chap on the cob either didn't hear him, or chose to ignore him and rode on. We, for our part, were terribly shocked and shushed old Kangaroo. Didn't he realise who he'd been shouting at? That was no way at all to go on at the sixth Duke of Portland! Where did Kangaroo think he was?

Kangaroo would have none of it.

"Sixth duke or no sixth duke, that beggar borrowed ten bob off me our last term at school and I never got it back. If he doesn't pay up, I'll sue him in front of his own ruddy House of Lords."

He seemed to feel the first thing Bentinck should have done when he came into the title was to scour the world looking for his old creditors, though the rest of us thought this was a pretty unlikely thing to happen.

But I'm happy to say it all ended well. The duke was delighted to see his old school-friend again, gave him an excellent lunch as well as his ten bob back, and put him on to a very good thing for the Two Thousand Guineas.

Chapter 14

Some Men of My Time – 2
Swears

Ernest Frederick Wells

SWEARS, renowned proprietor of the Pelican Club, began his career as a solicitor's clerk in Jimmy Davis's office. After a few weeks Jimmy noticed that the new clerk received far more letters than he did, instituted inquiries and discovered Swears was augmenting his salary by selling items by post. Swears assured him there was nothing untoward. He was always careful to word the advertisement so the customer could not claim redress. Articles like an 'aluminium telescope pencil case' costing ten pence, but advertised by Swears as 'worth three and sixpence – sold only because it is a duplicate birthday present', kept him nicely in the new shirts and startling ties that are so important to a young man.

As Swears maintained, people didn't have to buy his pencil cases. In any event, he was giving far better value than his trade rival, a fellow clerk around the corner in Great Marlborough Street, who did a roaring trade with a 'box containing two hundred bright and useful articles for ladies of all ages' for only half-a-crown. By return of post they received a small packet of pins!

Swears, whose nickname came from the firm of furriers Swears & Wells, decided his rôle in life was to run clubs. When Shifter Goldberg's Star Club closed in a sea of writs, Swears revived it as the immortal Pelican Club and, in an institution famous for its characters, he was the greatest character of all. He claimed the secret of successful club management was simple:

"Never contradict a member; circumvent him."

He cited the occasion when he ran a lunching club in the City and was called to the table of an indignant millionaire broker.

"Look here, Swears, do you call this thing a chop?"

"Certainly not," said Swears promptly. "Give it to me; I'll see to this myself."

He grabbed the plate, took it into the kitchen, counted ten slowly, turned the chop over and brought it back again.

The millionaire was delighted at such efficient service: "Ah! That's more like it. Thank you, Swears, most kind of you."

Swears smirked his gratification before returning to the kitchen to upbraid the chef:

"You damn fool, *always* serve a chop with the concave side underneath!"

One member who'd made his millions by watching every penny used to bring in his own materials for lunch. He was highly indignant at being charged ninepence to have his own sausages cooked and served.

"He only had to cook 'em – and there's nothing like ninepenn'orth of coal in cooking sausages!"

"That's not for coal, dear old boy," replied Swears promptly, "that's our standard charge for – er – skinnage."

One day Swears was driving his dog-cart in Richmond Park and collided with an aristocratic lady in a barouche. There was little damage done, but one of the barouche pair looked as though it might be hurt. Swears was profuse in his apologies and presented his card. He was startled to find the stern old lady at the door of his flat that evening, presumably checking the address on his card was correct. Swears ushered her in – she was, after all, a dowager countess – and offered her a cup of tea.

Swears had not drunk the stuff since childhood, so he was slightly taken aback when she accepted the invitation. However his manservant George, who had got his master out of far worse scrapes than this, scrounged some suspicious-looking dust from the landlady downstairs and produced a teapot of brown liquid at which Swears sniffed dubiously. Just to be on the safe side, he surreptitiously added a good dose of brandy and served it to the countess, who took three cups.

The following morning found the countess's footman at his door with a note from her ladyship. She was glad to announce that her bay mare seemed none the worse of her injury – and would Mr Wells kindly favour her ladyship with the name of his tea-merchant!

After the Pelican closed, Swears ran the City Athenaeum in Angel Court for some years. This soon became known as 'The Thieves'

Kitchen' because its members comprised the sharpest brokers on the Exchange.

Even though his record for financial misadventures was well-known, he had no difficulty in finding support for his last club, Wells, in Old Bond Street. Hughie Lonsdale became chairman, while Leopold Battenberg, Edward Grosvenor and the like were on the committee.

The financial prospects of the club were sound, indeed sounder than any other establishment with which Swears had been involved, but even in his last years, Swears believed in looking ahead. I was present when he made an impassioned address to the committee on the necessity of securing some really good pieces of silver and gold plate for the dining-room. Royalty might drop in, ambassadors would dine there; the club must start off giving the right impression.

"Besides," he concluded, "if the worst comes to the worst – gold always pawns awf'lly well!"

Ernest Wells, 'Swears' of the Pelican Club

Chapter 15

Hard Times for the House of Lords

Destitute dukes and barnstorming baronets

IN MY young days it was the understood thing that tradesmen submitted their bills to the aristocracy every two or three years; anything more frequent was taken as dunning and was NOT well received. But the War changed all that. I remember vividly the shock we all got when Billie Le Poer Trench was sent to prison for bouncing a cheque in a London restaurant. If it could happen to him in all his glory as 5th Earl of Clancarty, Viscount Dunlo, Baron Trench and all the rest of it, then what was the world coming to?

There is no doubt that things are getting very tight for the old aristocracy nowadays. What with Land Tax, Income Tax, Super Tax and Death Duties, it is getting harder and harder to keep anything in the family sock. As someone said somewhere – if England wants a happy, well-fed aristocracy she mustn't have wars. She can't have it both ways.

Peers of the Realm are having to get out and about and rustle up the ready just like everybody else. Some people find it surprising, but this has always happened. The newspapers nowadays make a big fuss about Percy Graves, the 6th baron, being the first noble bookmaker. Absolute rubbish, of course. Lord Granville Gordon, brother of my old Pelican chum Esmé Gordon, was doing very nicely as a bookmaker nearly forty years ago.

The stage has long been a useful source of income for members of the peerage, though it used to cause tremendous fuss and bother. The families tried to hush it up, the chaps concerned always adopted stage names, but there were a lot of them doing it. Basil Bartlett, the second baronet, is on the stage now, following in the footsteps of Sir George Power, Sir Randal Roberts, Earl Cowley, the Earl of Rosslyn and Lord Lyveden, while milords Lathom, Longford and Dunsany have added to their noble incomes considerably by writing plays. What with rent-rolls dropping and Death Duties knocking everybody sideways, every little bit added to what you've got makes just that little bit more.

Writing for the papers augments many a noble bank balance. Lady Vera Mace, for example, used to make quite a bit doing advertisements, telling the world how somebody's soap kept her beautiful, but she now specialises in 'happy pieces' for women's magazines. You know the sort of stuff: there's always sunshine somewhere and we ought to be as bright and cheerful as the little birds in the trees.

It was from her that I learned the big money nowadays comes from writing gossip columns. Apparently the papers can't get enough of:

> 'Amongst those present, I noticed the Duke of Knupple and Knopp enjoying a joke with the Earl of Croydon, who is of course soon to be married to the beauteous Miss Van Guggenheim of New York who is, of course, the daughter of the Canned Beans King.'

The result is that the House of Lords is full of young chaps practising their shorthand when they ought to be legislating their heads off for the good of the country.

Young Tubby Bridgnorth, the Duke of Hampshire's boy, and the Marquess of Donegall spend all their time at parties making notes on the back of their dance cards, while Lord Riddell reports the goings-on of the Smart Set for the readers of the *News of the World*. His rival in this dreadful trade is Viscount Castlerosse who performs the same office for the readers of the *Sunday Express*.

I can go along with most of their methods of raising the ready, but I feel it only right to warn readers against two of my fellow entries in Debrett. If you ever find yourself in the company of the Earl of Biddlecombe, be prepared to sell your life dearly.

The last time I was foolish enough to accept an invitation for a quick drink at his Berkeley Square house, I emerged an hour later the reluctant owner of a tie, a new scarf-pin, a bottle of Clark's Corn Cure, a combination mousetrap and pencil-sharpener ('Highly educational – not a toy'), plus a year's subscription to *Our Tots*. Yet in my Pelican Club days, I could take on the best con-men in the country and come out ahead of the game. I must be getting old.

It just shows that blood will tell. The 10th Earl of Biddlecombe brings to his salesmanship all the force, vigour and will to win that made his father the most feared Steward of the Jockey Club, before whose reproaches hardened bookies burst into tears and resolved to lead better lives.

Of the second aristocrat's method of earning the odd bob, I will simply say – never, ever play card games of any sort with Reginald Alexander James Bramfylde Tregennis Shipton-Bellinger, 5th Earl of Brangbolton.

Nearly all the young men I know are working at something. Look at young Rupert Grayson, son of the MP Henry Grayson who was made a baronet a few years back. Henry is reputed to be the only MP returned without making a single election speech, a fact which may be due to his extraordinary good looks. I was with him on the Town Hall balcony when he was declared elected with a 10,000 majority, and a shrill voice came from the crowd: "I wouldn't mind 'aving a kid by you, Mister!" Young Rupert did his bit in the War, thought about going into politics, but decided his future lay in serving as a deck-hand on a tramp-steamer off South America.

Sir Reginald Rankin is one of those energetic chaps who climb mountains, join in every war they can find, go into Parliament and write books of blank verse in their spare time. His son Hugh decided the life his father had chosen wasn't for him, so he ran away from Harrow to work in a Belfast shipyard. After that he joined the Royals as a trooper, became broadsword champion of the cavalry, was wounded in Ireland and took up farming. The last thing I heard, he was an itinerant sheep-shearer in Western Australia, with ten thousand square miles of desert as his bailiwick.

I think Gussie Perceval, 8th Earl of Egmont, must have the most unusual *curriculum vitae* in the House of Lords. He has been a sailor before the mast, a London fireman, caretaker of Southwark Town Hall and even did a spell in the Cheshire salt-mines. There aren't many of the aristocracy who can equal that.

Some chaps sell motor cars on commission, some run chicken farms, others sell paintings. One or two have even become interior decorators, a calling which would once have categorised them as effeminate. But the world is changing. Take Johnny Milbanke, commonly known as Buffles, who makes his living doing up people's houses and telling them their ancestral portraits don't go with the décor. From that information, one might fall into a certain train of thought, but it would be wrong to do so. He's the eleventh baronet, married to a delightful Australian girl, and is known as the Boxing Baronet with quite a few amateur championships to his name. As I say, it's unwise to jump to conclusions.

Yet how much money does one really need? I always think back to what my Pelican chum, The Mate (Sir John Astley), said when old Baron Brampton turned him down as flat as a bed-spread over a small loan. Brampton, better known as Hanging Harry Hawkins, was a fine judge but didn't like throwing his money about, especially when he knew he had little chance of ever getting it back. The Mate got the last word, as he usually did:

"What will you do with your money when you die? You have no children and you can't take it with you. And even if you could, it would melt!"

The last thirty years of the nineteenth century saw a lot of big spending; the Prince of Wales liked a bit of show and encouraged others to do the same. There's little show left in these drab post-war years, and even the most formal of households are relaxing the old rules. We all realised times were changing when the word went round in 1920 that Curzon had told his butler the footmen were to wear full livery and knee-breeches only when Royalty or more than twelve people sat down to dinner. That was the beginning of the end.

Devonshire House has gone now, the Court gives State Balls rarely and the world has become a greyer place. But at least Rutland keeps up sartorial standards, holding strong views on what a gentleman should and should not wear. An old friend remarked to him the other day that, in all the years he had known him, he had never seen the Duke dine in anything other than full evening dress. Did the Duke never wear a dinner jacket?

"Only when dining alone with my wife in her boudoir," was the impressive reply.

To see real spending nowadays, you have to go to India and stay with one of the Maharajahs. Freddie Hamilton, Abercorn's third son, was out in India with Hughie Lonsdale and came back with some tales of real high living.

The pair of them went to stay with Cooch Behar in one of his palaces, built as a copy of the Victoria and Albert Museum in South

Kensington. That was impressive enough, but they were even more struck when they were taken to meet the family in a 'summer-house' in the grounds. It turned out to be the size of the Alhambra theatre, laid out as a skating-rink, and there was the entire family, about thirty or forty of them, all skating round and round to a full-scale orchestra whose Viennese conductor had taught them every Strauss waltz to perfection. But then Freddie Hamilton always moved in exalted circles. He has five sisters, every one of whom married a duke, marquess or earl. That's a record to be proud of, if that sort of thing matters to you.

But you don't need money to make a splash or get yourself talked about. Old Lady Cardigan, who died a dozen years ago, made heads turn to the end of her days. She lived with Cardigan, the Balaclava hero, until his wife died and, although they were married after her death, they were never received at Court. The old Queen wasn't going to condone that sort of thing!

Cardigan died back in '68, but Lady Cardigan didn't repine. She knew everybody and everybody knew her. In her later years she startled London by riding a bicycle, dressed in her husband's old cavalry cuirass and trousers. She shocked people even more by her promenades in Hyde Park, wearing a curly blonde wig, a three-cornered hat and a leopard skin trailing on the ground behind her, while a tall footman walked ten paces to the rear, carrying her pet dog on a silk cushion.

She married a Portuguese nobleman, the Comte de Lancastre, five years after Cardigan died, and everybody was convinced she had done so merely to get her own back on Queen Victoria. You see, she was then able to anglicise her title to the Countess of Lancaster, which just happened to be the name Queen Victoria used when she wanted to travel *incognito*.

I knew Lady Cardigan slightly, and was invited to a shooting weekend at Deene to which her Portuguese husband had invited a lot of his compatriots. They were a pretty odd bunch and their shooting was abysmal, but the Countess had a ready solution, putting a row of her English pals behind the Portuguese to get all the birds they missed. And, to obviate the accidents that would certainly otherwise have occurred, the more wayward shots amongst the Portuguese guests were issued with cartridges filled with bran instead of shot!

To get her own back on the people who had ostracised her over the years, she published her *Recollections,* a series of splendid stories that caused more than a little embarrassment in various noble households, including those of the Earl of Strathmore and the Earl of Bradford. It created a sensation and, I recall, gave me the idea for this book.

She rehearsed her funeral for years, keeping a coffin in the ballroom for the purpose. Every so often, assisted by her butler, she would climb in to check it was comfortable and conduct a full-scale rehearsal of her lying-in-state, taking notes the while of any changes she considered necessary. In her dining-room was a bust of her as a young woman, in a dress cut so low that she appeared to be wearing nothing at all above the waist. She was immensely proud of it and lost no opportunity of drawing it to the attention of her male guests, telling them that it was cast from life. She used to urge their wives to have similar busts done, but 'only, of course, if they had something worth showing'.

Born in 1825, she provided a link with the old, bold Regency days till her death in 1915. A splendid old girl.

I mention elsewhere Billy Harris the Sausage King, who named his sons William I, William II, William III, to make sure his name didn't die out. It struck many people as comical, but he was only following the example of a fellow Pelican, Billy Fitzditto.

Billy Fitzditto was one of the eight sons of Lord Fitzwilliam, who also had six daughters. They were an odd family, all outdoor types, and they hardly ever spoke. I stayed with Billy a few times and found that everybody took breakfast in complete silence, which was restful, but a bit unnerving. The Earl sat at one end of the table with his hat pulled down over his eyes and his wife sat at the other, equally taciturn and always with an anxious look on her face. I realised why eventually. It was the perpetual worry of seeing her husband and eleven children go out hunting five times a week with the avowed aim of jumping every ditch, gate and hedge they might encounter. Enough to make any mother anxious.

But the point of the story is that each of the eight boys had the same first name – William – which made things very confusing sometimes, while all six daughters were called Mary. I never did find out why. My own theory is that their father wanted to commemorate William and Mary, who'd given the family their earldom, but Billy would never confirm it.

The de Crespignys do the same thing. There can't be anybody who doesn't know Sir Claude Champion de Crespigny, 'the Champion of England' as the newspapers call him, but I doubt if many people appreciate the different things he's done. He spent five years in the Navy, found it boring so he joined the Army, found that was too dull as well and decided he could find more amusement on his own.

He took up steeple-chasing but reckoned there were too many safety regulations in England, so he went off to Ireland and earned himself the title of 'The Mad Rider'. When he got fed up with that, he went out to India and set records for big-game hunting, which he always insisted on doing by himself and on foot. He wanted to go and look for Livingstone, but the Foreign Office wouldn't let him so, having got himself appointed war correspondent for the *Pink 'Un*, he joined the expedition to relieve Gordon at Khartoum.

In his mid-forties he swam the Nile rapids just to show it could be done. In his fifties he went out to fight in the Boer War, fitting in another spell of fighting in East Africa on the way home. In between wars he saved half a dozen people from drowning, crossed the North Sea in a balloon and was still steeple-chasing in his late sixties.

Two pieces of advice if you ever come into contact with him; never insult him and, if you want a job, go into training first. Every applicant for anything from hallboy to butler or head-gardener has to face Sir Claude in the boxing ring first – even though he is nearly eighty. They don't have to beat him, just put up a good fight. As for insults, Sir Claude still believes duelling is the only way to answer a slight. There was a tremendous row only a few years ago, when he took exception to something said by a cousin of his and called him out. But then, he takes a robust view on the mortality of man. It is not generally known that he once served as assistant to Calcraft the hangman. He only introduces the topic at particularly noisy dinner parties; he finds it produces at least five minutes of thoughtful silence.

When I asked him why he had done so many dangerous things, he said with perfect sincerity:

"Where there is a daring deed to be done in any part of the world, an Englishman should leap to the front to accomplish it."

An awesome creed to hold to.

So it comes as no surprise that he holds strong views on heredity as well. His five sons have all fought for their country with great bravery and distinction and, to make the point I started with, all the boys are called Claude – so there will be Claude Champion de Crespignys around for a long time yet.

My own name, Galahad, isn't everybody's choice, but at least I'm better off than poor Liar Tollemache. Liar's father was a clergyman and grandson of the Earl of Dysart, who traced his family back to before the Conquest. The old vicar, anxious his children shouldn't forget their Saxon roots in these decadent days, called his sons Lyonel, Lyulph, Leo, Leone, Lyonulph and his daughters Lyonesse, Lyona, Lyonela and Lyonetta.

Poor old Liar's full name was Lyulph Odwallo Odin Nestor Egbert Lyonel Tuedmay Hugh Erchenwyne Saxon Esa Cromwell Orma Nevill Dysart Plantagenet Tollemache. No wonder he felt impelled to leave England and emigrate to New Zealand. There has been some pretty rough stuff pulled on defenceless children at the font over the years.

My last anecdote concerns a family who took a very different view of their forebears. Edward Harris (Lord Malmesbury), who died in '99, enjoyed a drink as much as the next man, but knew when to stop, most of the time anyway. He and I once stayed with a noble Irish family who had nothing left but the family portraits, and they weren't worth selling.

As we sat down to dinner on the first night, we both noticed there were peculiar stains all over the pictures staring down at us. We didn't like to say anything and, in any event, we soon found out the reason. When the port came round, our host started to give a series of toasts to the family ancestors:

"Here's to the 4th earl, who sold the ships we got our money by – curse him!"

They all drank their port, seized the nearest comestible to hand and threw it at the 4th earl's portrait.

"Here's to the 6th earl – who sold all the timber in the vain hope he could train a Derby winner – curse him!"

Another glass went down and another fusillade of assorted foodstuffs hit the 6th earl's canvas. And so it went on.

The following morning, Malmesbury came along to my room in quite a state. He'd woken late and had asked his man if breakfast was being served.

"Yes, m'lord. They're having it now in the dining-room. It's 'addicks and champagne."

"Haddocks and champagne!" exclaimed Malmesbury, shocked. "That's a drunkard's breakfast! What shall I have, John?"

" 'Addicks and champagne, m'lord. That's all there is," replied the imperturbable John.

"This is too rich for me, Gally," said old Malmesbury. "I thought I'd seen a thing or two, but Romano's bar is a rest-home compared to this place. They told me last night how proud they were of the peace and quiet of dear old Ireland. If last night was peace and quiet, give me Piccadilly on Boat Race Night!"

Perhaps he was right, but the haddocks were excellent.

Chapter 16

The Pelicans Fly North – 1

How to shop, how not to pack

M Y SISTERS constantly tell me I spend all my time drinking and
smoking in frowsty bars and that I never get enough fresh air.
They may be right, but I've never yet found a free drink in a corn-field
or a good cigar in a cattle-meadow. The Pelican Club, Romano's or the
Empire, on a good night when you could hardly see your neighbour for
the smoke, has always been my idea of Heaven.

But the Pelicans did spread their wings outside London occasionally.
I missed the famous week at Henley, but I did take part in the club's trip
to the Highlands. A new member had joined us, with the two attributes
Swears Wells always looked for but rarely found. The chap came back
from Australia with a fortune and a willingness to spend it; the perfect
member as far as Swears was concerned.

Swears was telling the Major, Fatty Coleman, Hughie Drummond,
Stiffy Halliday and myself about him when Sam Lewis came over to see
what was going on. He listened for a while, then called for drinks:

"Well, Swears, for your sake and mine, I hope this man's as rich as
you say he is. It's about time somebody else around here had some
money to spend – perhaps Fatty will start looking somewhere else for
his Sunday supper."

There was a roar of laughter at this, because Fatty had tried to stick
Sam with the bill at Romano's once too often, and Sam had said it was
the last hot meal Fatty would get out of him. Although he was London's
biggest money-lender, Sam was a kind-hearted chap with a soft spot for
Fatty, of which Fatty took shameless advantage. But when Sam said
something he meant it; he took a pride in never going back on a promise
or a threat. Even Fatty, the most optimistic prosser in London, had
been discouraged and gone to ground for a while. A fortnight later he
appeared in Romano's and sat down at the table next to Sam's.

"It's all right, Sam. Quite all right. I know exactly where you stand.
You're a man of your word and you're never going to buy me a hot meal

again. But you never said anything about cold suppers, and to show I forgive you for your cruel and heartless words, which I'm sure you didn't mean, I'm prepared to take half a dozen oysters off you, with perhaps a slice of the cold game pie – and we'll say no more about it!"

He sat back with a complacent smile on his face, convinced he had helped Sam out of an embarrassing situation. Sam burst into laughter at his cheek and nodded to Luigi to serve the oysters.

The new member's name was Kingdom and, in common with most of us in the Pelican, he soon acquired a nickname, coined by Peter Blobbs (Shirley Brooks):

"Well, if he's that rich, Swears, it looks as if the Kingdom has come in answer to your prayers."

And The Prayer was how he was known thereafter.

He made no bones about spending his money, and started by buying the Royal Music Hall from old Sam Adams. He then looked for other diversions. Whether he was really keen on shooting, or simply wanted to establish himself as a country gentleman, I don't know. Whichever it was, he decided to acquire shooting rights somewhere, so went to Swears Wells to ask his advice.

Swears didn't know a grouse from a turkey unless it was on a plate in front of him, but he was a master at two things – enjoying himself at other people's expense and the art of screwing the best terms out of tradesmen. Nothing too much, you understand, just the odd fifteen or twenty per cent for his trouble.

Swears cheerfully agreed to take the whole matter off the Prayer's hands and convened a committee meeting to discuss ways and means. It was Arthur Roberts who commented how appropriate the title was – Swears wanted to have his way with the Prayer's means. I was co-opted on to the committee at the last moment, a great honour, or so I thought, until I discovered Swears had seen Fatty Coleman come in looking thirsty and reckoned I was cheaper to keep in free drink than Fatty was.

Free drinks at Pelican committee meetings had become a hallowed tradition since the time The Mate (Sir John Astley) and The Major (old Bob Hope-Johnstone) had threatened to leave unless they were properly compensated for their valuable time. Consequently committee meetings were popular events with the members, if not with Swears who had to pay for the drinks. He tried to add them to Sam Lewis's bill once, but

Sam was too sharp for that:

"Swears, old man, I've come across an odd little item in my account, some six pounds eighteen shillings for whisky at a committee meeting. And your man George tells me you wrote the bill yourself. Now, I don't mind that so much. What I really object to is your adding on the date as well! Any more little mistakes like that and I'll start looking through *my* account book and then you *will* be in trouble!"

Of course Swears protested his innocence, said it was an accident and generally soothed him down. But, as he told me afterwards, he was furious. He didn't mind Sam finding out about the false bill; what really shook him was that Sam had noticed the inclusion of the date:

"I gave the red-haired waiter at the Café Royal a fiver for telling me that trick, and it's worked like a charm ever since. Now Sam will tell everybody and I'll have to think of some other way of getting ahead of the game."

After the committee had rejected a motion put by Swears to serve us beer 'for the good of our stomachs' and made him give us whisky instead, we settled down to business.

The Prayer wanted a grouse moor and was willing to pay for it. Swears had never seen a grouse moor in his life, but was unwilling to let money or the chance of a free binge past him. What was our advice?

We put our heads together and agreed that Swears and Ned de Clifford, who knew about such things, should go round the agents, see what they could find and then report back – at another committee meeting. The motion was carried enthusiastically by everyone except Swears, who was thinking of his whisky.

Ned de Clifford found the right sort of place though, as he said, agents always exaggerate the amount of game to be shot. It was a 60,000 acre estate near Uig, with a lodge which sounded exactly what we wanted. The next task for the committee to decide was the equipment, staff and dogs we would need.

Swears insisted his fighting dog Dumb Jack was an obvious choice, while his two bulldogs Sister Mary and Jim were just what we wanted to retrieve grouse. Ned de Clifford had difficulty choking back his laughter, but Swears was quite convinced that his dogs, famous for their ratting and ability to kill any animal of their size and weight, would be perfect for a Highland grouse moor. And who were we to disagree with our proprietor?

Carried away by his enthusiasm, Swears became slightly confused whether he was organising a shooting party or a hunt. He decided more dogs would be needed and put the word out amongst his wide circle of acquaintances.

For the next week Denman Street resembled a down-at-heel zoo. Every animal on four legs in London was paraded before Swears's critical gaze. He inspected whippets, lurchers, terriers, retrievers, greyhounds, pekes, pugs and poodles. It went on till even Swears realised that hiring animals from the best-known dog-thief in London wasn't quite the way to go about things, so he reluctantly agreed it might be as well to leave that side of things to the ghillies in Scotland.

The Prayer was very taken with Swears's efforts and insisted that he buy the guns and supplies for the trip. This was right up Swears's street. With the comforting assurance to the Prayer:

"It's quite all right, old man. It is no bother at all. Leave it with me, I'll make sure you don't get diddled," Swears marched happily out with the Prayer's money in his pocket.

Using ready cash, which most of his suppliers hadn't seen for months, he bought food and drink for an army. I wouldn't claim he used the Prayer's money to pay off his own debts. Let's just say that the club food improved remarkably while George, who was in charge of the wine-cellar, started walking round with a smile on his face instead of his usual scowl.

Stiffy Halliday and I taxed Swears with it one night to his great indignation:

"Use another man's money! What a thing to suggest! You fellows have been listening to gossip again. Besides," he added, "there wasn't any need. Firstly, do you think I'd let the good old Prayer be stuck with food or wine I hadn't tested personally? Secondly, when you are lucky enough to go shopping for a rich man, there are often other little benefits as well as his gratitude."

Stiffy and I were naturally intrigued. We were both on our beam-ends at the time, what with the wrong horses winning right and left, and chorus girls who had once been grateful for a glass of stout and a pork chop in Soho getting all hoity-toity if they didn't get Bollinger and lobster at the Café Royal. If it wasn't that most head-waiters have a sporting streak, and I knew lots of race-horse owners who gave me tips I could pass on in lieu of cash, I don't know how I'd have managed. So we asked him to explain.

"It's perfectly simple," he began. "Imagine you are a shopkeeper in these hard times, and someone like me walks in with a pile of ready splosh clasped in my hot little fist. Firstly, you are glad to see me. I mean," he added, looking round the bar, "take Shifter over there. He doesn't use his money; that is, whenever he happens to have any. He spends it at Romano's or on that girl of his; he doesn't make it work for him. He'd get twice as much credit from tailors and the like if he showed his money around a bit. A shopkeeper will never serve a writ on you if he thinks you have got money, because he knows you'll never go to him again. He'll only set the duns on you when he thinks you've got nothing left. So when I walk in with ready money, your shopkeeper sees me as a gift from Heaven.

"I explain that I am buying on behalf of a friend, and I make it clear I want to compare the quality and price of rival establishments before I expend my friend's money. My *wealthy* friend's money, I add significantly.

"I let him brood on this for a bit and give me all the guff about quality and price, no better value in London and all the rest of it. Then I start talking in an offhand way about reductions for cash, the possible benefits to the shopkeeper of a firm recommendation from me to my wealthy friend so far as future business is concerned, and there you are.

"If I can't get at least fifteen per cent off for cash, PLUS the odd item for myself for bringing the business through the door, PLUS commission on everything else I put his way – then," Swears paused for emphasis, "I've been wasting my time and the shopkeeper's certainly been wasting his. And not a sniff of the Prayer's money does he get!

"And that, my young friends, is how you make money work for you. But – *always make sure it's someone else's money!*"

Swears went on buying stuff for the now famous shooting party including, we noted, lots of whisky. We told him this was definitely a case of carrying coals to Newcastle, but he laughed us to scorn:

"Where do you think this grouse moor is? There isn't an off-licence within twenty miles. Fat chance I'm going to walk halfway across Scotland every time I want a drink!"

He went off to the gunsmiths in Pall Mall and came back with some fearsome weapons and enough ammunition to defend Rorke's Drift; I'm sure now it was these that gave Hughie Drummond the idea. Hughie always denied it but, since Barmy Twistleton wasn't in London at the time, Hughie was the only man I know who could have instigated what became known as the Denman Street Disaster.

More and more stuff arrived at the club and Swears, who now saw himself as a sort of latter-day Stanley fitting out the expedition to find Livingstone, had it all carefully locked away upstairs. He felt that with the members we had in the Pelican, it would be morally wrong to put temptation in their way.

A few days before we were due to travel north, Hughie drew Swears to one side for a word of advice. With Hughie this could be anything from a complaint about the price of whisky, to a tip on a horse no one had ever heard of, but he had a serious look on his face and Swears and the rest of us listened intently.

"Swears, you're off next week on a trip to the other end of the country with a pile of equipment and food. Now, you've got a lot of stuff there," Hughie went on, "and I wouldn't like to see you lose it on the way."

Swears paled visibly at this terrible thought.

"So, this afternoon, Swears, purely on your behalf, old fellow – though I'll take a whisky for all my hard work – I went and had a word with the regimental quartermaster."

Hughie paused at this point to drink the whisky which the puzzled but deeply-attentive Swears procured for him. (Hughie had been in the Scots Guards and many of our Guardee members had joined on his recommendation. It should be said, however, that his eccentricities served to scare off as many members as he brought in.)

"He told me that the thing you must do is to put all the gear in ONE packing case! Absolutely vital, he said. The entire profit of the railway companies comes from the so-called losses of baggage along the way. Send that stuff up to Scotland in separate boxes and packages, and half of it will never arrive. You must put it all in one case and then the railway will have to get it there for you."

Swears was deeply impressed by this, coming as it did from a man who claimed to have four cousins in the War Office. The result was that we couldn't hear ourselves speak in the bar the next day, because of the banging and crashing upstairs as the special container was constructed to Swears's specifications.

The Prayer and the rest caught the train north, but Stiffy Halliday and I said we'd go up on a later train with Swears and the supplies. It was the Major who'd given us the tip; he'd been a Regular for forty years so we reckoned his advice was worth following:

"Swears may be able to run a club, but he hasn't done much campaigning outside London. My advice to you fellows is always to stay within reach of the supply wagon. It's the first rule of successful soldiering."

The next day Swears called us upstairs to see the special packing-case. It was special all right. It was enormous, occupying most of the room, and Swears was delighted with it, although his man George was not looking too happy.

"There you are," said Swears. "All in one box. The railway company isn't going to get anything out of me this trip!"

There was a pause, then Stiffy voiced the thought in all our minds:

"How," he asked, "are you going to get it downstairs?"

There was a silence broken by a hoot of laughter from Hughie, but Swears wasn't at all put out. If it couldn't go through the door, which was clearly impossible, then it must go out by the window – and George, looking gloomier than ever, was dispatched to find a carpenter.

The rest of us waited downstairs, while Swears superintended operations which entailed more bangs and crashes, prompting Hughie to remark:

"It's not often you hear breaking glass in the club this early in the day."

Then George, who'd been serving behind the bar, was called upstairs as Swears assembled the entire club staff, including the cook, poor woman, to form his team of packing-case lifters. He asked us to volunteer as well, but it all sounded far too energetic so we stayed where we were, especially as there was no one serving at the bar and we were able to help ourselves.

The cart arrived and we took our drinks outside to watch the proceedings. Above us was an enormous hole in the wall where Swears had had the window taken out and a winch with a rope and pulley fastened to it. Swears shouted orders, the rope tightened and the enormous box came slowly into view and rested on the edge.

By this time most of the residents of Denman Street were out on their doorsteps to see what was going on, the carter was looking up at the box with some apprehension, while a couple of policemen tried to control the traffic jams that were building up.

Swears shouted more instructions, the box came slowly out and, only just under control, started to move downwards. It must have been some ten feet from the ground when a voice, which I would swear in a Court of Law was Hughie Drummond's, shouted "Gee up!" and off the horses went. There was a shout from above, the rope slipped free and the box plummeted down.

That was bad enough. What really scared us was the bang that followed! The cartridges must have gone off, because the crunch of the box hitting the ground was followed by an explosion. There was a flash, an enormous cloud of black smoke which cleared slowly to reveal the box in pieces and about a ton of food, bottles and packages scattered all over the place.

You can imagine the pandemonium. The residents of Denman Street were shouting for the police, the police weren't too eager to come any nearer in case there was another explosion, Swears upstairs was calling on his Maker at the top of his voice, we were polishing off our drinks to reassure ourselves we were still alive and, through it all, Hughie Drummond was laughing as though he would never stop.

It all got sorted out eventually and Swears went off to do some more shopping, relieved things had not been worse. In fact his vanity had been tickled by Hughie's explanation to the police inspector who turned up. Hughie had been in tremendous form:

"I'm glad you came, Inspector. These Fenian outrages are striking at the very heart of Society. It is clear that those dreadful assassins have heard how many distinguished Members of Parliament belong to our club and decided to murder us in our beds. I am calling on my old friend the Home Secretary this afternoon to make a personal report. In the meantime, I look to you to provide the protection we have a right to expect."

The Inspector was very impressed by all this, especially when Hughie reminded him that we'd had Royalty to our boxing evenings.

"Remember, Inspector," Hughie concluded, "that John L. Sullivan honoured us with his presence – and that's more than you can say about the House of Lords!"

There was a policeman stationed outside the club for the next three weeks. There would have been one there still, but the Commissioner got to hear about it, and clearly knew more about the political importance of the club than the Inspector did.

Chapter 17

The Pelicans Fly North – 2

Rough shooting, rough walking, rough fishing

IT TOOK Swears three days to replace the stuff that had been damaged, and another two days for the 'Relief Force', as Stiffy Halliday christened us, to get to Uig on Skye.

We might have done it in less, but we took time off to look at Glasgow, which neither Stiffy nor I had visited before. Remembering Swears's advice, we spent the afternoon calling on whisky merchants, telling each that we represented the Prayer.

We took it very carefully. We said that we had come on his behalf to see if Messrs X's malt whisky was all it was cracked up to be, before we placed an order on behalf of our wealthy, our *very* wealthy, friend for a dozen cases or so. It was astonishing how many samples did not quite come up to our demanding standard. At the fifth establishment, Stiffy had a brainwave. As we tried our second free sample, he suddenly said: "That's it! This is the one we're after, Gally my boy."

I had no idea what he was playing at and I saw us getting lumbered with a ruddy great bill I could well do without. It was bad enough coping with London duns and bookies' minders, without adding irate Scotsmen to the list. So I disagreed; this was not the whisky we were after. We should keep on looking; our friend would never forgive us if we ordered the wrong brand.

Stiffy was adamant – this was the one. He would stake his reputation on it; he would brook no argument. I obviously knew nothing about whisky and he regretted allowing me to accompany him on such an important mission, which required a deep knowledge of whisky, a fine sense of judgement and a good palate, in all three of which I was clearly deficient.

I gave as good as I got until the whisky-merchant intervened. The matter could be easily settled. If we would be kind enough to take a couple of bottles with us for our friend, he could make up his own mind. I was about to dismiss the idea when I caught Stiffy's eye which was speaking volumes. So we reluctantly undertook the fag of lugging two bottles of the best twelve-year-old malt whisky away with us.

As we waited for the bottles to be packed, the chap asked the name of the gentleman we represented. Stiffy had his answer ready:

"Mr Hugh Drummond, The Pelican Club, Denman Street, Piccadilly, London. If he's not there, they'll forward it to his kinsman – the Earl of Perth, you know!"

The shopkeeper bowed, gave us the parcel and we left with a couple of bottles of the best possible antidote to travel sickness.

Stiffy reproached me as we walked back along Sauchiehall Street:

"For a moment in there, Gally, I thought you were going to let me down. Didn't you realise that as soon as we started arguing, he'd insist on us taking some to settle the matter?"

"Stiffy," I said humbly, "I give you best. What made you think of it?"

He looked at me pityingly.

"Don't tell me you've already forgotten what Swears told us the other night? Besides, I once saw Shifter and Fatty Coleman standing back to back in Covent Garden with an assorted bunch of heavies, duns and creditors round them baying for blood. It reminded me of those pictures of the British squares at Waterloo. Yet, after five minutes of Shifter at his best, there were the pair of them walking away through the market without a care in the world. It's all in the way you tell the tale – and not being too greedy. I was tempted to make it a case of whisky, but then that fellow might press for his money. Leave it at a measly couple of bottles and he'll just write it off when Hughie ignores his second letter."

At Uig we were warmly welcomed by the rest of the party, who couldn't wait to get out of the local hotel. This had proved more than a little shy in such matters as *haute cuisine* and hot water, so they were delighted to move into the shooting-lodge where we settled down to enjoy ourselves.

We had come for exercise and fresh air and there was plenty of both. There was a golf-course nearby but none of us played. In any event, we didn't want the locals to be able to say our game was as bad as Prince Leopold's had recently proved to be.

The big annual event at St Andrews, the home of golf, is the ceremony at which the new captain hits a ball down the first fairway. A cannon fires, the captain hits the ball as far as he can, and whoever retrieves it gets a sovereign for his pains. The club had persuaded Prince Leopold to accept office and, since he was a beginner at the game, he had some private coaching from the great Tom Morris. The day came, the crowd assembled, the cannon roared, the Prince swung his club and the ball went down the fairway – just.

It was such a miserable effort that the customary polite applause was late in starting. It came eventually, but only after the Prince and everybody else had heard a disgusted voice from the crowd:

"He may be the Queen's son and the Devil himself, but he can't play golf a damn."

So we stuck to shooting instead.

We weren't expert marksmen; I think we got only a dozen brace of grouse all the time we were there. The deer were too far away, or out of season, or something of the sort, so we didn't go after them either.

Stiffy did go out one day with a rifle, returning proudly with the mangled remains of what he swore was a rabbit. After a few whiskies he told us that he had seen a deer and stalked it for miles, before cornering it in a quarry. We were very impressed with this tale of high adventure and asked where the body was. He looked us straight in the eye and told us solemnly that when he saw that magnificent example of God's creation at close quarters, he felt unable to destroy it – so he had let it go.

It wasn't till months later that I learned the true story. He hadn't had to stalk the deer at all; he'd just walked round a rock, seen a pair of horns poking out of a bush and put a bullet into it. He hit it all right but, on subsequent investigation, decided not to bring it home.

"How was I to know they were the wrong sort of horns? When I got up to it, it wasn't a deer, it was a ruddy Blackface ram! I wasn't going to have you fellows ragging me rotten for going out after the Monarch of the Glen and coming back with Mary's Little Lamb."

Despite the shortage of game, we had a pleasant time. When the midges weren't biting, we used to sit outside in the evening, drinking our whisky while we admired the sunset on the mountain across the valley.

One evening Archie Drummond, Hughie's brother, decided to walk down to the village; to see the fishing-boats come in, he said. We rather thought it was the pretty girl at the hotel, but that's by the by. Swears waited till he had gone, then announced he'd taken a bet with Ned de Clifford that he, Swears, would ensure that Archie climbed to the top of the enormous mountain across the valley, and Swears would ensure there was proof that Archie had done it.

Ned was offering 4-1 Swears couldn't manage it since he knew, as did the rest of us, that Archie was the laziest man in London, with the possible exception of Fatty Coleman. I remembered what Pitcher had said about backing Swears so I placed a fiver on him, though for the life of me I didn't see how he was going to do it.

The next evening when we were outside after dinner, Swears started telling us what a great walker he had been in his youth. He told a few obvious stretchers, and then said that the mountain across the valley looked a good walk for an active man, indeed he thought of strolling up it. We knew he was working up to something so we kept quiet, waiting for Archie to react:

"You'll never walk up there, Swears. Not your sort of thing at all. You'll never do it."

"Oh, won't I?" said Swears. "Well, I've got a tenner here that says I will."

Archie took the bet and that was that. We still couldn't see what Swears was playing at and Ned increased the odds to 5-1.

I happened to be up early the next day, having a smoke in the sunshine, when I saw Swears walking furtively down the back path to the village. Something prompted me to follow him. He stopped at a cottage, a shepherd or somebody came out and they talked together for a bit, then I saw Swears give the chap his stick and what looked like a handkerchief. The shepherd started walking up the valley, while Swears vanished inside the cottage.

Late that evening he staggered in looking as though he'd been in a battle; his face was streaked with dirt and his boots and trousers caked with mud. He threw himself into a chair and shouted for whisky.

"Well, I've done it. I've climbed that mountain as I said I would. I want ten pounds off you, young Archie, and if you don't believe me, you'll see my handkerchief tied to my stick waving on the summit."

Archie grumbled a bit, but the following morning, when he got a telescope out and saw what Swears claimed was his handkerchief, he paid up. We all had a look and there was certainly something up there, though whether it was Swears's handkerchief or not, it was impossible to say.

The following morning there was no sign of Archie. We thought he'd got up early to exchange views with the girl at the hotel again, so we didn't let it bother us. We commented on the fact that Archie clearly didn't know the girl had five big strapping brothers, which was the reason the rest of us weren't down mashing her as well, but that was all. You can imagine our surprise when he staggered in after dinner, looking even worse than Swears had done and carrying Swears's stick in his hand!

"I must say, Swears, you're fitter than you look. I didn't believe you, so I went up to see and I've collected your blasted stick and handkerchief."

There was a shout of laughter from the rest of us and Swears explained about his bet with Ned. Archie took it in good part:

"All right, Swears conned me up that mountain. But he had to go up it himself first of all, so I reckon he's earned his money. Pay up, Ned."

I got Swears in a corner later, told him what I had seen the previous morning and asked how much he'd paid the shepherd to take his stick and handkerchief up the mountain. Swears took the point immediately:

"All right, Gally. I'll split Archie's tenner with you, less the sovereign I gave that shepherd. But it just shows you can't trust people nowadays. After he'd left, his wife told me he goes up that ruddy mountain every day and he'd have done it for a bob!"

There was a river nearby and some of us tried our skill with the rod, but without much luck. The ghillie told us that the only decent salmon were to be found in the Minister's Pool, a stretch of water halfway to the village, so we wandered down there one afternoon to see what we could see. There were no salmon visible but we met the minister, a burly, raw-boned chap with a fine pair of whiskers on him, whom we engaged in conversation, hoping that Christian charity and our natural charm might produce an invitation to fish his famous pool.

We heard a lot about the Disruption, whatever that might be, plus a well-turned homily on the evils of the flesh and the necessity of preparing ourselves for the Hereafter. Eventually Swears turned the conversation to fishing, and in particular, fishing in the inviting pool below us.

He didn't know what we were talking about. He'd been minister here for twenty years and not a single fish had he seen! It was a waste of time even to cast a line. There were no salmon or fish of any sort in the pool and never had been. And so it went on till we broke away and walked back to the lodge. Swears, who claims to have been on the stage once, voiced the opinion of us all:

"Methinks the Man of God doth protest too much. I don't know about you fellows, but I think that pool is well worth a quick sweep with a splash net."

One or two of us weren't quite sure whether poaching Church property was what we had come for. As Stiffy said:

"It's not like London where a hansom cab can get you away in a hurry, and most of the bars have a useful back door to slide out of. I'd hate to find myself legging it back to Glasgow across the heather."

Our minds were made up by the news Archie brought back on Sunday. He had gone to Morning Service because the pretty girl at the hotel had said he could walk her home afterwards, and he joined us at lunch in a state of high indignation:

"The damned hymn-singing hypocrite! He spent a good hour this morning on the evils of lying. He told us lies were condemned by God, were never, ever justified and finished by telling us that he had never uttered a knowing untruth in his life. And Flora told me that that pool has the finest salmon on the West Coast. Canting old humbug!"

After that it was simply a matter of planning. We invited the old rogue to dinner the following day and made sure he had plenty of 'the wine of the country'. We saw him off, mellow to put it charitably, about midnight, then sat around for another hour or so.

Going quietly down to the pool, we soon had twenty or more splendid salmon on the bank, with the help of an excellent sweep-net Swears's man George had acquired from somewhere.

The next day, our last on Skye as it happened, we invited the minister to dinner again. We served up salmon steaks so big they could hardly fit on the plate, and waxed extremely modest when he admired our skill with a rod.

This was nothing, we said, and we had George bring in some of the others to show him. He was flabbergasted, but recovered enough to accept our offer to take a couple of the biggest home with him.

The following morning we packed up and George, under Swears's careful eye, put the rest of the salmon in a large hamper. On the way down to the village, Swears stopped the brake at the Manse so we could bid the minister farewell. Swears was on top form:

"Mr Campbell," he said, "we bring you great news. The Lord blesseth those who bless His name and He must have blessed you!

"You told us there has not been a salmon in that pool of yours for twenty years. And we believed you, especially when you preached so eloquently on Sunday on the damnation that awaits all liars.

"Well, two nights ago the Lord saw fit to bless you with some of the finest salmon in Scotland. And since Divine Inspiration led us to make the discovery for you, we thought the labourer was worthy of his hire. So we hoicked them out, including the one you enjoyed so much last night!

"No," Swears went on, "please don't thank us. We are proud to have played a small part in a modern miracle of the loaves and fishes. The Lord giveth," he declaimed, "and the Lord also taketh away. Blessed be the name of the Lord. Come on, Gally."

And off we went.

You may wonder if our host, the hospitable Prayer, wasn't disappointed that he never got a stag. Swears, ever anxious to keep his members happy, especially when they had money, had organised that as well. When we got to Glasgow, Swears and his man George vanished into town with the hamper of salmon. An hour later they joined us in the station waiting-room without the salmon, but carrying an enormous parcel between them.

Swears stepped forward and called for attention.

"Prayer, old man, we've had a marvellous holiday and we owe it all to you. I know you're a bit sad you aren't going back with a stag's head to put on the Club wall – so I swapped the salmon and got one for you!"

And he pulled off the paper to reveal a mounted stag's head with the finest set of antlers you ever saw. The rest of us started applauding, but Swears hadn't finished:

"I've had the plaque inscribed with your name on it, Prayer, although you'll note it doesn't actually say you killed it. I never like lying unnecessarily! We'll hang it up in the Club, and the rest of us will swear blind you shot it, or strangled it with your bare hands – whichever you prefer. If anyone presses you about it, just look modest, tell the truth and say you got it with a splash-net!"

Chapter 18

The Church Militant,
The Church Triumphant

Where have the pale young curates gone?

THE OTHER day an American chum of mine asked me how vicars were appointed in the Church of England. By the time I had finished telling him, he didn't know whether to laugh or cry; I suppose certain aspects of the right of advowson are a trifle unusual. As my chum said, it does seem incongruous that a noble acquaintance of ours, notorious in his day as the biggest rake in London, holds the power of appointment to a dozen vicarages and rectories – and that's only one example. Earl Fitzwilliam appoints to twenty-eight livings, Hughie Lonsdale has sixteen and my brother Clarence has seven in his gift.

At one time my mother felt I should take Holy Orders, but nothing came of it; my years at Oxford made that clear to her. Still, the church made a decent niche for many a younger son like me, when the only careers open to us were politics, the Bar, the Diplomatic, the Services and the Cloth. Look at Lord Victor Seymour, the Marquess of Hertford's son; he's been curing souls all his life, but I don't think it would suit me.

I get along well with clergymen, though they can be overpowering *en masse*. My mother used to hold an annual garden party for the bishop and local clergy which could be very heavy going. I recall once hiding in the cottage in the East Wood to escape from an earnest curate who insisted on discussing the Apostolic claims of the Church in Abyssinia, and finding another fugitive there. In his case the reason for flight had been a lengthy dissertation on the Eusebian view of the Synoptic Gospels.

We discussed various aspects of the clergy, he having much to contribute from his experience of four clerical uncles who had looked after him while his parents were in Hong Kong. We agreed that neither of us would like the life; my ambition at the time was to run a night-club, and he wanted to leave his bank in the City and become a writer.

When I was young, most curates were pale and languishing, and the ladies of the parish took it in turns to see they were properly fed. Nowadays muscular Christianity is the thing, and curates all seem to be big, burly chaps with their rugger or boxing Blue.

Take my cousin Henry Threepwood, for instance. He would probably have languished as a curate for years if it hadn't been for his prowess in the hunting field. He was out one day with old Lord Burslem, one of those Masters with strong views on people getting ahead of him. He said it was because they rode over his hounds, but everybody knew he just liked to be in the lead. They were going well across country when old Burslem came a cropper at a nasty fence, and everybody held back to let him remount. Not Henry! As far as he was concerned, the pace was too good to inquire. With a shout of "Lie still, m'lord and I'll clear you," he sailed over the fence, over Burslem and Burslem's horse and went on without a thought.

The rest of the Hunt were horrified, but old Burslem was delighted. He caught up with Henry at the kill and presented him with the brush and a vicarage in the same breath. Burslem had had a row with the local bishop who didn't approve of hunting, so appointing Henry killed two birds with one stone. It annoyed the bishop and got Burslem a vicar he could rely on.

Henry built on his experience that day, and I still believe he got his bishopric – he's Bishop of Godalming now – from studying the habits of his ecclesiastical superiors. When he got his step up, I asked how on earth he'd managed it.

"A soft answer not only turneth away wrath, Gally, it can also improve one's chances of preferment. I suit my actions to the company, especially when they are my superiors in God."

He had a cure of souls near Lincoln at the time, and was due for an episcopal visitation. The bishop was all right, but his wife was another matter. Known to her husband's flock as 'the Lincolnshire Handicap', she made Mrs Proudie look a soft touch and Henry decided he would be better off without her. A letter was dispatched to the Palace stating that, as the vicarage was being re-decorated, Henry was unable to provide the facilities appropriate to a lady. Much as Henry regretted it, the Bishop would have to come on his own.

Everything went swimmingly. The churchwardens, all hunting men, assured the Bishop that Henry was the finest vicar they had ever had; the Sunday School sang a song especially composed in the Bishop's honour and the Mothers' Union asked him to dedicate a new banner with his name on it. The final touch, Henry said, was dinner at the vicarage that night. It was well-known that meals at the Palace were meagre, to put it mildly, so Henry pushed the boat out.

At the end of dinner Henry passed round the decanters, but kept a careful eye on his two curates. As one of them reached for the brandy, Henry stopped him:

"No, no, my boy, I don't think so. Claret for curates, port for parsons, but brandy is for bishops. Don't you agree, my lord?"

It was this simple declaration of sound churchmanship, Henry believes, that tipped the scales in his favour.

In the Shires they still like their vicars to ride to hounds, while elsewhere cricket and football can be equally useful. So long as landowners have the right of presentation to livings, there are advantages in being able to offer more than just a good sermon. And why not? Theology is all very well, but it does help if a clergyman can turn out for the local football team or lead the village cricket eleven. That's why one sees the occasional vacancy advertised in the *Church Times* with the vital proviso: 'Slow left-arm bowler preferred', or 'Ideally the applicant should be an experienced wicket-keeper or good opening bat'.

Lord Middleton, with whom I discussed the matter the other day, told me he'd filled one of his livings by advertising in *Horse and Hound*. He said the Archbishop wasn't too happy about it, but it got him the man he wanted. When I asked if the Archbishop had objected to the appointment, Middleton said:

"He started to, but I asked how he'd heard of the advertisement. It turned out he'd read it in *Horse and Hound* himself, so he decided to leave things as they were."

A good sporting record can be an advantage on the stage as well. Young Potter-Pirbright was telling me in Buck's the other day how he got his start in Frank Benson's Shakespearian company. Benson (he's Sir Frank nowadays) has always been an enthusiast for games, especially cricket. He couldn't do much in London, but his tours were a different matter; he arranged his bookings around places where he could get a game of cricket and chose his cast accordingly.

Potter-Pirbright, Catsmeat they call him, was just down from Oxford, doing the round of the agencies, when one of Benson's famous telegrams arrived: 'Urgent. Replacement needed for the Ghost in Hamlet. Must be able to field cover-point'.

Young Catsmeat told the chap about his cricket Blue and was off on the next train. He thoroughly enjoyed it, though things got a bit complicated when some fellow challenged Benson to a series of needle matches. All the matinées were cancelled, and cricketing skills became far more important than acting ability. Catsmeat recalled some of the telegrams that whizzed down to London:

'Replacement needed to play Laertes and keep wicket'; 'I need a new Polonius at once. Will accept anybody who knows the words so long as he can bowl googlies'!

Although hunting, cricket and football are an advantage in rural parishes, the tougher urban areas require different skills. I understand, for instance, that a boxing Blue is far more useful than the Thirty-Nine Articles in the Missions and Boys' Clubs of the East End.

I know a young curate, Bill Bailey, who's running a Mission down there now. He's the most mild-mannered of fellows, but they tell me that spreading the Word has certainly been helped by his ability, when necessary, to smite the heathen with an excellent left hook. Church attendances may not be all he would wish, but his boxing classes are filled to capacity.

Bill is not his real name, of course; like all Baileys, he's called Bill because of the song. [1] (Incidentally, I met the original Bill Bailey when I was in America. He was a music teacher in Michigan whose wife complained he spent too much time in the local bar.)

One archbishop made his mark in the East End by making his boxing classes financially, as well as spiritually, rewarding. He found one lad with a brilliant straight left and augmented the parish funds considerably by training him on sound Christian principles, i.e. cutting

---

(1) The origin of the famous song 'Won't you come home, Bill Bailey' was forgotten till 1973, when Mrs Bailey celebrated her 100th birthday. Married to Bill Bailey, a music teacher of Jackson, Michigan in 1893, she reproached him for spending so much of his time in the Whistler Bar. Hughie Cannon (1877-1917), the piano-player at the Whistler, heard him grumbling about his wife and wrote the famous song in 1902. Furious at the notoriety the song brought her, Mrs Bailey secured a divorce the following year. *Ed.*

down his beer consumption. He still boasts of his time as an impresario:

"We got a new spire, the altar rails and the West window through the skill of Battling Bob, the care we took in matching him properly and the fact that one of our churchwardens was the best hedger of bets in London. If Bob had been a heavy-weight, I'd have re-roofed St. Paul's by now."

Dr Wakefield, *quondam* Bishop of Birmingham, is an impressive example of the Church Militant. When visiting Boys' Clubs in his diocese, he used to go three rounds with anybody who would take him on. This incurred some adverse comment, but it cheered the boys up and showed the local curate what he should be doing. And there was never any shortage of opponents, because every boy in Birmingham wanted to be the one to give the Bishop a black eye.

Bishop McLaglen was a prelate with similar views. Although his sons didn't follow him into the Church, he was proud of the boxing skills he taught them. Jack Johnson saw Victor McLaglen fight at the NSC a few years ago and wanted him to turn pro, but Victor reckoned films paid better. They tell me he and his brother Clifford are both doing well in Hollywood now.

When I was a boy, we used to see a lot of our local bishop. One of his visits to Blandings coincided with the engagement of a new hall-boy, and our butler rehearsed young Herbert thoroughly in what to do when delivering the bishop's hot water in the morning. He was to knock on the door, wait for the bishop to reply and say:

"It is the boy, m'lord, with your hot water."

Unfortunately, Herbert was very nervous and his voice was breaking. When the bishop came down to breakfast, he told us that he had heard a knock on the door and asked who it was.

"You may imagine my surprise, indeed to be honest I must say my considerable alarm, when a deep voice declaimed: 'It is the Lord, my boy, you're in hot water!' "

He went on to enthrall the Blandings breakfast-table with details of the scandal that was rocking the Athenaeum at the time, having had the story direct from the injured party, Bishop Thorold of Rochester.

Bishop Thorold had a pair of gold-rimmed spectacles of which he was particularly fond; they had been given to him on his ordination or enthronement or something of the sort. He was in the reading-room of the Athenaeum and had put the spectacles down while he checked a reference.

When he looked for them a moment later, they had vanished. He went home in some distress and confided to his wife what had happened. She sympathised, but couldn't see why he should be so agitated over a pair of spectacles. Someone in the reading-room must have taken them; who else had been there?

"That," said the Bishop in anguish, "is why I am so distressed. The spectacles were certainly stolen – and the only other people in the room were the Bishop of London, the Bishop of St David's, the Archdeacon of Rochester and ... and Mr Gladstone. I fear for the well-being of Church and State!"

I suppose it was better than what happened to the venerable Bishop of Bath and Wells when he was staying at Daisy Warwick's place. It was when Daisy was more than chummy with the Prince, and weekend guests at Warwick were *very* carefully chosen. Somebody made a dreadful mistake with the room numbers, and the good bishop was awakened by a burly nobleman leaping on his bed in the middle of the night with a cry of 'Cock-a-doodle-doo!'

Bishops come in two categories: the worldly and the unworldly. I prefer the worldly ones myself, though I agree with old Beetle Kemble that bishops should dress as such. Beetle, one of the famous theatrical dynasty that goes back to Sarah Siddons and beyond, had a fine sense of his own dignity and an equally strong sense of other people's. While holidaying at Baden, he was introduced to a bishop who had discarded his normal clerical garb for a pepper-and-salt travelling suit. Old Beetle was deeply shocked and made his feelings clear to the entire hotel dining-room:

"Bishop? Call yourself a bishop? Where are your calves, sir? Where are your calves? Are you ashamed of your cloth, sir? They shall hear of this in Canterbury!"

He made such a fuss that the poor chap had to climb into his normal clobber and wear it for the remainder of Beetle's stay.

I have too much respect for the Cloth to tell all the stories I know about bishops. During his time at Oxford, the present Bishop of Bognor proved that he too was susceptible 'of such sins as do follow men'. Since my spies inform me that he has hopes of further advancement, I will omit the painful details.

However, there is one dignitary who is quite pleased to be the subject of the following lines by my pal, Nicols-Pigache of the Café Royal.

> 'There once was a bishop of Brum,
> A jovial clerical sport.
> He enjoyed his Baba au Rhum
> As well as a lady from Court.
> And although I won't tell her name,
> (To do so would be too disloyal.)
> On the stage she enjoyed quite some fame
> With others who dined at the Royal.'

I can see why my American chum laughed at some aspects of the old C of E, but I wouldn't change it. I admire its common sense, its realisation that things become complicated if one takes them too far.

For instance, look at the Stanleys, the Alderley lot who live over at Chelford. They took to religion in a variety of ways. Some stayed with the C of E, one turned to atheism, another became a Roman Catholic bishop and Henry, the third Baron, converted to Mohammedanism. His brother Algy refused to take Henry's conversion seriously and pulled his leg about it unmercifully. His most effective gambit involved the installation of a statue of Buddha in the dining-room. Having had his own breakfast, Algy would wait for Henry to come down and tell him that all the remaining food had been dedicated to Buddha.

"Have you dedicated all of it?" Henry would ask mournfully.

"All but the ham, dear boy," was Algy's heartless reply. "All but the ham."

Chapter 19

Dog Stealing and a Royal Duke

O LD BILL Larkins of Berwick Market died years ago, but I still count it an honour to have known him. Pre-eminent in his ancient profession, he was the finest dog-stealer this country has ever known.

Dog-stealing has shrunk to a shadow of its former self, but was once one of London's biggest industries. Indeed, it was so bad that a Royal Commission was set up, to which every section of society gave evidence. There were sporting editors, dog fanciers, captains of industry, policemen and known thieves including old Bill who, incidentally, thoroughly enjoyed the occasion.

I heard from a journalist chum that Bill gave the Commissioners quite a shock, with his simple claim that there was no dog in England he couldn't steal. They were even more shocked when Scotland Yard agreed, adding that they had been after Bill for fifty years and had never managed to catch him.

It was Bill who told me about Cherry, Queen Victoria's King Charles spaniel, whose theft caused an uproar many years ago. Bill had eventually found the stupid man who had stolen it and then been too scared to return it. Through Bill's intervention it all ended happily, I'm glad to say, and Cherry, stuffed by Rowland Ward, is still to be seen in a glass case at Windsor.

I think Bill's greatest coup was his deal with the Duke of Cambridge.

In private life the Duke was addicted to partridge shooting, taking a sinful pride in his pointers and setters. He was so proud of his dogs that the Press started writing about them – and that was enough for Bill Larkins. Every year, just before the shooting season started, Bill went down and stole them all. After a suitable interval, he sold them back again at a special discount rate of fifty quid for the lot.

The Duke called in the local police, Scotland Yard and everybody else he could think of, but the thefts went on year after year. Eventually the Duke gave in and asked Bill to come and see him. Would Bill accept fifty quid as a retainer to leave the Duke's setters alone? Bill accepted the *amende honorable* in the spirit in which it was offered and with all the respect due to a Royal Duke. He even guaranteed that no one else would steal them either.

He kept his word too. Until the Duke died in 1904, he never lost another dog and Bill was thinking of applying for a Royal Warrant. The problem was he couldn't work out the correct phraseology for not stealing dogs.

The Duke, Commander-in-Chief for forty years or so, was a fine old chap, though liable to express himself in very strong language. Yet he abhorred bad language in others. He felt very strongly about it, which once led him to cause consternation at a school prize-giving. He gave an impassioned address on the evils of swearing, the dangers of bad language and a stirring discourse on blasphemy, concluding with the moving words:

"Damn it all, boys, never swear!"

There was a moment's shocked silence before the delighted pupil body burst into uproarious applause.

It was the Duke who made my old Pelican colleague, Captain Fred Russell, famous when he was inspecting Fred's regiment, the 3rd Lancers. Although Fred was an energetic and efficient officer, nobody is perfect and the Duke was horrified to discover some cobwebs in the corners of Fred's troop stables:

"Captain Russell, why are these cobwebs here?"

Fred was a quick-thinking chap – he was, after all, a member of the Pelican Club – and facing a Royal Duke was nothing compared to coping with a bookie's plug-ugly out for blood because of a little account you had somehow overlooked since Goodwood.

"Perhaps you are not aware, sir, that flies annoy horses and spiders eat flies. These cobwebs provide homes for the spiders, sir, and keep our chargers happy and fly-free."

Which I still consider was a pretty good answer, though the Duke was not impressed. He became even angrier later when he turned to Fred and asked:

"And tell me, Captain Russell, what do you consider to be the role of cavalry in modern warfare?"

Fred looked at him and replied thoughtfully:

"Well, I suppose it's to give tone to what would otherwise be a mere vulgar brawl."

Punch made the reply famous around the country within the week, and my cavalry friends tell me it is still the standard response to busybodies questioning their role.

Chapter 20

Bookies and Bailiffs

I IMAGINE it has already become clear to the reader that bookies played a significant part in my early career. My old pal Dickie Dunn, the last of the big ready-money bookmakers who took thousands in cash on a single race, was a generous man and gave freely to any charity that approached him. His repartee was famous. On one occasion he took a double bet in fifties from a nervous plunger who looked like a bank manager on the eve of absconding. The first horse won and the frantic better rushed up to him:

"It's won! It's won!" he panted and fell over in a dead faint. Dickie and his clerk looked down at him in silence till the latter made a suggestion:

"Shall I fetch him a brandy, guv'nor?"

"Let the perisher be," commanded Dickie sternly, "and go and get a ruddy wreath!"

Dickie and his clerk, Bill Lakey, made an effective team. But, while Dickie's comments on the world were notable for their acerbity, Bill Lakey managed to retain a more charitable view of his fellow men.

I happened to be chatting to Bill at Newmarket one day when we saw Lillie Langtry putting a hundred on a horse that both of us knew had no chance. As she walked away, Bill shook his head sadly:

"What a lot of stable information women miss through not having to wait their turn for a shave on racing mornings."

He felt a similar benevolence towards the higher clergy. It was Pitcher Binstead who recounted Bill's comment to a friend as they watched the Archbishop of Canterbury pass by in his carriage. His companion expressed his disgust with the social order:

"These blurry bishops has a fine time of it and no mistake."

Bill took a more tolerant view:

"Oh, I dunno. In the speech he made during the Licensing Bill, he said he hadn't smelt a drop of beer for thirty years. 'Tisn't all jam, being a bishop!"

The other big London bookie in those days was Charlie Head, who took pride in never refusing a bet although, as he once told me, it could prove an expensive habit. In those days it was the custom not to settle bets during the Sussex fortnight (Goodwood, Brighton and Lewes) until after the second week. The result was that losing plungers bet desperately on the last Saturday at Lewes to try and recoup. Their bets were taken cautiously by the Ring because, as Charlie said of one hopeful:

"I knew he was never going to settle; he took any odds I offered him."

I remember once Sir Robert Peel of Drayton Manor, the father of the present chap, owed Charlie quite a packet and sent him a hamper of game as a temporary palliative. Charlie appreciated the gesture but did not want the habit to spread, so he sent a telegram in reply:

"Dear Sir Robert. Your game is high, my funds are low. Please remit."

Charlie was a dapper little man, very good company and possessed of a surprisingly soft heart for a bookmaker.

He roused the *habitués* of Romano's to unfeeling laughter and derision one day when he sought their collective advice on a letter he had just received from a peer of the realm, who everybody knew had owed him for six months and had little chance of ever paying.

"I had a letter from young Ponsonby this morning, and he is very sorry to keep me waiting and promises to let me have something on account before Goodwood. But he's put no address on the letter. I think that looks bad, don't you?"

I'll never forget the night when a fellow, clearly looking for trouble, came into Romano's with a gang of toughs. Relying on the gang behind him, he started to needle Charlie unmercifully. Charlie didn't want a fuss, so he took it all until the chap knocked the glass out of Charlie's hand and called him 'a welshing swine'.

Charlie looked up at him – he was nearly a foot taller than Charlie and big with it – and looked at the gang behind him.

"A welshing swine, am I?" said Charlie quietly, and took his wallet out of his pocket.

"And how much have I welshed you for? Go on – tell me!"

He advanced slowly on the man who was so surprised that he started to back towards the door, his eyes fixed on the money Charlie was pulling from his wallet.

"Tell me," said Charlie. "How much do I owe you? Go on, tell me."

By this time, the fellow was at the door and looked round for his toughs to jump on Charlie, but none of them moved. They were all mesmerised by the enormous roll of notes in Charlie's hand.

Charlie advanced again till he was inches away from the chap and said even more loudly:

"Nothing, sir? Nothing? Then take that as a tip from a welshing bookie!"

And he threw the bundle of notes in the chap's face. There was dead silence for a moment, broken by Pitcher Binstead's voice from the bar: "Out! Now!"

The chap and his gang looked round to see every man in the room on his feet; the corridor to the restaurant was crowded and every one of us had a bottle in his hand. He lurched out the door with his toughs and we never saw him again.

We cheered Charlie for the brave man he was; we even helped him to pick up the money he'd thrown, nearly two thousand quid it was, and we were so impressed he got it all back too!

You sometimes hear people say that bookies are heartless. Well, I must admit that most of the ones I've known have shown little sign of possessing that sympathetic organ, but there are exceptions. Dickie Dunn always treated me fair and square, and I recall that Charlie Head had a soft spot for Shifter Goldberg, as most people did. As Charlie said:

"At least when he's giving me ten good reasons why he can't pay me, he makes me laugh while he does it."

In fact, the more Shifter owed him – and he owed Charlie more than he could ever hope to repay – the more Charlie regretted it. I think he simply reckoned that Shifter was better off owing him than some of his fellow bookies.

But the event that really restored Shifter's faith in his star was the Monte Carlo earthquake. Charlie Head was in Monte Carlo on holiday when the Principality was struck by a series of earthquakes.

A few days later, Shifter marched into Romano's with the air of one to whom all the wonders of the world had been revealed. He jumped on to a table, called for silence and read aloud a letter he'd received from Charlie.

I don't remember the details but, roughly, Charlie had escaped injury in the earthquake and realised how lucky he was. He wrote about the bravery he had seen and the courage of the rescuers trying to save those buried in the rubble. It had made him appreciate how chequered his own life had been, and he wanted to make some gesture to show his gratitude for being spared. As a first step towards this end he had wiped all Shifter's debts off his slate!

Shifter finished the letter to an incredulous silence broken by shouts and cheers. Understandably so. As he said, looking as if he'd just single-handedly brought the good news from Ghent to Aix:

"Just one more bally earthquake and we'll all be back on the right side of the ledger!"

One pair of bookies I knew, who rejoiced in the names of Posh and Copp, had a client who lost regularly and paid up every Monday like a lamb. He never won and the two partners looked upon him as a sort of pension fund. One Monday his cheque didn't arrive and they decided to write him a letter, but they agreed it must be polite enough not to scare him into taking his business elsewhere. One partner sat down and struggled with composition.

"Is it polite enough?" asked his partner after a time.

The scribe looked up indignantly:

"Course it's polite – but – how many 'r's are there in bastard?"

They weren't the only bookmakers to keep a solicitous eye on their regular customers. Before the War, George Edwardes was famous for his betting; when he decided to back his fancy, he would do so in bets that would bring the odds down from 33-1 to 5-4 at a jump. One day when he was at Waterloo seeing some actress off to America, one of London's biggest bookmakers appeared, pale with anxiety:

"You're not going to America, Mr Edwardes, are you?"

"Oh, no," was the reply. "I'm just seeing some friends off."

The bookmaker mopped his forehead.

"Thank Gawd," he blurted out with heartfelt relief. "I thought we were going to lose you!"

One of the more unusual bookies I remember was old Joe Capp (T'Owd Mon) who reckoned the lowest point of his career was the time he was thrown off a race-course for fighting in front of Queen Victoria. Her carriage had just entered the enclosure at Ascot when someone made a remark to Joe that required a response more telling than his usual flow of invective. He went for his man and was dealing with him satisfactorily, when he found himself seized and frog-marched out by the two senior Stewards, Lord Coventry and Admiral Rous, each telling him exactly what they thought of his behaviour.

Joe Capp was a rough old bird but, amazingly, liked writing poetry. Since my Pelican chum, Nat Gubbins, controlled the fortunes of *The Bird of Freedom* newspaper, as well as possessing a strong sense of humour, Joe had an outlet for his verse, of which he was inordinately proud.

Here is a sample:

> *The sailor who clings to the icy shrouds,*
> *When his vessel is tossed to the lea,*
> *And with weary eye, looks up to the sky*
> *For the stars he may never see,*
> *Who feels his hand slipping, his strength near gone*
> *And he sees that his chance is lost*
> *Feels just as I did at Epsom last Wednesday,*
> *When I see Lord Marcus drop the flag in the October Handicap,*
> *and that dommed brewte Gay Hermit, whom I'd backed for*
> *seven pun ten, got left at the post!*

And he got fan letters about them too!

I think it is the thrill of the chase that keeps some bookmakers going. Dickie Dunn told me that it was the thought of all those stupid men who believed they knew which horse would run faster than another, that inspired him.

"I feel I've got a duty to show 'em they're wrong. If they are right, well, then I'm happy to pay 'em. But," he grinned, "not many of 'em are."

It was his quick wits that made Dickie a wealthy man. When he was at home one Sunday afternoon he saw a balloon crash into his orchard. Fearing that somebody might be hurt, he went out to help and recognised the unconscious balloonist as a chap who had owed him forty-seven quid for the last six months or so.

"What did you do?" I asked. "Go through his pockets?"

"Don't be silly," retorted Dickie. "And lose my good name by petty larceny? No ruddy fear. I called a policeman, brought the perisher round, then said I was giving him in charge for causing wilful damage to my orchard. Of course I offered to drop it if he'd pay for the damage. He was a bit indignant at first, but when the copper told him I'd the right to hang on to the balloon as evidence, he paid up like a lamb.

"And by an odd coincidence, the policeman agreed with me that forty-seven quid for the damage was just about right. Plus of course another fiver for legal fees!"

"What legal fees?" I asked.

"For the blooming policeman to remember what I told him to say, you juggins," retorted Dickie.

In my early days in London most of us had financial problems at one time or another, and Life could become a trifle fraught. Tipstaffs and bailiffs weren't so bad, and we all learned early on – NEVER RESIST A BAILIFF. If you can struggle free (Swears's top-coat was always cut on the loose side for this reason) and make a run for it, all well and good. But never hit him; that turns a civil claim into a criminal one, and we found things were exciting enough without getting the police on our trail as well.

Bookies' minders are a different matter. Because gambling bets aren't enforceable at law, bookies can't send in the bailiffs, so they just send their friends instead, and a right lot of bruisers they are.

It was a rule of thumb in our day that the one person you always paid was your bookmaker, otherwise you were liable to find yourself in hospital. Though I must admit that most bookies were reasonable men, in their fashion, and gave us fair warning. I never had any bother with Dickie Dunn but then, apart from the ten pounds credit he let me have for reasons recounted earlier, he simply wouldn't take my bets unless I produced cash.

I remember down at Goodwood one year there was a chap, a bit of a stinker in many ways, showing off to the girl he was mashing. He'd convinced her the only reason he wasn't at the Duke's house-party was that the invitation had been lost in the post, told her he knew every member of the Jockey Club by his first name and generally made her think he was the Great Panjandrum of the racing world.

Eventually she decided she wanted a bet placed on a horse, so our hero went off and found Dickie Dunn. He wanted to bet on credit but Dickie knew him of old; it was ready money or nothing. The chap persisted until Dickie lost his rag.

"Credit? Credit? To you?" he roared at the top of his voice. "What, me give credit to a shyster like you? Standing there in a frock-coat and top-hat you certainly never paid for and probably never will! I know you – you'd never be allowed on the course at all if I had my way. You still owe me for Hurst Park and you had the cheek to ask me for a lift home when you couldn't pay me then. I've never in my life seen you put your hand in your pocket! No, not even a ruddy bob to buy a rotten race-card.

"And I bet you borrowed the train fare today from that pretty little girl, who'd be better off at home with her Mama than spending the day with a whited sepulchre like you!"

He was a clever man was Dickie. The scamp *had* borrowed the fare from her, plus a bit more as well, and that was the end of that little affair.

On the regrettable occasions when I found myself unable to meet my financial commitments, I worked on the principle of dealing with the man up top, rather than through intermediaries. It was no good trying to soften up bookmakers at long range. One had to do it at close quarters, dusting specks off their suits, massaging their arms and generally exerting the old charm and personality. But when trouble did strike, desperate needs produced desperate measures.

I once found myself cast in the role of hunted fawn, with the heavy part being played by a plug-ugly called 'Erb, a brute of a fellow employed by Joe Timms, the Safe Man. It was only for twenty pounds or so, but charm of manner and a ready tongue proved insufficient.

The first time he cornered me I managed to convince him, with the aid of a stick of make-up, that I had small-pox. Unfortunately, later in the day I met him in the Strand, and only managed to get away by finding I was a better sprinter than he was. It was a week or so till I received my allowance and I spent a terrible time slinking round the West End, making sure there was a back entrance to every pub I used. I even had to shift my digs, first checking that my new abode had a good, sturdy drain-pipe outside the bedroom window.

We all went through it. Shirley Brooks was often in a bit of bother, and once had to send his articles for the *Pink 'Un* down by messenger because of the bruiser who was camping outside the office waiting for Shirley to settle 'his little account'.

Unfortunately, the fellow he sent hadn't had Shirley's affairs properly explained to him. He came back to announce that he'd met some 'friends' of Shirley's outside the *Pink 'Un* office who were most anxious to contact him. Eager to please, he had given them Shirley's address and they were on their way to see him!

Shirley didn't waste time in impassioned reproaches. In one minute flat, he'd sent the chap back again with an appeal to Shifter and Pitcher, grabbed a copy of a notice he'd picked up one day in the Law Courts, pinned it to the door, locked it behind him and retired to his bedroom, determined to sell his life dearly.

As I recall, his rapid action did earn him some time, because the notice read:

> No One To Enter This Room Under ANY Pretext
> Until The Inquest Has Been Held.
> By Order Of
> The Coroner.

It was Fruity Biffen, better known to the world today as Admiral George Johnson Biffen, late of His Majesty's Royal Navy, who showed us all the way. He felt that racing round London one jump ahead of assorted thugs was no way for a suave *boulevardier* to behave; a simple disguise was the answer in Fruity's opinion. A good bushy beard which concealed the salient features was his preferred method, and it worked very well. However, any reader who decides to follow in his footsteps should be warned of two things. Don't be too confident, and make sure you use a strong glue.

Fruity's beard worked so well in London that he decided to try it at Hurst Park. I told him he was pushing his luck, but he was adamant. So there he was, in the middle of Tattersall's Ring, surrounded by a dozen bookies who'd been looking for him for weeks, when there was a sudden heavy shower. Fruity automatically pulled out a handkerchief to wipe the rain from his face and wiped off the beard as well.

It was the roar of laughter from all the bookies that saved Fruity, affording him the five seconds head-start so essential on these occasions. But I still remember the look on his face as his pride and joy fell to the ground; Henry Irving at his best never displayed so much visible emotion.

Bailiffs with court orders and writs in their pockets were never quite so frightening. Indeed, people like Pitcher and Swears Wells became quite philosophical, and put them to work in the kitchen, or digging the garden. Swears tried putting them behind the bar in the Pelican, but found that temptation was too much for them.

One place you could always be sure of seeing bailiffs was at the *Pink 'Un* office on Fridays. Inside you might find an archdeacon remonstrating with Master on his refusal to print a review of the man of God's latest publication *Is There A Hell?* or some such title while, in another corner, there would be a couple of girls from the Gaiety abusing Shifter or Pot Stephens over the reviews they'd written – or hadn't written – about their new show.

In the street outside you could always reckon on at least two characters with 'tipstaff' or 'bailiff' written all over them. There was one old boy who specialised in serving writs on the *Pink 'Un* and Pelican crowd for, as I discovered, a very good reason.

"It's simple, sir. Take your average bloke who lives in Clapham and owes his butcher ten or fifteen quid. Serve him with his writ and what do you get? A cup of tea and maybe a biscuit, if you're lucky, and his wife thinks she can talk you round.

"But with this lot, Mr Goldberg, Mr Brooks and the rest of 'em, it's different. I don't get my money, but it's a poor old day if I don't get at least a whisky or a beer while they're writing another cheque that they know, and I know, will bounce all the way back from the bank! So the next week I'm back again, and there's another beer for me and we're all nice and cosy."

On one famous occasion, he called in at the *Pink 'Un* office just before Christmas. Standing in the doorway, he grandly announced that though he had 'several little papers in his pocket', he wouldn't bother with them today. He had merely looked in to wish all his old clients the compliments of the season, and to collect his Christmas box!

Chapter 21

Some Men of My Time – 3
Presto

Brighton again and Harry Preston, its uncrowned king

I HAVE mentioned elsewhere the part that Brighton played in my education in the ways of the world. Like anywhere else, it has a smart side and a seamy side. Harry Preston ruled over the former; my jellied eel pal, Charlie, was at the centre of the latter.

Charlie continued to take his barrow around race-meetings, while his wife looked after the shop in Aldgate that my sisters had paid for. As he said, there's something about racing that makes people hungry for jellied eels. So we used to run into each other at Brighton and Goodwood, and he proved an invaluable source of information on such vital matters as racing-tips, which three-card trick men would let you win twice before they started switching, and the true story of what happened during the fire alarm at the Grand Hotel in Brighton which led to four fights and three divorces.

Of course some of Charlie's acquaintances were a bit too rough even for me, and I nearly became a receiver of stolen goods through doing a small favour for a pal of his. Very embarrassing it could have been, although I suppose it reflected credit on somebody, I'm still not sure whom.

Brighton Races were notorious for the London gangs which congregated there for a day out. They were a really tough lot, and you made sure your wallet and your watch were left at home or inside your shirt. If a gang decided you were worthy of their attention, it was useless to resist. It was at least six to one and the chance of a knife if you fought back.

I managed to steer clear of trouble most of the time, and one day Charlie introduced me to a character whom he called the Captain. This did not mean he held Her Majesty's commission, it was simply the courtesy title accorded to many gang-leaders in my day. It usually meant that they used their head as well as their muscle; their gang did the actual thieving from a prospect the Captain had spotted.

The Captain was clearly off duty, or maybe there were too many policemen nearby, but he was affability itself, especially when he found out I was a chum of Pitcher Binstead for whom he had tremendous admiration. The three of us chatted of this and that till the conversation turned to more sombre things, the recent death of someone called 'Arry. Charlie and the Captain both shook their heads sorrowfully over his sad end, drowned off Wapping Dock after a drunken brawl, it transpired. They agreed that while 'Arry was no great loss, his wife was a splendid woman who had been far too good for him. She was expecting their fourth and her mother had died, so there was no one to look after the family.

The Captain told us that a collection was being taken up to help the widow and Charlie, rather to my surprise, promptly reached into his pocket and gave him five bob towards it. I'd had a good day, four winners including a very good outsider, and I felt that if Charlie could afford five bob, the least I could do was to put in my little bit as well, so I gave the Captain a fiver.

I could see Charlie was very pleased and I must admit that there was a certain amount of self-interest involved. Being on the right side of someone like the Captain could be useful one day. And so it turned out, though not quite in the way I had envisaged.

It must have been some weeks later, at Hurst Park I think it was, just before the second race, that I found the Captain at my side. 'Arry's wife had had her baby and things were working out for her nicely. Quite a bit of money had been raised but:

"No one else gave a fiver, Mr Threepwood. It was real good of you, you not even being a friend of the family. And to show our appreciation, the boys and me thought you might like a nice little tie-pin."

Of course I demurred and said it was quite unnecessary, but he was adamant.

"We were thinking that a nice diamond cat's-eye pin would look good on you," he said, "and if it isn't troubling you too much, just step over to the paddock gate and I'll point out the feller that's wearing it, and you can see if it's your style before we grab it off 'im!"

It needed all my tact and discretion to turn down *that* kind offer without causing offence. But now I can claim acquaintance with most of the pickpockets and three-card trick men around London, and very useful it has been too.

So, what with Charlie keeping me informed on things at his end of the social scale, and Harry Preston at the Royal York knowing everything else, there wasn't much going on in Brighton I didn't hear about.

Brighton was Harry Preston's in those days, as it still is. I can't think of anybody who doesn't know Harry Preston, but since such unfortunates may exist, I'll describe him. Harry is proprietor of the Royal York and the Royal Albion hotels. If you visit him you are likely to find yourself in the company of the Prince of Wales, George Robey, E.V. Lucas, Bertram Mills or Sir Alfred Fripp, who is surgeon to the King as well as being president of the Ancient Order of Frothblowers. Those 'also present', as they say in the Society papers, may include Seymour Hicks, Viscount Castlerosse, Edgar Wallace, Charlie Cochran, Hilaire Belloc, Arnold Bennett and even Jack Dempsey.

They will be there because of the extraordinary magnetism Harry Preston seems to radiate. I can think of no one else to whom it seemed perfectly natural to take Edward VII for a drive in his motor-car, at a speed the King had never experienced before. The King loved it, but old Ponsonby, his secretary, was furious when he found out, and muttered that Harry was clearly a dangerous Republican trying out a new method of assassination!

Nor was I at all surprised when I heard that when King George V visited the Fleet during the war, he used Harry's motor yacht in which to do it. And to continue the royal connection, Harry is the only man I know who has been rescued from a jammed lift in Buckingham Palace by the present Prince of Wales, and who repaid the kindness by taking the Prince out to the end of Brighton pier one dark night to see his first Follies show.

Harry must be seventy by now. He is small, bald, has the heart of a lion and the liver of a ten-year-old. He still rides, sails, takes regular runs, has a session with a punchball every morning and will go three rounds in the ring with anybody. He broke two ribs recently, but spent a busy day in Town presiding at charity committees, then danced at a night club till three in the morning before he thought of going to a doctor about the slight pain he was experiencing.

There does not seem to be anyone he does not know. It was from him I learned that Maurice Baring likes to celebrate his birthday by walking into the sea at Brighton in full evening dress, a remarkable sight which used to alarm the local gendarmerie considerably, till Harry reassured them it was a regular ritual.

I don't know whether Baring still walks into the sea, but I was at a dinner in Buck's Club the other day when he demonstrated his steadiness of hand after an excellent dinner by placing a bottle of champagne on his head and then balancing a glass of brandy on top of it. Young Buck (Herbert Buckmaster) has the menu card on which Orpen recorded the event.

Baring told us that night of the occasion when he had brought London to a standstill during the War. He was in the Air Service, as it was then, and he and his chief Trenchard were called over from France to a conference in London. Each flew over in his own plane, but Trenchard got lost in a thick fog over the Channel and landed somewhere in Kent. Baring, however, kept to his route and flew on to London. Unfortunately nobody knew he was coming, and his arrival over the capital was greeted by the maroons and every gun in the area opening up on him. He said it was the only time in his life he was grateful for the inaccuracy of our anti-aircraft guns.

It was Harry Preston who gave W.G. Grace his first ride in a motor-car, a treat for which Grace let himself be bowled early in a match, and it was Harry who organised the first official RAC car-race along the sea-front from the Palace Pier to Black Rock. There was tremendous opposition since a special tarmac coating had to be laid along the entire length, but Harry Preston was behind it and that was enough. The tarmac was laid and the races went ahead. That was back in 1905 and I suppose it all seems very old hat now, but it was a tremendous thing then and lots of us went down for it.

The Madeira Terrace was the main grandstand, and we spent three days watching the racing, collisions and breakdowns. Some of the cars reached 70 miles an hour, which for those of us who had been brought up in the era of the horse, was incredible. We attended the closing dinner and were fortunate enough to find ourselves in the company of Daisy Hampson and Victoria Godwin, two of the first women racing drivers.

Daisy had a enormous beast of a car, a Mercedes I recall, and insisted on taking us for a spin during which she scared us half to death. A most determined young lady, not at all the type I felt I could settle down with.

Cars were still regarded with deep suspicion in those days, as we learnt at dinner from Sir Arthur Stanley, president of the RAC. A few weeks previously one of his members, an MP, had tried to drive his new car into Parliament Yard and was firmly evicted by the police, who classified it as an explosive machine.

I was talking about car-racing and flying the other day to Buffles Milbanke (Sir John Milbanke) and realised old age was creeping up on me. I saw his mother, Leila Crichton as was, board the balloon in which she flew from London to Paris back in '04 or '05. And just to top things off, she carried on to the Riviera and went up with Graham-White in the first of those planes that take off from water.

It shows how things have changed. For Leila Milbanke, a baronet's wife, to go up in a balloon was front-page news in those days. Nowadays everybody's doing it and the Duchess of Bedford, who didn't take up flying till she was sixty-two, is setting records all over the place. (Yet she only took it up because she found flying relieved her deafness and the constant pain in her ears.) And, speaking of flying, it was of course Harry Preston who organised the first British cross-country flight from Brooklands to Brighton.

I am sure it is Harry's influence that has kept Brighton the cheerful place it is. Certainly the authorities down there have been remarkably skilful at drawing the right balance between liberty and licence.

I think it was about 1907 that King Edward came down to stay with his daughter, the Duchess of Fife, at her house in Lewes Crescent. It was a private visit and everybody respected the King's wishes, but the news soon spread that he liked strolling on the open terrace of the Duke's house which overlooked the sea. The result was that the seats at that end of Madeira Drive became extremely popular. The Chief Constable, a man of tact and understanding, went to Harry Preston for some quiet advice.

Nothing was said; nobody was moved on. A coat of fresh paint on the seats each day was all that was necessary.

Chapter 22

The Café Royal

PEOPLE sometimes ask me if there was any difference between Romano's and the Café Royal in the old days. There was all the difference in the world, though it might not be obvious to the casual observer who saw them both as the haunts of Bohemia. We lunched at the Café Royal but we always had supper at Romano's; we would never have dreamt of doing it the other way round.

Romano's was always more raffish, more fights in the bar and that kind of thing. It was the place for the sporting set, the Pink 'Uns and Pelicans, racing journalists and their crowd, plus members of the lighter stage. The Café Royal was more pretentious; it was for the artistic lot who preferred absinthe to whisky, and would rather talk about Beauty in the abstract than take a pretty girl out to dinner and do something about it.

Perhaps the best way to illustrate the difference is that George Moore, Oscar Wilde and their friends patronised the Café Royal. Gus Moore and Willie Wilde, their Bohemian brothers, and their pals frequented Romano's. (I suppose Pagani's occupied similar pride of place with the musical lot, probably because it was old Tosti's favourite haunt.)

Nevertheless, many of the Café Royal's customers were as odd as those at Romano's, which made them very odd indeed. Jimmy Glover, leading light of the Empire Theatre and Drury Lane, always lunched at the Café Royal, would have half a dozen whiskies with it and go peacefully to sleep at the table, till he was woken up by the waiters at 5 p.m. in time to get ready for his evening's work. The pretty little brunette who usually accompanied him would tactfully withdraw for a couple of hours and join him again for the awakening.

Another regular was old Sir Blundell Maple, the furniture chap, whose son-in-law was Baron von Eckhardstein, First Secretary at the German Embassy. The Baron was a decent enough chap, but his habit of eating every comestible in sight once caused a sad romantic rift.

It happened in '98 at a house-party at Chatsworth. It was a big affair, fifty guests or so, shooting, amateur theatricals, dancing and all the rest of it, and Joseph Chamberlain had got Eckhardstein invited so they could use all the activity as a cover for some secret talks on Anglo-German relations, which were a bit strained at the time.

Amongst the party was a young couple who were infatuated with each other. They decided to meet later that night in her room and, because Chatsworth is such a large place, the girl said she would leave a plate of sandwiches outside the door so her lover would know which was her room.

They weren't to know, poor things, about Eckhardstein and his appetite. As he crept along the corridors to his assignation with Chamberlain, he saw the sandwiches on the floor and promptly wolfed them down. The unfortunate young man found the empty plate, decided the girl was telling him she'd changed her mind, and returned sadly to his own room. The following morning she reproached him bitterly for his lack of enterprise, refused to listen to his excuses, told him he was a wet fish not worth bothering about and returned him to store forthwith. And that was the end of that. The next thing he knew she had become engaged to somebody else.

Another regular at the Café Royal was Barney Lewis, the South African diamond millionaire. Lewis was morose, bad-tempered and mean. He dined at the Café Royal every night, ordered the set meal at fifteen and six and, every night, he asked for a reduction. Eventually he wore them down and got his dinner at fourteen shillings on condition he ate there seven nights a week.

I didn't believe the stories I'd heard about him till the night he came in and, to the great surprise of the staff, kept his cab standing at the door. Freguglia noticed it, had a closer look, then went over to Lewis to make sure he hadn't forgotten it. I saw Lewis growl and shake his head and Freguglia turned away, shrugging his shoulders. When he brought me the wine, I asked what it was all about.

Lewis had picked up a girl on the way home, and she was out there in the cab waiting for him. When Freguglia asked Lewis if she was coming in, the millionaire's reply was:

"Leave her where she is. If I brought her in, she'd want dinner and I can't afford it." He was a miserable old beggar.

The Marquess of Clanricarde was equally stingy. It was his habit to walk across the restaurant wearing his shabby top hat, take the best table in the corner, then solemnly order a single bread roll. When this appeared, he would take from his pocket a jar of fish-paste and spread a thin layer on the roll. That was the Marquess's regular lunch, yet he left three million pounds to young Lascelles and made possible his marriage to Princess Mary.

Although the Café Royal staff wished Barney Lewis and old Clanricarde would go elsewhere, I happen to know that the man who really makes them shudder when he comes through the door is Arnold Bennett. He may be a famous writer, but he is the worst judge of food and wine in London. The Café Royal staff could live with that; what they object to is his insistence on telling them at considerable length that their choice of food and wine is always wrong and his is always right.

Whenever men of spirit foregather you will get the odd fight, and we had plenty in Romano's and the Pelican. I am glad to say the tradition still lingers, even in these degenerate days. I forget whether it was Augustus John or Jimmy Pryde who was recently banned from the Café Royal for six months for his forceful expression of artistic opinion. The management don't mind the odd row, but they draw the line at hitting people over the head with champagne bottles simply because they hold differing views on *chiaroscuro*, or tempera, or whatever it was.

My spies tell me there was another incident recently which caused some concern. A young Fusilier officer held his stag-party in one of the upper banqueting-rooms, and two Messes came along to help him enjoy it. About two o'clock in the morning, they decided their one aim in life was to throw the grand piano on to the street below to find out what sort of noise it would make as it landed. It could have been quite serious, because old Fumagali, the head waiter, was spreadeagled across the top of it, but he was rescued just in time, as was the piano. The Café Royal might have overlooked that; the problem was that the French ambassador was holding a reception in the next room and it was he who blew the whistle on them – literally. Vine Street police station hadn't been so full since Boat Race night, and two regiments of the British Army didn't have a single officer on parade the next day.

One of the Café's more unusual customers is Jim Carney, sometime lightweight champion of England. If, in the corner of the bar, you see a small, quiet, elderly man with skin like teak, wearing a respectable, if shabby, blue suit – that's Jim Carney. He must be in his seventies now, but I'd hesitate to cross him. After retiring undefeated from the ring, he joined a firm of bookmakers as debt collector and does it very well. Because he always pays his own debts, he honestly can't understand why everyone doesn't do the same. It is no good trying to fob him off with excuses; in his eyes, if you haven't got the money, you shouldn't have bet.

Since a lot of his clientèle patronise the Café Royal, Jim patronises it too, drinking soda-water or lemonade in a corner, causing no bother at all. He rarely speaks to anybody and, if he does, it is in the mildest of tones. To Jim the Café Royal is special and he would die rather than disturb its tranquillity. They don't make much profit out of him, but they were glad enough to have him around a couple of years ago. It was the end of Brighton Race Week and two of London's largest and nastiest race-gangs decided to celebrate in the Café Royal. They were deadly rivals and, for ten minutes or so, it looked as if the restaurant was going to become a blood-bath.

Just as Fumagali was clearing the other customers from the room, all he could do in the circumstances, Jim Carney got up from his corner, walked over to one gang-leader, whispered in his ear, then crossed the room and did the same to his rival. There was a pause of half a minute or so, then each led his gang quietly out of the restaurant.

Fumagali and his waiters were all over Jim and asked him what he'd said. Jim was still furious:

"Who do these boys think they are, coming in to the Café Royal to do their fighting? You'd think they'd know better. What did I tell 'em? I just told them I was Jim Carney and if they didn't walk out of here in one minute, I'd have every pug in London here in five minutes to make sure they never walked again. Blooming cheek of them!"

I'll conclude this section with two ladies who played an important part in the Café Royal's history. People will tell you that the story of Lillie Langtry's famous row with the Prince of Wales is apocryphal; that she never dropped a lump of ice down his neck and that the incident had nothing to do with his leaving her. If the story is apocryphal, then so too is the old boy I was talking to just the other day, who remembers delivering the ice-bucket in question and seeing Mrs Langtry perpetrate the most ill-advised joke of her life.

To appreciate the story of the second lady, you must remember that, in my day, the head waiter in the Café Royal was a power in the land. I recall an MP telling me that people talked with bated breath about the power of the Chief Whip. He said he was far more frightened of the head waiters at the Café Royal, the Savoy or the Ritz. They could bar you from their doors, which is more than any Chief Whip could do – and then where would you be?

Old Freguglia, head waiter in the Café Royal Grill Room, was a man of immense dignity and presence, but I was lucky enough to be there when he ran for his life like a startled rabbit – and from a woman too.

One of the regular lunchers in the Grill Room was Marie Lloyd. She tipped well, she was popular, but she had one idiosyncrasy – she did not like paying for her brandy. For some reason she had got it into her head that when she ordered brandy, she would pay for one glass. That was all right, so long as she drank only one glass, which she normally did.

But if she lunched with a party, she insisted on the bottle being left so everybody could help themselves. When the bill arrived, Marie would insist that brandy for three people was three single brandies, and that was all she would pay for. Old Freguglia let her get away with it most of the time, but one day she went too far.

It was in the summer of 1913 and I was lunching with Charlie Foster and Stiffy Halliday, while Marie Lloyd was two tables away with George Edwardes, Archie Haddon and a few others. At the end of the meal, Marie ordered brandy for them all and old Freguglia bowed, took the order and returned with a tray with seven brandies on it. Marie Lloyd wasn't having that!

"Take those away," she declaimed. "Bring the bottle and some glasses."

Freguglia did so with an impassive face, but the air of a man who sees storm-clouds ahead.

Eventually Marie got the bill. We waited for the explosion which duly came: "What's all this? Twenty-one brandies! Nonsense! Send for the manager!"

Freguglia did all a man could. Madam and her friends had consumed a bottle of brandy; the bottle had been opened at her table, it was now empty. There were twenty-one measures in a bottle and that was what madam was being charged for. Marie didn't see it like that at all. So far as she was concerned, brandy for seven people meant seven brandies, and that was all she was going to pay. Freguglia tried again but it was no good; with three brandies inside her, Marie grew angrier and angrier.

She called old Freguglia every name under the sun; she summed up his appearance, his ancestry and his personal habits with a wealth of description I hadn't heard since the time a Covent Garden porter tried to express his feelings about the cabbie who'd driven over his foot.

But Freguglia had decided enough was enough and he stood his ground. He didn't do so for long. Realising that words were getting her nowhere, Marie Lloyd decided on action. She put her hands up to her head, pulled out two evil-looking hatpins a foot long and went for him.

The next thing we knew, the dignified Freguglia was running in and out of the tables at top speed with Marie Lloyd after him in full voice. You never heard such a row. I don't know how many circuits of the room they did, with everybody cheering them on, before Freguglia came to his senses and vanished through the service door, which is what he should have done in the first place.

I have to admit that if I'd been six inches ahead of Marie Lloyd's hatpins, I would have lost my presence of mind as well. Even the fortitude of spirit and coolness of nerve engendered by membership of the Pelican Club doesn't give one the courage to stand one's ground in the face of that kind of threat.

Chapter 23

The Servant Question

Baronets and butlers, viscounts and valets

IT HAS always struck me as odd that none of these clever historian chaps has written about the vital role that servants have played in our Island Story. Some of them maintain our destiny is governed by our weather, which made us the colonists we are because we simply couldn't stand the climate of our native heath. They prove the point by quoting the Scots, whose weather is even worse and who, consequently, are to be found running every financial and engineering enterprise in warmer climes around the world.

Other historians tell us we are what we eat, and maintain the British diet of roast beef, cabbage and steamed puddings has given us the phlegmatic common sense that is the envy of the world.

I believe the true glory of my Native Land stems from the butlers, stewards, grooms of chambers and valets who control the destinies of our great households. When you think about it, most of the Empire was won in the nineteenth century, and you can take it from me that it wasn't in Parliament that the important decisions were taken. They were made in the Stately Homes of England, during grouse shoots, week-ends, Hunt Balls and dinner parties. It was the butlers, stewards and valets who oiled the wheels; without them there would be no diplomacy, no quiet get-togethers to agree Government policy; nothing would ever have got done. The more sensible of our statesmen realised it too.

Take the Duke of Wellington. He knew his worth, but he always made it plain, often to the discomfort of Ministers, that it wasn't he or his generals who won battles, it was the soldiers they commanded. And he wasn't above taking good advice when he had to.

There was the time Queen Victoria decided to visit him at Stratfield Saye and asked when she could come. The Duke, loyal chap that he was, told her to come as soon as she liked, and sent a message to his housekeeper to prepare for a Royal visit.

When he returned to Stratfield Saye the next day, the housekeeper let him have his lunch in peace, then sent in word she wanted an interview. She started by stating that she was proud of her position in his household, and that she hoped to continue in his service for the foreseeable future. However, his grace would understand from his military experience that his subordinates had a right, indeed a duty, to advise him on those matters that were their responsibility. The old Duke gravely assented to this and asked what point she wanted to make.

She told him bluntly that he had made a mistake in inviting the Queen. Since he lived so simply himself, he had no idea what was involved in a Royal visit. The house was not big enough, the dining-room was too small and the Duke did not possess a dinner service suitable for the occasion. While he paid little attention to such things, she said, other people did. And, whether he liked it or not, the nation expected a duke to entertain in a ducal manner. If he was not prepared to do so, he must withdraw the invitation to her majesty!

The Duke listened, thought about it and took her advice. The Queen's visit was postponed, a new wing was built, more china was bought and the dining-room enlarged. Six months later the Queen and Prince Albert paid their delayed visit. As they were leaving and saying how much they had enjoyed their stay, the Duke told them the story and presented his housekeeper to receive her Sovereign's formal thanks.

People say it wouldn't happen nowadays, but I'm not so sure. Look at Morton, the butler I met in New York, who wielded immense influence. He decided who was on Mrs Fish's dining list, and you can be pretty sure that if a chap wasn't on that list, he wasn't going to be accepted socially, and *that* meant he was never going to be appointed ambassador or Secretary of State or whatever it was. That's real power for you.

Dahlia Travers tells me her nephew has a wonder-man called Jeeves who has sorted out all kinds of problems for her, as well as acting as consultant to the entire membership of Buck's Club. She says there seem to be no limits to his genius, and that she expects any day to see him wearing a jewelled tie-pin for his services to Royalty, just like Sherlock Holmes.

The other day Beach, our butler, told me he had received a letter from an old friend, another of the splendid race of butlers without whom this country would be as nothing. Apparently this chap, Brown his name was, had been with the same family for thirty years, become revered as the prop and stay of the establishment, yet had suddenly decided to give in his notice.

His employer, naturally very upset, asked him to change his mind but Brown was adamant. When asked why he was giving up his portfolio after so many years, he was unwilling to answer that either. It was a personal matter, he saw no need to give a reason, he just wanted to leave. Eventually he gave way:

"Well, sir, if you insist, I will tell you. I've been with you now for thirty years as you say – and the fact is I am sick and tired of the sight of you and every member of your damned family."

Which is reasonable enough, when you come to think of it.

Binger Abinger (5th Baron Abinger) told me he once had a similar problem. Binger, for those who don't know him, was a nice old boy who enjoyed his food, and was famous for wearing the tightest white spats in London; they always looked as if a single breath would burst their buttons. He came home one night to find his wife upset because the second footman had upped and given notice after only three months. So Binger sent for him and instituted a probe or quiz to find out why. Eventually the chap came out with what I always thought was an excellent reason, even if Binger didn't:

"Well, m'lord, if you must have it. When I was in service at Mr Joel's before I came here, we used to pour more champagne down the sink than you drink here! I'm sorry to say it, m'lord, but I don't think you can afford my tastes."

Servants can be colossal snobs sometimes. Even in these modern times, a duke is a duke and many servants still like the cachet of a ducal establishment. Johnny Roxburghe (8th Duke of Roxburghe) who married the American girl May Goelet in '03, was telling me the other day that he met an ex-footman of his in Piccadilly. He'd given the chap a good reference to go to a munitions millionaire with a large place in Park Lane, so he asked how he was getting on and the man replied:

"Oh, quite well, thank you, your grace. We entertain largely but I still regret leaving your grace. Last night I helped serve dinner to a hundred and twenty people – and I didn't know one of them!"

I get on well with servants, most of the time anyway. The secret is to realise that you have no secrets from them. In 1895 Puffy Benger and I were staying at old Wivenhoe's place at Hammer's Easton for the partridge shooting. After the Bachelors' Ball, at which it had become clear that Plug Basham was losing his old zip and go, we decided to cheer him up by putting old Wivenhoe's prize pig in his bedroom. We covered it with phosphorescent paint to make sure he didn't miss it and the wheeze worked very well. Took Plug right out of himself and he became teetotal for at least two weeks.

We thought we had got away with it, but old Wivenhoe found out and was furious. Puffy Benger eventually admitted he had probably given the game away, albeit unwittingly. He had written to tell Hughie Drummond all about it and that was enough. When I expressed surprise, Puffy was incredulous. Didn't I realise the one thing never to do in somebody else's house was to write important letters? He'd forgotten the housemaid who changed the blotting paper every day. When I asked what he meant, he replied:

"If you read the Divorce Court proceedings as keenly as you read the racing news, Gally, you'd know that unchanged blotting paper is the single biggest source of proof of divorce proceedings in this country. That's how Lillie Langtry's husband found out."

George Cornwallis-West, the man probably best known for being Winston Churchill's step-father, told me his valet had given him the same advice when they were at Petworth or some other enormous place for a big week-end party. This was before the war, when house parties *were* house parties and you would have sixty sitting down to dinner, which meant at least the same number of servants in the Housekeeper's Room downstairs.

George had spent a pretty boring evening, cold food and poor port followed by bad singing and worse piano playing. When he eventually got back to his room, he asked his valet how he had spent his evening. He never forgot the reply:

"Well, sir, one of our favourite amusements is piecing together the letters found in the waste-paper baskets in the morning. Better than any jigsaw-puzzle, I can assure you, and much more entertaining. But it's quite all right, sir, I always dispose of yours myself!

"Though, since you have been kind enough to inquire, I would venture to advise against playing cards again with Mr Smithers. He has sent a note to his bookmaker in London, saying he won fifty pounds off you last night and hopes to get a couple of hundred more off you before Monday morning!"

What with Income Tax and hard times all round, one doesn't see so many footmen as one used to. People don't bother about their height any more either, I've noticed, but I remember when the going rate was so many bob extra wages for each inch over six foot. I think it was the Londonderrys who used to have a dozen or so matched chaps, each one six and a half feet tall, lining the corridor as you went in. Most impressive it was.

I used to be puzzled how footmen half my age acquired that disconcerting habit of looking right through me. I learned the secret from Beach, who tells me it was standard procedure when he was a slip of a lad. It was always difficult to make a new footman, usually an ex-hall-boy or boot-boy, stand up really straight and look dignified, but it made all the difference. It was a simple enough trick; for a month the butler shadowed the new footman wherever he went, whispering fiercely in his ear:

"Hold your head up and look as if you had ten thousand a year and a deer-park – and despise anybody who doesn't!"

Of course some fellows rely on their servants for all sorts of things. Old Charlie Stanhope, 8th Earl of Harrington to give him his formal title, had a couple of country places, one of which was Elvaston in Derbyshire. He spent a lot of his time there, while his wife used to live at their other place near Chester, or at Harrington House, their London house in Craig's Court in Whitehall. Craig's Court isn't a particularly smart address but Charlie was very proud of it; he claimed it was the oldest nobleman's house in London.

Anyway, if you went to stay with Charlie at Elvaston expecting all the splendour of a stately home, you were in for a surprise. The front door was fastened with bits of rope and the whole place was very run down, although the cooking was excellent. The reason was that Charlie selected his servants for their polo-playing abilities, and fielded an Elvaston team of himself, his butler, his valet and his cook. Very good they were, too, and the smart cavalry regiments hated them, because they loathed being beaten by a team of servants.

Charlie took them out hunting as well, although that led to difficulties because the cook was a brilliant horseman, mad on hunting and always in the lead. That meant that if the meet was the wrong side of the county, Charlie had to wait till midnight for his dinner, so he had to restrict the chap's outings to local meets.

Young Horace Pendlebury-Davenport was telling me the other day of the bad luck he'd had with his valet. He was playing squash down at Queen's Club, when the chap telephoned him to say he was leaving his service immediately and would be taking Horace's more valuable trinkets with him.

He said he much regretted doing so, but circumstances dictated. He concluded by apologising for leaving without notice, stated that he would, of course, set out Horace's evening clothes and rang off. When Horace got back to his flat he found everything of value had gone, but his dress clothes were laid out with bone cufflinks and studs carefully in place, just as the chap had promised.

People look for different things in their servants. My old Pelican chum Brer Rabbit (Captain Fred Russell) had a manservant he swore by, because he met Brabbit's particular needs:

"He's slow, he's not particularly sure. I'm hanged if he's honest and he sleeps with a corkscrew chained around his neck. But it is my firm belief that that chap could get you a cheque cashed in the middle of the Sahara Desert!"

I agree with him. Make sure your man does what you want him to do, rather than what he thinks he ought to do. Of course if you are staying in someone else's house, it can be a little awkward but the half-crown in season or, if desperate, the odd sovereign, works wonders.

Look at what happened when I stayed with Venetia James. She was born into the purple as a Cavendish-Bentinck, she's married to a very wealthy man with a house in Grafton Street and a country place at Coton near Rugby, yet she's one of the meanest women in England. Hughie Lonsdale told me he'd never go there again after a dinner when one chicken was served to ten people. I thought he was exaggerating, had a row with her or something, so I didn't take any notice and accepted an invitation from her husband whom I see in the Bachelors' occasionally.

Everybody told me to take a fur coat AND my woollen underwear because I would freeze to death, but I thought I knew better and didn't bother. I was wrong. When shown to my room on a freezing February evening, there was no fire in the grate, so I naturally turned to the footman and asked to have a fire lit.

"I'm extremely sorry, sir, but madam only allows fires in bedrooms in cases of severe illness or pregnancy."

There was only one thing to be done. I produced a couple of half-crowns and chinked them together:

"I think I have a touch of my old malaria coming on," I said firmly and waited. The rascal took me up to ten bob before he'd budge! Even then I had to throw in an extra half-crown for the maid who cleaned out the fire in the morning. And the dinner was just as bad as Hughie Lonsdale had said.

When I got back to Blandings I recounted the story with great indignation, but received no sympathy from my sisters; women don't seem to feel the cold like men, I have noticed. My brother Clarence, however, showed much more fellow-feeling and expressed his concern in a most gratifying manner.

Some weeks later he received an invitation to stay at Coton as well; I think Venetia had a nephew in Holy Orders and she wanted to talk Clarence into giving him one of his livings. Now my brother Clarence, though he is the ninth earl, is the shyest of men, and told me he was far too nervous to look a footman in the eye and bargain for a fire in his bedroom.

He had considered the matter most carefully, he said, and he had taken steps, but he refused to tell me what they were. So off he went and I thought no more about it, until he returned late that same night with the look of one who has been hit on the back of the head with a sandbag wielded by an efficient hand.

My sister Constance immediately instituted one of her Courts of Inquiry, reminiscent of Torquemada's training school for the Inquisition, but Clarence refused to explain. Eventually she went off to bed in a huff and I got Clarence alone. I poured an enormous brandy down him, counted twenty slowly and started my own investigation.

With patience and more doses of brandy judiciously administered, I managed to get it out of him. As he said, it was sheer bad luck and he blamed it all on that blasted Persian cat!

He had remembered my ordeal and wondered what measures he should take. Eventually he had the brilliant idea of taking his own materials with him, so he'd told Beach to fill an old suitcase with the best household coal plus paper and sticks for kindling. I congratulated him on his ingenuity and asked what had gone wrong.

Apparently he had arrived at the right time to be greeted warmly by his hostess, although she had eyed with some doubt the suitcase he refused to hand over to the footman. They exchanged the usual pleasantries and Clarence had asked to be shown to his room, wishing to get the suitcase out of sight as soon as possible. Venetia summoned her butler, who led the way up the staircase with Clarence behind him, still clinging like a limpet to his suitcase full of coal. He grew quite animated at this point:

"It was like smuggling tuck back into my prep school years ago, Galahad. The same old feeling that the gaoler would stop and search you at any moment, and the feeling of triumph when you realised you were going to get away with it."

Fate decreed otherwise. Just as Clarence reached the top of the staircase, a Persian cat appeared from nowhere and decided the best way to descend was through Clarence's legs! Over went Clarence and rolled all the way down the staircase, finishing flat on the hall floor with his hostess glaring at him. Unfortunately he had clung to his suitcase throughout. Each time he rolled, so did the suitcase, until the jolting was too much for its frail strength and it burst, spreading its contents all the way down the stairs and across the hall!

It was at this point that Clarence lost his presence of mind. Instead of expressing amazement at the contents and cursing someone for mixing the bags up, he made some remark about New Year and a dark man bringing luck into the house with a lump of coal. Since it was April, this seemed to lack credibility, and eventually he just gave up and admitted the truth.

Naturally his furious hostess said that in that case, she supposed he'd rather spend the night in his own bed. Anyone else would have recognised this as a rhetorical question, but Clarence took her at her word and came home right away. Never the most socially adept of men, my brother Clarence.

Some of my acquaintances take a tough line with their servants. I remember being terribly impressed by the story I heard about Captain Thistlethwayte. He was the Guards officer who caused a tremendous rumpus when he married Laura Bell, notorious in her day as one of the most expensive 'ladies of the town'.

She was the woman who screwed a quarter of a million quid out of the King of Nepal's brother before dumping him. There was a tremendous diplomatic fuss, but there was no way she was going to give the money back, so the Foreign Office paid it themselves. Just as well as it turned out, or there wouldn't be any Gurkha regiments in the Indian Army. Anyway, Laura Bell bought a house in Grosvenor Square and left cards with all her new neighbours. This induced tremendous attacks of the vapours in the wives of half the aristocracy and, it is rumoured, caused the local house prices to drop. (She got religion later on and spent all her money saving the new generation of fallen women.)

The point of the story is that Thistlethwayte had the unusual habit of summoning his servants by gunfire. He slept with a revolver under his pillow, and when he wanted his breakfast in the morning, he simply discharged a shot into the ceiling. I suppose it kept everybody on their tocs. But one day the inevitable happened. He woke up, reached for his revolver and fired it, but was too drowsy to notice which way it was pointing. Blew his head off, poor chap.

I have mentioned elsewhere how William Bentinck, now 6th Duke of Portland, whom I see occasionally at the Bachelors', greeted the news of his unexpected succession to the dukedom. The cousin he succeeded was the hermit who built those extraordinary vast underground State Rooms at Welbeck. He couldn't stand the sight of servants; whenever they saw him coming, they had to get out of the way sharpish. If they didn't, they were promptly sacked.

I don't know whether they hoped for a change when the present chap took over, but they certainly got one, even if it wasn't quite in the manner they expected. While his predecessor had a mania for privacy, William had one for physical fitness. There was a skating-rink in the grounds, and if William came across a housemaid anywhere, he promptly ordered her off for an hour's roller-skating.

His wife was just as bad. Winifred, one of the Lincolnshire Dallas-Yorkes she used to be, decided the footmen at Welbeck were getting too fat on their beer allowance, and she bought each of them a bicycle and a set of golf clubs so they could take exercise in their time off. That didn't work, because they sold the bicycles and broke all the clubs. So then she decided more direct methods were called for, and hired a Japanese judo expert for regular sessions chucking the footmen all around the Welbeck gymnasium.

She told me the other day that she still thinks it was a good idea. The staff cricket team started winning all their matches, and she found it very useful having a couple of wrestling experts on the box of her carriage when she went to her charity work in the East End. She never had much bother, but on the few occasions it occurred, she said it was a treat to see the way her footmen could dispose of the biggest tough in seconds!

And of course the Servants' Balls at Welbeck were famous, especially for the tact with which the Duke and Duchess left the house early in the morning, so as not to spoil people's pleasure by expecting breakfast or anything else to be provided the following day. That's what I call real consideration.

We didn't have such grandeur at Blandings, though things were very strictly ordered in my father's day. For example, I know that Beach doesn't insist any longer on visiting valets bringing their own evening-dress, which certainly used to be the rule in the '90s. I remember Ned de Clifford telling me once that his valet had had to borrow one of his evening suits before he, the valet that is, was allowed to join the upper servants in the Housekeeper's Room.

Although Blandings is a big place, it isn't in the same league as the really grand establishments that used to employ a hundred servants or more. I remember once talking to old Strike, Salisbury's steward, on one of the rare occasions when he unbent to young fellows like me. He told me that he and Burgh, the Abercorns' groom of chambers, worked to a rule of thumb. If you could seat a hundred people at dinner without having to send out for any of the food, wine, linen, china, plate or servants to serve it, you worked in a Great House. It's one of the biggest changes I've seen in my time. I don't suppose there are more than half a dozen houses in the country in this Year of Grace 1929 where you will still find that sort of style.

Say what you like about the decadent aristocracy, they certainly provided employment. I remember when I stayed in Belvoir in the '90s, the place was so big and there were so many people and servants around the place, that they used a trumpeter to announce the time of meals. Very military it was, and the older fellows who had been in the Army thoroughly enjoyed it; they said it took them back to their youth.

I suppose Chatsworth is most people's idea of a Great House and they would be right. Home of the Cavendishes, who got their dukedom of Devonshire in 1694, it is certainly a big place, but they have had their problems with servants too. I was talking to Victor, the present Duke the other day (he was a year ahead of me at Eton) and he told me he had been astonished by some of things he had found in the family archives.

For some reason it was always the Cavendish valets who caused problems. One valet helped himself to £500 of the housekeeping money and spent it on gambling. Another valet had bad luck at Doncaster Races, borrowed a twelve-bore from the gun-room and shot himself. And there was a secretary to the sixth Duke, Kuhlback, who appeared in court accused of keeping a houseful of prostitutes. Then there was Meynell, another valet, who was always drunk and was eventually dismissed for being found in a brothel. What got him dismissed was not being found in the brothel, but the fact that he'd taken the Duke's favourite spaniel in with him!

Of course they did have Paxton, the famous gardener, renowned for designing the Crystal Palace and all the rest of it, but they had to pay for it. Victor told me that when they had the King of Portugal to stay, it meant a hundred guests and over two hundred servants eating and sleeping around the place. I used to grumble about my father not entertaining enough, but perhaps I misjudged him. If he'd lived like that, there would be little left for us to get by on.

We haven't had many eccentric servants at Blandings. Our head-gardener, McAllister, can be pretty curmudgeonly, but that's the way with all Scottish head-gardeners. As I read somewhere recently, it is never difficult to distinguish between a Scotsman with a grievance and a ray of sunshine.

We did have one chap whose eccentricity took a most bizarre form. His name was Baxter, secretary to my brother a few years ago. I was away from Blandings at the time, but Clarence told me all about it. There was a big house-party at Blandings and my sister Constance's diamond necklace was stolen. It caused some excitement, as you might imagine, and my personal opinion is that the strain was too much for Baxter, an unstable character like so many clever fellows who work too hard.

At four o'clock the following morning my brother Clarence was rudely awakened by, of all things, a flower-pot hitting him in the small of the back as he lay in bed. As he sat up, wondering whether he was in the middle of an unusually realistic nightmare, another sailed through the window, crashing against the wall like a shell. When Clarence looked out, there was Baxter dressed in lemon-coloured pyjamas glaring up at him with the light of madness shining through his spectacles. A sight to alarm the most courageous of earls, let alone my brother Clarence, who has always preferred the quiet life.

Baxter made up some weird story about looking for the missing necklace in the garden and then finding himself locked out. This, he maintained, was sufficient excuse to bombard his harmless employer with flowerpots. All my eye and Betty Martin! 'Mad as a coot' was the term used by my brother at the time, an expression with which I am fully in accord.

Why, even as I was originally drafting this chapter, this same Baxter whom my sister Constance had, with mistaken sympathy, allowed back into the castle, took it into his head to jump out of the library window on to the flower bed fifteen feet below. A man of strange whims.

Although Dahlia Travers, old George Yaxley and others keep telling me what a master mind this chap Jeeves is, I cannot speak from personal experience. So I shall finish this chapter with the best man servant I ever met – Swears Wells's man, George. I don't know where Swears found him, but I firmly believe that George made more money for Swears than any of Swears's schemes did; and Swears had more schemes for making money that anyone I have ever known.

George had an instinct which enabled him to sense duns, bailiffs and bookies' minders half a mile away in a thick fog, and he could fob off a landlord looking for his rent better than anyone in London. When the inevitable happened, he could smuggle Swears's clothes and baggage out of lodgings or hotels like a magician.

I think George must have been a professional pugilist at one time. When Swears decided it was time the Pelican Club gave a dance, George was made responsible for looking after the band. They enjoyed their supper, but some of them didn't like the cigars George provided and complained. George took full responsibility and asked them what they were going to do about it. The first violin decided to reinforce his argument with his fists, but he never stood a chance. George flattened him with a left hook, then did the same to the bassoon player and the pianist when they tried to intervene. He had no bother after that. Now that's the sort of manservant to have!

Chapter 24

Rats!

R ATTING isn't as popular as it used to be; I don't know why.
Maybe it is all the hygiene inspectors who check on everything
nowadays, or perhaps people have just become lily-livered. The rats are
still there, you can be sure of that, but nowadays people call the Council
ratcatcher in to do a job that we used to do ourselves. In my day we all
had a 'smart little dog', bred and trained to kill rats, and had plenty of
fun with them.

When we were boys, my brother Clarence and I used to pot rats in
the stables with airguns; he was an excellent shot, far better than I was.
He told me the other day that he had got in some recent practice, but
was strangely reluctant to give me any details. I got the impression that
our butler, Beach, was involved, but I haven't managed to get the full
story yet. [1]

The first time I saw a ratting match in London was, of all places, in
the foyer of the Haymarket Theatre. I used to tease Beerbohm Tree
about it whenever I met him, telling him it drew more money and gave
more innocent pleasure than his beloved Shakespeare ever did. It was
when Lillie Langtry went on the stage, causing a considerable social stir
by doing so. I can't remember what the play was, but the Bancrofts were
producing it and Abington Baird, who was paying Mrs Langtry's rent at
the time, had persuaded them (gossip said a thousand quid) to give
Lillie Langtry her chance.

The trouble was that Baird thought the deal had given him the right
to do what he liked in the theatre. This meant that when the Jersey Lily
swept in to collect her letters one Saturday morning, she found herself
in the middle of a crowd of toughs very different from her usual
respectful admirers. Pushing her way through the scrum, demanding

---

(1) Mr Threepwood has a footnote to this page:
' Splendid story. Baxter-potting all over the castle. Must get further details out of
Beach.' *Ed.*

explanations, she arrived at a ratting ring into which Baird was just putting his best terrier to deal with a dozen assorted rats.

She screamed and tried to make a fast exit, but the crush was too great and she was forced to stay where she was until the rats had been dealt with. In the relative calm that followed, she enthralled the crowd by telling Baird exactly what she thought of him, then relieved her feelings with a dramatic faint. Unfortunately, she fainted into the ratting ring, so she decided to recover and fight her way out, using her parasol in the manner of a foil to do so. She never spoke to Baird again nor, I believe, did she feel able to enter the Haymarket Theatre for a considerable time after.

Before they rebuilt it, Simpson's Restaurant used to be infested with rats, as were most of the places on the river side of the Strand. Sometimes it seemed to be a race between the rats and the customers as to who got first go at the famous saddle of mutton. But we were used to it and got on with our meals; the rats had been there far longer than we had. I hasten to add that I have never seen a rat in the present building – but I'm sure they must still be there somewhere.

Nicols-Pigache (Pig-Ash we used to call him), manager of the Café Royal till the big row some years back, used to run popular late-night ratting parties in the Café Royal but laid down one condition – no one taking part was to admit it in public. (This was before they rebuilt the place in 1923.)

Pig-Ash began killing the rats on his own but found there were too many of them, so he called in an assistant and they worked as a team with a couple of terriers. He told us about it one night in Romano's and found himself with a dozen willing volunteers.

We used to troop along about midnight with our favourite terriers; Pig-Ash would let us in by the back door, allocate us each a room to clear and let us get on with it. Guns weren't allowed – not after the time Barmy Twistleton brought his six-guns and every policeman at Vine Street rushed along, thinking there was a robbery in progress. Luckily, Barmy had been working in one of the private rooms upstairs but the bullet holes in the furniture and the shattered mirrors didn't help things.

The biggest *battue*, if that's the right word, we ever had was when Pig-Ash found out that the rats had secured access to the Café Royal's larders. This was serious and we dealt with it accordingly. We killed over two thousand in seven nights before they decided to go elsewhere, and Pig-Ash gave us a splendid dinner as well.

What really annoyed the Café Royal was that the rats were coming in from a rival establishment though, in a perverse sort of way, they were flattered. They knew their food was far superior to that at Oddenino's. They hadn't realised the fact was equally clear to the Oddenino's rats, who showed their excellent taste by tunnelling under Glasshouse Street to reach the epicurean delights of the Café Royal's larders.

The tunnels were blocked up, but then the rats started using the surface route and came over the street. It was a sight I was introduced to by a policeman chum of mine, memorable for his first name, Egbert, and his astonishingly red hair. He was the chap, as I relate elsewhere, who showed me how to avoid getting hurt when being thrown out of places of amusement. I used to see him on his beat occasionally and one day he invited me to join him in a little nocturnal amusement; I was to meet him at the back entrance to the Café Royal, bringing a strong stick, not my usual evening cane.

When I arrived, he stood me in one corner of the entrance while he stood in the other, and after a few minutes we saw a fine big rat sauntering towards us across the street as though it belonged to him. There was a swish, a thud and Egbert had his first kill of the evening. We got thirteen between us that night.

Old Joey Chandler used to divert his guests in the interval before dinner by loosing a dozen rats on his billiard table and showing us how his little Skye terrier could deal with the whole lot in under a minute. (His dinners in Old Bond Street were always bachelor affairs; his wife preferred to stay at their country place where rats were at least kept outside the house.) Sometimes the odd rat would escape and hide in the most ingenious places – including, on one occasion, my evening coat, a fact I did not discover till it emerged from my pocket in the middle of the Alhambra ballet and the girl I was with started screaming her head off and got us both chucked out.

We used to have contests, matching our dogs against all comers, with an independent timekeeper to decide who killed most rats in the time. I won quite a bit of money with my Towser, whose sole defeat was due to the worst chicanery the ratting world has ever seen, perpetrated by that man of wrath – Tubby Parsloe, now Sir Gregory Parsloe of Matchingham Hall, Much Matchingham, Shropshire.

It happened in the upper room of the Black Footman in Gossiter Street, where most of the big matches were held. Tubby Parsloe had challenged my Towser against his Banjo for a hundred pounds a side, and I'd taken it like a shot; Banjo was a nice little animal, but not a patch on my Towser. When the big night came, I had Towser trained to a hair. He would have taken on Jumbo the elephant and the entire Brigade of Guards if I'd asked him to.

We tossed for starting, Parsloe won, and Banjo killed his twenty-four rats in just over two minutes. Then it was Towser's turn. I opened his box, got him out and set him in the ring. As I live and breathe, he just lay down, closed his eyes and went to sleep! The rats were dropped in the ring, but Towser didn't stir; he just sprawled there, out like a light. I shouted, whistled, urged, cajoled to no avail. Not a movement did Towser make and Parsloe pouched the hundred quid.

If ever a dog had been nobbled, Towser had; when I sniffed his breath, it was like a Soho chop-house on a hot night. There must have been six pounds of steak and onions inside him, undoubtedly fed to him by the twister Parsloe while the rest of us were having a drink downstairs before the match.

It quite spoilt ratting for me. It is a good clean sport when not ruined by men like Parsloe, who wouldn't recognise the spirit of fair play if it was served up to them in aspic on a bed of lettuce. When one realises that, through no effort or merit on his part, he has now become a baronet, a land-owner and pillar of county society, it makes one sympathise with the views put forward by anarchists and republicans.

I then tried cock-fighting for a bit, but it wasn't the same. In passing, don't believe people who tell you cock-fighting doesn't happen nowadays. Not a hundred yards from the doors of the Garrick Club is a popular and well-used cock-pit which holds regular mains. My acquaintances in the Garrick tell me they know nothing of it, but I am not so sure. [2]

Even in these decadent post-war days, it is possible to enjoy a little ratting. All you have to do is to persuade a member of the Eccentric Club to take you along to their premises in Ryder Street. It used to be the old Dieudonne Hotel, a well-known *maison de rendezvous*, and the rooms on the upper floors are still linked by concealed doors, but that's by the way and definitely another story.

My old pal George Graves, famous for creating the part of Baron Popoff in 'The Merry Widow', is probably the best chap to approach. Give George an hour's notice and he'll be there with his famous terrier David. The arrangements are in the hands of Powell, the head waiter, who will arrange a ring of tables laid on their sides in the hall between the telephone boxes and the cloakroom. He can also be relied upon to produce a dozen rats as and when required.

Powell was famous during the war as the best mess-corporal in the Army. If there was anything edible within half a mile of his Mess, it was caught, plucked and cooked before the Provost Marshal could say "What's all this, then?"

I don't suppose there's much enthusiasm for it in the Athenaeum or the Reform, but it's reassuring to know one can still get a little ratting in at least one London club when one wants to. But then I suppose it's only to be expected, because the Eccentric is the direct successor to my beloved Pelican Club.

---

(2) I can confirm Mr Threepwood's story. There is (in 1992) a new shoe shop ten doors along from the Garrick Club. I explored the building when it was refurbished in 1978 and found a small room in the cellar with wooden benches set around a cock-pit, which showed signs of comparatively recent use. The offices above had the unusual facility of no fewer than three back doors. Since cock-fighting has been illegal in England since 1849, the precaution was a sensible one. *Ed.*

Chapter 25

Some Men of My Time – 4
Willie Clarkson

IN 1905 I attended the opening of Willie Clarkson's new establishment at 41 Wardour Street, which provides over 10,000 wigs to its customers during the Christmas season as well as supplying theatrical and fancy-dress costumes to the world. (Willie is particularly proud of the fact that Crippen and Charlie Peace came to him for their wigs.)

No one has ever seen him in anything other than tail coat and striped trousers, and you'll find him behind the scenes at every theatrical dress rehearsal or fancy-dress ball in London.

Willie takes a pride in meeting all his customers' requests, but his relationship with Beerbohm Tree was often difficult. Tree used to drive his staff to distraction by changing his mind up to and including the dress rehearsal. The result was that Willie would suddenly find that the thirty wigs Tree had demanded on a Monday had to be replaced by thirty different models on the Thursday.

I was there the night the Carlton Hotel went up in flames, and a group of us were looking at the blaze and wondering if the fire would spread to Tree's theatre next door. At one point the flames moved that way and we were shocked to hear Willie shout "Thank Heavens!" We were outraged by his callousness till his second shout explained all.

"Thank Heavens! I knew Tree would change his mind again – so I never delivered the wigs!"

Still, he did get his own back on Tree sometimes. At one Haymarket dress rehearsal everything had gone swimmingly until Tree took Maud Jeffreys through her big scene. He suddenly stopped and started shouting for Willie:

"Where's Clarkson? Where's the wig man?"

Willie, who had been sitting at the back of the theatre, came down to see what the matter was.

"Look at her! Look at her! I wanted a real wig! A wig that looked like real hair. I wanted a wig that looked as though it was growing from her head – but how would you know what hair is?"

Willie was ready with the answer every wigmaker must hope to make:

"Really, Mr Tree, it's not my fault! I made her a wig. A beautiful wig – but she wouldn't wear it and that's her real hair you're looking at now!"

Willie was full of bright ideas, one of which made him extremely unpopular in our Imperial outposts. He had some fake sovereigns made out of cardboard for an advertising stunt, showing King Edward's head on one side and Willie's on the other. Somebody going out East secured a bagful of them and convinced the rickshaw men of Ceylon they were a new model introduced by the British Government. The authorities had considerable difficulty in sorting it all out, especially when it transpired that the rickshaw men preferred Willie's version to the real thing. Willie was delighted when the news got back, but was rather put out when I suggested it was a bit of a cheek putting his head on the back of a sovereign.

"On the back!" protested Willie. "On the back! My dear boy, can't you see it's on the front?"

It was Wuffalo Will (Willie Wilde) who told me of the time Willie Clarkson was called down to Windsor to attend to the royal head-dresses before some State function. When he had finished, a lady-in-waiting told him one of the Princesses needed his advice on her hair and escorted Willie to her room. Watched by the lady-in-waiting and the Princess's maid, Willie did whatever it was and was shown into the corridor to find his own way out.

As he turned away from the Princess's door, he walked straight into Queen Victoria, who looked curiously at this unknown man leaving her daughter's room. Willie, anxious she should not jump to the wrong conclusion, said the first thing that came into his head:

"Honi soit qui mal y pense, your Majesty!"

This seems an appropriate place for me to refute the widely-held belief that Queen Victoria had no sense of humour. While she took a poor view of the Marlborough House set, she knew the world better than people give her credit for and enjoyed a joke as well as anybody.

I had the story from one of the heroes of the following tale, who told me he is proud to have made Her Majesty laugh uproariously, even though he still wakes up sweating at the memory of it.

It happened in the '90s when the Court was at Balmoral. As usual, a Highland regiment provided the guard of honour, and the two subalterns of the Argyll and Sutherlands on duty were told they would be presented to their Queen after dinner. The summons came and the two young men, tall and shining in their dress uniforms, kilts swaying bravely, marched down the corridor to the drawing-room. They had been told what to do. The door would be opened, they were to march straight across to the fireplace where the Queen would be standing, and halt on the small rug a few feet in front of her.

Unfortunately they had *not* been told that the drawing-room had a particularly well-polished floor. They were ushered in and marched across the room towards the Queen, who stood there ready to greet them. As they halted together on the small rug, disaster struck. The rug shot from beneath their feet and both of them went down flat on their backs, with their legs whirling wildly in the air.

They scrambled frantically to their feet while the Queen gave vent to peal after peal of laughter, followed by everybody else in the room.

The presentation went ahead and they withdrew with but one thought in their minds – to shoot or otherwise dispose of themselves as soon as conveniently possible. As they sat despondently in the ante-room, brooding over their fate, a senior member of the Household came out. With tears in their eyes they asked what they could do by way of apology to the Queen.

The wise old man reassured them. No apologies were needed. On the contrary, the Queen was delighted. She wanted them to know that she was pleased to see that the officers of the 91st were just as fine men as their fathers had been. She had been greatly entertained and impressed by what she had witnessed!

Chapter 26

Some London Theatres and Some Men Who Ran Them

Tierney, Jupp, Blake, George, Buncle and Bungay

THERE are lots of books of reminiscences about the great actors of the past, Irving, Tree and the rest of them. They became famous and made their theatres famous as well, but the fellows who counted with us, who really controlled things, were the stage-doormen, the porters and the chuckers-out.

When George Edwardes took over the Gaiety, he made his old nurse the theatre housekeeper, and installed her sailor husband, Tierney, as stage-doorman. As custodian of the most popular theatre in London, Tierney did very well out of it, saved his money and built the street of houses in Streatham that now bears his name.

'Tierney the Terror', as we called him, was succeeded by Jupp, a warrant officer of the 8th Hussars. He had learned the sergeant-major's trick of seeming to look into your very soul and, most of the time, he was right in what he saw there. He had a sense of humour and no tip, no matter how large, would get you past Jupp unless he approved of you; we sought his good opinion more eagerly than we sought that of Royalty itself.

At Her Majesty's Theatre the man who counted was Beerbohm Tree, an extraordinary chap who, unlike any other theatrical manager I ever knew, couldn't stand long runs. They made money, but they bored him. The result was that we all used to attend his first nights, and then we'd go again a couple of months later to see what changes he'd made.

His cast would be as curious as we were, because they wouldn't know what was going to happen till Tree did it on stage! He said it kept them on their toes; they called it driving them mad. I think he did it just because he was bored, but it certainly kept his cast on the *qui vive*.

I was lucky enough to be there the night he drove them frantic in 'The Darling of the Gods'. It was a play in which he took the part of the villain Zakkuri. In the opening scene the whole cast were on stage, and were supposed to surge about a bit, the way crowds do on these occasions. Then they all turned towards the rostrum above them and started shouting his name. On the third shout, Tree was to appear on the rostrum – all good dramatic stuff.

The night I was there the curtain went up, the crowd appeared, swarmed to and fro for a time, then turned towards the rostrum and started to shout:

"Zakkuri! Zakkuri! Zakkuri!" Nothing happened – no Tree.

Thinking he was late for his cue they tried again:

"Zakkuri! Zakkuri! Zakkuri!" Still no Tree.

They had another go and this time they really shouted; if Tree was within half a mile, he was certainly going to hear them. Still no Tree!

It wasn't till they'd shouted themselves hoarse and were wondering what on earth to do next, that a quiet voice from behind them said:

"Were you looking for somebody?" and Tree walked quietly on stage, having proved to his own satisfaction that his cast would stick to their lines and business even if he didn't.

It was always worthwhile cadging an invitation to Tree's rehearsals, which were often more exciting than the final version. Sometimes they became too exciting which is why, if you mention the battle scene in 'Macbeth', the staff at His Majesty's still shudder slightly and try to change the subject.

Tree took great pride in making Shakespeare popular, doing it in the way he was sure Shakespeare would have liked – with lots of spectacle and action. He decided to stage the battle scene in Macbeth with as many combatants as he could squeeze on to the stage, and hired a hundred or so Guardsmen for the purpose. Over the protests of his stage-manager they were all fitted out with uniforms, pikes, swords and shields, after which Tree shoved them on stage and let them get on with it. (I did hear a rumour that he'd taken the NCOs to one side and promised a bonus to the winning army, but he always denied it.)

All I can say is that I never saw a fiercer theatrical battle in my life. It was pandemonium. I saw one chap, an unpopular lance-sergeant I discovered later, who was picked on from the start, and his flight from the stage after a tremendous thump from a pike followed by a dozen round-arm blows in his ribs, had an authenticity rarely seen in the theatre.

It stopped only when the frantic stage-manager saw his scenery was being cut to ribbons from the sword-slashes. Tree blew a whistle half a dozen times, managed to restore order and announced some new rules:

"Soldiers! Remember this! Play fair – never hit a back cloth when it's down. Oh, yes! Anybody actually drawing blood will be fined. This is a theatre, not the Battle of Waterloo.

"But you all did very well. It was in the finest traditions of this theatre and of your own famous regiment. No wonder England is so proud of you."

He stepped down and said quietly to the stage-manager:

"Most satisfactory – but I think it might be wise to make sure the pikes and swords are really blunt before the next rehearsal. I had no idea amateurs could be so enthusiastic."

There is one thing every actor and actress agrees upon. People never remember how good you were; they never mention the night you jumped in and saved the show. But they always remember the disasters, the night when everything went wrong. I've seen at least half a dozen plays ruined by dogs or horses which decided that the big emotional scene was the moment to perform their natural functions on stage, thereby earning roars of applause from the audience and the undying hatred of the unfortunate Thespians involved.

I've seen realism carried too far as well. It was years ago, a thing called 'Ecarte' by Lord Newry, who, as I recall, never wrote another play and I can see why. As with so many productions where amateurs play too large a part, it went wrong from the start. The first act finished with the entire cast enjoying a picnic and somebody, probably Newry himself, decided to add realism by providing real food and real champagne. It went well, too well, and the second act started with most of the cast carried away on a sea of alcohol, and in no mood to meet the demands and discipline of the play. By the third act the heroine had to play four parts by herself and the hero never appeared at all!

Such disasters become legends. On one glittering first night, Cynthia Brook played a duchess who was to make a stately entrance in the first act. Her opening line to Charles Wyndham, the most dignified of men, was to be :

"Kit! Kit! I've been dining with ..." whoever it was.

Unfortunately nobody had told her that the door in the back-cloth, which had stuck badly during rehearsals, had been fixed to open easily.

As she had done at every rehearsal, she pushed at the door with all her might; it shot open and she staggered across the stage to fall full-length in front of the startled Wyndham. Her determination to stick to her lines, though laudable, was ill-judged. Lying prostrate on the stage, she gasped out the words :

"Kit! Kit! I've been dining ..." before the roar of laughter cut her off.

Stage-doors often cause problems, and the more eminent the actor, the more we enjoyed such disasters; I suppose we were simply pleased to see that great men could make mistakes. After Irving died, George Alexander of the St James's Theatre became London's leading actor-manager. He had a tremendous following and took great pride in ensuring that nothing ever went wrong on the St James's stage – ever! He could be a bit pompous sometimes but, after that fatal night, we could always bring him down to earth.

It happened during his 'Rupert of Hentzau', which pulled in the crowds for months and had gone so well that Alexander's stage-manager had clearly relaxed his vigilance. It was the climax of the play, the famous duel scene when Alexander and Harry Irving (son of Sir Henry) were to fight to the death in a locked cellar. Desperate for his life, Irving was supposed to throw himself at the door, find it locked and be forced to turn and fight like a trapped animal.

To the huge joy of those of us lucky enough to be there that night, Irving shouted his lines: "Locked! Locked, by Heavens!" and threw himself at the door. It promptly gave way and he vanished through it to the biggest shout of laughter in London.

Arthur Roberts, the finest comedian of my day and a fellow Pelican, could be relied upon to get a laugh, no matter how inappropriate, and no matter how much the author had urged him not to.

He once appeared in a charity performance of 'Money', playing the part of the butler. The audience was the sort that actors hate, lots of wealthy people who had paid to get their names on the subscription list, but far too self-conscious to applaud unless someone else, preferably Royalty, did it first. Arthur's part as the butler was a small one, but he made the most of it.

Just before the curtain fell on the first act, the hero declaimed with all the pathos at his command:

"Who will lend me ten pounds for my old nurse?"

In the dramatic pause that followed, Arthur stepped forward:

"I will!" he cried. "I will! I got the old girl into trouble – and I'll see her through!"

He turned a tear-jerking melodrama into a knockabout farce in three seconds flat.

The stage-door of the Palace Theatre, which provided a different type of entertainment, was guarded by Blake, a ferocious individual who hated women, call-boys and education of any sort. He exercised rigid discipline amongst the young exquisites who lined the passage outside his door, and his fierce "Put that cigarette out and stop talking", cowed the proudest of peers and the bravest of Guardees.

The Palace hit the headlines with Maud Allen's dance 'The Vision of Salome'; it was the sensation of the day. The theatre-going public reeled at a spectacle best described in a review by Augustus Moore:

'... the ropes of pearls and plaques of jewels that enviously hide the exquisite delights of her form ... Her naked feet, slender and arched ... the sheen of her smooth hips ... Salome dances even as a snake eager for her prey, panting with hot passion, the fire of her eyes scorching like a living furnace.'

Everybody was terribly shocked, and we crowded the place out to see if the throbbing review was justified. London had even more to talk about when Margot Asquith invited her to give a private performance at Downing Street; then the Mrs Grundys knew the country was going to the dogs.

At least Maud Allen was a professional. When Lady Constance Stewart-Richardson started doing the same thing in 1910, people wondered where it was all going to end. Some of my friends even blamed her for the 1911 constitutional crisis in which the House of Lords lost its veto. If an earl's daughter could appear on the stage of the Palace Theatre cavorting in few clothes and bare feet, how could anybody respect the House of Lords any more?

It never bothered me, but it certainly bothered Edward VII who threatened to call her sister, the Countess of Cromartie, down to London for a royal ticking-off. But when he discovered the Countess was artistic as well, and the author of several 'unusual' novels, he didn't

HOW WINSTON CHURCHILL NEARLY LOST ANOTHER SEAT.

think it would do any good.

The Hippodrome rivalled the Palace in speciality acts. Some of them were pretty weird: Consul the Almost Human, Russian giants, African pygmies, and two chaps and their sister who dived from the roof of the theatre into a tank of water. When Maud Allen started displaying the body beautiful at the Palace, the Hippodrome responded with a lady who went under the name of La Belle Titcomb.

She also showed off her figure but, because the Hippodrome specialised in animal turns, she did it on a horse, riding round and round the stage wearing a sort of Greek toga with very little, if anything, beneath it. Nobody could decide which was the more shocking till La Belle Titcomb pulled off a publicity stunt that was a tremendous success and put her well ahead of Maud Allen. One morning the crowd in Hyde Park were electrified to see her riding along Rotten Row, wearing the same flimsy outfit she wore on stage.

Halfway along the Row, she met Winston Churchill riding the other way. He was so startled by this near-naked apparition coming towards him that he jabbed his spurs into his horse, which promptly reared and threw him. He wasn't hurt, but the Press had a field day:

'Member of Parliament Dramatically Unseated', 'Churchill Thrown Off His High Horse', 'Minister Thrown Off Balance By a Pretty Face' were just some of the headlines that we enjoyed.

The leading lady of the Alhambra in Leicester Square was Valerie Rhys, whose engagement party to the brewer Sir Henry Meux is mentioned elsewhere. After her husband's death she took over the brewery, and her business acumen became the talk of London, while her habit of wearing at least £30,000 of jewellery whenever she dined in public made a deep impression on the Society ladies who had initially snubbed her. Quite a few City financiers got the shock of their lives when they were called to account by the lady they had dismissed as 'that chorus girl'.

She had an endearing characteristic. She was an enthusiastic dairy farmer and all her cows were given Biblical names, Naomi, Vashti, Esther, etc. Her favourite was named Ruth, because the cow insisted on following a few steps behind the bull – 'whither thou goest, I will go'.

The guardian of the Alhambra stage-door was George, who served there forty years. He saw it through all its phases of circus, music-hall, theatre, Wild West shows, picture-house and music-hall again. He was a gloomy man and disapproved strongly of Wild West shows and circuses, probably because he was unable to exercise the same terrifying authority over animals as he did over his fellow men. He used to recount with acute resentment how an elephant had once had the impertinence not only to remove his cap from his head, but to swallow it as well. This, in his view, was nearly as reprehensible as the time a sea-lion had chased him out of his own stage-door.

One of the most popular turns at the Alhambra was the Zancigs, a mind-reading act. Zancig would wander down into the audience, be given a letter by someone, hold it in his hand and Madame Z, up on the stage fifty feet away, would then declaim its contents. It was most impressive and, as far as we could see, authentic. One night a supercilious young chap, hoping to show them up in front of his girl, called Zancig over and told him to choose any one from a bundle of letters he pulled from his evening coat. Zancig looked at him and quietly advised him to choose the letter himself.

The young chap wasn't having any of that. The whole thing was obviously a put-up job, so Zancig could choose any letter he liked.

Zancig smiled and bowed, riffled through the envelopes, selected one and asked permission to use it. The fellow sneered his agreement and Zancig turned to his wife on the stage and asked her what was in the envelope he had in his hand.

There was a pause, then Madame started to recite the most torrid slush you ever heard. She got three sentences out before the young chap leaped to his feet, snatched the letter out of Zancig's hand and stormed out of the theatre to roars of applause.

As Pitcher pointed out in the Cavour later that evening, Zancig's gift could cause problems. We'd invited Zancig to dinner, because we were all anxious to find out if the famous mind-reading act could work with bookmakers and racehorse-owners. Zancig said it was all very simple:

"It is simply zis – zat at any hour or any place, whatever I gaze upon or place my hand upon, Madame can see clearly."

There was silence while we digested this remark, then Pitcher voiced what was in all our minds:

"I hope, for your own sake," he said gravely, "that if you are not a strictly moral husband, you have the ability to – er – ring Madame off occasionally."

Apart from Romano's and the Café Royal, I suppose the Criterion was the most popular place for men about Town to have their lunchtime snifter. Charlie, the bar-keeper, presided over the prettiest, blondest barmaids in London, with whom we used to chaff and flirt, thinking what devils of fellows we were. And they smiled back at us because it was good for trade and I suppose we were harmless enough.

Despite the free-and-easy atmosphere, drunkenness was rare. It was the extraordinary mix of society that was the Criterion's attraction, though I remember vividly Stiffy Halliday's demonstration of loyalty at the time of the Jubilee. He spent the entire day drinking in the Criterion bar, deaf to our suggestions that he take a little soda with it. He was adamant, producing one of the best reasons for heavy drinking I have heard:

"Not on y'r life. The Queen, God blesh her, hash given orders f'r all public houses to remain open till 2 a.m. and I'm ruddy well going to stay here and drink her health till then to show I'm not a blurry republican!"

In those days leading actors were admired and imitated by every young man in London. People wanted to look like Henry Irving, Wilson Barrett or Bill Terriss; they tapped out their cigarettes like Tree or Gerald du Maurier.

I think Bobby Averill was the last actor whose clothes were imitated all over London. He had been just about everything in his short life, runaway schoolboy, mounted rifleman in the Cape, sailor, strolling player in a fit-up company and then a leading man in the West End. But he was always stony-broke and always light-hearted. He came into his own in 'The Girl In The Taxi' in 1913, where he had a line that always brought a roar of laughter:

"Here, hang it, I say, how's a fellow to see high life on five bob a week?"

What his audience didn't know was that it was true for Bobby in real life. Although he wore his dress-clothes on stage better than any man in London, he didn't have enough cash to buy an overcoat.

That's why so many fellows preferred musical shows to straight plays. I don't know if it still applies, but the rule used to be that in an ordinary play, an actor provided his own kit. But if he had to sing a single bar of music, then the management became responsible for his clothes. And if you were lucky enough to work for George Edwardes, you were allowed to keep them at the end of the run; that's why you heard people speaking of their 'G.B. suits', which was short for 'God Bless George Edwardes'.

While we admired the great actors, and respected the equally great men who guarded their stage-doors, we saw them from the outside. There were, however, two places where we were able to take part in the proceedings – Covent Garden and the Empire. I mention elsewhere how the Covent Garden Balls filled a great need. You could take along the girl of your dreams, pay your guinea, dance with her all night and then take her to breakfast the following morning at Hammond's.

It could get a bit rough, of course, and if it wasn't rough inside, then we could be pretty sure that the porters in the Covent Garden Market would start something when we came out in the morning. I suppose the sight of a couple of hundred top hats was a bit of a temptation if you happened to have a potato or an orange handy. So one could usually rely on a bit of a turn-up to round the night off. Some of the porters were pretty good with their fists too; in fact that is where the phrase 'cauliflower ear' came from, since so many had them from their various pugilistic encounters.

But they were splendid evenings. The last Covent Garden Ball I went to was in '06 in the company of young Buck Buckmaster, Stiffy Halliday and a few others. I can't recall what the occasion was, but everybody was there from Shuggy de Bathe (who hated being called Mr Lillie Langtry) to Countess Randall, Gabrielle Ray, Biddy Brett, the rest of the Gaiety chorus and Marie Lloyd, who delivered a speech from the balcony.

At some time during the evening I recounted how, on a previous occasion, it had taken four chaps to chuck me out. Tim Curtis and young Buck took it into their heads to see if they could improve on this, and started a spoof fight which soon had the heavies moving in from all directions. They put up a very good show but Rendle and Forsythe, the two chaps in charge at Covent Garden, had at their beck and call some of the burliest firemen and commissionaires you ever saw. They also took what we considered to be an unfair advantage of the Bow Street police station's being just across the road.

Buck won by occupying the full attentions of two commissionaires, one fireman and two policemen; Tim Curtis only had three to look after him. Although Buck went out fast when they eventually mastered him, I was glad to see he remembered the tip I'd given him.

When you are being frog-marched out of anywhere, watch out for the swing-doors. The chaps frog-marching you will use your face to open them; the trick is to put your foot out and kick them open first. Saves quite a few bruises. I was given the advice by a policeman, who had chucked me out of the Criterion three nights running and with whom I became pally. He was the red-haired chap who had the kindly habit of making sure my top hat was restored to me after I'd been consigned to the outer darkness. You may remember our joint ratting expedition at the Café Royal.

In my day the Empire Theatre in Leicester Square was London's greatest meeting-place. You went to the Gaiety to look at the chorus; you went to the Empire to meet your friends. You might look at the show, but most of the time you strolled through the promenade where you would be sure to meet half a dozen of your pals. I know it had a reputation because many ladies of easy virtue foregathered there, but the atmosphere of the promenade was more that of a man's club than anything else.

The Empire's great days started in '87, when Augustus Harris and George Edwardes took it over and installed H.J. Hitchins (universally known as Scratchums) as manager. It is no exaggeration to say that, for thirty years, the Empire promenade was the real centre of the British Empire. Up to 1914, whenever you said goodbye to some chap who had finished his home leave and was off to some God-forsaken spot in West Africa or India, the parting words were always the same: "Cheerio, old man. See you in the Empire some time." And you always did.

Everybody knows what happened when they partitioned off the promenade in '94. There were protests, letters in the papers, questions in Parliament, but it needed a party of Sandhurst cadets to do what had to be done. They came up to London one night and simply tore it down; their leader, incidentally, was Officer Cadet Winston Churchill. My part in the Empire's history wasn't quite so dramatic, but I'm still proud of it.

If you wanted a quiet evening there were two nights to avoid the Empire, Boat Race Night and the night of the Varsity Rugger match when the fittest young men in England came up to Town to measure themselves against the two most famous chuckers-out in London – Buncle and Bungay of the Empire.

They were legends along the Isis and the Cam. Both big men, both late of the Royal Horse Guards, they had immense good humour and tact, but even Buncle and Bungay could not be expected to cope with two hundred rowdy undergraduates. So crafty old Scratchums worked out a system of dealing with trouble before it had started.

Scratchums would wander round the bars and promenade, keeping an eye out for anybody he thought was getting a little too lively. He would approach the over-excited youth and murmur a few courteous words while, at the same time, patting him gently on the back. *And his heavily-chalked evening glove left a glaring white mark on the fellow's coat.* As soon as Buncle or Bungay saw that mark, the chap was out in Leicester Square before he knew what was happening.

It must have been in '97, after I'd been turfed out of the Empire three nights in a row, that I was in Romano's grumbling about the unfairness of life in general and of Scratchums in particular. Pitcher Binstead listened, laughed at my indignation, showed me the chalk on my back and told me of Scratchum's low cunning. While I admired his methods, I felt cheated. Being chucked out, just 'on appro' as it were, might be a great compliment but I felt it was basically unjust. I burned for revenge.

I remembered all the stories I'd heard from chaps who shot lions, tigers and other dangerous fauna; I bided my time and stalked Scratchums round the Empire every night for a week. Pitcher was right. If that chalk mark appeared on a chap's coat, there was no appeal, he was out as soon as Buncle or Bungay saw it.

My chance came a month later. I happened to hear that the Empire was to be honoured by an official 'unofficial' visit from the Benchers of the Middle Temple. They were giving a dinner for the new French ambassador and his suite which was to conclude with an introduction to London's night life.

That evening found me in the Empire promenade with Pitcher Binstead, Stiffy Halliday and Puffy Benger. It was their task to keep Scratchums, Buncle and Bungay out of the way while I carried out my grand counterstroke.

With one of my kid gloves heavily chalked, I made my way along the promenade, touching various eminent members of the legal profession on their back as I went. Each encounter was followed by profuse apologies; I had dropped my cigar, I had stumbled, I thought it was an old friend. I was charm and courtesy itself. Then I rejoined Pitcher and the others and waited. It didn't take long.

Buncle and Bungay came along on their regular tour, saw the chalk marks and swung into action. It was beautifully done. They picked off each chap so smoothly the others hardly noticed he had gone. One big fellow, a newly-appointed circuit judge, tried to fight back, but Buncle and Bungay just smiled pityingly and the learned justice was sailing through the door into Leicester Square before he could say *Habeas Corpus* – though those weren't the words I heard as he felt the toe of their boots.

I look back on the evening with quiet pride. It isn't given to many to get three judges, four Queen's Counsel, a French *Chargé d'Affaires* AND a Home Secretary chucked out of the Empire. Scratchums was a bit more circumspect with his chalked glove after that.

And now the Empire has gone.

I went to the last night to watch those two young Americans, Adele and Fred Astaire, dance their way through the 326th performance of 'Lady Be Good'. The Prince of Wales was in one box and Adeline Genée, the *prima ballerina* at the Empire for twenty years, was in another.

I suppose the audience enjoyed it; some went back to a party at St James's Palace afterwards, but I didn't join them. For me, for Adeline Genée and many others, it was the end of an era; the biggest loss to London, my London, since Romano's and the old Pelican Club closed down. I have happy memories of them all.

The Empire Promenade

Chapter 27

Some Men of My Time – 5
Jimmy Davis

otherwise known as
The Brickbat, The Stalled Ox, Pan, Owen Hall and Payne Nunn

JIMMY DAVIS was one of the many gifted men with whom I rubbed shoulders in the old days. I just wish some of their gifts had rubbed off on me. He was at various times a solicitor, publisher, editor, author, librettist, playwright and race-horse owner. He owned a succession of big houses at the last of which he gave a colossal party for the team of broker's men who came to evict him. His nicknames reflect his changes of career.

Jimmy Davis came from a talented family. His two sisters (Frank Danby and Mrs Aria) both wrote, while his nephews Ronald and Gilbert Frankau have made their names in journalism and the stage.

Jimmy started as a respectable solicitor, practising in an office in Conduit Street. One of his clerks in those early days was a tall youth of fifteen called Ernest Wells, later to become famous as Swears of the Pelican Club. Although he did well at the law, Jimmy's evenings at Romano's introduced him to a world which seemed far more enjoyable than that of conveyancing and affidavits.

He became legal adviser to Gus Harris at Drury Lane, and was always much in evidence when the important matter of selecting chorus girls was in progress. He then decided the law was boring and took up full-time journalism instead.

He secured Pot Stephens's job as dramatic critic (The Brickbat) of the *Pink 'Un* in circumstances I relate elsewhere, but soon found a single column was insufficient for his talents. When the proprietor, John Corlett, went away on holiday, Jimmy published an open letter to him in the 'Notes to Queries' column:

'Enjoy your holiday, dear boy. Things are going swimmingly here on the old paper. The man we saw being thrown out of the Criterion has been prevailed upon to write an article explaining how all the members of the Jockey Club pull their horses and, as he has given us names and dates, the article will be a sensation.

'News is scarce, but by calling two Bishops daylight robbers, a Cabinet Minister a liar and listing the heirs to at least eighteen peerages who were not born in wedlock, we hope to cheer up your public and yourself. Don't worry about a thing!'

While the *Pink 'Un* readers found this amusing, Corlett ruefully reflected that the letter wasn't too far from the truth so far as Jimmy's articles were concerned.

Jimmy, who viewed the theatre with a jaundiced eye, took full advantage of the licence old John Corlett gave his eccentric staff. Eventually his special form of criticism under another pseudonym (The Stalled Ox) became too much even for the easy-going Master, who found he was no longer on speaking terms with any of his theatrical friends. While Master didn't mind the odd libel writ, Jimmy's articles were producing too many too fast.

I remember one review which stated that the leading lady could not act, sing or dance, but went on to say she must have had something, or else why should she have been for so long the mistress of a well-known lecherous marquess? It was good ripe stuff, as well as being perfectly true, and helped the circulation figures considerably, but it was too much for Master. He called Jimmy in, gave him the sack and six hundred pounds "to go and start a little hell of your own".

Jimmy promptly founded *Pan,* a society journal, in partnership with Alfred Thompson, an ex-captain of Heavy Dragoons who astonished us all by becoming an excellent dress-designer. *Pan* collapsed in a welter of lawsuits, so Jimmy bought *The Cuckoo* from Edmund Yates and continued to purvey snappy Society gossip. This produced such a brandishing of horsewhips and writs that Jimmy closed it down and cheerfully set about raising the money for yet another periodical, *The Bat,* persuading some of the more irresponsible members of the *Pink 'Un* staff to join him on a part-time basis.

One evening I accompanied Jimmy into his drawing-room which doubled up as *The Bat's* editorial office. We found Shifter, The Pagan and Sir Walter (Willie Goldberg, George Moore and Cecil Raleigh) in the middle of a tremendous argument over a Society paragraph. It so happened that as well as being three of the liveliest journalists in London, they were also undoubtedly the three worst spellers. As Jimmy opened the door, they yelled at him:

"Here, you decide it! How many 't's are there in Duchess?"

The combination of such erratic free spirits and Jimmy's decision to turn his attention to the iniquities, real or imagined, of race-horse owners meant that *The Bat's* existence was as short as its predecessors, and Jimmy had to make a hurried journey to France a couple of hours ahead of a writ for criminal libel from Lord Durham. When that little problem was sorted out, Jimmy came back to start his last paper, *The Phoenix*.

In its turn this also failed, the main creditor being the printer, who found himself out of sympathy with Jimmy's historic dictum :

"What? Pay my printers? Sir, I NEVER pay printers!"

Yet in his own way, he was a brilliant journalist. It was while he was editing *The Bat* that Jimmy pulled off the journalistic coup of the decade. He got wind of something interesting, followed it up, extracted information from people who had sworn never to reveal it – and the world learned of the Tranby Croft scandal and the Prince of Wales's weakness for baccarat.

It was typical of Jimmy that he started his third career to settle a bet. Finding himself in a railway carriage with George Edwardes, whose musical comedies at the Gaiety had been delighting London for years, Jimmy started on his hobby-horse of the poor state of the theatre, how a child could do better, etcetera, etcetera. George Edwardes made the natural reply – if Jimmy felt like that, then why didn't he do something about it? Writing librettos for musical comedies was not as easy as it seemed. If Jimmy thought he could do better, then he, Edwardes, had twenty pounds to say he couldn't.

It was the best bet either ever made, because Edwardes's biggest hit that year was Jimmy's 'The Gaiety Girl', followed by 'An Artist's Model'. Jimmy went on to write half a dozen more shows, including 'Floradora' and 'Sergeant Brue'. I remember the first night of 'Sergeant Brue' with Willie Edouin playing the lead. It went well, and I was pleased to see that the young bank-clerk-turned-writer who used to live near us in Shropshire had written one of the lyrics – I can't remember which one.

'Floradora' made a fortune for Jimmy, although you won't find it credited to him in the reference books. It was about this time that he made himself into a limited company under the name Owen Hall, probably as a legal trick to fob off his creditors. Whatever it was, the name and his permanent state of indebtedness tickled the whole of London, and Owing All was how he was known thereafter. In order to drive home the point that his old creditors would get little from his newly-won theatrical gains, he later registered himself as another company, Payne Nunn Ltd.

Jimmy Davis was a man of many parts. His attitude to life is summed up in the reply he once gave to a startled Inspector of Bankruptcy:

"Trust me? Of course you can trust me – with anything except a pretty girl and a sovereign."

Chapter 28

The Battle of Clayton Square

O NE OF the regulars at Romano's in my time was Charlie Mitchell, the boxer who fought for the world championship half a dozen times, and would have won it if he'd gone into proper training. He was a magnificent fighter, but not good enough to beat the undisputed champion, John L. Sullivan, the Boston Strong Boy. Sullivan dominated the boxing world for ten years, and I was lucky enough to be in the Pelican club the night he fought an exhibition bout before the Prince of Wales.

After his defeat by Corbett, Sullivan left the ring to go on the stage, as did many boxers, and delighted his audiences with the song some American chap wrote about his evening at the Pelican – 'Let me shake the hand that shook the hand of the Prince of Wales'. He toured for years in something called 'Heavy Hearts and Horny Hands' and took himself very seriously as an actor. When the newspapers asked for his comments on the death of Henry Irving, he sighed, shook his head sadly and reflected:

"Hully gee, but it's a great loss. There'll be damn few of us left presently."

Towards the end of his life he became a fervent temperance advocate and had no hesitation in name-dropping to help the cause:

"Boys, let whisky alone. I'm saying this at the request of a friend and admirer of mine who saw me box before the Prince of Wales. The Prince is King Edward of England now, and I mean to see these articles of mine on whisky get into his hands if I have to send them to him myself. Like a good many other men, he will be benefited by them. When I met him I talked affably to him and put him at his ease, and I have no doubt that he will be glad to hear from me after all these years. Boys, remember my words and give whisky the mitt. I thank you for your kind attention."

Of course boxing was illegal in those days; it could take place only in private or on registered club premises. That's why the Pelican boxing matches were so popular. At least we could ensure there was no funny business that you used to get in some places, the ropes being cut or a crowd of toughs suddenly deciding to interfere when they saw their man losing.

I've never known why boxing was banned whereas wrestling was allowed but, whatever the reason, it was the wrestling matches that used to pull in the crowds. To be a successful wrestler, you had to be a foreigner with an exotic name, so they were always billed as The Terrible Turk (there were dozens of these), The Abominable Armenian, The Fearsome Frenchman or The Cruel Crimean.

Yousouf the Terrible Turk, billed as The Sultan's Favourite although he was really a docker from Marseilles, was the first I remember. He was famous for three things; the biggest appetite anyone in London had ever seen, his insistence on being paid in gold sovereigns which he carried in a belt round his waist, and the distasteful fact that he hated washing. This last attribute at least ensured that his admirers did not crowd around him after his matches – they stayed at a respectful distance. Everybody said the weight of gold around his waist would be the death of him one day, and it was. He died by drowning when his ship went down in the Atlantic.

It was about that time that C.B. Cochran appeared on the scene, and since Cockie Cochran is still going strong, there is no need for me to introduce him here. All I will say is that he is the best showman in the country, and I honestly believe he could get ten thousand people to pay to watch tortoises racing if he put his mind to it. William Brady, and perhaps Ziegfeld, are the only fellows I know with the same gift. Whether it's boxing matches, ballet, circuses, shows or concerts, Cochran will pull in the crowds to all of them.

There is no doubt the wrestling craze in Britain from about 1900 to 1914 was all due to Cochran. He became Hackenschmidt's manager in 1901, and made wrestling the thing people wanted to see by keeping Hackenschmidt in the public eye and stage-managing his appearances as though the wrestler was a *prima donna*. When things got slack, he always had a heavy tucked away in the audience to challenge, and then be beaten by, Hackenschmidt. But I believe the secret of Cochran's success is his gift for publicity.

During one series of matches Cochran, having made sure the Press were present, suddenly stopped the fight and announced that Hackenschmidt's opponent had oiled his body, thereby making it difficult to throw him. There was a tremendous fuss, and Cochran made a packet out of the Pear's Soap people by letting the Press photograph him washing down both wrestlers with 'the only soap that really gets you clean'.

When Hackenschmidt left for America, Cochran found a replacement in Zbysco and made him equally famous as 'the most hated man in England'. Since everyone wanted to beat Zbysco, Cochran did even better with him than he had with the popular and likeable Hackenschmidt.

It wasn't all easy money though, even with a wrestler as famous as Hackenschmidt. I was in Liverpool, for the Waterloo Cup I suppose it would have been, when The Battle of Clayton Square took place. Nobody remembers it nowadays so it's worth recounting what happened. I saw it from the inside and, looking back, I think I was lucky to get away with my life.

At that time Cochran and Hackenschmidt were on their uppers. They'd run out of halls in London to fight in, because Hackenschmidt couldn't fake his wrestling and tended to win his matches in about two minutes flat. Since Cochran knew wrestling was popular in Lancashire, he hired the Prince of Wales Theatre in Liverpool for a week and announced a great new event – but he didn't say what it was. Only when he had arrived a couple of nights before the fight, did he put up posters all over Liverpool saying that the giant Hackenschmidt was to fight a series of matches with the local champion Tom Cannon.

Cochran was right to have kept his intentions quiet, because the manager of the theatre had never staged a wrestling match before and was frightened he would lose his licence. So he started off by trying to cancel Cochran's agreement.

Cochran simply ignored this and hired hundreds of men to carry boards all over Liverpool to advertise the fight. The manager, in his turn, hired hundreds of other men to carry boards around the city announcing the fight had been cancelled. All that did was to arouse tremendous publicity, and dozens of private fights when the rival sandwich-board men met each other. In the meantime Cochran had taken over the theatre, and Hackenschmidt and a dozen other toughs were guarding the doors to stop the manager and his fellows getting in.

Cochran seemed to have the situation under control until about three hours before the fight, when the crowds were already at the doors, clamouring to pay double prices to get in. That was when all the lights went off because the manager had cut the gas-pipes.

Cochran solved that problem by sending out messengers for gas-fitters, and persuaded one to mend the pipes with the promise that he could act as time-keeper for the big fight. The chap, protected by a bodyguard organised by Cockie, mended the pipes while Cochran himself made a speech from the balcony outside the theatre to the biggest, angriest crowd I've ever had the misfortune to see. I should add that I'd bumped into Cochran in the Adelphi Hotel, and he'd invited me along for what he said 'should be an interesting evening'!

I finished up beside Cochran on the balcony, trying to protect him from the eggs, oranges, missiles of all sorts coming up from below and wishing I was back at dear old Blandings. The gas came through, the lights went on and the fight went ahead with Hackenschmidt winning easily.

But the manager wasn't finished yet. The next day he went to a solicitor, who found a clause in the contract stating that Cochran and his wrestlers had to be out of the theatre by midnight. After the fight on the second night, the police enforced the clause and escorted us all out. As soon as we were clear of the place, the manager and his team promptly charged in and locked the doors.

Next morning we went down to be met by shouts of defiance from behind barricades. Cochran thought of what Napoleon would do in similar circumstances and did it. He got hold of the local newspaper people, made sure they had good positions from which to watch, then proceeded to storm the building, leading the charge himself.

Hackenschmidt proved extremely handy with a telegraph pole as a battering-ram, and we soon broke down the door and fought our way through to the stage. Then the opposition rallied and we were met by firehoses and a counter-attack force in a foray which ended with Cockie being thrown down a flight of stairs. It was the biggest free-for-all I've ever seen in my life; Hackenschmidt and the rest of the gang against forty or fifty Liverpool stevedores – and no rules!

Cockie and I were right out of our league, but we did have the satisfaction of dealing with the manager, whom we found cowering in his office, telephoning for reinforcements. Cockie chased him round and round the room, eventually managing to stuff his head into his own waste-paper basket, before Hackenschmidt came in to report that he and the rest of the troupe had regained possession.

But it was all for nothing. During the night the manager had not only cut the gas-pipes again, he'd removed all the seats from the theatre as well. Cochran lost the battle but, being Cochran, got what he wanted – publicity. The newspapers splashed The Battle of Clayton Square all over their front pages, every theatre in the North wanted Hackenschmidt at £100 a night, and Cochran went back to London with enough money to start him on the extraordinary career he has pursued ever since.

Chapter 29

Love and Marriage

'Wisest men
Have erred, and by bad women been deceived;
And shall again, pretend they ne'er so wise.'
'Samson Agonistes', John Milton

ALL OF US fall in love at one time or another; some chaps I knew seemed to do it on the first of every month. Even my brother Clarence, who has spent the last thirty years trying to avoid the opposite sex, was once the victim of Cupid's arrow. It never came to anything, just as well as it turned out, but that story cannot be told quite yet.

On the other hand, there were some fellows whose passions could only be described as volcanic. They took young Lochinvar as their model and pursued the girl of their dreams all over the country. They'd fall in love in London, the girl's parents would find out and the next thing you knew, she was on the train back to darkest Yorkshire or Devonshire or wherever the old home happened to be. Of course the chap would follow, but illicit meetings in the country are far more difficult than in London. Some fellows used to rent a cottage nearby and rely on mere propinquity; others took a more positive line and adopted a rude disguise to deceive her parents.

There was an inherent problem with the latter course; sometimes the girl didn't recognise him either. I know a baronet who still bears the scars of a pitchfork administered on the old spot by a Yorkshire landowner who took exception to a complete stranger kissing his daughter in the rose garden. He'd never have found out, if it hadn't been for the girl screaming her head off at this excessive courtesy from a bearded individual bearing no resemblance to the suave *boulevardier* she had admired so much in London.

Some fellows adopted an even more forceful course of action, and broke into the girl's house to press their suit. All very romantic, but there is always one great danger – getting the wrong room! Young Billy Mandeville climbed up a ladder to a window to exchange views with old

General Magnus's youngest girl, and found he'd got the General instead. The old boy chased him round the lawn three times with a bread-knife, and would certainly have got home if he hadn't fallen into the goldfish pond on the fourth circuit.

So it's always worthwhile getting your facts right. Look at Boko Bagshot who was greatly enamoured of a charming girl he'd met at some charity function. He eventually persuaded her to accompany him to the theatre and supper afterwards. Everything went as merry as a marriage bell and there they were, sipping their liqueurs in the Gardenia, when this furious old chap charged in and started calling Boko every name under the sun.

Boko decided to take the chivalrous line and stood there, looking like Sidney Carton in one of his more noble moods:

"Have no fear, sir. I am a man of honour! I shall marry your daughter."

That only made things worse. The old boy grew even more purple in the face and shouted:

"Daughter? Daughter? Damn it, that's my wife."

It quite spoilt the evening for Boko and he didn't look at another girl for at least a fortnight.

Tubby Parsloe had a similar experience with Lord Burper's second wife. He had no idea who she was, till old Burper found them trying to keep each other warm on the terrace during the County Ball. Burper was a big chap, the terrace overlooked a moat, and before Tubby could explain they were merely practising a new dance step, he found himself in six feet of water.

He got his own back though. A month or so later Clarence and I attended the annual dinner of the Loyal Sons of Shropshire, at which old Burper was to speak. As the port came round, the chairman got up to announce that, due to the sudden indisposition of Lord Burper, the Bishop of Shrewsbury would oblige instead. We thought no more about it till we met a jubilant Tubby in Romano's later that night.

From his pocket he produced a small cigar-box in which reposed old Burper's false teeth! Tubby had grabbed them off the basin in the wash-room while Burper had been otherwise engaged, and his only regret was that he hadn't hung around to hear Burper make his speech without them. He was furious when Clarence and I told him the bishop had taken his place.

"What! Copping out for a little thing like that! He ought to be ashamed of himself. If it was left to chaps like him, we'd never have won the Empire. It makes you ashamed of the House of Lords. Well, he doesn't deserve to get them back and he's not going to. I'll pop them at a little place I know in the Edgware Road."

Which is what he did. He got five bob out of the chap once he'd told him where they came from, and we all trooped along to admire them in the window. They had a notice underneath:

Property of the Right Honourable Lord Burper

Munch like a marquess,

Eat like an earl

ONLY £2

Unrepeatable Offer!!!

Sometimes, of course, the thought of marriage never entered into things. Why should it when female society of a sort was readily available?

'Professional' ladies have always been part of Society, even if Society doesn't like to acknowledge the fact. But there is no denying that such ladies have their uses, both practical and educational, if you take my meaning.

Look at Charlie Yarborough (he's the fourth earl) whom I met one day in the Bachelors', back in the early '90s it must have been. He had been a bit of a goer in his time, but he had certainly sobered down after marrying Marcia Conyers. Not surprising really, she was descended from Marlborough and a baroness in her own right, with a hundred and fifty-three quarterings on the old coat of arms, all that sort of thing. By the time I knew Charlie, he had become a bit stuffy and we made only desultory conversation as we walked up Park Lane.

We were crossing South Street, when who should come along in her carriage but Skittles (Catherine Walters) herself. I don't know what age she was then, but she was still a handsome woman, and you could see why she had been the most famous courtesan in London, although I prefer the French phrase *grande horizontale*. She had an annuity of £2000 a year from old Devonshire and lived in style, though her social life was restricted for obvious reasons. (Devonshire became the very pillar of respectability in his later years. He turned down the premiership three times, held just about every other Government post there was but, like Clarence, was far prouder of the prizes his pig won at the Yorkshire Show.)

I got the distinct impression that Charlie didn't want to catch her eye, but that didn't put Skittles off. She leaned forward and shouted cheerfully:

"Hallo, Charlie! How's it going? Three little boys now, I hear. Well done! I told you it was easy once you learned how."

As her carriage began to move off, she added:

"Never mind what the *Pink 'Un's* saying this week. Just make sure that wife of yours doesn't see it. Still, with the ancestors she's got, she's probably heard the facts of life before. Willie Goldberg promised not to put names in, but I'm afraid yours slipped out! Never mind – if anybody asks me, I'll swear blind it was your old dad instead. Can't stop, I'm off to have tea with Mr Gladstone. Bet you never thought you'd see me doing that!"

And off she went, leaving Charlie as red as a beetroot and spluttering to himself. I hadn't seen the *Pink 'Un* that day, but as soon as I did, I realised why Charlie looked so stricken.

Shifter had gone along to South Street to interview Skittles for his series 'Famous Women of Our Time'. She was a bit dubious at first but, when Shifter told her the other ladies included the Princess of Wales (a downright lie, but it opened doors), Mrs Besant, Mrs Gladstone and the like, Skittles had been delighted with the idea. She'd been afraid it would simply be another Lillie Langtry series, with people like Kate Cook, Dolly Tester and Lady Colin Campbell. Anyway, she gave Shifter all he wanted to hear and more.

Shifter claimed it was one of the great interviews of the century. The imbroglio of the Prince of Wales and the Tranby Croft baccarat scandal had nothing on what Skittles told him. The trouble was that revelations of the extremely private habits of Royalty and the House of Lords were too hot, even for the *Pink 'Un*. Although he knew Shifter to be the most irresponsible journalist in London, Master nearly fainted when he saw it.

"Shif," he roared, "you must be mad to think we could print this. I've known for a long time that you were going to be the death of me, but I'm damned if you're going to kill the paper off as well!"

And he tore up the article there and then to be on the safe side. Shifter managed to persuade him to leave one snippet. In the centre of the next *Pink 'Un* front page was a small box with the entry:

'Many London hostesses boast of having the Cabinet to dinner. But can anybody equal the claim of Miss C ... W ... of South Street who is proud of her record of entertaining, in a more personal capacity, the entire House of Lords from A to Z?

When your humble correspondent ventured to query the letters Y and Z, he received the prompt reply: "Yarborough and Zetland, you fool!" '

No wonder Charlie had been so upset. But it didn't do him any harm, rather the reverse in fact. His wife never saw it, everybody at the Bachelors' thought him a hell of a gay dog, and his social life improved no end. Even his wife benefited because an invitation to Marlborough House arrived within the week, and she'd been after that for years.

The Yarborough name has entered the language now. It was Charlie's grandfather, the second earl, who made the famous bet giving odds of a thousand to one against a hand at whist being dealt with no honours in it. It's been called a Yarborough ever since, and they tell me that with this new Bridge craze, you'll hear the term everywhere.

My father and Charlie's had a good deal in common. I remember Father ticking off our local vicar (not the present fellow, but his predecessor Mr Deane) about the parable of the labourers in the vineyard. He said it showed a disgraceful lack of economic sense, and went against every principle of good farming and estate management.

He used to recount, with every sign of approval, what he heard Yarborough say while reading the Lesson at a Christmas Service. Yarborough announced the text, and told the assembled congregation that it was about the shepherds leaving their flocks to go to the stable:

"And I'd just like to say, before reading this Lesson, that if they'd been my shepherds, I'd have sacked them."

A sentiment which my father had seen fit to applaud with a sonorous "Hear! Hear!"

I sometimes think the New Women and the Suffragettes had a point when they claimed there was little difference between matrimony and the other thing. With the first, you set a girl up in a house from which she couldn't escape; with the second, you set her up in a house in St John's Wood from which she could walk out whenever she liked. Why should Society recognise one but not the other? If it's a matter of expense, then some fellows paid a great deal for either option.

I recall a dinner party given by Jimmy Davis's sister, Julia Frankau. She always provided splendid meals and, unusually for the period, coffee and liqueurs were served with the ladies still at table. She also had a remarkable gift for putting people at their ease, so much so that they forgot where they were and came out with some astonishing information.

On this occasion the conversation had turned to a famous, probably the most famous, ex-Royal favourite and her various romantic attachments with people like Hughie Lonsdale and Abington Baird. The question that intrigued the company was – what rewards, financial or otherwise, had the lady received for her favours?

Flushed with brandy and warmed by happy memories, a gallant colonel at the table was able to enlighten us:

"It was three hundred pounds for a couple of hours. But, by Gad, Mrs Frankau, she was worth every penny of it!"

Some fellows spent much more and received much less. There was a marquess I knew who once sent a certain famous 'lady' a necklace for which he'd paid £20,000. She returned it the next day with a charming note, saying she had plenty of necklaces already, so would he please send a cheque instead? He did as she asked and was delighted to receive an invitation to tea as a reward. And two cups of tea was all he got for his money!

Foreign travel seems to have an odd effect on some fellows; they do things they'd never dream of doing in England. It is not too long since a certain Royal equerry was thrown out, without his trousers, from a house of ill repute in Canada for being unable to pay for services rendered. His noble father-in-law, whom I mention elsewhere in this volume, would have shot him if he'd known.

Some people marry for love, some for money and I've known a few who managed to combine both. But sometimes things can go badly wrong, as happened to old Donegall, father of the present Marquess who's become a gossip writer.

Back in 1864 he married a farmer's daughter called Mary Cobb. It didn't work out; she turned to drink and had some other nasty habits. In 1873 she left him for somebody else and went downhill fast. She was regularly arrested for being drunk and disorderly, and always insisted on being charged under her title of Marchioness of Donegall.

The climax came at a workhouse one Christmas, when the Lord Mayor and the Prince of Wales visited the place to see the paupers' Christmas dinner being served. One of the paupers present was the Marchioness who, with a pint of gin inside her, decided to exercise her rights. She lurched up to the platform and tried to push the Lord Mayor out of his chair.

"I am the Marchioness of Donegall," she shouted. "Get out of my way. I take precedence over any vulgar Lord Mayor. I won't have any common City people putting on airs over me!"

In theory, of course, she was absolutely right, but the workhouse staff saw things differently. They succeeded in pulling her away, though not before she had managed to throw a bowl of weak tea at the Lord Mayor, doing the mayoral robes no good at all. Donegall tried to get a divorce, but it didn't go through and he was stuck with her till she died in the East End in 1901.

So that was the end of his first marriage. He was 79 years old, and some years before had been declared bankrupt for over half a million. All he had left was his title, so he decided to use that. In 1902, the readers of *The Daily Telegraph* were surprised to read an advertisement from a nobleman offering to marry any woman who would pay him twenty-five thousand pounds. Violet Twining, an American girl, took him up on his offer and produced an heir for him just after his 81st

---

(1) John, fifth Baron Grantley, was born in 1855 and died in 1943. While his elopement of 1879 scandalised Society, his citing as co-respondent sixty-four years later attracted incredulous admiration. The Judge infuriated Lord Grantley by adjourning the proceedings to consider whether the grounds given in the action could be admitted at the age of eighty-seven. "You'd think," he growled, "the fellah was implying I was past it."

The decree was granted, much to Lord Grantley's satisfaction. *Ed.*

birthday!

Happy marriages can stem from extraordinary beginnings. Look at Lord Grantley, whose cousin and heir brought along his new bride to be introduced to Grantley as head of the family. They arrived at one o'clock; at four o'clock the bride eloped with Grantley to the Greek Islands. The cousin eventually divorced her and she and Grantley married just in time to celebrate the birth of their first child five days later. That was cutting things a bit fine. [1]

Some women seem to devote their affections to their household pets rather than their husbands. When in America I was invited to stay at Newport, and there was one old lady, a Vanderbilt I think she was, who had a pet pig which she took for daily drives in her carriage. But at least pigs have a useful function; it is a predilection for reptiles that I cannot understand.

I've already mentioned Connie Stewart-Richardson, the Countess of Cromartie's sister, who scandalised London with her Greek dancing, whirling about the Palace Theatre stage wearing very little but a wisp of muslin. Her weakness was for snakes, which accompanied her everywhere, even on country-house visits. It wouldn't have been so bad if she'd kept them in their cages or whatever they lived in, but she insisted on their being let out for exercise.

The result was that you never knew when you weren't going to find a reptile sharing your bath or curling up in your bed. Daisy Warwick found one under her pillow one morning, and subsequent investigation revealed it had been there all night. She was a lady of considerable fortitude and determination, but snakes were too much for her and she left the house before breakfast.

Snakes tend to affect people that way. In his bachelor days Legs Ponderby fell madly in love with a girl who did a snake act on the halls. Legs was terrified of them but, despite his protests, the girl insisted on bringing the troupe with her when they met for supper after the show. One night the inevitable happened. A small boa-constrictor escaped from its basket and poked its head up over the side of the table, just as Legs was telling the girl how much he loved her. Legs lost his nerve completely, threw his glass at it and then tried to finish it off with a French stick. The girl was horrified at what she called his unfeeling cruelty to a dumb animal and never spoke to him again.

As I've said elsewhere, I've seen a lot of girls from the stage marry into the aristocracy, and I reckon the aristocracy was lucky to get them. (I wanted to marry one myself but my family put the kibosh on it.) Some people think chorus-girls are just empty-headed blondes with good looks and nothing else, but most of the ones I knew were far cleverer than the men they married. Look at Val Rhys of the Holborn Casino, who married into the brewery business, took it over after her husband died and ran it better than he ever had.

She was one of the few people who ever got the better of Whistler. He did two portraits of her – 'Arrangement in Black and White' and 'Pink and Grey' – which were a great success and Whistler asked her to sit for a third.

Whether he was ill or just thought she wasn't worth being polite to, I don't know, but, as the sittings went on, he became more and more impertinent. One day she'd had enough:

"See here, Jimmy Whistler! Keep a civil tongue in that head of yours, or I'll get someone in to *finish* those portraits of yours!"

She couldn't have said anything more calculated to infuriate him and marched out in triumph, leaving Whistler gibbering with rage.

One of the wittiest women I know is Hazel Lavery, wife of John Lavery, the painter. She's a beautiful woman and her husband's portrait of her has been a feature of the Summer Exhibition for years; it's her face you see on Irish banknotes and stamps.

She told us the following story when they came to dinner at Norfolk Street. Clarence and I thought it was very funny, but it did not amuse those of our sisters who were present.

Shortly after Lavery was knighted she was invited to a reception at Londonderry House, and was a little nervous because it was the first time she had gone anywhere as Lady Lavery. She gave her name to the footman at the door and that was all right. But as she got to the top of the grand staircase to greet her hostess she became even more nervous, and when the steward asked her name again she lost her voice and had to whisper "Lady Lavery".

Upon which he bowed, lowered his voice in response and whispered:

"At the bottom of the staircase, madam, and through the baize door on the left."

She was delighted to answer to 'Lady Lavatory' from then on.

I've heard many reasons for entering into the blessed state of matrimony, but the oddest was that given by Frank Otter, seemingly a confirmed bachelor. He spoke with a slow drawl, was a keen gambler and huntsman and followed a strict and impressive daily regime. He was woken every morning with half a bottle of champagne; for breakfast he had another half bottle, and a full bottle at lunch. Around half past four he enjoyed another half bottle, had a bottle for dinner and another half bottle in the Empire in the evening. After sticking to the routine like glue for years, he amazed us all by suddenly getting married. We were all terribly curious because he seemed the last chap to fall victim to the divine passion. What had happened? He just said:

"Well, it was a horrible wet and miserable day and we had nothing to do, so we thought we had better get married."

I think the girl must have given him ambition or something, because the next thing we heard he had gone out to the Balkans to report on the conflict there as war correspondent for the *Pink 'Un*. He turned up at Sarajevo wearing a fez on top of correct morning dress, carrying a large umbrella in one hand and a box of cigars in the other. The Austrian general in charge had never heard of the *Pink 'Un* and was a bit suspicious at first, but Frank soon reassured him:

"The *Pink 'Un* is the leading British military journal. It takes its name from the colour of the jackets worn by the British Army!"

The general was terribly impressed by this, chucked the *Times* correspondent out of the special office he'd been given and installed Frank there instead.

I have made little mention of the marital or extra-marital adventures of the Threepwood family, mainly because we haven't had many. Apart from Daredevil Dick Threepwood, who married an actress back in the early part of the last century, we have been a pretty unromantic lot. But some of our in-laws had their moments. Look at my brother-in-law, Major General Sir Miles Fish, CVO, late of the Grenadier Guards.

Marriage to my sister Julia slowed him down considerably but, when I first met him, Fishy Fish was as bright a young man about Town as you could wish to meet; no Pelican club gathering or race-meeting was complete without his presence.

After an enjoyable and alcoholic lunch in Romano's in the summer of '97, he took it into his head that the perfect camouflage for the British

Army was not khaki but sky blue. To prove the point he insisted on cycling down Piccadilly in his underwear, which happened to be that particular shade. He made it down to Hyde Park all right, but we had to take forcible measures to prevent him continuing his journey to the War Office in order to tell them all about it.

He was a pleasure to have around the place when there was any gambling or heavy drinking to be done, but he had one problem; he was extremely shy of girls. Nothing wrong with that, but it certainly looked as if the name of Fish wasn't going to continue if it was left to him! However, an incident on New Year's Eve in '02 changed all that.

Although Fishy reacted perfectly normally to beer or spirits, port had an extraordinary effect on him. For some reason it aroused his martial spirit, and he became convinced that he was surrounded by Boers or some other enemy whom it was his duty to confront. It was a habit that used to cause a bit of bother at country-house parties, I recall, but they soon learned either to lock the gun-room before dinner, or give him brandy instead.

I was in Stiffy Halliday's flat having a nightcap when we heard Fishy come in and stumble upstairs to his flat above. It was clear he was in a bad way, so we went up to settle him down, arriving just in time to see him shoot the coal-bucket with the fire-tongs, under the impression it was a mad dog. We did our best to convince him he'd killed it, but Fishy was in fighting mood, and started buckling on his sword preparatory to fighting some other phantom battle.

Since it was clear that we were going to get no sleep that night unless we took firm measures, firm measures are what we took. We got him on the bed, stripped him and tied him down. His braces held one arm, his sword belt served for the other and his trousers and shirt sufficed for his legs. He looked like a plucked turkey but at least he was immobilised, so we went to bed.

The following morning Stiffy and I were having our hair of the dog when we heard his landlady go upstairs. (She was a pleasant enough woman, quite a good-looker in a mature way, but Stiffy had always found her very stand-offish.) We didn't think anything of it till we heard her try Fishy's door. Then we remembered how we'd left Fishy, stark naked and trussed to his bed, and we looked at each other in wild surmise. We heard a slight scream, followed by a silence that seemed to go on forever, then we heard the sound of the door being locked.

And that was that till, half an hour later, we heard her unlock the door and come downstairs again. Fishy never told us what had happened but, from that day on, he was a changed man. He joined the rest of us at our regular gatherings outside the stage-door of the Gaiety, became a keen admirer of the Alhambra ballet and proposed to my sister Julia within the year. An odd way to gain a brother-in-law, I've always thought.

Chapter 30

Some Men of My Time – 6
George Edwardes and G.P. Huntley

WE ALL look back at our youth through rose-coloured spectacles, but I would still argue that the turn of the century was the Golden Age of the London theatre. We had Irving at the Lyceum, Augustus Harris at Drury Lane and we had George Edwardes at the Gaiety. Irving got the first theatrical knighthood, Harris produced the most spectacular shows London had ever seen but, if someone talked about The Guv'nor, you knew they meant George Edwardes of the Gaiety.

George Edwardes came into the theatre by accident. He had tried business and the law before his cousin, Michael Gunn, constrained by family duty rather than anything else, put him in charge of the box-office at the Opéra Comique. It was a small beginning for a man who was eventually to have 3000 people on his salary list.

In 1896 Edwardes joined Hollingshead at the Gaiety to produce 'Little Jack Sheppard', acquired sole interest in the theatre soon afterwards, put on 'Dorothy' and went on to success after success.

At one stage he even got the religious lot going to the Gaiety. Realising that chapel-goers normally shunned theatres and music-halls, he decided to tempt them with religious masques, illustrating stories from the Bible in *tableau* form.

Although Edwardes lost some of his regular audience (one millionaire who booked his box at the Gaiety by the year was very annoyed), he did rather well out of it. Clergymen brought along their congregations, the bar started making a profit on lemonade and tea, normally very poor sellers, and families came to marvel at such *tableaux* as Rebecca in the Cornfield, Joseph and his Brethren and The Soul's Awakening. A particular favourite was the Rock of Ages, a girl clinging to a big stone cross in the waves (Edwardes was very proud of the wave-machine) while the rest of the Gaiety company sang hymns off-stage.

Unfortunately the news got out that the bashful, spiritual maidens the chapel-goers admired so much were really the famous stage beauties Constance Collier, Poppie Harris and Agatha Roze and ticket sales fell dramatically.

Edwardes made the Gaiety famous across the country by picking beautiful girls for his shows and leaving the rest to Nature. Starting with Belle Bilton hitching up with Lord Dunlo, and Connie Gilchrist becoming the Countess of Orkney, I've seen a couple of dozen chorus girls marry into the peerage. And most of them fit the part to the manner born.

Look at Julia Mannering-Phipps, who used to wear tights and knock them cold at the Tivoli with her rendition of 'Rumpty-tiddley-umpty-ay'. She married Mannering-Phipps, settled down to queen it in county society and did it very well too; no one could freeze you better with a single glare through her lorgnettes. But blood will out. Although her husband left her comparatively wealthy, I hear she's going back to join her son in vaudeville.

There is no doubt that by allowing their gentlemen friends to take certain liberties, some of the girls in 'thinking' parts did very well for themselves. For the benefit of the younger generation, I should add that a 'thinking' part at the Gaiety meant that your main task was to come on stage, walk languidly across it and stand there looking beautiful.

I was at a dinner party one night, at Solly Joel's I think it was, where there happened to be quite a few theatrical ladies present. One of them, who had adorned the Shakespearian stage for years, was wearing a splendid pearl necklace. During a pause in the conversation, the fellow on her right turned to her and admired it. She had obviously had a good look at the other actresses around the table and didn't think much of them, because she replied in the ringing tones for which she was renowned:

"Yes, I am proud of this necklace, very proud. It was given to me by the ladies of England" – with tremendous emphasis, unmistakeable in its significance – "for being the most moral woman on the English stage!"

There was silence while the company digested this remark. It was broken by Hughie Drummond, who was sitting next to a beautiful and notoriously warm-hearted Gaiety Girl wearing a superb diamond necklace that outshone the other as the sun outshines the moon.

"That is a beautiful necklace you are wearing," said Hughie. "You must be very proud of it."

She took her cue right away. "Yes, I am. Very proud. It was given to me by an English gentleman for being the most beautiful – and the least hypocritical – woman on the English stage!"

I was in the Savage Club the other day talking to Herman Finck, who has been composing and directing the orchestra at the Palace Theatre for longer than I care to remember. We were having a drink to the memory of G.P. Huntley, who rivalled George Grossmith in portraying knuts, dudes and mashers on stage.

Grossmith is in management at the Winter Garden now, but still turns in an excellent performance in silly ass parts. Huntley used to play the same sort of thing – if someone dashed on stage waving a tennis racket and shouting "Hullo, girls! Anyone for tennis?" then you could be sure it was Huntley. Nowadays it's probably young Catsmeat Potter-Pirbright, or Claude Hulbert who's playing the Duke of Datchet in 'Oh Kay!' as I write.

Finck reminded me of the catch-phrase 'Yip-i-addy-i-ay' that Grossmith had made so popular, and wondered how long such things lasted. Would people still use them in fifty years' time? As he said, neither of us had heard 'Teuf, teuf!' since the War but, from about 1905 till 1914, everybody in our crowd used it to say goodbye.

In the interests of posterity, I should add that 'teuf-teuf-teuf' was the sound early motor cars made. So, if you had a motor car, you indicated your intention to leave by saying you would have to 'teuf-teuf' away. Funny how something like that can just vanish from the language.

Apropos of this, I mentioned the phrase Huntley had made fashionable: 'I knew it! I knew it!'. Finck smiled and told me Huntley had never intended to say it at all; it was a sheer accident which came about like this.

Unlike most of the actors I know, Huntley didn't drink much; enough to be sociable, but no more, seemed to be his rule. It transpired that this was because he'd never found a drink that he really liked. Finck had discovered this unusual fact in the Café Royal one day when he saw Huntley sitting at a table with the wine list in front of him and a gloomy expression on his face. Finck asked what the trouble was and Huntley had screwed his monocle a bit tighter into his eye:

"I have in front of me this huge volume entitled 'Café Royal Wine List'. Well, old thing, what on earth am I to choose?"

Finck, who had lunched very well himself, thought about this for a bit and offered the humorous suggestion that Huntley should tackle it methodically; start at the beginning of the wine list and work his way to the end. He was never so surprised in his life when Huntley said it was a splendid idea, and he would start there and then with number one! He was sure Huntley was pulling his leg, but no – he called the waiter and ordered a bottle of the house pale sherry and Finck left, still wondering whether Huntley was spoofing him or not.

A few weeks later he was lunching there again, and Huntley called him over to say he was up to No 42 or 43, somewhere amongst the burgundies. Huntley still hadn't found anything that he really liked, though some of the old champagnes had been quite enjoyable. Finck tried to tell him it had been a joke, but Huntley waved him aside. It was an excellent idea; he was only sorry he hadn't thought of it himself.

I expressed incredulity but Finck swore it was perfectly true. He tried to keep an eye on Huntley's progress, but it wasn't till some months later he realised the danger.

He was lunching with some of the livelier element, and it wasn't till they were having coffee that he remembered Huntley. There was no sign of him, so Finck sent for old Freguglia and asked if Huntley had been in. Apparently he had and, to the great surprise and admiration of the staff, he had managed to walk out of the restaurant unaided!

Finck asked what he meant and Freguglia told him that Huntley's progress through the wine list had now reached the liqueurs.

"What's wrong with that?" asked Finck. "Nothing wrong with a glass of liqueur with your lunch."

"Nothing whatsoever," replied Freguglia, "but Mr Huntley always orders a bottle – and today was no exception."

This was a bit of a facer for Finck, who was beginning to regret his little joke more than ever.

"What did he drink today, then?" he asked, and Freguglia gave the answer he most feared.

"Today, sir, with his soup, Dover sole, steak and fruit, Mr Huntley consumed an entire bottle of absinthe! May I suggest that as a friend of his, you keep an eye on him."

Well, Finck dashed around everywhere, the theatre, Huntley's flat, but there was no sign of him. (It later transpired that he'd spent the afternoon flat on his back at his club.) As curtain-up time approached, the theatre people were getting worried, the stand-in was told to get ready and poor old Finck was wishing he'd never opened his mouth.

Just as the show was about to begin, Huntley rolled up, pale but perfectly lucid, went to his dressing-room, changed and came on stage on cue. Everybody breathed a sigh of relief – for the first five minutes. Huntley was giving an excellent performance, but said everything twice!

"Why he wasn't booed off the stage, I shall never know," said Finck. "It was chaos. Luckily somebody started laughing, thinking he was doing it as a gag and the more he did it, the more everybody laughed. The rest of the cast went through hell, but the audience loved it. And when he came to the line 'I knew it!', he rolled it out twice and it caught on right away."

"And that," concluded Finck, "was how I introduced a catch-phrase into the language."

And we raised our glasses to the memory of Huntley.

Chapter 31

Tubby Parsloe and the Prawns

*An incident in the early life of Sir Gregory Parsloe-Parsloe
of Matchingham Hall, Shropshire*

ALTHOUGH many of us in the Pelican were often in straitened circumstances, we were in them together. If anyone had some oof to help out, we shared it around; assuming, of course, there was enough to share around.

While fellows like Shifter and Fatty Coleman were noted for their scrounging, Tubby Parsloe outshone them all; when he entered the club, strong men shuddered and hid their wallets. Even Fatty Coleman restricted his activities to a weekly touch and a regular tariff. Once you'd persuaded Fatty that five bob was your limit, he left it at that. But young Tubby Parsloe was different. No matter how little you had, he would try and screw it out of you. His was a simple creed – what was yours ought to be his.

Pitcher Binstead said once: "You've got to admire Tubby Parsloe. He seems able to sense exactly how much you've got in your pocket and he'll go to any lengths to get it into his." But then, Pitcher always took an indulgent view of his fellow men.

After the fiasco of the ratting match between my dog Towser and his Banjo, Tubby dropped out of circulation for a time. It wasn't till later that we heard the reason for his unlamented absence. He received an allowance from his father, but it wasn't enough and he employed a variety of methods to remedy the deficiency, including trying to pay for a bottle of champagne in the Café de l'Europe by raffling his trousers, a feat for which he was promptly chucked out on his ear by an indignant management.

Tubby suddenly realised the advantages of having a dean for a father. Apart from an archbishop or duke, a dean is about the best reference a shopkeeper could look for, especially as some dukes were going through a rough patch then. Even the Marlboroughs were feeling the pinch; the 7th duke left only a few thousand quid, and that was after he'd sold off his library, the Marlborough gems and quite a lot of land.

When Kim Mandeville, the present Duke of Manchester, came into the title, he grumbled that his credit was as bad as ever.

"Here I am with a ruddy title going back hundreds of years, two country seats where the blasted Trustees won't let me sell a single tree and I can't raise a penny anywhere in London. Being a duke nowadays isn't worth the candle."

His father had gone bankrupt with tremendous publicity years before, and only got himself straight by marrying an American heiress. It was clear that things weren't much better for Kim, so I suggested that the ducal coronet should be good for something.

"It was the first thing I thought of, Gally. I went along to Garrards last week to sound them out on the going rate and d'you know what they said? They were glad I'd raised the matter, because they had been going to write to me anyway. My father raised a monkey on it with them fifteen years ago and, if I wanted it back, an early settlement would oblige. I knew the old man had been a bit strapped, but what sort of father deprives his son of the ruddy ducal coronet!"

So, compared to some of the dukes we had around, Tubby's father was a very good bet and Tubby decided to cash in. He started buying things on his father's account from the shops the Dean used. Just small stuff at first, a shirt here, some socks there, and the Dean paid the bills like a lamb. But then Tubby got greedy and started buying whisky from Fortnum's wholesale. His orders must have raised one or two eyebrows at the drinking habits of senior Church dignitaries, but they let him have the stuff and the bills went off to the Deanery.

That put the cat among the pigeons. The Dean may have been absent-minded, but even he knew he hadn't ordered a case of champagne for a young lady at the Gaiety Theatre. Tubby was summoned home, given a tremendous decanal dressing-down and sent into exile. His allowance was stopped and digs were found for him at Shepperton on the river. He got his room, two meals a day and that was all; anything else he had to earn himself. I imagine the Dean thought this would be the making of Tubby, but he clearly didn't know his pride and joy very well.

In between scrounging drinks off strangers in the Shepperton pubs and running up bills in the local shops, Tubby taught his dog Banjo to do tricks. Walking on its hind legs, dying for the Queen, the usual things, but Banjo was a clever little dog, far too good for Tubby, and learned them all quickly.

Tubby used to hang around the river-bank by the hotel, waiting for a steam launch to arrive for lunch, then he'd send Banjo out to start doing his tricks. Of course the people would say what a clever dog he was and start making a fuss of him. At the psychological moment, Tubby would appear and say he hoped his little dog wasn't annoying them or getting in the way, etc. The next thing they knew, they were in the hotel with Tubby in their midst, graciously thanking them for an offer of lunch they couldn't recall having made, and telling the waiter to make sure the hock was properly cooled.

He never missed a trick, did Tubby Parsloe. But he made the mistake of so many greedy men – he went *too far*.

One day Bill Lister, a journalist pal of mine, invited me to a trip on the river. He had just got engaged to a charming girl who did a Strong Woman act on the halls and wanted me to make up a four. I saw myself escorting his future mother-in-law all day, but Blister assured me the girl's sister would be acting as chaperone. The sister was even prettier than Blister's girl, and when I discovered their father was a bookmaker with the excellent habit of confiding inside information to his family, things became quite enjoyable.

We rowed up to Shepperton and Blister and I went to see about lunch. When we came out, there was Tubby mashing the girls. His face fell for a moment, then he saw the way out and was all over us. Two old friends! How splendid! At last he was able to congratulate Blister on his engagement to a charming girl of whom he'd heard so much, and so on and so forth. After that there wasn't much we could do without a fuss in front of the girls, so we had to go in and watch Tubby filling himself at our expense.

We were a bit annoyed, but Tubby hadn't finished yet. He told us he had an important engagement in town, an interview for a job he said, and scrounged the fare off me, promising to pay it back the next day at the Two Goslings pub off the Haymarket.

He duly turned up, much to my surprise, and suggested a little sporting diversion before getting down to business. He pulled out a thing shaped like a top, with the words PUT on one side and TAKE on the other, and explained that you spun the thing and if it finished with PUT on top, you put your money on the table. If it said TAKE, you picked up what was on the table and so on. When he suggested we should try it at half-a-crown a go, I saw the chance to get my own back. I should have known better. In five minutes flat I was a tenner down the hole and Tubby picked the thing up and said he'd have to be going.

I told Blister about it in the Pelican that night, and he confirmed my suspicions that there was dirty work at the crossroads. Apparently the gadgets were taking the place of the three-card trick; some had been fixed so that a twist of the stem made the thing always come down with TAKE showing – and Tubby had clearly got hold of one. To add insult to injury, Blister's girl told us Tubby had persuaded her to pass on her father's confidential advice regarding Bounding Bertie, a long-priced cert at Sandown Park which duly came in at 14-1.

"Tubby Parsloe has gone too far," declared Blister, "and must be taught the lesson of a lifetime. We must do something that he will never forget; something that will make him wake up in the middle of the night and wince for the rest of his life.

"Do you remember what Tubby told the girls at lunch? They were saying how nice it was by the river, and he said the two things he was terrified of were water and crawly things inside his clothes. If I can't work something out from that, my name isn't William Lemuel Lister."

Apart from telling everybody of Tubby's black-hearted chicanery and warning them off his PUT and TAKE gadget, I didn't see what more we could do, but Blister was determined to wreak revenge, as I learned when I met him at Ascot the day Martingale won the Gold Cup.

"Gally," he said, "it's all arranged. It's Henley next week. Make sure you're in the Stewards' Enclosure on Friday; you'll find it well worthwhile. Tubby Parsloe is going to get the lesson he so richly deserves."

The following Friday saw Stiffy Halliday, Buffy Struggles, Hughie Drummond and myself down at Henley, sporting our best bib-and-tucker and bursting with curiosity to see what Blister would do.

I hadn't been to Henley for a couple of years, not since my natural history lesson there from a charming girl, but there were plenty of people I knew. I passed the time of day with Dickie Dunn, who told me that a couple of Stewards had tried to warn him off the towpath where he was plying his trade. He told them he'd be delighted to do so if they would care to settle their own little accounts which had somehow been overlooked from the last Newmarket Meeting. And what with meeting old pals and the excitement of the arrival of the Prince of Wales in the Enclosure, I almost forgot Blister's scheme.

It was just before the last race that it happened. In those days the river used to be crowded with young fellows and their girls in punts. Everybody knew the Prince had arrived, so the bank in front of the Enclosure was five deep with punts and boats, full of people hoping to see him. It was quite a sight, all the men in their blazers and whites, and the girls looking charming in the Dolly Varden hats and parasols that were all the rage that year.

Suddenly Hughie Drummond appeared and grabbed my arm: "Gally, look over there."

On the far bank I saw Blister getting into a punt, with Tubby gingerly climbing in after him. As I watched, Tubby sat down hurriedly and turned round to help two girls whom I recognised as Blister's *fiancée* and her sister. Then it happened! Blister's girl, the Strong Woman, grabbed Tubby's arms and held them behind his back while her sister reached forward, pulled open Tubby's shirt and tipped a jug of something down his chest. As the girls jumped back, Blister heaved on the pole and he and Tubby were out on the river, heading straight towards us.

Hughie and I stared at each other and then back at the punt. We saw Tubby look down inside his shirt, then leap to his feet and begin to tear his clothes off.

It was a hot day and he was in flannels, so it took him only a few seconds to get down to his trousers. All this, mark you, in the middle of the river in front of thousands of people on whom a sudden hush had fallen.

The silence was broken by a tremendous shout from Dickie Dunn on the bridge: "I'll lay 3-1 on the Henley Pink 'Un!"

There was a roar of laughter from every man in the crowd, drowning out the screams of the girls who hid behind their parasols, though I did notice that most of them peeped out from underneath to see what was going on.

Blister timed it perfectly. He crashed into the line of punts below the

Enclosure just as Tubby got his drawers off. Tubby was thrown forward on his face, staggered to his feet, and stood there stark naked with the whole of Henley staring at him. He looked round wildly and saw sanctuary ahead. Dressed in nothing but his socks, he sprinted straight up the bank to the shelter of the Stewards' tent. How he made it, I don't know; I think everybody was laughing too much to stop him.

Hughie and I dashed in behind him to see what happened next. It was all we could have hoped for.

As Tubby charged in, he must have seen the cloths on the lunch-tables. He wrenched one off, whipped it round him and turned to see who else was there. At the sight of the group of men in the corner, his jaw dropped, then he whirled round and vanished under the tent-flap at the back. There was a moment's silence before the Prince's unmistakeable voice rang out:

"Gentlemen, was the fellow who just paid us a brief visit really as naked as he appeared to be?"

Hughie and I didn't wait for the answer. We quietly withdrew, leaving the Stewards to deal with the matter as they thought best.

That night Blister and his girl were guests of honour at Romano's. He told us of the invitation to a day at Henley, eagerly accepted by Tubby, and the vital importance of timing. The jug emptied inside Tubby's shirt had contained a couple of dozen live prawns, calculated to disturb anybody's equanimity, let alone Tubby's who, it will be remembered, couldn't stand wriggly things inside his clothes.

Blister refused to take credit for the part played by the heir to the Throne: "I had no idea the Prince would be there. Clearly Providence takes the same view of Tubby Parsloe as we do."

Nobody saw Tubby for a couple of months, till he wandered into the club one night with a defiant look on his face as though daring somebody to start something. We knew he'd have to come back some time, so we had worked it all out. Nobody said a word out of place; people engaged him in conversation and we watched him slowly relax.

At last Pitcher decided the time was ripe and nodded to Swears. A couple of minutes later, the club page-boy came through the door with a basket in his hand and marched up to Tubby.

"Mr Parsloe, sir?"

Tubby looked around. Everybody had stopped talking, every eye was on him. He knew something was up but there was nothing he could do.

"Yes, my name's Parsloe."

The page held the basket out and repeated the words Swears had coached him in so carefully.

"Message from Marlborough House, sir, from 'Is Royal Highness. There's a couple of quarts of best fresh prawns in 'ere with the Prince's compliments and 'e says - 'Next time, will you please be good enough to make sure they're cooked before you deliver them!' "

There was a shout of laughter round the room as Tubby grabbed the basket, threw it at Swears and stormed out. We didn't see him again that year, probably because I sent him a menu of a club dinner with one course heavily underlined:

'Fresh prawns (hereinafter to be called Henley Pink 'Uns)'.

My sister Constance is puzzled at my insistence that we serve prawns whenever Tubby comes to dinner at Blandings. I told her they are his favourite dish and she hasn't yet queried this unusual solicitude on my part. The expression on his face is a delight to see. With men like Tubby Parsloe, it is a pleasure and a privilege to keep old memories alive.

Chapter 32

Some Men of My Time – 7
The Immortal Shifter

William Farn Goldberg

B Y FAR and away the most popular section of the *Pink 'Un* was the 'Notes and Queries' column written by Office Boy, otherwise known as William Farn Goldberg – the Shifter. The weekly account of his trials and tribulations at the hands of bookmakers and head waiters who wouldn't give credit, together with his sardonic comments on topics of the day, were enjoyed by an enthusiastic readership stretching from St James's Palace to the tea plantations of Ceylon.

Shifter, a prizeman of Lincoln College, Oxford, took his degree, to the slight surprise of those who knew him, and began his career in the dreadful trade of private tutor. His employer was a widow anxious to ensure her eighteen-year-old pride and joy was warned against the world and its evils before going up to the University.

On Shifter's first morning she crept up to the study door behind which he was instructing the young hopeful. Shifter always maintained he was only passing on the maxims essential for any young man about to enter Society. I set some of them out here without comment:

1. Never dodge a tradesman to whom you owe money. Keep going back to him and if he cuts up rough, threaten him by saying you'll go bankrupt and he won't get a penny.

2. Never go into bankruptcy without making sure you have sizeable assets on paper. For a fiver you can pick up worthless Stock Exchange shares with a nominal value of three hundred quid or more. With those in your pocket you can always claim that your financial embarrassment is temporary.

3. Never dodge a friend to whom you owe money. On the contrary, whenever you see him, dash up to him, grab him by both hands and weep over his kindness to you. After you have done this a few times, he will get so sick of it, he will run a mile whenever he sees you coming.

4. Never take a small knock with a bookmaker. To owe one of them a tenner is as bad as owing ten thousand. Wait till you can bet on credit with the big bookies in the club enclosures; at least they'll come after their money with a better class of plug-ugly than the lesser fry. Meanwhile, keep betting in ready money on a very small scale.

5. Never let yourself be seen shabbily dressed; it's the biggest mistake in the world! A shabby man may get the odd loan out of pity, a well-dressed man can make it seem as though he's doing the lender a favour.

6. Never listen to what your elderly relatives say; they have probably been wrong 'uns themselves in their time. Now they can't enjoy themselves any more, they want to make sure you don't.

It was at this point that a distraught mother burst into the room to inform a bewildered Shifter that his services were no longer required. Still, as he said, a month's pay in lieu of notice came in very welcome.

He came to the *Pink 'Un* from a lucrative billet at the Foreign Office. I don't know how long it lasted, but Shifter told me that, like Jimmy Davis, he felt the golden days of youth were not granted to us to be spent in a dark office, with nothing but dull papers on the trade figures of Lower Mongolia to feed the bold free spirit that animates us all. It was soon after he reached this conclusion that Fate brought together John Corlett, the proprietor of the *Pink 'Un*, and his most famous contributor.

By the time Shifter's third or fourth column appeared, he was famous throughout the country. His wit, philosophy and outlook on life were all his own, and the weekly account of the tribulations undergone by Shifter and Peter Blobbs (Shirley Brooks) were the talk of London and the British Empire.

Shifter's smartness of dress used to puzzle those of us aware of his straitened circumstances. Enlightenment came with his invariable reply to all queries as to the cost of his latest frock-coat:

"I don't know. They haven't issued the writ yet."

But even Shifter's standards lapsed occasionally. When Shiny Bill, an admirer who ran a hotel in Margate, invited him down to lunch, a dozen or so faithful readers came along to meet their hero. Whatever they expected, it was not a small man with a long nose and two days' growth of beard, who carried with some awkwardness a very shabby portmanteau, three disreputable hats, a billiard cue, a large haddock in a basket, two dormice in a cage and a tame squirrel in his breast-pocket.

Shifter once found himself involved in an argument concerning the exact date of the Bishop of Hereford's Betting Bill. In an attempt to settle the'matter, he wrote the bishop a most civil letter beginning:

'In order to settle a bet, will your lordship kindly state ...' and the readers of the following week's *Pink 'Un* read of his disappointment at the heartlessness and lack of sporting spirit of the Bishop in not replying.

Just about all the *Pink 'Un* staff tried their hand at dramatic criticism at one time or another, and Shifter didn't want to be left out. As he said:

"A dramatic critic is given the best seats and in these hard times, every little bit helps. Besides, if I make a go of it, they'll start giving me free passes and you can swap those for a bottle of the best in most places."

Eventually he persuaded Master to let him review Gus Harris's new show 'Pleasure', and was highly indignant when even the indulgent John Corlett refused to publish the result. Shifter's piece began:

' 'Pleasure', the new autumn drama at Drury Lane is claimed by Augustus Harris to be taken straight from life. It is. The first act starts well, with the beautiful and virtuous heroine clearly in the family way. This is about as near real life as you can get ...'

But normally his upper lip was the stiffest in London. On one of the occasions when the writs caught up with him, I was in the rescue party which managed to raise the thirty-odd quid to secure his release from durance vile. Despite his grim surroundings and the imminent prospect of prison, we found Shifter as cheerful as ever in the bailiff's office. He was busy on a snappy article, which duly appeared in the next edition of the *Pink 'Un*, dealing with the amorous adventures of the tipstaff's cat.

Apart from Swears Wells, I never knew anybody so ingenious in his attempts to raise money. Few of them ever worked, but his exploits in this direction always gave us something to talk about over the bar at Romano's and the Pelican. One of his most notable feats resulted in his being banned by the Jockey Club. Their official statement said it was because he hadn't paid the entrance fee for a horse to race at Alexandra Park. Well, anybody could make a mistake like that, and lots of my chums did. What kept Shifter's name on the Forfeit List so long was that the horse in question was one Shifter had never seen, which he had bought for nothing from a man to whom it didn't belong, and which was stolen from the paddock while Shifter and Pitcher Binstead were trying to persuade a jockey to ride it on a sale or return basis, i.e. no win, no fee!

Until Legs Ponderby won the title of the Pelican Club's biggest liar, an event I recount elsewhere, the honour was held by Shifter Goldberg, who achieved it at a lunch at the Tower of London. With tremendous sincerity, coupled with apparently limitless historical knowledge and the purported ability to read ancient Hebrew scrolls, he convinced three Aldermen, their ladies, the City Marshal, the Captain of the Queen's Guard and assorted Guards officers that the Bloody Tower was so named because it was the site of the famous massacre by King Herod of the Babes in the Wood!

Chapter 33

Clubs

'The lower classes live in pubs,
The upper classes die in clubs.'

WHEN people ask me about the clubs I have known, I always think of the retired judge I met on the steps of his club in St James's. Looking back at the building he had just left, he said;

"Forty years ago, when they elected me, I was the only bounder in the place. Now it's simply full of them."

In my experience clubs that have no bounders amongst their members are pretty dull places; all you have to do is look at the Athenaeum, the Reform or the Carlton. I was talking just the other day to a chap who's been a member of the Reform for forty years, and he told me he couldn't remember a single instance of disorderly behaviour. What sort of club is that?

I've been a member of the Bachelors' and the Eccentric for longer than I care to remember but, in my younger days, it was the livelier institutions that attracted me, somewhere you could get a little boxing or gambling or simply a drink. Since the apparent aim of Parliament over the last fifty years has been to stop people buying a drink when they want one, an oasis in the desert of London's licensing laws was imperative.

There have always been nightclubs, and there always will be, so long as there are young men and women who want to meet in informal surroundings. As the Zoo's official description of a small bird from the Solomon Islands says:

'The sexes are distinctly different, the males being distinctly green, and the females are extremely red.'

It may seem odd to today's generation but, in my time, it was almost impossible to dance in public. Most dances were held in private houses where you had to be on your best behaviour. If you weren't invited to these, and many of us weren't, the only dancing available was at Covent Garden Balls or subscription dances at the Empress Rooms in Kensington. The result was that nightclubs, where one met young ladies who were not only willing to dance with you but were also kind enough to let you pay for their supper, did very well.

The Lotus, to which I was first taken by Hugh Wilson, the chap who married Julia Foster of Apley Park near Blandings, was one of the earliest dancing clubs; 'cock and hen clubs' we used to call them. The Lotus stood at the upper end of Regent Street and was financed by various men about Town, although its nominal proprietor was John Hollingshead (Honesty John), then owner and manager of the Gaiety Theatre.

The secretary was the unforgettable Fatty (Stephen) Coleman, who took over the year Hughie Lonsdale came into the title. The night I first went there, Fatty had gone to bed early, which was most unlike him. Some of the members decided he should be downstairs looking after them so they hoicked him out of bed, assisted by half a dozen members of the Gaiety chorus. Fatty joined us, disgruntled and still half-asleep, and got it into his head that someone had accused him of having done away with his wife and of having been a cornet in the Blues. For some reason, Fatty viewed both charges with equal disfavour.

The nearest rival to the Lotus was the Corinthian, which had a great vogue in the '90s. The food was good, the band was one of the best and its membership included half the peerage, but it did too well, became too noisy and was eventually closed down by Lord Egerton of Tatton who lived next door. The Sports Club is there now, quite a reasonable place but a bit hearty for my taste.

There were other dancing clubs where things were more free and easy like the Gardenia, next to the Alhambra in Leicester Square. The Gardenia was started by the Negro Bohee Brothers, banjoists who first came over here with Haverley's Minstrels when they filled Drury Lane. The banjo became fashionable and one Bohee brother gave lessons to the Prince of Wales, but with little success. The Bohees eventually sold it to Dudley Ward, father of the Southampton MP, and during his control of the place the Gardenia was a merry, if rowdy, place.

We had a routine, not a particularly healthy one, I admit, of times and places where we could be sure of meeting our pals, and one paper even published our time-table:

8 p.m.	– Dinner at the Savoy or the Berkeley
10 p.m.	– The Gaiety or the Empire
11.30 p.m.	– Supper at Romano's, Rules or Gow's.
12.30 a.m.	– Call in at the Pelican
1.30 a.m.	– Second supper at the Corinthian Club
2.30 a.m.	– Third supper at the Gardenia
Last Scene	– The Raleigh.

And pretty exhausting it could be, but it passed the time and kept us in touch with what was going on.

I was asked the other day to categorise the nightclubs I knew in order of respectability. It was a difficult question to answer; if they had been that respectable, we wouldn't have wanted to join. I think the Corinthian would come first as the smartest, then in descending order it would be the Lotus, the Palm, the Alsatian, the Percy Supper Club in Percy Street, the Nell Gwynne, the Waterloo, the Arlington, the White Beer Club and at the bottom, the Red Beer Club in Soho, an unusual establishment to which I was introduced by Pills Holloway.

We were having a drink in the Pelican one night when Pills announced he was going on to a dance at the Red Beer and asked if I would care to join him. I was still a shy young chap in those days, and demurred since I was not a member nor did I have a ticket. His retort gave a fair indication of the membership qualifications required for the Red Beer Club:

"Ticket! Member! You don't need to be a member or have a ruddy ticket. All you need for the Red Beer is a good stout stick! Come on!"

And off we went. The evening fully justified his view and I made sure that any subsequent visits were made in the company of good brawny chaps. I'd never have stood a chance on my own.

Although I still consider the Pelican to have been the finest club of all, I have a soft spot for the old Raleigh.

The Raleigh was a men-only club in Lower Regent Street of a type that would horrify a Home Secretary of today. It opened at 9 p.m. and closed nominally at 4 a.m. No food beyond toasted bacon sandwiches was attempted, but the wines and cigars were famous, while the gambling became so ruinously high that it was the talk of London.

There was great excitement once when the newspapers announced that a member of the Raleigh, 'a well-known baronet' (Legs Ponderby, who else?) had vanished. There was a tremendous to-do, the police were informed and rewards were offered. He was found after three days, still dead drunk, in a disused passage between the Raleigh smoking-room and the kitchens.

The Raleigh wasn't for namby-pambies, but the members did have a softer side. One day someone brought in an injured bulldog that had been run over by a hansom in Waterloo Place. It was promptly made a member of the club on the understanding that it paid its subscription in rats' tails.

So you can see why at one time I wanted to make my name as proprietor of a nightclub. It came to nothing; the money went out but didn't come in, and my father had to pay a thousand quid to get me clear. It looks as if I was not cut out to be a business man and must continue to exist as a lily of the field. I think such lack of financial acumen must run in the family; my nephew Ronald has just suffered the same fate with a similar venture. He called his club The Hot Spot; it lasted an even shorter time than mine did.

What people forget is that when a group of chaps join a club, they grow old together; they become used to each other's company and tend to shun the younger member. As a result the young chaps go off and start their own club.

Look at the Constitutional and Buck's; one specialises in age, the other in youth. The Constitutional began as a club for country landowners whose political activities didn't go beyond expressing their support for the *status quo*, old port and good crops. It is really just a club for senior Conservatives, which is what some people call it; when I say that my brother Clarence is a typical member, I have said it all.

The Constitutional, an enormous place halfway down Northumberland Avenue on the left, looks like the head office of a bank. It has the biggest staircase in London, the rooms are fifty feet high and the whole place is decked out in that peculiar type of marble that looks like Gorgonzola cheese. It has about four thousand members, the majority of whom seem to be bald-headed politicians or be-whiskered financiers. I don't suppose any of them have set a booby-trap for a bishop in their lives; they probably don't even now what a booby-trap is.

The food is excellent and Adams, the dining-room steward, can be relied upon to tell you what is the best choice. And that is about all that can be said for it.

I used to wonder why any young fellow should ever want to join the Constitutional. Calling there once to collect Clarence, I met the chap whom I'd last seen in the cottage in the East Wood at Blandings, where we had both taken refuge from one of my mother's ecclesiastical garden parties. He had left his bank as intended, become a writer, and told me the Constitutional library was the best place in London in which to work uninterrupted. The dark recesses of the library, a place of vast silence like the Sahara desert in brown calf, suited him down to the ground.

Nobody ever worked in the old Pelican; the nearest thing we had to a library was a battered copy of *Ruff's Guide to the Turf* which Shifter had pinched from the *Pink 'Un* office. So perhaps there are some advantages in belonging to a club where you don't speak to anybody unless his grandfather and yours served in the Crimea together - and even then the most you would dream of saying is: "Mornin' ", or perhaps "Evenin' ".

In contrast there is Buck's Club in Clifford Street, founded by young Herbert Buckmaster after the war. I suppose there may be some members over forty years of age but I never seem to see them. It is an odd sensation being invited there; so many of the members are sons or nephews of my old Pelican chums that I feel as if I'm looking at ghosts.

I approve of Buck's. Their bar-tender McGarry mixes the best cocktails in London, they throw bread, they make a noise, they have the odd fight and they get out and about. They started golfing weekends down at Sandwich, found they worked very well and now hold them at Le Touquet. An excellent idea if you like golf, an even better idea if you don't, because one can always visit the casino or look at the girls bathing.

With so many young chaps working nowadays, selling motor cars on commission, reading for the Bar and so on, some people consider the Buck's membership to be a lot of drones, who toil not neither do they spin. But, as a young chap there told me, if he had enough money to get by on, why bother to take a job from someone who needed it more? They are a likeable lot, and I'm told by my nephews that they still have the occasional spot of bother with bookmakers or tailors, and their rear entrance is highly valued for strategic withdrawals when the odd bailiff camps outside. I like to see these fine old traditions preserved.

So there you have two typical London clubs today. One for the staid and elderly, the other for the young and noisy. Perhaps the Bath Club in Dover Street has the right balance. It started in '94 when Billy Grenfell, Henniker-Heaton and Jack Wodehouse were grumbling about having nowhere in London where they could swim. Of course Grenfell, he's Lord Desborough now, has always liked that sort of thing. He got his Blue at Oxford in all sorts of strenuous activities, hunted the draghounds, swam across Niagara twice, and is never happier than when swimming or climbing mountains in great discomfort.

They bought the Marquess of Abergavenny's house in Dover Street, turned the ballroom into a swimming-pool and added squash courts and Turkish baths. All far too energetic for me, especially as the swimming-pool doubles up as a gymnasium and there are bars on the walls and ropes and swings hanging from the roof.

After a good dinner, it is the custom of the younger members to race each other down the pool, swinging from one to another of the rings suspended above the water. If someone has had too much, it isn't long before he is restored to instant sobriety by falling into the water. And I hear that it is not unknown for some kindly spirit to tie back the last ring so the unfortunate athlete finds himself faced with the same prospect. Now that's a custom I do approve of.

While men's clubs go on for ever, nightclubs are far more ephemeral. They die out every few years, but always come back with new people and new names and I'm sure their *habitués* are just as thrilled with them as we were with ours forty years ago.

Another sign of the times is the names they give these places nowadays. My nephews inform me that currently they patronise the Mottled Oyster, the Smiling Mushroom, Lamb's, the Bat, The Not, the Hambone, the Silver Slipper, Uncle's, the Manhattan and the Gargoyle, to name but a few.

I have been to the Gargoyle a few times. It's an odd place, founded a few years ago by Margot Asquith's nephew, David Tennant, and his wife, the actress Hermione Baddeley. It is one of those arty-Bohemian clubs where the women wear berets instead of hats, and the men make a point of wearing soft collars or even open-necked shirts instead of evening dress. Pretty scruffy they look too; they would never have got into the old Pelican dressed like that. We might have been raffish, but when we stepped high, wide and handsome our shirt-fronts were as stiff as our upper lips.

The Gargoyle started off as a second Chelsea Arts Club, to foment the feast of reason and flow of soul amongst painters, musicians and writers. It isn't my style, and my view is shared by Rosa Lewis of the Cavendish, a lady for whose judgement I have the highest respect. She is not a member of the Gargoyle any more than I am, but she descends on it occasionally and sweeps past the doorman with the remark : "Just tell young Tennant I've come to take a look at his place."

She can get away with it because she's been confidante and friend to Margot Asquith's family for years. Tennant is one of the several score of youngsters to whom Rosa Lewis can say: "I knew you before you were born." That puts them in their place, especially when she adds: "I knew your real father as well!"

The other nightclub making the headlines nowadays is the 43 Club in Gerrard Street. Everybody goes there, so I'm told, King Carol of Rumania, Valentino, Joseph Conrad, Tallulah Bankhead, Jack Buchanan, Epstein, J.B. Priestley and Augustus John. Its owner, Mrs Merrick, has been in and out of the courts so often that her faithful members have an anthem :

> *'Come all you birds*
> *And sing a roundelay*
> *Now Mrs Meyrick's*
> *Out of Holloway.'*

Though why everybody calls her Mrs Meyrick when her name is Merrick is beyond me. I don't know how many times she has been jugged now, but Jix (Sir William Joynson-Hicks, Home Secretary) has let it be known that he believes no one should be allowed to buy alcohol after midnight. I have news for him. No government in the history of the world has managed to prevent young men and women having a drink after midnight – and they never will.

The Press and the Pussyfoots see Mrs Merrick as the spirit of evil, but her background couldn't be more respectable. She is the widow of an Irish doctor, her two boys were at Harrow, her four girls went to Roedean and three of them have married into the peerage. May married

Lord Kinnoull, the racing motorist; Gwendoline married the Earl of Craven and Dorothy is now Lady de Clifford.[1] I sent a wedding present along to Dorothy because young Ned, the 26th baron, is the grandson of my old comrade in arms, Ned de Clifford. It made me realise how the years are slipping by.

In passing, it is strange how the de Cliffords die off so young. Ned, (every de Clifford is called Edward) the present baron is the sixth holder of the title in a hundred years. Dorothy Merrick is a delightful girl with the admirable habit of listening attentively to my stories and laughing at the right moments. Old Ned would have liked her.

I suppose the leading nightclubs today are the Café de Paris and the Embassy. The Café de Paris became a success when the owner, Poulsen, persuaded the Prince of Wales to patronise it, and when the news got out that the Prince went there in the afternoons for private lessons in the Charleston which is now all the rage, everybody wanted to go there.

There is one thing to be said for the Café de Paris; they do have standards and you have to be properly dressed to get in. The place was built as a replica of the Palm Court of the old *Lusitania* with a balcony running round three sides. Only those in evening dress are allowed on the dance floor, those in day clothes are consigned to the balcony. My nephew Ronald tested the rule recently and found the management were prepared to employ three waiters, a head waiter, a commissionaire and a passing policeman to enforce it. Ronnie finished up with a black eye and a fine in Court to prove it.

The Café de Paris has a long way to go before it overtakes the Embassy, which is not at all surprising since the Embassy's guiding spirit is none other than my old friend Luigi Naintre, the famous Luigi of Romano's.

He holds London's Society night-life in the palm of his hand and does it very well. But, every so often, the mask slips and he is the old Luigi who coped with the Pink 'Uns and Pelicans in the past. We have

---

(1) The de Clifford-Merrick marriage in 1926 was the sensation of the day, since Lord de Clifford was under age and his mother tried to have the marriage annulled. He achieved legal immortality in 1935 when he became the last English nobleman to be tried by his peers in the House of Lords. Like Mr Threepwood's nephew Frederick, Lord de Clifford became a dog-food salesman. *Ed.*

seen a lot together, Luigi and I, over the years. I remember once asking him who the group of heavy-jowled men were at a corner table in the Embassy and was told they were tradesmen whom he always put there. When I raised an eyebrow at the unsuspected snobbery, he reassured me. Surely I remembered the rule in Romano's in the old days? Always put a tradesman in a corner so his presence will not interfere with the enjoyment of those other customers who might owe him money.

They don't have a cabaret at the Embassy. Luigi sees no need for it; all he has to do is to put the latest *divorcée* at a table by the dance floor and the rest of London comes along to see her with her new boyfriend.

When Buck had a celebration dinner at the Embassy the other day, to which he was kind enough to invite me, he decided the quickest way to go and greet another guest was to jump over the table. His foot caught in the cloth and brought the whole table crashing down.

There was silence across the room – Royalty was there that night and not too sure how to regard the incident, but Luigi whisked across to reassure us. It was nothing! Nothing at all! Indeed, the sound of breaking glass revived happy memories. The Embassy might be smart but nobody threw things, nobody emptied their soup over each other in an argument over a horse; he had never even had a fight in the bar. The sound of breaking glass brought back happy memories of Romano's, when a night without a fight was something to talk about.

It is an odd twist of Fate that, if I want to revive memories of the Bohemia I once knew, I have to go to London's newest and certainly most un-Bohemian club to be served by the man who served me then. My Romano's is nearly a lifetime away but Luigi is still with us, still tactful, still making it clear that though he cannot accept your IOU, he would rather take one from you than from anyone else.

A great man. He's come a long way from the days when he used to lend Shifter a fiver to put on a horse and then have to lend him a penny to buy a paper to find out it had come in last.

Epilogue

At the back of the package containing Mr Threepwood's draft was an envelope, containing a second letter to Mrs Ronald Fish. After lengthy consideration and consultation with the Threepwood family's legal advisers, Mrs Fish has decided it can now be put in the public domain. It is reprinted without comment.

'My dear Sue,

By the time you read this, you will have worked your way through my memoirs. I hope you like them. There is little of moral value in them; rather the reverse I suspect. But it does no harm to know what sort of family you are marrying into.

I wrote the memoirs to amuse my fellow-beings and to show that even the highest in the land are as other men are, very much so in some cases. If you ever decide to publish them, you have my blessing.

I have, however, omitted two incidents in the Threepwood family history. They are known only to my brother Clarence and myself – and he, dear old chap, has almost certainly forgotten them both. Although I was tempted to take them with me to the grave, I have decided, after much heart-searching, that it would be wrong to leave them unrecorded.

You won't find much mention of the Threepwoods in our country's annals, but on two occasions Clarence has brushed with History.

As you know from your acquaintanceship with him, nobody could call Clarence a lady's man. His marriage, though short, was reasonably happy, but since then he has tended to forsake female company. But there was once a great love in his life. Like mine for your mother, it came to nothing.

It happened back in 1891 when Clarence was staying with the Lygons at Madresfield in Worcestershire. My mother received a letter from the Countess saying how much they enjoyed having him and all the rest of it. She was startled to read that the Beauchamps were delighted 'to see that dear Clarence has quite come out of his shell and is being most attentive to a young lady whose family is at present staying at Malvern'.

As you can imagine, this caused considerable comment around the Blandings breakfast table, but we heard no more. When Clarence returned some weeks later, we tried to get further details, but he was saying nothing. All we could discover was that he had met a girl, had ridden with her, gone for walks with her and even danced with her. And that's all he would say, but it was clear he had got it badly.

My mother, as mothers will, persisted. Any girl who affected her first-born as this one obviously had, was clearly out of the ordinary. All Clarence would say was that the girl's mother had put her foot down and it was over. That was all there was to it.

We let it drop and gradually forgot about it, as families do. It wasn't till some considerable time later that I came across a group photograph in Clarence's desk when I was scrounging some stamps.

It was clearly a picture of the Lygons' house-party. The Earl and Countess sat in the middle and there was Clarence, at the end of the row behind them. He wasn't looking at the camera; his gaze was fixed on the only other youngster in the picture, a tall, slim girl in the front row, sitting next to a stern-looking woman.

I recognised her at once. I thought about it, put the photograph back in the desk and I have never said a word till now.

In those days she was just the daughter of minor Royalty with a Grace and Favour residence and not much else. You, my dear Sue, know her better as the erstwhile Princess May of Teck, now Her Majesty Queen Mary.

I read a biography the other day which said:

'Her Majesty still looks back fondly on her visit to Malvern in 1891. During her stay at the Foley Arms, Her Majesty met many local families and joined in all the social activities of the neighbourhood. In 1895, she appointed Lady Mary Lygon as her first Lady In Waiting, saying that her stay in Worcestershire had been one of the happiest periods of her life. It was, she says, the last time she was able to lead a normal private life and walk, ride and dance with whom she liked, just like any other English girl.'

The second incident took place in 1914. Clarence had been invited on a cruise to the Greek Islands, but his susceptibility to sea-sickness led him to land at Athens and make his way back to England overland.

He travelled by train through the Balkans, stopping off at various places to collect botanical specimens.

In June he found himself in Sarajevo. He did all the usual things, put up at the main hotel, reported in to the British Consul and engaged some locals to act as servants and guides for his trips up the mountains. He must have been there a couple of weeks when the Austrian archduke was assassinated.

There was a tremendous fuss locally but, like most of us, Clarence thought it was just another minor Balkan incident. It wasn't till the Consul warned all the British visitors to go home, that he realised something might be up.

When he got back to Blandings, I watched him unpack his luggage and his botanical specimens. Perhaps because it was clear that war was coming, I asked him idly:

"Clarence, where's that revolver of Father's you took with you?"

He couldn't find it anywhere and eventually dropped his bombshell:

"I remember now, Galahad. I gave it to that young fellow to clean when I was staying in Sarajevo. He was most obliging and promised to check the ammunition as well. I wonder what on earth he can have done with it?"

I kept my emotions in check as best I could.

"Clarence," I said, "do you happen to remember the name of this paragon who seems to have stolen your pistol?"

He replied with the words I had feared:

"Yes, yes, I can, Galahad. I remember because at the time, I thought it reminded me of yours. It was Gabriel. Gabriel something. Why? Is it important?"

I took a deep breath and thought of the long line of honourable, blameless Threepwoods across the centuries and the unsullied family name.

"No, Clarence, no. It's not important."

Yes, Sue, I regret to say it's true. You may remember that I went to the Continent a couple of years ago, saying I was off to Monte Carlo. In fact I took the train to Yugoslavia and paid a visit to the museum in Sarajevo.

In a glass case there is a large revolver with an inscription in four languages, saying this was the weapon with which Gabriel Princep shot the Archduke Franz Ferdinand and started the War of Independence against Austrian repression, and all the rest of it. Engraved on the butt, for all to see, is an earl's coronet and the letter E.

One day, when you feel the time is right, you might pass the information on. I leave it to you.

Gally'

Supporting Bibliography

In addition to the books listed below, much of the corroboration
of Mr Threepwood's memoirs came from the excellent obituary
columns of *The Daily Telegraph*,
an invaluable source of information for all social historians.

Binstead, Arthur, *Pitcher In Paradise*, Sands 1903
Binstead, Arthur & Ernest Wells, *A Pink 'Un and A Pelican*, Sands 1898
Booth, J.B., *London Town*, T Werner Laurie 1929
Booth, J.B., *A Pink 'Un Remembers*, T Werner Laurie 1937
Booth, J.B., *Old Pink 'Un Days*, Richards Press 1924
Boyd, Frank M., *A Pelican's Tale*, Herbert Jenkins 1919
Burke, Sir Bernard, *Peerage & Baronetage*, Harrison & Sons 1911
Burke, Thomas, *English Night Life*, Batsford 1941
Cardigan and Lancastre, Countess of, *My Recollections*, Eveleigh Nash
   1909
Cartland, Dame Barbara, *We Danced All Night*, Hutchinson 1971
Caufield, Catherine, *The Emperor of America and other Magnificent
   British Eccentrics*, Routledge & Paul 1981
Deghy, Guy, *Paradise In The Strand*, Richards Press 1958
Frankau, Gilbert, *Self-Portrait*, Hutchinson 1939
Grantley, Lord, *Silver Spoon*, Hutchinson 1954
Harrison, Michael, *Painful Details*, Max Parrish 1962
Kent, Graham, *A Pictorial History of Wrestling*, Spring Books 1968
Leslie, Anita, *Edwardians In Love*, Hutchinson 1972
Leslie, Seymour, *The Jerome Connexion*, John Murray 1964
MacColl, Gail & Carol Wallace, *To Marry An English Lord*, Sidgwick &
   Jackson 1989
Macqueen Pope, W., *Gaiety, Theatre of Enchantment*, W.H. Allen 1949
Nicols-Pigache, Captain D., *Café Royal Days*, Hutchinson 1934
Portsmouth, Earl of, *A Knot of Roots*, Geoffrey Bles 1965
Petrie, Sir Charles, *Scenes of Edwardian Life*, Eyre & Spottiswoode 1965
Preston, Sir Harry, *Leaves from My Unwritten Diary*, Hutchinson 1933
Preston, Sir Harry, *Memories*, Constable 1928
Sutherland, Douglas, *The Yellow Earl*, Cassell 1965
Wodehouse, P.G., *Heavy Weather*, Herbert Jenkins 1933
Wodehouse, P.G., *Summer Lightning*, Herbert Jenkins 1929
Woods, Lawrence M., *British Gentlemen in the Wild West*, Robson Books
   1990

Index